Sophie Pembroke has been dreaming, reading and writing romance ever since she read her first Mills & Boon as part of her English Literature degree at Lancaster University, so getting to write romantic fiction for a living really is a dream come true! Born in Abu Dhabi, Sophie grew up in Wales and now lives in a little Hertfordshire market town with her scientist husband, her incredibly imaginative and creative daughter, and her adventurous, adorable little boy. In Sophie's world, happy is for ever after, everything stops for tea, and there's always time for one more page...

Christine Rimmer came to her profession the long way around. She tried everything from acting to teaching to telephone sales. Now she's finally found work that suits her perfectly. She insists she never had a problem keeping a job—she was merely gaining "life experience" for her future as a novelist. Christine lives with her family in Oregon. Visit her at christinerimmer.com

Also by Sophie Pembroke

A Proposal Worth Millions
The Unexpected Holiday Gift
Newborn Under the Christmas Tree
Island Fling to Forever
Road Trip with the Best Man
CEO's Marriage Miracle
Slow Dance with the Best Man
Proposal for the Wedding Planner

Also by Christine Rimmer

The Nanny's Double Trouble
Almost a Bravo
Same Time, Next Christmas
Not Quite Married
The Good Girl's Second Chance
Carter Bravo's Christmas Bride
James Bravo's Shotgun Bride
Ms. Bravo and the Boss
A Bravo for Christmas
The Lawman's Convenient Bride

Discover more at millsandboon.co.uk

CARRYING HER MILLIONAIRE'S BABY

SOPHIE PEMBROKE

For Hayley,
with love and takeaway curry x

CHAPTER ONE

ZOEY HEPBURN SHOVED the hotel window a little further open, hoisted her bare foot up onto the sill and cursed as her hem got caught on the latch—again. She was beginning to regret the strapless hot pink dress she'd chosen for her rehearsal dinner. However pretty the lacy skirt was, it was not getaway-friendly.

Of course, when she bought it, she hadn't been planning on escaping through a back window the night before her wedding. But then, she never did.

'People are looking for you, you know.' The calm, almost lazy voice behind her made Zoey jump just enough to whack her head on the window frame. *Ow*. 'Also, you made me promise I wouldn't let you do this again this time.'

'Again feels a little harsh. I've never actually climbed out of a window before.' Maybe her shoulders would fit through the small gap better if she twisted them more to the left.

Zoey tried it. They wouldn't.

Ash sighed. His usual, *What did I do in a past life to get lumbered with you as my friend?* sigh. Zoey was alarmingly familiar with it.

'They want to do the speeches,' he said. As if the idea

of hearing David's father waffle on about how important his family was—to him and to the world at large—might tempt her back into the hotel restaurant. Everyone in there knew what trouble his company was in anyway, whatever tall tales he told about famous people he'd met once and who would never remember his name.

David didn't do that, she reminded herself. David was reasonably modest. Well, compared to his father anyway, which wasn't a *very* high bar, she had to admit.

Still, it meant she probably couldn't use 'pompous name-dropper' as a reason for not marrying him.

'Since when did speeches become a must for rehearsal dinners, anyway?' she asked, eyeing the window again. 'Can't they save them for tomorrow? You know, the *actual* wedding.'

'Seems to me they're being sensible getting them in early,' Ash said, and she just *knew* he was raising an eyebrow at her, the way he always used to when she and Grace came home from the pub tipsy and tried to deny that last bottle of wine they'd shared. 'Tomorrow is not looking like a sure thing right now.'

Outside, a warm breeze fluttered past like butterfly wings. She was in paradise—a luxurious island in the middle of the Indian ocean, a boutique hotel filled with her and David's friends and family, private villas on stilts stretching out into the azure sea from a wooden boardwalk for all her guests.

It was just unfortunate that, from the minute she'd arrived three days ago for the last-minute wedding preparations, she'd felt as if she'd been trapped in purgatory.

But she wasn't going to escape hell through this window—even if she *had* followed any of those 'Lose Ten Pounds for your Wedding Day' diets her mother had kept leaving strategically around the house. Which she hadn't.

Resigned, Zoey pulled her head back through the open window, turned to face her best friend's husband and sat down on the windowsill. 'I can't go back in there, Ash.'

Ash took a seat on the table she'd climbed up on to reach the window. 'Because rehearsal dinners are a terrible tradition that should be banned, or because you don't want to marry David tomorrow?'

'Both,' Zoey replied promptly. 'And I should know. I've had three rehearsal dinners, including this one.'

'And not a wedding between them,' Ash said mournfully. 'Not to mention the two other broken engagements.'

Zoey winced. 'Three, actually. One of them was before Grace and I met you.'

'The musician, right?' Ash tilted his head to the side as he looked at her. 'Grace told me about him. I think calling that one off was legit.'

'As opposed to the others?' She gave him a sideways look. 'Do you honestly think I should have married Harry, or Julian, or Fred?'

'I suppose not.' Leaning back, Ash rested his elbows on the table and looked up at her. His bright blue eyes were too knowing, and Zoey had to work to resist the urge to brush his sooty hair away from them. He really was absurdly good-looking. The thought registered, as it always did—an acknowledgement of a fact, like saying the ocean was blue.

She'd never let herself dwell on it beyond that. That way lay madness and misery.

'It's just a shame you never figured out that they weren't the right guy for you until the morning of the wedding,' Ash went on, and she focused on his words rather than his looks again. 'As much as *I* love a last-minute runaway bride drama, I think some other people might be thinking it's gone a little far now.'

He could have a point, Zoey allowed. In fact, she had a nagging suspicion that David might have had an ulterior motive for insisting the wedding took place on an island in the middle of nowhere.

She frowned. Ash would know. 'When David spoke to you about booking the wedding, did he say why he wanted to have it here?' She hadn't wanted to ask before. But if not now, when?

Ash, as heir to the Carmichael Luxury Travel business, had organised the use of the island hotel as his wedding present to them. She was pretty sure his company actually owned the island, as well as the hotel, when it came down to it. Zoey wondered if she'd have to pay him back for that if the wedding didn't go ahead. She hoped not. Her job as an art gallery assistant in London was her dream, but the benefits weren't all entirely financial.

'He might have mentioned the advantages of having control over which boats and sea planes arrived at—and more pertinently left—the island,' Ash said diplomatically.

'You mean he was trying to make sure I couldn't run away.' Zoey frowned. Was *He manipulated my wed-*

ding venue choice a good enough excuse not to marry him? And why did she need an excuse at all beyond *I don't want to*?

Because your mother is going to pitch a fit. Not to mention all the other people you're letting down.

Not Ash, though. Even if he had gone along with David's possibly nefarious scheme.

'Why didn't you tell me that sooner?' she asked, trying to feel outraged and failing. 'I mean, you'd let me marry a man who didn't give me an out on my wedding day? What kind of a friend are you?'

Ash rolled his eyes. 'Yes, obviously this is my fault. Zoey, you know that if you told me you wanted out then I would get you out—planes, boats and automobiles be damned. But, if you recall, you also told me—quite definitely—when we had dinner last month that David was *absolutely* the one, and that I wasn't to let you get cold feet this time, because you'd regret it for the rest of your life.'

Had she really said that? It was hard to imagine somehow, here and now. Impossible to summon up that certainty again—and not because of the island, or his father's pompous speeches. But because now it came down to it she simply could not picture spending the rest of her life with David.

But she *had* been able to once. She must have done, to say yes to his proposal. She'd loved him—or believed she did—and had been planning their life together right up until the moment they had arrived in paradise to get married.

People might laugh at her history of running out

on weddings—and, yes, there had been a few family members who'd refused to even come to this one, just in case—but when she said yes to a guy on one knee with a sparkly ring, she always, *always* meant it.

It was just getting from 'yes' to 'I do' that seemed to cause her problems.

Her whole life with just one person—that was a big ask. And Zoey had seen first-hand what a disaster it could be if she picked the wrong one. Her own parents were a shining example of how not to do marriage.

And then there was Ash.

Ash, her only friend, who had been her best friend's husband. Ash, who'd had the perfect marriage—until it had been ripped away from him and had left him broken.

Zoey bit her lip, contemplating the question she wanted to ask but didn't know if she dared.

'What?' Ash sat up straighter, watching her. 'Whatever it is, just ask, Zoey. You know I'll help if I can.'

He always had. Ash was one of only two people she'd known beyond doubt that she'd always be able to rely on, ever since she and Grace had met him in the student union over a decade earlier. But she didn't want to hurt him by bringing up painful memories.

On the other hand, she needed to know the answer, if she were to make a real decision about what to do next—not just bash her way through a window and hope for the best.

'When you and Grace…on your wedding day. Weren't you nervous?'

Unbidden, memories of that perfect English summer day came back to her. Grace, her best friend since junior school, ethereally beautiful in her delicate lace dress. Zoey's rose-pink bridesmaid's dress, a perfect match for the tea roses in Grace's bouquet. The tiny stone chapel in their home village. The afternoon tea reception on the village green, with mismatched china and bunting strung all around.

And, through it all, Ash and Grace smiling at each other as if their hearts were on show. So in love, so certain that the future would be perfect, as long as they were together.

It hurt now to think of how happy they'd all been, never imagining that it could all be torn away from them in a heartbeat.

'Nervous?' Ash shook his head. 'I was terrified.'

He hadn't looked it. He'd seemed like a man whose every dream had come true.

If Ash had been nervous, maybe it was okay that she was too?

Or maybe it depended on why. Because Ash had gone through with it. He'd said 'I do' and promised his whole life to another person.

And six diamond rings later, that was something Zoey still hadn't managed.

Ash took in the look of confusion on Zoey's face and wondered how he could make her understand, when the depth and strength of his love for Grace had always been something he'd just had to take on faith, rather than pick apart and puzzle out.

He was telling the truth when he said he'd been nervous, but perhaps not in the way Zoey meant the question. It hadn't been the wedding—all those people there looking at him—that had worried him, or the fear of anything going wrong. And it definitely hadn't been the concept of marriage itself; the idea of spending the rest of his life with Grace had only ever made him smile.

No, he'd never been scared of committing to Grace. But he'd been petrified of not being good enough to deserve her. Even now she was gone, the idea of not living up to the man she'd believed he could be kept him awake some nights.

Sometimes, he wondered if it was only Grace's belief in him, in what he could become, that kept him going after her death. That, and Zoey's blind determination to drag him out of the pit he'd buried himself in the moment the doctor had told him the news.

But that was him. It was all so different for Zoey. For her, it was the commitment she was terrified of. The idea of forever with one person.

Not that she'd ever told him that. But Grace had tried to explain it to him once, back when they were blissfully happy in their extended honeymoon period, and Zoey had just run out on her latest fiancé.

'It's not that she doesn't want to get married. She does, desperately, I think. It's just that after so many years of watching her parents perform the perfect How Not to Be a Happy Couple *show, she's terrified of getting it wrong.'*

That had been three fiancés ago and now, sitting in a tiny storeroom of a luxury hotel, watching Zoey eye up the too-small window as a viable escape route again, Ash had to admit that his wife had been right. As usual.

Hardly surprising, he supposed. Grace had known Zoey better than anyone in the world. Almost as well as she'd known him.

And now he and Zoey were all that was left, trying to muddle through together. She'd literally picked him up off the floor after Grace was pronounced dead following a frantic ambulance ride from the scene of a multi-car pileup that stole three other lives. In return, he tried to be the best friend he could to Zoey, to make up for the much better one that she'd lost that day.

Some days he was better at it than others. He hoped today was a good day. Zoey looked as if she needed it.

And she was still waiting for him to explain his fears.

'It never occurred to me *not* to marry Grace.' Ash stretched out his legs along the table, turning so he could see Zoey as he talked. 'From the first moment I met her, she was my future. She was all I could think about.'

'I remember,' Zoey said, her voice dry. 'You had to be reminded that you'd actually met *me* that night too, when you both finally came up for air a week or so later.'

Ash winced. His eighteen-year-old self might not have been entirely aware of other people's feelings. But Zoey was smiling at the memory, so he figured he must have made up for it in the decade or so since then.

'So, why were you scared?' Zoey asked.

'Because…everything was so perfect. *Grace* was so perfect. I was scared I'd screw it up. That I wouldn't be enough.'

'*That* I get.' Zoey pulled her knees up against her chest, her bare toes with their sparkly aqua nails peeking out from under the hot pink dress. Ash spotted her high heels discarded by the door.

She looked about twelve, sitting like that. Ash felt the familiar protective instinct rising up in him. Ever since Grace died, it had just been him and Zoey, looking out for each other. His parents, as much as they loved him, were generally more concerned with Ash's ability to perform his role in the family business than the state of his psyche, and Zoey's parents were worse than useless.

Which meant it was up to him to fix the latest twist in Zoey's romantic life.

Starting with figuring out which side of that window she *really* wanted to be on.

'Is that what this is about?' He scooted closer to sit beside her. The warm breeze from the open window brushed against the back of his neck. 'You're scared that you can't be what David needs?'

If anything, Ash thought it was the other way around. Of all her fiancés, David was his…second least favourite. Not that he was keeping a list. Well, not a written one.

But then, he and Grace had never thought anyone was good enough for their Zoey.

Zoey pulled a face. 'Not exactly. It's more… I don't think that our marriage will be what either of us are hoping for.'

'But you didn't feel that way when you said yes to his proposal. Or when you told me that David was different, and that you'd absolutely go through with it and I wasn't to let you climb out of a window to escape getting married this time.'

'Hey! I told you. I've never climbed out of a window before.'

Ash raised an eyebrow to remind her that the window really wasn't the point here.

Because this was the part that Ash couldn't understand. When they'd had dinner a couple of weeks ago, when he'd been home in London between business trips, Zoey had been *so* certain, so sure of her love for David and their future together, that he'd resigned himself to boring dinners and holidays with the man for the rest of his existence. Because he wasn't losing Zoey in his life, whatever idiot she finally married.

He'd really thought that this time she'd go through with it.

But maybe that just meant he didn't know Zoey as well as he'd thought he did.

'Zoey. Tell me. What changed in the last two weeks?' he asked.

What always changes? Every damn time.

Zoey sighed as she tried to find the words. Find the reasons. How could she explain it to him when it didn't even make sense to her? It wasn't one thing that had changed. It was a hundred tiny things she'd finally noticed, all building on each other.

'Nothing. And everything.' She shook her head to try and clear the whirlwind of thoughts that seemed to have filled it since she arrived on the island. 'I really thought I could go through with it this time, Ash. That I could make it work. But then we landed here a few days ago to get everything ready for the wedding…and everything started feeling wrong.' Pit of her stomach wrong. Instincts telling her to run wrong.

She'd always trusted her instincts. Even when they led her into another engagement, or away from another wedding. At the time, they always seemed right.

'Everything?'

No. That wasn't fair to David. He was a good man. She loved him. Had loved him. One or the other.

'Well, little things, I guess. Like suddenly he wasn't happy with the ceremony plan and wanted to change it—even though it was what we'd both agreed *months* ago.'

'Last-minute nerves?' Ash suggested.

'Probably. But then I realised, all the changes he wanted to make, they involved me being with him all the time. Every single second. Even tonight, even though he *knows* my mother will freak out about it being bad luck.' And even though they were still doing the stupid abstinence thing the 'engagement counsellor' he'd hired had insisted on. Zoey hadn't even realised that engagement counsellor was an actual job, but David had been adamant that he wasn't taking any chances. Whatever the counsellor had suggested, he'd instantly implemented. Including the no sex for six weeks before the wedding rule.

No wonder they were both so tetchy and stressed.

'And why do you think that's bothering you so much?' Ash asked, sounding eerily like the relationship psychologist her ex-boss had introduced her to after her third near miss with marriage.

Really, with all these marriage professionals in her

life Zoey would think she'd have the mental strength and tools to get through an actual wedding by now.

Of course, getting engaged to said relationship psychologist then calling it off three days before the wedding probably didn't help.

But she was getting side-tracked. This wasn't about past mistakes. It was about the one she might be about to make. Whichever way she jumped.

'Because…' Why *was* it bothering her? She was marrying the guy, so why would spending time together be a problem?

Then she realised. The reason behind that feeling in the pit of her stomach.

Ash had already told her, but she hadn't been listening. It was why she was on this stupid island in the first place.

'Because he's not doing it because he wants to be close to me. He's doing it because he wants to stop me running away.' God, he'd even planned the wedding for unfashionably early in the day to give her less time to bolt.

Zoey bit the inside of her cheek and stared down at her perfectly pedicured toenails. A waste of polish, really, if she didn't go through with the wedding. Not to mention all the time, money and energy that had gone into the planning. David might not need to worry about money right now—the company wasn't doing *that* badly—but Zoey had put her meagre savings on the line again for her dress and shoes, hair, beauty and all the rest. She couldn't ask her parents to pay for anything again. Not after all the times before. Even if they did seem strangely more enthusiastic about her marrying David than they had about anyone she'd been engaged to before.

She'd skipped a hen night this time—with Grace gone, it felt wrong anyway—and she'd only invited the hardcore friends and family who could make it through another one of her maybe-weddings. Ash, her aunt and uncle, a couple of cousins who were also friends. But David and his parents had invited *everyone*. She'd be letting a lot of people down.

But…

'It hurts to know he doesn't trust you.' Ash said the words softly, and for a moment Zoey could almost imagine that it was Grace, putting Zoey's own thoughts into words better than she ever could, just like she had since they were children.

Every time Zoey had shown up on Grace's doorstep as kids, with some story ready about why they urgently needed to hang out, Grace had just tilted her head and said, 'They're fighting again, right? Come in, come in.' Then they'd sat eating cookies or watching movies or anything to distract Zoey from what was going on at home.

'My home is your home,' Grace had told her when Zoey had run away at sixteen. And again at seventeen. Then she'd made sure they ended up at the same university, so Zoey wouldn't be alone when her parents flaked on her again, because they were too busy with their own misery.

Zoey had done what she could to keep her relationship with her parents going, but she'd always known that

Grace was her real family. And Ash, once it became clear that he and Grace were a package deal.

She'd had visions of being part of their family for life. Christmases, birthdays. She'd be Auntie Zoey to their kids… She swallowed hard at the memory, knowing how close that one had been to coming true.

Before the crash. Before they all lost Grace for good, and the world had grown a little colder.

Zoey let her head fall to Ash's shoulder, taking comfort from the arm he placed around her. He might not be Grace, but he was still family.

And right now she couldn't afford to dwell in the past. She had to decide what to do about David.

'I know I'm a flight risk. I know I have form. And I know I'm proving him right at this very moment. It's just…if David doesn't trust me now, what if he doesn't ever? What if he's always just waiting for me to run? I can't live like that.'

'Nor should you,' Ash said. 'I can understand his reasons, but I can understand yours too.'

She looked up at him, into those strange, light blue eyes that stood out so clearly against his pale skin and black hair. 'So what do I do?'

'Well, that's up to you. Do you love him enough to convince him? Do you love him enough to take a chance? I mean, he obviously knew that asking you to marry him was risky. And, whatever steps he's been taking this week to make sure it happens, he was only doing it to make sure you go through with it.'

Zoey smiled. Although Ash was obviously trying to be fair to both sides of the story, playing devil's advocate, she could hear his distaste for David's methods in his tone.

Suddenly, they heard a voice in the corridor outside their store cupboard. 'Zoey? Come on, Zo, this isn't funny. My dad's waiting to give his speech. Where are you?'

'Decision time,' Ash whispered. 'What do you want to do?'

All at once a feeling of rightness settled over her.

'Get me out of here, Ash.'

CHAPTER TWO

SO THEY WERE RUNNING. Right.

Ash gave a sharp nod, then whispered, 'Stay here.'

Easing himself off the table, he opened the door to the cupboard an inch and peered out. David stood with his back to him, staring down two identical-looking corridors branching off from the main one at the far end of the hall.

Perfect.

Ash slipped through the door and closed it silently behind him. Then he took a few steps forward before calling, 'David! I've been looking for you everywhere.'

David spun around. 'Have you seen Zoey? She's been missing for fifteen whole minutes.'

If he'd sounded less irritated and more concerned, Ash might have felt guiltier about lying to him. Or if David had realised that Zoey had actually been gone for more than half an hour. As it was…

'That's why I was looking for you. She had a migraine so went up to her room to lie down.'

'A migraine? Tonight?' David pulled an exasperated face. 'Zoey doesn't even get migraines!'

Okay, now Ash barely felt guilty at all. 'She's had them since she was twelve. She had to take a make-up exam our last year at university when she missed one of her finals because of a migraine.' How could David not know that about her? Wasn't he supposed to be in love with her?

'Well, she's never had one in the eighteen months I've known her!' David snapped. Then he ran a hand over his hair, looking away. 'Sorry. I'm just…a little anxious right now.'

'Wedding eve nerves,' Ash said sagely. 'I remember them well. Look, why don't you go back and tell your guests what's going on. I'm sure Zoey will feel much better in the morning.'

'Yeah. Yeah, you're right,' David said, already turning back the way he'd come. Ash smiled to himself. Sometimes, people just wanted someone else to tell them what to do. 'I could do with an early night, anyway. I'll go say goodnight then head up and check on Zoey. See if there's anything she needs.'

Okay, that wasn't *exactly* what he'd hoped for, but Ash would take it. It bought them a little time, at least.

'Great. I'll…see you back in there.' He waved a hand in what he thought was the direction of the bathrooms and hoped that David would get the hint.

He did. The moment David turned the corner towards the restaurant, Ash slipped back into the cupboard to find Zoey listening anxiously at the door.

'I definitely told him about the migraines,' she said indignantly.

'He forgot an important medical condition; you're skipping out on your absurdly expensive wedding,' Ash pointed out. 'I think you can call it even. And unless you want him following you, we need to go. *Now*.'

Getting out of the hotel, it turned out, was the easy part. Leaving behind the store cupboard and the too-small window, Ash guided them out through the kitchens instead. He'd spent enough of his formative years in hotels, when his father took him along on business trips, to know the ins and outs of most of them. And as a growing teenage boy he'd always, always found the kitchen first.

'Why didn't I think of this?' Zoey said as they weaved their way through the busy kitchens, apologising to the sous chefs and kitchen underlings as they went.

'Because you're only used to seeing hotels as a guest,' Ash pointed out. 'When you're staying somewhere as luxurious as this, people tend to forget that there's a whole world behind the scenes, working hard to make your holiday happen.'

'But not you?' Zoey's eyebrows were raised and Ash recognised that expression all too well. That *You're a rich kid and you're lecturing me on how the other half live?* look.

'I spent a lot of time in hotels growing up,' he said. 'I got to know how they operate pretty well. And that was before I started working in the kitchens of one at the age of fifteen.'

Zoey stared at him incredulously as they burst through the final set of doors and into the only slighter cooler night air of the island. 'You? Ash Carmichael, heir to the Carmichael millions, worked as a hotel cook?'

'It's billions, actually. Or will be soon, if my father gets his way. And I was deputy washer-upper for three months before I was allowed anywhere near the food.' Ash scouted around the back of the hotel, making sure there were no loitering guests to see them run. 'My father is a firm believer in earning your place—even if you're born into it. I worked in every part of a hotel in the three years before I went to university, and after that I worked my way up through every department of Carmichael Luxury Travel before I was allowed anywhere near the top offices.'

'Huh. Grace always said you worked hard, but she never mentioned all that.'

Ash shrugged. 'Why would she? It was just a job.'

And his job—and his money, for that matter—had always been the least interesting thing about him to Grace. Which was one of the reasons he'd fallen so hard and so fast for her. She'd loved him in spite of his name, not because of it.

'So, where do we go now?' Zoey looked out at the darkening skies, a nervous line marring the skin between her eyes.

A gnawing feeling of doubt settled in Ash's stomach. Was he doing the right thing, taking her away from this wedding? He'd promised her just two weeks ago that he'd make sure she went through with it. But even then he'd not felt entirely comfortable making that promise.

Watching her with David, he'd been worried. Or unsettled, perhaps. Nothing Ash could put a finger on, but just a sense of wrongness. Maybe it was the way that David's eyes never left her, especially when she was talking to other people. Or perhaps the way that they only ever said yes to engagements he wanted to go to, and arrived and left on his clock, not Zoey's.

Or maybe it was just that Ash didn't like him much.

Whatever it was, Ash had to admit that he was glad Zoey wasn't marrying him. If she'd gone through with it, there was an interminable future of boring dinners listening to David talking about how important he was, and how magnanimous, supporting Zoey in her little job at the gallery.

Yeah, he was definitely doing the right thing.

'The company has a villa on a private island, not far from this one. Freshly refurbished and awaiting inspection by yours truly next week. I even know where the spare key is hidden. We could borrow one of your guest's boats and be there before bedtime.' He nodded to the array of boats moored up at the hotel, ranging from small speedboats to large private yachts. Many of the wedding guests had decided to make a longer trip of the event and hired boats for the occasion to tour the region—relishing the excitement of island-hopping in the tropics instead of yachting around the Med for a change. Ash had been hoping for a chance to take a trip out on one of the boats anyway, so really he was killing two birds with one stone.

Actually, this all sounded like a pretty good plan for one he'd just come up with on the spur of the moment. Hopefully the villa had an equally luxurious drinks cabinet, and he and Zoey could wait out the wedding sipping cocktails by the pool before they headed back to face the music.

'Borrow a boat from somebody?' Zoey asked, sounding less enamoured of his plan. 'Doesn't that mean going back *into* the hotel we just escaped from and *telling* one of my guests that we're leaving? Kind of defeats the object, don't you think?'

'Well, I wasn't exactly going to ask,' Ash admitted. He'd always found it better to seek forgiveness rather than permission in situations like these.

'So you want to *steal* a boat. From one of David's friends and family? Because I can't see that making me any more popular with them.' As if she thought running out on her own wedding wasn't going to achieve that on its own. Sometimes Zoey had no sense of priorities.

'No,' Ash explained patiently. 'We'll bring it back tomorrow. *After* the wedding that won't be. And we'll only borrow a small one, anyway. They probably won't even notice it's gone.'

'I'm not sure—' Zoey broke off abruptly as another voice filled the air. David's.

'Zoey? Are you out here?'

'Boat?' Ash whispered.

Zoey nodded. 'Boat.'

And then they ran.

As if she wasn't feeling guilty enough already, now she had boat theft to add to her weighty conscience.

Ash had commandeered a small yacht with surprisingly little trouble—one that had been hired, she had a feeling, by David's boss—which made Zoey wonder if he'd actually done this before. Funny, if she'd been asked this morning she'd have said that she knew everything there was to know about Ash Carmichael. After all, Grace had talked about him *incessantly* since the moment they met, so it was hard not to. And that was even before Grace died, and suddenly all they had was each other.

A tragedy like that brought people together. Made them close. Helped them know and understand each other in a way they never would have done, otherwise.

But somehow she still hadn't known that he'd worked in a hotel kitchen, or that he knew how to hotwire a boat, or whatever it was he'd done to steal this one.

It was a nice boat, Zoey decided, standing by the rail looking out at the rapidly receding island hotel where she wouldn't be getting married tomorrow. Stretching out from the main island itself was the long wooden bridge out over the water that led to twenty or so individual hotel suites on stilts, looking as if they almost floated on the waves.

It was an incredible place, Zoey had to admit. Under other circumstances, she'd be sorry to leave.

As it was…

She sighed and turned away, back to where Ash was steering the boat. And frowning. A lot.

'What's the matter?' she asked, drawing closer. 'Having second thoughts?'

He flashed her a smile. 'I'm pretty sure I'm supposed to be asking you that.'

Zoey considered, taking a reading on her internal feelings. A lot of guilt, as usual—and, really, who had a 'usual' for a situation like this?—but no regrets. No second thoughts.

She might regret letting her relationship with David reach this point, but not walking away. Her whole body sang with the rightness of that decision.

But that didn't explain Ash's frown.

'I'm absolutely fine. What's up with you?'

'Not me,' Ash said shortly. 'The weather.'

Zoey looked up and saw the sky ahead was a different colour to the sky behind. And, from Ash's expression, it wasn't just the usual gradients of colour of sunset in paradise.

'A storm?' she asked.

He gave a short nod. 'A squall, at least. Basically, out of the frying pan…'

'Into the dangerous weather systems.' Hadn't someone at the hotel said something about incoming weather that morning? Yes! They'd been talking about possibly having to bring the ceremony in from the beach into the hotel itself. David had been furious. She'd been so caught up in her own doubts and concerns she hadn't listened. She'd tuned out the way she always did when David was rude to someone he considered less important than himself. Which was basically everyone except his father. And her own parents, actually, which was probably why they liked him.

For someone who could be so sweet when it was just the two of them, he didn't go over so well with other people. Something else she should have considered sooner.

Maybe she was just an incredibly lousy judge of character. That would explain a lot.

But personal revelations didn't change the past. Or the squall in their future.

'I knew it was coming,' Zoey berated herself. 'I had a conversation with the wedding planner about it this morning—well, David did. But I was there. I should have remembered.'

'You've had a lot on your mind,' Ash said drily, but Zoey could feel the wind lifting her hair, and saw the way Ash gripped the boat's controls.

It was coming.

Looking over the side, Zoey could see the waves rising higher, crashing against the side of their boat. How on earth was she going to explain to David that she'd not only run out on their wedding but also destroyed his boss's boat in the process?

Maybe this was divine retribution. Fate taking its revenge for her messing up other people's lives and plans one time too many; taking control of her future for her, since she couldn't ever seem to stick to any of the decisions she made herself.

Maybe she deserved it.

'I should have checked the forecast before bringing you out here.' Ash's knuckles were white, Zoey realised, and his face pinched. Strain, fear or both? 'You should get down in the cabin. There's not much space down there, but it's a lot safer than up on deck.'

Or maybe fate was a load of bunk, and the future was hers to control.

'I'll stay here with you.' Zoey grabbed a hold of the railing beside Ash, planting her feet firmly on the deck. 'I mean, I have no idea how to drive a boat, so you'll have to tell me what to do so I can actually help you.

But it's my fault we're out here. I'm not leaving you up here alone.'

Ash looked at her, his gaze steady despite whatever fear he was feeling. Zoey gazed back just as evenly, so he'd know she meant it.

Then the wind kicked up again and a wave crashed into their side, making them both stumble a little.

'Okay,' Ash said, his eyes back on the water, his hands firm on the controls. 'We're not far from the island. Let's see if we can get there before this storm gets any worse.'

'We'll get there,' Zoey said with a confidence she wasn't sure she truly felt.

Fate could go hang.

What kind of idiot took a random boat out in these waters at night without checking the forecast? Ash berated himself mentally as he clung to his tenuous control of the boat. The waves crashed against the sides and Ash tried desperately to focus on the task in hand and not get distracted by images of his late wife giving him hell in the afterlife for getting her best friend killed.

With Grace gone, he was responsible for Zoey. It wasn't as if her parents had ever been able to let their own issues go long enough to care about her, and since the odds of her actually finding true love and settling down—at least long enough to get through a wedding reception—seemed to be getting slimmer, he was it. He was all the support she had left—and he was doing a lousy job of it so far.

The sky was growing blacker, the kind of doomed

darkness that foretold of disaster to come. Maybe he should just have let her marry David after all. Sure, he'd probably have been throwing her a divorce party within six months, but at least she'd be alive to celebrate it, instead of dead at the bottom of the ocean.

He glanced to his left. Zoey was holding on tight to the rail beside him, obviously determined to stand by him—as much as he wished she'd just get to safety below. The waves weren't too big yet, but they were going to get bigger...

Then, suddenly, he got a glimpse of what he was looking for. Refuge. Safety. A fully stocked drinks cabinet, he hoped.

'There!' He risked raising one hand from the controls to point. 'Do you see that?'

Zoey leant forward over the rail, squinting into the distance and almost giving Ash a heart attack at the same time. 'Is that the island?'

'I hope so.' Ash braced himself and started to turn the boat. He'd studied the online maps and satellite footage well enough to know that the new acquisition was the nearest island to the one he'd recommended to David for the wedding. It had to be the right one. Hopefully. 'And if all else fails, it's *an* island.' Dry land had to be better than water right now.

As they grew closer, Ash could make out the outline of a wooden villa at the water's edge, the traditional stilts meaning it was half over the ocean and half on land. The roof looked to be the usual thatch, and he recognised the terrace layout from the photos of the recently acquired property he'd been looking at a few days before. This was the place they'd been searching for.

Best of all, there was even a mooring point for the boat. Ash just hoped it would hold overnight.

Once the wedding was over, Zoey was going to want to leave again, after all. Well, eventually, anyway.

Getting the boat moored securely was a battle in itself as the threatened rain began to fall.

'Run up to the house,' he yelled at Zoey, his throat sore with the effort of getting her to hear over the storm. But Zoey shook her head, her wet hair whipping around her as she held on tight to one of the stern lines as he crossed them to tie up.

Stubborn. Just like Grace. No wonder they'd been such good friends.

Finally, finally, the yacht was as secure as he could make it. He'd just have to hope that was as secure as it needed to be. It was too late to do any more. The wind that had been steadily rising had reached a screaming pitch now, whistling and screeching through the trees and across the water. Looking back out to sea, Ash couldn't tell where the rain stopped and the waves started.

'Come on.' Grabbing Zoey's hand, he dragged her up from the small jetty towards the front door of the villa, already dreaming of what they'd find inside as he fumbled for the hidden key and tried to recall the security code he'd saved on his phone.

This place was perfect. Ash had read all the specs on the flight out. The villa was the newest jewel in his father's property crown, freshly refurbished to Arthur

Carmichael's exacting standards. If a person had to take refuge from a storm and a potentially furious bridegroom, this was the spot.

He flung open the doors.

Zoey crashed into his back as he stopped, still on the threshold, and stared in.

Okay. So this place *would* be perfect. Once the renovation was *actually finished.*

'Can we get inside already?' Zoey asked. Ash could feel her shaking, shivering with cold as she pressed against him.

The storm was on them. There was no going back.

'You might wish you'd stayed and married David,' he muttered as he moved aside to let her in.

Zoey pushed past him, then stopped in the middle of what Ash assumed would be the lounge. Eventually.

'So, when you said that this place had just been re-furbished…' She turned around slowly, taking in the room. Ash winced. Even in the darkness of the storm raging outside, he knew this didn't look good.

'I might have been a little optimistic.'

He tried to see the villa through her eyes. The half-built kitchen area off to one side. The random pieces of wood stacked up against the far wall. The windows still covered in tape but no blinds. The complete lack of furniture.

Zoey sighed. 'I suppose it's too much to hope for a fully stocked drinks cabinet, then?'

CHAPTER THREE

THERE WAS OFFICIALLY nothing luxury about the luxury villa Ash had promised her. Even without the storm raging outside, this would have been a disaster. As it was…

Well. They'd just have to make the best of it. After all, it had to be better than going back to the hotel and admitting to David that she'd tried to run out on their wedding but been driven back by bad weather and incomplete renovations. Besides, if she had to get on another boat again this lifetime it might be too soon for her seasick stomach.

Of course, she would have to. But not yet.

They had to make it through the night first.

'Maybe the builders have left some useful stuff lying around,' Zoey said. Although, looking around her, mostly they seemed to have left splintering wood and a lot of rubbish. 'Like blankets or tea or something. I'll go look.'

'And I'll go check the boat.' Ash didn't sound particularly excited at the prospect. 'Probably a better chance of finding things we need there anyway. Maybe even some dry clothes.'

Zoey glanced reflexively down at her beautiful strapless pink dress—now dark and sodden with water, streaked with sandy mud and clinging unflatteringly to her body. She imagined her hair must look even worse.

Good job that Ash had seen her in some seriously unflattering positions before, really—especially at university. At least he wouldn't be surprised. Or too horrified, hopefully.

'Wish me luck.' Ash flashed her a bright grin before pushing open the wide glass door and stepping out into the storm again.

'Good luck!' she called after him, but she doubted he could hear her over the wind. She tried to watch him go, but he was swallowed up by the darkness of the storm in no time.

Suddenly, Zoey felt very alone.

Well, that was what she'd wanted, wasn't it? To escape from the pressure and crush of all the people at the hotel, waiting for her to walk down the aisle in another white dress that didn't feel quite right, to marry a man who used to give her butterflies in her stomach but now gave her moths. Still unsettling but darker and somehow not right.

Oh, God, she'd done it again.

Her knees shaky, Zoey sank to the ground, her soaked pink dress pooling around her and leaving a puddle on the dusty, splinter-laden floor. Her hands twisted in the wet material as she tried to stop the tears threatening to spill over her cheeks.

Why was she *crying*, for heaven's sake? *She* hadn't been left at the altar, or the night before at least. *She* hadn't been abandoned, hadn't suddenly lost the future she'd imagined for her and David.

She'd chosen to run. Again.

She'd made her choice and now she'd live with it.

It was just... How could she have let this happen again?

The first time, with Kevin, it had been so hard. But she'd known it was the right decision. He told her he loved her, that he couldn't imagine his life without her, that he'd die if he couldn't have her...but he'd wanted her to give up her dreams of university, of a future career, to stay with him and see if he could make it as a rock star.

It had taken everything she had to hand him back his ring and walk away, but she'd never worried that she'd made a mistake. And whenever she'd missed him, she'd had Grace there to remind her why she'd done it.

The second time had been more complicated. She'd met Harry at university, not long after Grace and Ash became Grace-and-Ash. Maybe she'd been feeling left out, or maybe she'd just wanted something of the happiness they'd found, because it had been easy to fall into an echo of their relationship herself, with Harry. Except Harry wasn't Ash and she wasn't Grace. They weren't the perfect fit that their friends were, and they'd argued about almost everything.

They'd got engaged six months after they graduated, and Zoey had made it as far as addressing the envelopes for the invitations before she stopped and asked herself what on earth she was doing.

Grace and Ash had been waiting for her with a bottle of wine and a home-cooked meal at their new flat when she showed up, still gripping one of those damn invitations, and told them she didn't think she could go through with it.

Disentangling their lives together had been hard, and Harry hadn't understood what the problem was anyway, why she'd changed her mind so suddenly. But just one evening with Ash and Grace, seeing them clearly and realising everything they were that she and Harry weren't, had made up Zoey's mind for good.

She'd seen what marrying the wrong person could do to a couple—she'd lived with it growing up and, since her parents were apparently violently opposed to divorce, continued to witness it every time she went home. She hadn't understood, for years, what had kept them together, but she thought she did now. It was fear. Fear of scandal and gossip. Fear of losing the very comfortable lifestyle they had from the business they'd built up together—nothing on the scale of Ash's family business, of course, but enough that they didn't want to lose it in a bitter divorce battle. And, given how bitter their marriage had become, Zoey had no doubt that if either one of them ever caved and left, it would be horrific.

She didn't want that for herself, wouldn't let herself settle for a marriage held together by fear of how much worse things might be apart.

She wanted what Grace and Ash had, or it wasn't worth the bother of the fancy dress and the name changing.

She'd thought she'd found it over and over since then, with men who said they worshipped her, or men who promised to respect her, or even men who claimed they wanted them each to live their own lives, just together.

But, in the end, something always changed. There was always a moment when she looked at them and realised that, behind their words, they all wanted the same thing: to lock her in to a life that would no longer be her own.

Every time, it came down to the same problem. Marriage meant sharing a life, letting someone else have equal say in her decisions. It meant giving up control—and most of all it meant risk.

Risking everything on the promise that this guy would be different. That this man meant it when he said that he just wanted her to be happy—rather than *actually* meaning that he wanted her to be happy as long as it fitted in with what *he* wanted.

She'd seen how awful marriage could be if you made the wrong choice, and she wouldn't do that. If she ever finally made it to the altar and said 'I do' it would be because she was certain. That the risk was gone, because there were no doubts left.

Which seemed like a pretty impossible bar to reach.

Zoey sighed. Maybe she should just give up on the whole idea of marriage. It wasn't as if she hadn't had the thought before. But every time she did…she remembered Grace's radiant happiness on her wedding day, and the way Ash had looked like the proudest, most joyous man in the world, and she knew it was possible.

True happiness, true love, was possible—and Zoey wanted it.

It just seemed she was going to have to keep looking to find it.

Slowly, she forced herself back to her feet, brushing the sawdust from her hands on her soaked dress before wiping away her tears. True love would have to take a back seat for a while. Right now she had bigger problems.

First things first. Survive the night. Then go back after the wedding was scheduled to happen and explain everything to David. Given the lengths he'd gone to in order to make sure she was there for the wedding, he presumably wouldn't be entirely surprised by her absence. In fact, he'd already know she was gone by now. Still, it wasn't a conversation she was looking forward to.

But she'd get through it, all the same. Then get back to London and her normal life as soon as possible.

Starting with finding somewhere to live. Oh, hell, she'd probably have to move back in with her parents, in the house and the village where she grew up, at least until she found her own place. And that was after she'd braved returning to David's flat to rescue her stuff. Well, it wouldn't be fun, but it would be necessary—and all steps towards a better future.

She could focus on her job, her future—what *she* wanted in life—and forget all about men.

After they made it through tonight.

With a firm nod to herself, Zoey set off to search the other rooms of the villa in the hope of finding some towels, blankets, food, and maybe alcohol.

Not necessarily in that order.

Ash ducked into the interior of the small yacht, the door slamming behind him in the wind. Water dripped from his hair, his clothes, his skin, all pooling around his very wet feet. It was just as well he hadn't taken the time to dry off while they were at the villa—it would have been a wasted effort. Right now, every inch of him was more water than man, and it was hard to imagine ever being dry again.

First priority: towels. And something waterproof to carry them in back up to the villa. Then maybe clothes.

He found a stash of beach towels in a cupboard under the bed and towelled off his hair as he hunted around for something to hold them while he dashed back to the villa. In the end, the best he could come up with was a bin bag from under the bathroom sink. At least, given the yacht's current owner, it was a high quality one, and Ash trusted it not to break.

There was no sign of anything to wear beyond a couple of towelling robes that wouldn't fit in his bin bag, so he made a mental note to come back for them once the rain had passed. As he placed them back in the cupboard, an image of Zoey wearing one, barefoot and fresh from the shower, popped into his head and he quickly shook it away. '*Not* the time for that sort of thought,' he muttered to himself. Zoey was his best friend. What would she say if she knew he was thinking of her that way—especially the day before she was supposed to get married?

Back on his quest, Ash raided cupboards and lock boxes for food—not much…all packaged and long-life—a torch and matches, a thick blanket, a two pack of toothbrushes and a tube of toothpaste, some tiny hotel-sized toiletries, and finally, in the last cupboard he checked, a bottle of single malt Scotch whisky.

Perfect.

It was only as he hoisted the bag onto his shoulder that he realised fully how ill prepared they'd been for running away. Zoey had left her handbag, her passport, everything at the hotel—including her high-heeled shoes. Did she even have her phone with her? He wasn't sure. Even if she did, reception had been so bad on the islands, he couldn't imagine there was any at all in a storm like this.

He hadn't stopped to grab his passport either, or anything that might have been actually useful, like an extra phone charger. All they had was the contents of his pockets, since he was pretty sure Zoey's dress didn't even have those, which amounted to his wallet, his phone—probably nearly out of battery, but hopefully still working after the rain—and his hotel room key.

That was it.

Had Zoey even thought about it before she'd tried to squeeze through that cupboard window? Had she considered what she was asking when she said, 'Get me out of here, Ash'? Probably not.

Grace had always said that for someone who acted on gut instinct so much, it was a shame that Zoey's intestines were such lousy decision makers.

Ash wondered now if that was right, though. Because Zoey didn't seem to be acting on the say-so of her gut, but her heart. And the heart, he knew, was a far more complicated organ. At least, when it came to relationships.

He liked to think he knew Zoey pretty well. She was the only person who truly knew how much he'd lost the day Grace died. Even if they'd never openly spoken about it.

Before, he'd always known that if there was ever a cause to choose sides, Zoey would be on Grace's, whatever the story. But now, now she was *his* best friend. The person he relied on, the one person he knew would always take his side.

Which was why he'd known, from the moment he'd found her trying to climb out of that window, that tonight wouldn't end the way he'd planned. Not that he'd honestly believed, deep down, that any pre-wedding night involving Zoey was likely to end the traditional way. Him buying David one last whisky in the bar, giving Zoey a hug and a pep talk and getting an early night, ready for the wedding first thing in the morning, had never really been on the cards. More likely sitting up drinking too late with Zoey, reassuring her that she could do this. He'd been prepared for some last-minute jitters.

He just hadn't expected those jitters to lead to them spending the night in a dilapidated villa on a deserted island in the middle of a storm.

When was the last time they'd spent the night together, just the two of them? Had they ever?

Probably in those first days after Grace's accident, although he didn't remember it well if they had. Before that it had always been the three of them. And since then, well, Zoey had a very uncomfortable sofa bed in her lounge he'd slept on a few times before he sold the house he'd shared with Grace and bought a new flat, without the memories. But somehow that felt very different from tonight. Maybe that was what had prompted his brain to imagine Zoey in a bathrobe and nothing underneath…

Tonight, they'd be huddled together avoiding the storm, sharing blankets and body heat, probably. With another woman, anything could happen.

But this was Zoey. Not only was she his wife's best friend, but she'd literally just left a longstanding serious relationship. He shouldn't even be *imagining* anything like that.

Instead, he made himself remember the last time Zoey had called off an engagement at the eleventh hour. And the time before that, actually. Both times, she'd shown up at the house, looking distraught, and Grace had taken care of her. She'd listened, offered advice with no pressure to take it, tried to present different points of view, all without ever being less than one hundred per cent behind whatever Zoey decided to do next.

All Ash had needed to do was pour the wine and order the pizza.

He had a feeling that wasn't going to cut it tonight.

She was going to need to talk about things. That was how Zoey worked. And the only person she had to talk to was him.

I hope I can live up to your standards, Grace.

Except he was fairly sure he couldn't. In fact, he had a sinking feeling he was going to screw this up magnificently—if he hadn't already achieved that by taking them to an abandoned villa on a stolen boat in the middle of a storm.

Ash hefted the bag up to his shoulder again and heard the whisky clank against something satisfactorily. At least he was still providing booze and food—his usual job.

As for the rest…he'd just have to wing it.

Zoey was his friend. She'd forgive him if he got it wrong. Right?

By the time Ash returned from the boat, Zoey had almost managed to make the villa habitable. Well, one small part of it, anyway.

She'd tried the lights first, but either the power was out because of the storm or it wasn't properly connected yet, because the villa stayed resolutely dark.

Using the torch on her phone—the only thing she'd grabbed from the table to take with her when she'd run—she'd explored the whole building, but most of it seemed in a worse state than the main room and with even less furniture, so she figured the open-plan central space at the front of the villa was probably the best place for them to set up camp for the night.

She'd found a large brush and tried to clear the worst of the sawdust and rubbish from the middle of the floor, and even discovered a couple of folding chairs that the crew presumably used for breaks, so set them out too. The biggest and best discovery had been the kettle, mugs and teabags on one of the half-built kitchen counters. Zoey hated to stereotype, but she had a feeling that old Mr Carmichael might have hired his favourite British builders for this job. No wonder they weren't in a hurry to get it finished if they got to hang out in paradise when they were done working for the day.

'Honey, I'm home,' Ash said drily as he shoved open

the large glass doors again. Zoey turned. His voice was the only dry thing about him. Apparently the rain hadn't let up any since they'd arrived. Now she listened for it, Zoey could hear the raindrops hammering down against the windows and walls. The sound was so familiar already she'd stopped hearing it.

'What did you find for us?' She was hoping for food. Maybe vodka.

Ash threw her a towel. She supposed that was a start.

'Let's just say you're going to wish you'd waited until *after* the rehearsal dinner to run,' he said, towelling off his own hair then wrapping the towel around the back of his neck to catch the drips. 'But I did find this.'

He held up a bottle. Zoey grinned. She wasn't much of a drinker—beyond a couple of glasses of wine on occasional girls' nights or dinners out. Whisky definitely wasn't her favourite, but she supposed it *was* warming, and really, runaway bride beggars couldn't be choosers.

'Excellent. I found, well, not much. These chairs, and a couple of old blankets. Oh, and a kettle, so there can be tea in the morning.'

'Great minds…' Ash pulled a stash of teabags and some single serve UHT milk cartons from his pockets. 'That's all the important things covered. What do you want to do now?'

It turned out there really wasn't much *to* do in the middle of a storm on a desert island in a half-renovated villa. Drinking seemed categorically like the best option, especially considering the day she'd had, so they settled into their camping chairs and Ash distributed liberal amounts of whisky into the mugs Zoey had found. Zoey took a sip and pulled a face. Well, at least it seemed like the whisky would last them the night. She couldn't imagine drinking more than a tablespoon or two.

'So,' Ash said after a few quiet moments. 'As I recall from past experience, this is usually the point in the proceedings where you start talking.'

'Past experience?' Zoey raised her eyebrows. 'Have I forgotten all the other times we stole a boat together?'

'I was thinking more of all the other times you ran out on an unsuspecting fiancé.'

'Oh.'

Ash's gaze was measuring, as if he was watching to see which way she was going to jump. Zoey couldn't help but remember those other times he'd mentioned— how she'd always turned to Grace in times of crisis. About how Grace wasn't here to pick her up this time.

Tears burned behind her eyes. Maybe the whisky hadn't been such a good idea after all. Grace always said she was a total lightweight.

'I miss her, you know,' she said around the tightness in her throat. 'Every single day.'

Ash, to his credit, wasn't thrown by her non-sequitur. 'So do I.'

'Of course you do. She was your wife.' And he'd loved her so much. That had been obvious to anyone with eyes. 'Of course you're still grieving and stuff. But me...she was my best friend, and I don't have anyone else. But apparently I should be over this by now.'

Ash's face turned stony. 'According to who?'

'David.' Zoey took another sip of whisky, and then

a bigger gulp. It burned her throat, but somehow that felt like a good thing, now. David would tell her that expensive whisky was wasted on her if she didn't enjoy it. But she didn't have to worry about what David thought any more.

The relief that flowed over her at the realisation was probably a sign that she really should have figured out the not-marrying-him thing sooner.

'In that case, I'm more pleased than ever that I helped you escape marrying him.' Ash scraped his chair across the floor to get closer to her, resting a hand on the plastic arm of her seat. Without thinking, she covered it with her own. 'You said it yourself, Grace was your best friend. You're allowed to mourn and grieve for her as long as you need to.'

It had already been nearly two years. Every morning, Zoey wondered if today would be the day she passed a full twenty-four hours without thinking about her friend, and all she'd lost. Without feeling the hole Grace had left in her life.

It never was.

'But you're wrong about one thing.' Ash turned his hand palm up under hers and gripped her fingers. 'You said you don't have anyone else. That's not true.'

'Isn't it?' Zoey raised her eyebrows as she looked at him, waiting for a joke about the barista she had a crush on at the coffee shop they went to together sometimes.

'No. You've got me.'

The sincerity in his gaze almost broke her. She knew, of course, that she'd sort of adopted him after Grace died—he'd needed someone, anyone, and she was the only other person who felt the loss of Grace so keenly.

But she'd never quite realised until now how much support and love Ash had given her in return. She'd imagined herself as more of an obligation to him—someone Grace would want him to check in on from time to time, to make sure she was okay—once the initial period of chaos and grief was over.

Looking into his eyes now, though, she knew it was more than that. *She* was more than that. More than just an old university friend he'd known for too many years and through too many wild nights out.

They were all each other had any more. Grace might have brought them together, but it was the loss of her that would keep them linked for ever.

She should have seen it sooner. Like when her heating had broken and she'd texted both David and Ash to moan, but David was in a meeting so just sent a sad face emoji text, and it was Ash who showed up with chocolate, blankets and the number of a recommended plumber.

Or her birthday, David had been out of town on business so sent flowers. Ash had been on the other side of the world, at some fancy resort in Australia, but he'd sent a basket with popcorn, wine and a Victoria sponge cake, complete with candles and a party hat, then video called her at six in the morning his time, just as she was getting home from work, so they could watch Netflix together and he could sing 'Happy Birthday' before she blew out her candles. He'd even worn a matching party hat to make her laugh.

Ash was the best friend she had in the world. And now, looking into his bright blue eyes, Zoey wondered how she'd never realised quite *how* good a friend he was. Maybe because she'd always been comparing him to Grace, or thinking of him as an extension of her old friend.

But he wasn't. He was Ash. She smiled, and he returned it with a bright grin of his own that made her throat go tight and her blood feel too warm. And suddenly Zoey realised that there was no one else in the world she'd rather be stranded with tonight.

CHAPTER FOUR

ASH LET GO of Zoey's hand and sat back in his rickety folding chair. That whisky must be stronger than he was used to, or at least faster acting, because he'd only had a couple of sips—not enough to affect him. Or maybe it was the after-effects of stress and excitement from the escape and the boat ride. Yeah, that was probably it. A delayed response to a near-death, or at least near-maiming, experience.

Nothing else would explain the strange feeling that just ran through his body as Zoey smiled at him. The one that seemed to fizz in his blood and brush across his skin with a feather touch.

A feeling he hadn't experienced in two long years.

The problem now wasn't imagining Zoey in a bath-robe. It was the sudden flash of an image of her *out* of one that he couldn't shake.

Zoey. Best friend. Not someone to be imagining naked. Certainly not thinking about stripping that wet dress away from her skin…

He looked away, staring down at the whisky in his mug instead of at his best friend's face.

Zoey was a very lovely woman—he'd never denied that. But he'd never let himself think about her this way before—and he really couldn't afford to start now. She needed him as a friend tonight. That was all.

Maybe more alcohol would help.

Fortunately, it seemed Zoey was on the same wavelength, as she leant over to grab the bottle and top up both their mugs with considerably more liquor than he'd given them the first time.

What had they been talking about before? Something important. Something they should get back to…

Right. Zoey running out on her wedding. That definitely had precedence over any strange feelings he was experiencing.

'So, anyway. Talking. Do you want to? Talk about it, I mean?' Not his most elegant phrasing ever, but it seemed to get the intention across at least.

Zoey shrugged. 'What is there to say?'

What had Grace always done to draw Zoey out? Or did she just naturally talk to her in a way she didn't feel comfortable doing with Ash?

'Well, how are you feeling about everything? I mean, now we're on a completely different island from your fiancé, with no hope of getting back until after you're due to get married unless this weather breaks.' Even then, it might be a push. He wasn't sure how seaworthy that yacht would be after the storm had finished punishing it. The jetty he'd moored it at was rather more exposed than he'd like.

'Honestly?' Zoey said, still staring into her mug. 'Mostly I'm just feeling relieved.'

Ash's shoulders relaxed just a little at that. At least she wasn't regretting her decision. Because *that* would have been a problem he'd have no idea how to fix under the circumstances.

'He wasn't the right guy for you, Zoey,' he said softly.

She looked up with a sad half smile. 'They never are. That's the problem.'

'One of them will be, one day.'

'You can't know that.' Zoey shook her head, then took another gulp of whisky. 'Maybe there just *isn't* a right guy out there for me.'

'But maybe there is,' Ash countered. 'And if you stop looking, you'll never find him.'

She squinted up at him. 'Have you been reading self-help relationship blogs again?'

'No!' Well, not often, anyway. 'I just can't imagine someone as brilliant as you being alone for ever.'

Her cheeks turned a little pink at that, almost matching her still damp dress. It was funny, even drenched and bedraggled, shoeless and tipsy, she looked more beautiful than ever tonight. She always did, he supposed. He just hadn't ever let himself look before.

'What about you?' she asked, and the question threw him right back into the present with a jolt.

'How do you mean? I'm fine. Wet, but fine.' The towels hadn't been nearly good enough. He really wished he'd been able to bring the towelling robes as well—the stress it might have put on his imagination notwithstanding. At least then they could have got out of their soaked clothes.

Let me help you out of that wet dress...

Ash choked on a mouthful of whisky as the image of him undressing Zoey flashed through his mind.

Really not the time.

'I mean, do you think there will ever be anyone else for you? After Grace, I mean?'

Ash put down his mug. What did it say about him that the idea had hardly even crossed his mind in the last two years?

'I… I don't know. I mean, it's hard to imagine it. I can imagine dating, maybe even sex with someone else.' Hell, he'd been doing that right here, right now, at the most inappropriate time ever, curse his imagination. 'But the idea of loving someone else. Marrying them. Making a life with them…that's… I just can't see it. Literally. I can't picture it in my mind. You know?' When Grace had died, he'd lost not just his wife, but his whole future. The family he'd hoped to have one day was gone for ever.

'I know,' Zoey said sadly. 'That's the problem I have. I can see myself in the future, with a family, a home, a happy life. And there's always a vague figure in the background—a husband or partner or whatever. But I can never quite *see* him.'

'Not even when you're getting ready to walk down the aisle to meet him?'

Zoey shook her head. 'I guess I always think it'll come together. That everything will come into focus once I have that dress on and the ring on my finger. But then it comes to the day and the picture still isn't there. I can't ever see how to get from where I am to where I want to be.'

'So you *do* want to get married, then?' Ash asked. Grace had always said that Zoey wanted a happy marriage but, given how many times she'd walked out on the possibility of one, Ash had to wonder. 'Are you sure that marriage isn't just something you think you're supposed to want but don't really? I mean, it isn't for everyone. It doesn't have to be.'

'I know that.' Zoey looked up, straight into his eyes, and he felt a jolt go through him at the intensity of her gaze. 'But I want it. I want the whole thing—true love, marriage, a happy-ever-after. I want that more than anything.'

And he knew she meant every single word.

She'd never told anyone this before—except Grace. She let people believe that it was fear of commitment that made her run, let them think she just had the worst relationship style in the world. She never let on that it was only *because* she wanted that happily-ever-after so badly that she kept running out on it.

Zoey knew how much it was worth, how much it mattered—and how much it could hurt to settle for anything less. And that was why she couldn't marry anyone if she had a shred of doubt about how it would end up.

People wouldn't get it, she knew, which was why she didn't talk about it. The few times she'd discussed true love and happy ever afters with other people—usually after drinks—the reactions had not been encouraging.

Most people tended to fall into one of two camps. On the one side were those who believed that true love and soulmates were a fallacy, probably put about by greeting card companies and romance novelists. On the other were those who told her that marriage took work, that no one was happy all the time and that she should be grateful for what she had.

In the end, they were both saying the same thing, Zoey had realised eventually.

Stop wanting so much.

But she *did* want. And it wasn't about the ring or the ceremony or the big party or whatever happened next. It was about having the right person next to her when it happened.

And maybe some people truly believed that soulmates didn't exist—or maybe they were just saying it because they hadn't been lucky enough to find theirs. But Zoey knew for a fact that soulmates were real.

Because she'd watched Ash and Grace fall in love.

Even now, she used them as a benchmark. She thought back to how they'd been in their early days together and tested each of her own new relationships against the memories. And, for a while, they'd often match up—or perhaps she'd just convince herself that they did, half through optimism and half through desperation.

But there always came the point where she had to admit the truth to herself—her relationships were never that picture-perfect, soft-focus, tumbling headlong into love that she'd seen Ash and Grace manage at eighteen.

That wouldn't stop her looking, though.

'I want what you had with Grace,' she whispered, looking down at the mug in her hands. 'More than anything, that's what I want. That perfect happiness.'

There was an awkward silence emanating from the other folding chair. When she risked looking up, Ash's expression was conflicted, as if he couldn't decide whether or not to say what he was thinking.

'What?' she asked.

'Zoey, you know how much I loved Grace. And how much she loved me. But that doesn't mean things were perfect all the time. I mean, we fought, just like any couple. Stupid fights over whose turn it was to put the bin out, or whose fault it was we slipped into our overdraft that month. And bigger things too, like whether we should move house, or when we should have kids.' His voice caught on the last word and Zoey felt guilty for even making him remember how much he'd lost. She started to interrupt, to tell him he didn't need to say this, but he shook his head and continued. 'If I'd known how things would end, believe me, I'd take back every single one of those arguments and let her get her own way every time.'

'No, you wouldn't.' Zoey felt a small smile tugging at her lips. 'Because that's not who you two were together. Of course I know it wasn't perfect happy families every second. That's not what I mean.'

'Oh? Then what *do* you mean?'

Zoey cast around for the right words. 'When you two argued, it was because you were working something out between you. You were building a partnership—one that was far deeper and more important than the bins or the overdraft, but those things still had to be dealt with. Every row you had, it brought you closer together. Closer to the people you wanted to be for each other.'

Ash looked a little stunned at her words. Zoey allowed herself a small smile. Had he really never thought about how the two of them looked to the outside world?

The perfect couple, made to be together. Hashtag relationship goals, for sure.

'It wasn't…it wasn't ever about being perfect, you know. I just loved her so much I wanted her to be happy. For us to be happy together.'

'And you'd do anything to get there, I know. Sadly, I think you've ruined me for other men. The pair of you, I mean,' she added hurriedly. 'As a couple.' The last thing she needed was for him to get the wrong idea now. Even if a few impure thoughts had flashed through her head as he sat there, hair wet and shirt clinging to his body. Not that she was admitting to them.

'Right. Sorry…what?'

Even as she looked up at his adorably confused face, Zoey could feel a blush rising to her cheeks.

'I just meant, I want what you and Grace had. I know that sort of love is possible and I'm not willing to settle for anything less. That's all.'

Ash shook his head. 'So it's *my* fault you keep walking out on your weddings? Please, don't ever let any of your ex-fiancés hear you say that.'

'Well, yours *and* Grace's,' Zoey corrected, but that only made him laugh.

'I'm not sure if that makes it better or worse.'

Suddenly restless, Zoey jumped to her feet, cradling her mug against her chest as she paced to the window to watch the rain and the dark. 'Do you think I'm crazy? I mean, you wouldn't be the first person to suggest that my approach to love might actually qualify me for some serious free therapy.'

'How could I? I mean, it's my marriage that you're basing your theories on. It's just…'

'You can't see anyone falling for *me* like that,' Zoey finished for him. 'Don't worry, it's not like I haven't had the same thought myself.'

'No.' Suddenly, he was right beside her and she stopped staring out at the rain to turn towards him as he grabbed her hand. 'That's not what I was going to say at all.'

Zoey stared up into Ash's strange light blue eyes and wondered at the chain of events that had brought them to this moment. She couldn't, wouldn't have predicted any of them. In fact, she'd have avoided or stopped most of them if she could.

But now she was there, she couldn't imagine her life going any other way.

She was meant to be here, now; she could feel it in her bones.

Even if she had no idea why.

'What were you going to say?' Zoey asked, the words coming out strangely breathless.

Ash gave a sad smile. 'Only that I know how lucky I was. How rare it is to find the one person you're truly meant to be with. I honestly hope that you do, and when it happens I'll be there to catch the bouquet.'

'But?' There was always a but, in Zoey's experience.

'No buts, not for you, anyway.' He shrugged. 'But, whether I catch the bouquet or not, I know it won't happen for me again. The odds are too astronomical. And I'm like you. I know what true love feels like now so I can't accept anything less.'

It wasn't new information. He'd already told her he couldn't imagine loving again, after Grace. But somehow, standing with her hand in his in the darkness, Zoey felt his words deep in her heart, like gouges.

Which was ridiculous. She'd literally never thought of Ash that way—not as someone she could fall in love with. Of course she'd noticed he was gorgeous—that kind of thing was hard to miss. And there had been one or two dreams that had made their next get-togethers very uncomfortable for her. But he was Grace's. Always had been, always would be. Zoey had never forgotten that for an instant.

She pulled her hand away from his. It was just the emotion of the day—the craziness and the changes—getting to her. That was all.

But then Ash grabbed her hand back again and held it against his chest, and her treacherous heart skipped a beat.

'Zoey...' Ash trailed off, uncertain of what he even wanted to say. Just something. Anything that would wipe that hopeless look from her face.

This was why she needed Grace. He couldn't even get further than her name. What kind of comfort was that?

'It's okay, Ash.' Zoey started to pull away again, but instinctively Ash clung on.

There was something in this moment. Something important. And he knew, suddenly, that if he didn't tell her now what her friendship meant to him, he never would. And Zoey deserved to know.

'No. I want to tell you… I wouldn't be here without you.' He poured all the sincerity he felt into the words.

Zoey laughed in response, which wasn't quite what he'd intended. 'Well, no, Ash. If it weren't for me and my ridiculous inability to get married, you wouldn't be stuck here in some mystery island renovation project in the middle of a storm.'

'That's not what I mean either.' Taking the mug from her, he put it down on the half-built counter and took both her hands in his. 'I mean, after Grace. If it hadn't been for you, pulling me up, talking me through it, making sure I got out of bed in the mornings, I don't know if I'd have been able to keep going.'

'You would,' Zoey said, with more certainty than Ash felt. 'You know how furious Grace would have been if you didn't.'

'That's true.' His wife had been a stern believer in living your best life, even if the circumstances sucked. She never gave up on anything—until that last, awful ambulance ride. 'But you made it easier. You made it seem possible.'

Zoey shrugged, her gaze sliding away from his. 'I didn't do much. I had no idea *what* to do. For weeks, I just kept hoping it was a mistake. That the universe meant to take me instead of her.'

Her matter-of-fact tone made Ash's blood run cold. As much as he would give to have his wife back—up to and including his own life—he couldn't wish away Zoey's in such a manner.

'You know, you're the only other person who knows

how much was taken from me that day. Not just Grace, but—' He broke off, unable to say it.

'The baby,' Zoey whispered for him, and he nodded.

Grace had just turned twelve weeks pregnant; he or she had still been a tiny, perfect embryo. Zoey was the only other person Grace had told, wanting to wait until after the scan to make a big announcement. And afterwards, Ash hadn't been able to bring himself to mention it. But knowing that she knew, that his child was real for someone other than just him, that helped, a little.

'You knew what I'd lost. But still, you reminded me that the world was worth living for,' he said softly. 'Every day, you showed me everything that was still with me. From a sunny day in the park, to the best ice cream from that place by the canal, to just having a great friend to watch movies with on a Sunday afternoon. You never told me to smile, or to be happy. You were just there. Spending time with me, expecting nothing, but reminding me every single day that the world went on, and that was a good thing.'

Zoey stared up at him, her eyes wide and amazed. He didn't blame her. Ash wasn't entirely sure where those words had come from, either. But now he'd said them, he knew they were absolutely true.

'I want to do the same for you.' He pulled her close by their joined hands, until their hands were the only thing separating the two of them. 'Zoey, you've been my constant friend and support ever since that day at the hospital, and I'm not sure I've been anything close to the same for you.'

'You have!' she protested. 'Remember the long-distance Netflix binge on my birthday? With the cakes and the hats?'

Ash smiled, despite himself. 'I do.' Grace had always made such a big deal about people's birthdays—especially Zoey's. She always said it was because Zoey deserved a fuss, and no one else in her life was going to give it to her. When a reminder popped up on the electronic calendar he and Grace had shared, a week before the big event, he'd realised that, without Grace there, Zoey's birthday could go unmarked altogether. For some reason, it hadn't even occurred to him that David might celebrate it properly—and, of course, he hadn't.

So Ash had taken up the challenge. Even if he had to be thousands of miles away on the day, that was no excuse not to celebrate.

That was what Grace would have said.

'That was just a tiny drop in the ocean compared to all the things you've done for me,' he pointed out.

Zoey looked shyly down at their clasped hands. 'Maybe. But it meant the world to me.'

Releasing one hand from her fingers, Ash tucked it under her chin, forcing her to look up at him. 'You are worth far, far more.'

He could see incredulous disbelief vying with hope in her eyes. Ash wished he could convince her. Could show her that she was worthy of so much more than the men who just wanted a ring on her finger, but not the full Zoey experience. Worth more than countless last-minute escapes at the altar. Worth more than a long-distance video call and some cake on her birthday.

He wanted to show her that she was worth *everything*.

'There's no one in the world I'd rather be stranded in paradise with.' He'd meant it as a joke, something to lighten the mood, but it didn't come out that way. Instead, it came out serious, heavy with meaning. The words reverberated around his chest, surrounding his heart, filling him with a feeling he couldn't quite identify. And from the way Zoey bit her lower lip, she felt it too.

'Me either,' she whispered, her gaze never leaving his for a moment.

And then...then it was as if his mind shut down altogether and his body took over. Or maybe, maybe it was his long-ignored heart.

All Ash knew was that suddenly he was kissing Zoey Hepburn. And it was glorious.

CHAPTER FIVE

THE STORM HAD stopped.

As Zoey raised her aching head from her pillow, the first thing she noticed was the lack of rain hammering on the roof and windows. The second was the blazing sunlight that was making her eyeballs throb.

The third was that her pillow wasn't a pillow.

Oh, I've really done it this time.

Her head hurt too much to process the sight of Ash Carmichael lying beneath her, a rough towel draped across his hips and the rest of him probably—*definitely*—naked.

Naked. Her best friend was naked.

And, oh, hell, so was she.

Okay, this might be her biggest screw-up yet. Forget running out on multiple fiancés. *This* was the act that was going to send her to hell.

She had slept with Grace's husband. Her body, through the whisky hangover, was very sure about that much, at least. And as she sat, stunned, looking down at the perfection of his torso, the sweep of his dark eyelashes against his pale cheeks, his tousled black hair, all sorts of other memories started coming back.

Memories that made her chest tight and her cheeks red.

Memories that, under literally any other circumstances, would be very fond ones. Ones to relive in private, later. Ones to keep her warm on cold winter nights.

As it was…

'Oh, hell, I slept with Grace's husband,' she whispered, then clapped a hand over her mouth to try and keep from waking him. The last thing she needed was an awake and alert Ash before she'd figured out what the hell she was going to do next.

Grabbing the second towel they'd been using as a blanket, which had been thrown aside at some point during the night—she wasn't thinking about *which* point— Zoey wrapped it tightly around herself and tucked in the ends so it covered everything important. Somewhere, her pink dress must be lying abandoned, but even if she could find it Zoey wasn't sure how she could ever wear it again without remembering Ash stripping it from her body with long, capable fingers…

No. She wasn't thinking about that.

She was thinking about how to fix this.

Zoey paced to the window, rested her sore head against the cool glass and tried to focus.

This was a mistake. They must both know that, surely. And when Ash woke up he'd be embarrassed and confused, just like she was. They'd laugh about it, put it all down to the whisky and the drama of the storm, then they'd make a pact never to mention it again. Easy.

Except not mentioning it wasn't the same as forgetting.

And she knew all too well that the whisky wasn't responsible for what had happened last night. Not on her part, anyway.

She'd wanted him—wanted Ash to kiss her, to touch her, to make love to her, long before the whisky had taken effect. Alcohol had just given her brain permission to take what she wanted—had helped her forget all the reasons she shouldn't.

Guilt swamped her, heavy as a raincloud fit to burst. It wasn't just Grace she'd betrayed, it was her friendship with Ash too. Never mind that Grace was dead. Sleeping with Ash now…it undermined everything they'd had before. Suddenly, she couldn't look back at all those happy memories of the three of them without wondering if the lust and passion of last night was lurking there too, under the surface.

If she'd always been thinking of this, planning it even, all along—however subconsciously.

Had she?

She didn't think so. But then, she'd never have thought she'd sleep with Ash at all, let alone the night before she was supposed to marry someone else.

Slipping out through the bi-fold doors that opened onto the veranda over the ocean, Zoey gulped in the fresh sea air to try and clear her head. Closing the door as silently behind her as she could, she moved across to sit on the edge, her feet trailing just above the water, so the odd wave lapped against her toes.

She needed to think. To figure out what the hell had just happened—and why.

Leaning back on her hands, she let the morning wind ruffle her hair and awaken her skin. The last vestiges of the previous night's storm still lingered in the air—a cooler, fresher breeze than she was used to out here in the Indian Ocean, and the tang of salt in her mouth with each breath. The waves were higher too—not the crashing, terrifying crests of water they'd experienced sailing in the night before, but enough to show that nothing was calm, that it wasn't all over yet.

In fact, Zoey was rather afraid it might only be beginning.

Alone on the deck, she couldn't resist the urge to relive the night before in her mind. After all, how was she going to fully understand what had happened—or figure out what she should do next—if she didn't fully examine what she'd done? The fact that her heart-rate picked up at the memories was just an aside.

It had started with that kiss.

That stupid, ill-thought-out, spur-of-the-moment, mind-blowing kiss.

Zoey had never spent much time before imagining what it would be like to kiss Ash—she hadn't needed to. Grace had described it in absurd detail the first time she'd kissed him.

But the kiss Zoey had experienced was nothing like that decade-old description.

'It was perfect, Zoey,' Grace had said, bouncing a little on her bed in their tiny shared university flat. *'Like flowers and white wine and romance and rose petals. Not too much—you know, some guys can just get a little over-enthusiastic with their tongue?'*

Zoey had nodded at that. She knew.

'But Ash... He was gentle and careful and responsive and...'

She'd sighed, a dreamy look on her face, and Zoey had thought she understood exactly what she meant.

But that wasn't the kiss that Zoey had received last night.

When Ash kissed her there were no rose petals or romance. No holding back or being gentle.

But if she was honest with herself that had only made it better. Hotter.

Her eyes fluttered closed as she remembered.

Even as his lips had brushed hers for the first time, she'd felt her blood heating up. That first touch had sent her wild—and it seemed to have the same effect on Ash too. Within moments, his hands were at her back, holding her closer as his mouth worked over hers.

He'd pulled back for a half second, just long enough to meet her eyes and murmur, '*Okay?*' But the moment she'd nodded he'd been on her again, a drowning man who needed her kisses to survive.

Zoey had to admit it had been hot as all hell.

But a huge mistake.

Her eyes snapped open and she focused on the cool blue of the ocean, on the breeze against her skin, reminding her treacherous body of all the reasons why sleeping with Ash was the worst idea possible.

One: I just ran out on my own wedding. Again.

Two: I might technically still be engaged to David. Hell, she was still wearing his ring. Shame burning her cheeks, she tugged the diamond solitaire from her finger, realised she had nowhere safe to put it, and shoved it back onto her right hand instead as a compromise.

Three: he's my best friend's husband. That was the

biggie, of course. It didn't seem to make any difference to her heart or head that Grace had been dead for two years. It still felt like the worst and grossest betrayal.

Four: everything is different now.

They'd grown so close as friends. Ash was the only person she knew who was always in her corner. And now? She'd ruined that.

No, *they'd* ruined it. This was very much his fault too.

Zoey sighed, and tried to think her way out of the muddle her brain was in. But, before she could get further than *We need to fix this,* the bifold doors opened again and Ash stood there, wearing just his trousers from the night before, topless and gorgeous, his hair mussed from sleeping on the floor and his eyes knowing and heavy.

Oh, God, now what do I do?

Ash's first thought upon waking was, *We need to do that again. Soon.*

Then his brain—and his hangover—caught up with his libido, and he winced.

Cracking open his eyes—slowly—he took in his surroundings. Mid-refurbishment luxury villa. Hard and chilly tiled floors against his bare arse where the towels they'd lain on had shifted in the night. Wide glass windows and doors exposing him to the world outside, except for the towel laid across his middle, just about covering his modesty.

No Zoey.

Really, apart from that last part, he'd had worse morning-afters. But not for a long time—not since before he'd married Grace.

Grace.

Guilt flooded him with a heat that beat any tropical summer, and he sat up slowly as he took stock of what he'd done.

For the first time in two years, Grace hadn't been his first thought on waking. It wasn't that he'd forgotten her, of course, just that the memory hadn't been top of his brain the moment his eyes opened.

After she died, for the first few months, he'd often wake up expecting her to be lying beside him. Those mornings were even worse than the others—the ones where he woke up with the knowledge of her death already heavy on his chest. At least with the second sort he didn't have to deal with hope leaving him all over again.

But this morning—this morning he'd thought about last night first. And that had never happened before.

Wrapping the towel more securely around his waist, he stood up, wishing he'd raided the first-aid kit on the boat for some painkillers.

Where was Zoey? It wasn't as if she could have gone far, unless she'd been desperate enough to try and sail the boat back alone, which seemed unlikely. Not least because the storm had probably battered the little yacht enough that it would need some attention before it could go anywhere. Also, because she didn't know how.

So that meant she was still on the island somewhere, and they were going to have to talk about it.

I slept with Zoey Hepburn.

God, he was an idiot. What kind of guy seduced a woman who'd just run out on her wedding? He was pretty sure that wasn't in Grace's handbook for How

To Look After Zoey. Or wouldn't have been, if she'd ever written such a thing.

He wished, not for the first time, that Grace *had* written him a guidebook on how to live life without her. Maybe then he wouldn't be screwing up the only real friendship he had left so damn badly.

Okay, so. First step. Talking.

No, first step—clothes. Otherwise nothing about this was going to get any easier.

Tugging on his suit trousers, he headed for the large glass doors that led out to the veranda. As he opened them, he spotted Zoey, sitting on the deck just out of sight from the villa, her feet dangling over the water.

She turned to look at him as he approached and he saw everything she was feeling in her eyes. Zoey had always been an open book, unable to stop her every emotion showing on her face. He studied her, to get a read on how she was feeling.

There was guilt there, unsurprisingly. And confusion and…fear?

Ash's insides tensed at the last one. Why was she afraid? And what sort of terrible friend was he to have left her feeling that way?

Mild panic setting in, he quickly ran over the previous night in his head. They might both be thinking better of it this morning, but in the moment she'd wanted it as much as he had, hadn't she? He'd checked. Repeatedly. With every step forward they'd taken.

Her responses—physical and verbal—had been enthusiastic enough for him to relax a little. Whatever she was afraid of, it wasn't his behaviour the night before, he was sure.

'Good morning.' His voice came out scratchy from last night's whisky and he cleared his throat as he sat down beside her—close enough for friends, not so close as to spook her.

'Hey.' She gave him a small half smile. 'Sleep well?'

'Surprisingly, yes,' he replied. 'Given the lack of comfort and the luxury I was promised here.' Of course, the vigorous exercise and whisky before bed had probably helped with that. But he didn't mention it. Even though she had to be thinking it too.

Could he blame the whisky? They'd certainly drunk enough of it. But Ash knew himself too well for that. Whisky might lower his inhibitions, but there wasn't enough in a whole bottle to make him do something he didn't want to do anyway.

And, oh, God, he'd wanted Zoey. If he was honest with himself, he still did. Even hung-over and regretting putting their friendship on the line—it didn't change the fact that he saw her in a new light now. He knew how it felt to kiss her, to touch her, to feel her. And that wasn't something any amount of alcohol could wash away.

They sat in awkward silence for a long moment, looking out over the water as sea birds swooped low and waves crashed high.

'Do you think the boat is okay?' Zoey asked suddenly. 'I mean, for us to sail back this morning?'

'I'll go take a look when my head's stopped pounding so much,' Ash replied. His head hurt a little more just thinking about it.

'What will we do if it's not okay?' There was panic rising in her voice now, Ash could hear it.

'You mean, how will we explain it to the guest who hired it? They'll have insurance, Zo, don't worry. And if there's a problem, I'll pay.' He used his most soothing voice, trying to calm her, but somehow every word only seemed to make her more agitated.

'I mean, how will we get off this island!' She jumped to her feet. 'I need to get back there, Ash. Now.'

He blinked. 'Back to… David?' *Surely* she didn't mean what he thought she meant.

'The wedding is supposed to start in two hours,' she said. 'If the boat is okay—'

'You could get back and marry the man you already told me you'd be unhappy with?' Ash raised his eyebrows. 'Zoey, sit down. Let's talk about this.'

She shook her head, her dark hair whipping around her face in the wind. Wrapped in a towel that barely covered the tops of her tanned thighs, she looked wild, unpredictable.

And gorgeous. Utterly, utterly gorgeous.

Ash looked away and waited for her to sit. She didn't.

'I don't want to talk. I want to get back to where I'm supposed to be.' Her eyes were wide and wild too, he realised when he looked back. As if control was slipping from her grasp and she wasn't even trying to catch it.

'You're not supposed to marry David today,' Ash said calmly.

'What? So now you're a big believer in fate and destiny? And you've decided mine?' She threw the words at him, and he wondered if she knew how much they stung.

'You know I'm not,' he said softly, remembering the people who'd told him, after Grace's death, that all things happened for a reason, that God had a plan.

He'd known they were trying to offer comfort, which was the only reason he hadn't screamed at them that whatever plan this was, he hadn't agreed to it. That any God who had a reason for taking his wife and unborn child from him had better start explaining Himself pretty damn fast.

Sometimes, there were no reasons. And talk of fate and destiny only tried to hem people in to decisions they shouldn't be making, in his opinion.

Zoey's expression turned contrite. 'I'm sorry. I just…'

She trailed off, so he tried to find the words for her. 'You're scared and confused. Just like me. Which is why we should talk.'

But Zoey shook her head again. 'I can't. I'm sorry.'

Then, with a whirl of hair and towel, she'd turned and gone, disappearing back into the house and slamming the door shut behind her, before he could even think of following.

Ash stared out at the water.

'Well. That could have gone better.'

Yes, fine, okay, so technically she was running away again. At least she had a *theme*. Like, a personal calling card. If you wanted her, she was already gone.

And Ash had only wanted to *talk* to her. Imagine if he'd wanted to *marry* her.

Don't think about it. Don't think about it.

Too late. The idea was already there in her head. Festering.

Quickly, Zoey dragged on her still damp pink dress, ignoring the streaks of dirt from the boat, the storm and the sawdust, and let her towel drop to the floor. She needed real clothes to face today, however ruined they were.

Matches my mood.

Without looking back to see if Ash was following—*please don't let him be following*—she dashed out of the front door of the villa, away from the veranda and towards the beach.

'I need to go check on the boat,' she told herself under her breath as she marched away from the villa—away from *him.* 'See how bad the storm damage is to the island too. It's the responsible thing to do.'

And just because she hadn't been the responsible one at any point up until now, that didn't mean it was too late to start, did it?

Her determination and sense of righteousness lasted until she reached the edge of the sea and realised she'd stormed off in the wrong direction for checking on the boat and had no idea what the island had looked like *before* the storm hit.

Gathering her dusty and windswept hair into a knot at the base of her neck, she pulled it through itself until it stayed in place, held by dirt and sea salt, she supposed. Then her wobbly legs gave way and she dropped down to the sand, her legs folded under her.

She'd thought—she'd hoped—that they'd look at each other this morning and laugh. Brush away the events of last night as a drunken mistake, one that wouldn't affect their friendship in the least.

But then she'd seen him again and known, without a shadow of a doubt, that however *he* felt about their indiscretion, she wasn't going to be able to brush it aside or forget it at all. Ever.

His touch was burned into her skin. His kisses owned her brain now—she could think of nothing else when she saw his lips. And his body... How had she never touched it before? Been touched by it. Felt it sliding against hers—

Because he was married to someone else. Because he *loved* someone else. Still, even now. Grace was it for him—he'd told her as much.

So what was the point in pretending otherwise? In imagining—even for a moment—that things could be different.

What was wrong with her that a man kissed her and her thoughts instantly went to white dresses and diamond rings?

'It doesn't have to be all or nothing, Zoey,' Grace had told her once. *'You can have love without marriage, the same way you can have marriage without love. And not every potential relationship has to go the distance. Some are only meant for right now.'*

And some could only ever be one stupid, drunken night of passion.

Because, whatever Grace said, Zoey *wanted* that for ever kind of happiness. And Ash was the last person who could give that to her—because he'd already had it. Lightning didn't strike twice and all that.

And, even if it could, she couldn't live with always knowing that she was second choice, that she'd never live up to Grace's memory, whatever she did. Grace had been a ridiculously hard act to follow as a friend. But as a lover? A wife?

'There's no one in the world I'd rather be stranded in paradise with.'

Ash's words came back to her, as if on the wind, and in them she heard what he wasn't saying. No one in the world. No one left living, he meant.

Zoey shook her head and tendrils of hair slipped out of the knot and whipped around her face.

Okay. So, however incredible last night had been, one night was what it had to stay. That part was easy.

Forgetting how good it had been…that might be a little harder.

But she had to. For the sake of their friendship.

Dragging herself to her feet, she started back along the beach, towards the jetty where they'd moored the boat the night before. She could already make out a figure standing there, running a hand over the boat. Her heart contracted a little at the sight.

Ash.

Yeah, this might be harder than she'd hoped.

The problem, she mused as she walked, was that Grace had set Ash up as the perfect husband. In her head, Zoey saw the two of them as the ideals of marriage—everything she was looking for. It was only natural, really, that she should fall a little bit in love with him too. Or at least with the idea of him.

That was the part she had to focus on. The *idea* of Ash

as part of Ash-and-Grace, couple of the year, was one thing. The *reality* was something different altogether.

Ash the idea was perfect, unattainable, a dream—and he belonged to Grace. She could admire and adore him from afar, like she might a movie star. That was easy.

Ash the reality was her best friend, broken by the loss of his family, who needed her as a shoulder to cry on, as a support network and as someone to remember Grace with. She could do all that—she had been doing it for two years.

But the first wasn't real. And the second… He didn't need a best friend lusting over him or making things weird just because they got carried away with the romance of being stranded on a desert island, and the adrenaline of running out on yet another wedding. He didn't need a friend idealising him, or imagining him naked all the time.

He just needed her to be his friend. And she could do that.

With a sharp nod to herself, Zoey quickened her step. They'd check out the boat and head back to the hotel—not so she could marry David, but so she could set things right there.

Then she could go home, and she and Ash could go back to being friends again. Just friends.

The only problem with her plan, she realised as she reached the jetty, was that she wasn't entirely sure which of the two Ashes she'd slept with last night.

The ideal or the best friend.

CHAPTER SIX

'HOW'S IT LOOKING?' Zoey's voice called out, closer than he expected, and Ash spun around so fast he clocked his head on the side of the boat. 'Ouch.' She winced. 'Sorry.'

Okay, that was *not* going to help his headache. One he was pretty sure was caused more by stress and confusion and the lack of a pillow than alcohol.

'You surprised me.' Rubbing his temple, he stepped away from the boat and closer to her, eyeing her warily. Which Zoey was this? The carefree one he'd made love to last night, or the frightened one who'd run away from him this morning?

Careful scrutiny revealed neither. This Zoey looked cautious, but not afraid. She also looked determined.

Ash decided not to worry just yet about what she was determined to *do*. As long as it wasn't marrying David, how bad could it be?

'I'm sorry I ran out on you before.' She bit her bottom lip as she watched him from under her lashes. 'It's sort of a bad habit of mine.'

Ash couldn't help the bark of laughter that escaped from him. 'Well, at least you were wearing a towel instead of a white dress this time.'

Zoey laughed and the sound made his heart feel lighter.

'So? How is the boat looking?'

Okay, so they were avoiding the subject of them for a while. Probably for the best, Ash acknowledged. He wasn't sure he could talk rationally about it until the urge to kiss her again had left his system.

He just wished he knew how long that would take.

It was crazy. He'd never looked at Zoey this way before last night. And now…now it was all he could see.

For distraction, Ash glanced back at the stolen yacht. She wanted to know how it was. He needed to focus on that, and how they were going to get off the island. If that was actually their best move, right now.

'Well, that depends,' he said.

'On what?'

'On what you want to use it for.' He was not above some boat sabotage if it meant keeping her from a wedding he *knew* she didn't really want to go through with. Especially not if her reason for going back was because he'd screwed up and kissed her last night. Not to mention all the other stuff he'd done to her…

Focus on the boat, Ash.

Zoey rolled her eyes. 'I'm not planning on marrying David, if that's what you're worried about.'

'Good.' Relief washed over him. 'Because I was starting to worry about how truly awful last night was for you if your first instinct was to run back to him.'

Colour flooded Zoey's cheeks and Ash started to regret the joke—until she said, almost to herself, '*That* wasn't the problem at all.'

Interesting. Very interesting.

Okay, so not thinking about it and not talking about it wasn't working—in fact, the not thinking part seemed pretty much impossible.

Which meant they needed to deal with it head-on.

Moving closer, Ash couldn't stop himself pressing the point. Male pride, perhaps, he admitted to himself. Or maybe just a desperate need to fix things with his best friend.

'So what was the problem, Zo? Why did you run away from me this morning?'

'I wasn't running away—' she started, then broke off and sighed. 'Okay, fine, I was. I just… I needed to figure some stuff out in my head. Last night was… unexpected.'

'It definitely was,' Ash agreed. He could never have predicted they'd end up here. But now they were, he couldn't imagine how things could be any different. How he could ever get back to looking at Zoey and only seeing a friend.

What had changed the way he saw her? He wasn't even sure. But he had a feeling it had something to do with the way she'd looked at him in that damn cupboard and told him to get her out of there.

Suddenly, it had been the two of them against the world. And that had felt…right.

Zoey was still talking. God, *where* was his focus today?

Still in bed with Zoey Hepburn.

'And I get that we need to talk about it,' Zoey went on as he forced himself to tune back in. This was important. 'So I figure we should probably get that over and done with before we head back to the hotel.'

Over and done with. Well, that was a telling phrase. Ash felt his spirits sink as he realised what she was doing.

She was going to try and brush the whole night under the carpet. Talk about it and then pretend it never happened. And he could understand why, really he could. It wasn't exactly the best timing, or the ideal circumstances. But he knew how not talking about things could fester.

Ash tried to live without regrets these days. And while he certainly wasn't going to regret making love to Zoey Hepburn—how could he, when it had been the best thing to happen to him in two long years?—Ash knew that if they didn't resolve things properly between them now, he'd regret that later.

He looked back at the boat again. It wasn't in bad shape, considering the battering it had taken in the wind. But he was no expert. It would probably be reckless and irresponsible to try to sail it back now, with the winds still so high, right?

Wiping his hands on the towel he held, he tossed it back into the boat carelessly and smiled. 'Well, then, the good news is we have all the time we need to talk. The boat took a real beating in the storm. Better to wait until I can contact someone to come out and pick us— and it—up safely, I think. Don't you?'

Zoey's eyes went wide at the suggestion and she stammered her way through an agreement. 'Uh, right. Yeah. Sure. I guess.'

'So? Do you want to talk in the villa or shall we take a walk on the beach?' he asked, still smiling easily. He didn't want to spook her any more than necessary.

The way she glanced over at the villa then shook her head told him all he needed to know. She wasn't ready to return to the scene of the crime just yet. Or maybe she was worried about what they'd be tempted to do, alone in there.

He didn't blame her. Just the idea of it had his blood heating and images of her naked in his arms filling his brain.

Ash swallowed. 'Beach it is, then.'

Yeah, the villa was *not* a good idea.

It wasn't that Zoey didn't trust Ash there. She didn't trust herself. Just one kiss from him last night and she'd been clawing his clothes off. Blaming the whisky or the adrenaline or whatever didn't change the truth, now she'd acknowledged it to herself.

She wanted him.

But she couldn't let herself have him.

That way lay a broken heart, for certain.

She'd always been the runner before, but this time she knew she wouldn't be able to outrun her feelings for Ash if she let herself fall any deeper. He couldn't give her what she craved—a happy marriage, a happily-ever-after. And she couldn't ask him for it either.

He'd given it once, to the person who she'd loved most in the whole world.

It wasn't hers to want.

So she wouldn't.

It had been one night. One stupid night. And that was what it would stay.

Which meant she needed to get them both firmly back on friendship ground again. Quickly.

It would have been easier back in the real world—although there she'd have had her ex-fiancé and both their families to deal with first. So maybe this was for the best.

However tempting it was to just drag him back to the villa…

No. Focus on the friendship.

They strolled back along the beach she'd explored that morning but this time, less preoccupied with her own thoughts, Zoey noticed more signs of the storm. Palm leaves strewn over the sand, some wood she assumed the builders had been using for the villa had blown out and got stuck in a palm tree. Plants were reduced to sticks, and she could see signs where the waves had crashed far higher than usual, hitting parts of the island usually safe from the sea's ravages.

No wonder the boat wasn't fit to sail.

'So. Are we going to talk?' Ash asked after they'd been walking in awkward silence for a while.

Zoey looked away so he wouldn't see her wince. 'Absolutely. I'll go first.'

'Okay.' Was that amusement she heard in his voice? Well, she was ignoring it. She had a plan here, dammit, and she intended to follow it.

'Right. Well, first off, I think it's really important we agree that this doesn't affect our friendship,' she said, in what she thought was a reasonable tone.

'And you have an idea for how we can do that?' Ash guessed.

Zoey nodded. 'Absolutely. What happened on this island *stays* on this island. As far as the rest of the world is concerned—hell, as far as *we're* concerned once we get off here—it never happened. Okay?'

He didn't answer. Zoey walked a few more steps before she realised he wasn't with her either.

She turned to face him, her bare feet sinking into the sand. She should have known he'd make this difficult.

'What?' She placed her hands on her hips and tried not to scowl.

'You're beautiful when you scowl, you know.' He was smiling. Why was he smiling?

'I'm not scowling. And did you not hear me on the forgetting all about it part?'

'I heard.' He stepped closer. 'In fact, I heard you say—very clearly—that we had to forget this *once we get off the island.*'

Zoey swallowed. Hard. 'What are you saying?'

Ash's smile was almost wolfish. 'We're still on the island, Zo.'

She looked around her. Sea. Sand. Sun. No one else for miles and miles of water...

'So we are,' she said faintly.

Another step and he was right before her, his hands coming to rest on her hips. 'Look, I'm not saying you're wrong. Our timing sucks, and you have a million things to sort out when we get back to the real world. And your friendship is worth more to me than anything else.'

'But?' There was always a but. She could tell from the heat in his eyes he wasn't *actually* agreeing with her.

Hell, she wasn't sure even *she* agreed with herself right now.

'But all I can think of right now is stripping that lovely pink dress from your skin again.'

A shiver went through her at his words, and Ash chuckled. 'You thinking about it too?' he asked.

Words were beyond her, so she just nodded.

There was no alcohol this time. No runaway adrenaline still coursing through their veins. No excuses left between them. If they did this again it was on them. Their choice, their want.

And oh, she wanted.

Besides, she reasoned in her lust-addled mind, if this was all she could ever have of Ash Carmichael—this strange stolen time away from real world—shouldn't she make the most of it?

Later she'd get back to reality. To worrying about where she was going to live and what she was going to do about David, and how to repair her and Ash's friendship after they fractured it once more.

But right now...

Zoey stopped thinking, stretched up on her tiptoes and kissed her best friend.

His heart was still racing. He had sand in places sand should never go, he was covered in sweat, his bare skin was probably burning in the sun and he couldn't bring himself to care. Because Zoey was draped over him, naked and more relaxed than he'd ever seen her in his life.

And this time they'd been sober. This time he had no doubts at all about her state of mind or whether this was a good idea.

It was an *excellent* idea. They should definitely do it more often.

Quite how that would work out with Zoey's 'we should focus on our friendship' plan he wasn't sure, but he figured he had time. He wasn't going anywhere, after all—and she wasn't wrong. Their friendship *was* the most important thing.

But if, once they'd got back to the real world and Zoey had set things straight with David and moved on properly, they decided to try this again, in an actual bed next time…would that really be such a bad thing?

He didn't think so. And he hoped that, over time, Zoey might come to think the same way.

He just had to be patient.

Ash ran a hand down Zoey's naked side and cursed the fact that patience wasn't one of his many virtues. But he could do it. If it meant he got to have Zoey this way again.

'You okay?' he asked softly.

'Mmm,' she responded, rubbing her cheek against his bare chest.

See? That was a good start, right?

'So, do you still want to talk some more?' Personally, he had some much better ideas for how they could spend their time on the island, but if she needed to talk to feel comfortable with things between them then he'd talk.

But Zoey shook her head, her dark, tangled hair tickling his chin. 'What else is there to say? The minute we get off this island, this is over and we go back to being just friends. Right?'

A chill settled over him, despite the sunshine. 'If that's what you want.'

Zoey pushed herself up against his chest, leaning over him and frowning. 'It's what needs to happen.'

'So you said.' Ash shielded his eyes from the sun as he took in her expression. 'Remind me why that is again?'

'Because…because we're friends. And that's all.'

There was something behind her eyes. Something he couldn't quite interpret. But, whatever it was, it was holding her back.

Ash sat up, pulling her with him so she sat curled up against him. 'What's the matter, Zoey? Is it David? Or…' Grace. It must be Grace.

Of course this was weird—for him as well as her. But he'd lived without his wife for two years now, and he knew that she'd want him to find happiness wherever he could.

But for Zoey… Grace had been more family to her than her own parents. Closer than a sibling even, for a lonely only child. It stood to reason that she'd feel she was betraying her friend, even now Grace was gone.

Well, hopefully, that was something she'd come to terms with in time.

Time. Time passed, whatever he chose to do with it.

For two years he'd never even imagined himself with another woman, despite the blind dates people tried to arrange, or the obvious set up dinner parties his mother kept throwing whenever he was in London.

Now…now it was hard to imagine *not* being with Zoey again, not having her in his life, his bed.

Maybe it was because she'd always been there. A constant part of his life. Familiar and comfortable and easy. And okay, maybe the last twenty-four hours had seen their relationship take on a different aspect, but in some ways it felt perfectly natural.

Ash had no illusions about for ever or true love—like he'd told Zoey, he'd already found that once and didn't expect to again. But a friendship that also had passion, the way his and Zoey's did, that was something more than he'd ever imagined having again.

Quite honestly, now he'd had her in his arms this way, it was hard to imagine letting her go.

But Zoey was already pulling away.

'It's not David. Or anything else, really. I just think that we'd be better off as friends. Like I said, your friendship is too important to me to risk it on a fling.'

A fling. Was that what this was? Probably, he supposed. It wasn't as if he was lining up to be the next groom Zoey ran away from, anyway. He just wanted to enjoy what they had right now.

Ash didn't spend much time thinking about the future. He'd learned the hard way how easily it could be ripped away from him. He wasn't imagining for ever or happily-ever-after.

He just knew he didn't want this to end yet.

But was that just his libido talking? Quite possibly.

And Zoey was right. They couldn't risk their friendship. It was all either of them had, some days.

'If that's how you feel,' he said neutrally. Because, to

be honest, he wasn't entirely sure how *he* felt. So maybe they'd better go with her instincts.

'It is,' she said firmly.

Except Zoey's instincts were notoriously awful. Could he really rely on them for something as important as this?

'Just…promise me we'll keep talking,' he said, looking up at her as she stood, gloriously naked in the sunshine on the deserted beach. 'That you won't shut me out or start avoiding me now. That you'll always be honest with me about how you're feeling.'

She needed to be able to talk to someone and he was it. Which meant they couldn't let a little sex make things difficult between them now.

'Absolutely,' Zoey said with a firm nod.

'Good.' Plus, as long as they kept talking, stayed close, it would give them a chance to figure this out.

Whatever was between them, Ash had a feeling it wouldn't be put back in its box as easily as Zoey seemed to think it would.

He just wished he could shake the feeling that she was keeping something from him. That her reasons for calling things off weren't as simple as she was making out. They made sense, of course, whether he fully agreed with them or not.

Still, he was certain there was something else.

'Zo?' he asked softly. She bit her lip as she looked down at him. 'Is there something else? Anything else that's bothering you. That you're worried about?'

Her lips parted just a fraction, as if she were about to say something. Then her gaze darted away from him and out towards the ocean beyond, her eyes widening.

'Look! A boat!' Bounding over him in a move that caused her body to sway in a way that made Ash catch his breath, Zoey waved her hot pink dress over her head at the sailors. Ash reached for his trousers and pulled them on, less comfortable with his own nudity than Zoey apparently was.

Or perhaps she's just so desperate to get away from me, from this conversation, that she doesn't care about being naked in front of strangers.

He shook the thought away. Why would she be running from him?

Except she was. Tugging her dress over her head as she ran, Zoey raced towards the boat—a rescue service from one of the local hotels, by the look of things—laughing and calling out to their rescuers.

Apparently, their escape to paradise together was over.

CHAPTER SEVEN

IT WASN'T UNTIL she was safely on the boat that Zoey considered what she was heading back to.

Until then she'd been far too busy remembering what she was leaving behind.

Ash was quiet on the journey, and she knew the question she hadn't answered had to be weighing as heavily on him as it was on her. But how was she supposed to say, *I'm terrified that if I spend any longer with you this way I'll fall so deeply in love I can't get out again*?

He didn't want for ever—he'd had that. She knew that Ash made a point of living in the moment these days—even if it drove his father, and shareholders, crazy when it came to the business. He'd already had what she was still searching for.

And she had to believe that one day, against all the odds, she'd find it.

Then maybe she could make it through an actual wedding of her own.

'Want me to come with you to talk to David?' Ash asked quietly from beside her as the stood at the rail and watched the hotel grow closer and closer.

Zoey shook her head. 'I think I'd better do this one alone.' She looked down at herself. 'Hopefully after a shower and a change of clothes.'

The boat docked and two men jumped over the rail to tie it up. Ash helped her step over onto the jetty, just like he had the night before, in the middle of the storm. How different things were now, though.

Since last night *everything* felt different. Most of all Zoey herself.

'Where the hell have you been?'

Zoey winced at the voice. She'd been expecting David, but no. First on the scene were her parents. Just perfect.

Her father's face was bright red as he stalked down the jetty towards them. Part sunburn, part fury, Zoey decided dispassionately.

'We didn't fly all the way out here just so you could run off with some other bloke the night before your wedding!' He waved a hand vaguely at Ash, who sensibly put his hands in his pockets and looked away.

No, you came here for the free bar and the chance to cosy up to potential clients, Zoey thought, but didn't say.

'I'm sorry, Dad. I couldn't go through with it. Ash— You remember Ash, right? Grace's husband?' Her father looked blankly at him. Zoey wasn't all that surprised. It wasn't as if she'd spent a lot of time socialising with her parents and friends together, or filling her mum and dad in on the events of her life.

They were far more preoccupied with their own lives and dramas, anyway.

'You ran off with your *best friend's husband?'* her mother shrieked, because clearly this whole situation wasn't embarrassing enough as it was.

'Widower,' Ash corrected calmly. 'And all I did was help Zoey find some time and space to decide what she wanted to do next.' Which wasn't *entirely* true, unless Ash counted fantastic sex as some sort of decision matrix.

Which it might have been, really. There was no way Zoey could go back to the same old boring sex she'd had with David after one night with Ash.

Her parents weren't listening to him, though. Or to her, really. They'd turned the whole event into the Hugh and Tanya show, as usual.

'I always knew you were just like your father,' her mother, Tanya, said, looking accusingly at her husband.

'Oh, really?' Hugh replied, his tone sharp. 'Because I was just thinking she was just like her mother. Which one of us was it that ran off with the waiter at our anniversary dinner?'

'And who had a three-year affair with my best friend?' Tanya shot back.

'You know, I can't help but think sometimes the world would be a better place if one of *you* hadn't shown up at the church on your wedding day,' Zoey said, safe in the knowledge that neither of them were listening to her. They were too busy throwing past misdeeds in each other's faces.

They'd make up later, Zoey knew from bitter past experience. They'd be all over each other in the bar for at least an hour or two before something else set them at each other's throats.

'Except if they hadn't married you'd have never been born,' Ash pointed out. At least someone listened to her.

Then Zoey caught sight of David, pale and with huge circles under his eyes, approaching them on the jetty.

'Even so,' Zoey murmured, 'it might have been for the best.'

* * *

Ash watched, helpless, as David led Zoey away, back towards the hotel.

Their wedding venue, if she'd stayed. Was he taking her back to the bridal suite right now? What would he do? Say?

Ash knew he had absolutely no right in the world to feel jealous, but that didn't seem to be stopping him.

Zoey couldn't go back to him, could she? Not because of last night, or what they'd shared. But because he wanted her to be happy—and he was more sure than ever now that David couldn't give her that.

Mr and Mrs Hepburn were still at each other's throats, filling the air with accusations and curses that Ash didn't care to hear. Leaving them behind, he headed towards the hotel, hoping a hot shower would help wash away some of the emotions last night had raised.

'You.' The word—spat at him with real venom— gave him pause.

With a small sigh, he turned to the speaker. 'Benji. Hi.' David's best man was a small rat of a guy who seemed to want to compensate for his lack of size with sheer volume and theatrics. Not unlike Zoey's parents, Ash decided, hiding a lack of love with an excess of showy passion.

'David always said that you were trouble. That you had a thing for Zoey.' Benji was trying to get up in his space— at least that was what Ash thought he was doing. Being a full head shorter than him meant that Benji had to maintain some distance just to be able to look him in the eye.

Ash thought about crouching down to make things

easier for him, but figured that would just be patronising. Tempting though it was.

'Look, Benji, whatever you think was going on here…' Ash trailed off. How could he truly complete that sentence without lying horribly? Sure, maybe his intentions in taking Zoey away from the island had been entirely honourable, but that didn't change what had actually happened next.

'I think you wanted Zoey for yourself, so you stole her away when she was vulnerable. David says you never liked him, never thought he was good enough for Zoey—as if *she* wasn't the one with the track record for destroying lives!'

'Hey,' Ash snapped. 'That's enough. Zoey made a decision—I just helped her out.'

'I'm sure you did,' Benji said, with enough sleaze in his voice to make Ash feel even dirtier than he already did.

Suddenly, the full implications of their actions seemed to settle on his shoulders and he felt older, more tired and more disgusted with himself than he'd been in years.

Whatever his intentions, he'd made things harder for Zoey. He should have just insisted she *talk* to David, like any normal person would if they were having doubts the night before their wedding. Like Grace would have persuaded her to do.

Why hadn't he? Was Benji right? Had he wanted Zoey for himself?

He'd never really thought about Zoey that way until yesterday. She was Grace's friend, so would have been completely off-limits even if he *hadn't* been totally in love with his wife. But when Grace was alive he'd never looked beyond her—he hadn't needed or wanted to. She'd been his world.

And since his world had come crashing down around him, romance had honestly been the last thing on his mind. Even if it hadn't, he doubted he would have even considered Zoey a possibility.

She was his friend. His best friend. Possibly his only friend.

It had taken some pretty extreme circumstances to get him to see beyond that. To look at her in the light of the storm and really see her—wild and free and stubborn and so, so beautiful. Someone who trusted him to help her, who could laugh with him even when everything was falling apart.

And now? What was she now?

Still his friend, he hoped.

And she was right. They had to forget everything that had happened on the island.

Because back here in the real world, with David waiting on the dock, Ash could see at last the answer Zoey hadn't given him on the island—the real reason they couldn't carry this on.

She wanted a happily-ever-after marriage—she wanted for ever. And he'd already given his away with his heart.

He loved Zoey, of course he did. She was family, practically. And he wanted her—that much was obvious after last night.

But neither of those things added up to what Zoey wanted from her future. Not to mention that he had no idea if she'd even *want* him to feature in that future.

He had to let her go so she could find the true love she was looking for. However much his selfish heart wanted to keep her for himself.

They hadn't talked about the repercussions of their actions before they took them. If they had, they'd probably never have even kissed. Overthinking things was a definite passion-killer.

Except…oh, God. There was definitely one thing that they *should* have talked about before sleeping together. Ash hadn't thought beyond making sure that Zoey was happy with what they were doing.

He hadn't thought about protection at all, too overcome with lust to remember even that basic necessity.

Probably because he hadn't needed to, for years. Two years of celibacy had been preceded by Grace being pregnant or them trying. And even before that Grace had been on the Pill, and they'd both been tested and clean. He hadn't thought about contraceptives since he was a *teenager*.

And he couldn't think about them right now. He had to focus on getting Zoey through the next twenty-four hours first.

Most of all, she needed to get through this latest wedding breakdown with her sanity intact, and without ruining her reputation more than ever. A runaway bride was one thing. A cheating runaway bride was another. Plus, there were the practicalities to consider—she was living with David, had given up her flat last year. So where was she planning on going?

'Look, Benji. Here's the full story, okay? Zoey had cold feet. She wanted to get away from here to think, so I took her out on the boat. A storm came up so we sheltered in a half-renovated villa my company owns. It was dusty, dirty and the least romantic place you can imagine.' And yet… 'This morning we waited for a rescue boat as ours had been damaged in the storm. Then we came back so that Zoey could talk to David. It was as simple and as boring as that. Okay?'

All true—except for the major omissions. But Benji had no right to that information anyway, so Ash didn't feel too guilty about keeping it from him.

'That's really all?' Benji asked, his tone both doubtful and disappointed.

Ash gave a sharp nod. 'Now, if you don't mind, I am in desperate need of a shower.'

He brushed past the best man, heading for his room and hoping that hot water could wash away memories.

And guilt.

This. This was the part she hated the most. Explaining herself. Justifying her unjustifiable actions.

'David…'

'No.' David cut her off as he jabbed at the button, waiting for the lift that would take them all the way to the honeymoon suite on the top floor.

Zoey looked down at her ruined pink dress and thought about the beautiful ivory lace one that was hanging from the wardrobe in the suite. The dress she'd never wear now. Just like all the others.

They rode the lift in silence. Zoey stared straight ahead, avoiding catching her own eye in any of the reflections glinting from the mirror-lined walls. She didn't want to see the guilt there.

Finally, after what seemed like an eternity, the lift doors opened onto the top corridor and David strode out towards the honeymoon suite door. Zoey followed, her steps more hesitant.

She wished she'd spent more of the time since she'd left on that boat preparing for this conversation. But instead she'd found herself debating and stressing over an entirely different problem. One she couldn't even have predicted having twenty-four hours earlier.

But at least her night with Ash had made one thing very, very clear: there was no way she could marry David now.

Even if she confessed all and he still wanted her, she knew it wouldn't be fair—to either of them. She might not be able to find a future with Ash, but she was damned if she was going to settle for anything less than she'd felt with him last night.

How depressing was it that her most fulfilling relationship might actually be a one-night stand?

She stepped into the bridal suite and the door swung shut behind her, closing with an almost inaudible click. No slammed doors, no drama.

Except that David looked like he might explode any second now. Even standing with his back to her, staring out of the window at the blue, blue sea that surrounded them, Zoey could read the tension and the anger in his shoulders, his arms, even his legs.

David was furious. Understandably.

'I'm sorry,' she said quickly. It was best to get that

one out immediately, although she was under no illusion that it was the last time she'd be saying it in this conversation.

'Do you ever wonder what it says about you that you have to say that so often?' David spun around from the window, his handsome face ugly with hatred.

Zoey recoiled. David had always been an attractive man in a bland, easy way. No sharp features, just neat hair, neat jaw line, regularly spaced eyes and so on. Like a stock image, or one of those photos that came in a picture frame when you bought it.

He looked ordinary, in an attractive way.

But not now.

'I shouldn't have run. I should have talked to you first. I'm sorry,' she repeated, trying to keep her tone calm and conciliatory, even though her heart was racing.

'What you should have done was go through with the damned wedding!' he yelled, slamming his hand down on the desk at the window.

Zoey flinched at the crack of his palm against the wood. 'I'm sorry. I got cold feet. I just… I don't think we would have made each other happy for the rest of our lives.'

'So? Marriage isn't about being *happy,* Zoey. You've always had some sort of idealised view of what a relationship should be, but it's not all roses and sunshine all the time. Nobody has that!'

'I know. I don't want perfect,' she said softly. 'I just want perfect *for me.*'

'And I'm not, is that it?' David shook his head, his face red with anger as he stalked forward towards her. 'You *cannot* truly be trying to tell me this is *my fault.*'

The last two words came out as a yell, and Zoey shrank back against the door.

'No, no. That's not what I'm saying.'

But David was past listening. He took another slow, deliberate step forward and Zoey found her hands moving instinctively in front of her as if to ward him off.

Calm down, Zo, she told herself, trying to keep her breathing even. *It's just David. Nothing to be scared of.*

Except she was.

'Do you know, there's an actual support group.' David's voice was low and dangerous. 'For your exes. For all the men you've tried to destroy with your cheating, lying ways.'

Zoey swallowed. She wanted to deny the cheating accusation but, after last night, how could she?

'I… No. I didn't know that.'

'Oh, yes.' Another step closer. 'They reached out to me after I proposed to you. As soon as they heard you'd said yes. They keep tabs on you, you see.'

'They're spying on me?' Because that was creepy as all get-out. How many of them were there? Did they meet up for coffee or something, just to talk about how awful she was? Zoey wanted to ask more questions but she suspected this wasn't quite the time.

Still. The idea of a support group for men she'd dumped at the altar, or just before, was frankly terrifying.

What sort of an awful person was she, anyway?

'They said they wanted to try and save other poor fools from their fate.' David's mouth twisted up in a sneer. 'Of course, I told them this time was different. That *I* was different.'

'I wasn't planning on running out on you,' Zoey said miserably.

David scoffed. 'Oh, of course not. What was it you told me on our third date? When we talked about past relationships?' He put one finger to his jaw as if trying to remember. 'That's right. You told me that all those other men hadn't been right for you—and you weren't right for them either. Funny how you were the only one to realise that—and not until you'd dragged them all the way to the altar with you. Tell me honestly, Zoey. Do you get a kick out of destroying men's lives?'

'No!' Zoey's eyes widened as his words hit home. 'No, David, you've got it wrong. I didn't… I never meant to hurt you. Any of you. I just… I couldn't go through with it. It's me, not—'

'Don't say it,' David snapped. 'I know this isn't *my* fault. What I don't understand is how you think you can keep doing this to people.'

'Would it have been better to marry you knowing we'd both be unhappy?' she asked softly.

'Yes! Of course it would!'

Zoey blinked. 'I don't… I don't understand.'

'Because you're just thinking about *you*.' David spat the words out, his eyes filled with hatred where she'd seen love only days before. How could she have got this so wrong?

'So explain it to me,' she said.

'Every marriage has, at best, a fifty-fifty shot, right?' David said.

'I guess.' Of course, she suspected it was rather less

if the bride ran away and slept with another man the night before.

'So why not just give it a go? Would it have killed you to have just *shown up* for once? To *not* run when your stupid instincts told you to? To go through with what you promised for *my* sake?' His hands moved as he spoke, growing more animated as he explained. He had to have been thinking about this all night, Zoey realised.

'You would have wanted me to marry you even if I was having doubts?' *Serious* doubts. 'Why?'

'Because at least then I wouldn't be the laughing stock of my company, my family and all our friends!' David yelled and the words echoed off the walls, making Zoey's ears ring.

'I'm sorry if you feel embarrassed...' she started, but David wasn't done talking yet.

'Do you even realise how much was riding on this marriage? Why do you think I went to such lengths to make sure it happened? It wasn't just for my sake—it was for the sake of the company. Mine and your parents', for that matter. We had *plans,* Zoey.'

'Wait.' Zoey frowned, trying to make sense of his words. 'You wanted to marry me because of Mum and Dad's *company*? I was a business deal?'

David waved a hand to dismiss her incredulity. 'Not only for that, of course. It was just convenient that our industries lined up nicely. The company needs a boost right now and your parents are hoping to take early retirement, so I could have taken it over and built it up ready for when my own father retires, and I become CEO of the whole empire.'

'Not *only* for that,' she repeated faintly. Then she felt the anger rising, her instincts screaming that they'd been right all along. 'Was anything about this relationship actually about me?'

David rolled his eyes. 'Of course it was. I wouldn't have proposed if you weren't beautiful, and good company—in bed and out.'

'Or if you weren't in love with me,' Zoey pressed, but David didn't even dignify that one with an answer. Zoey's guilt started ebbing away, like water down a storm drain.

'And, to be honest, the fact that you were a challenge—that other people said you wouldn't go through with it—that only made me keener.'

Zoey tried to get her head around all the new information swirling around her brain. Tried to reconcile the man in front of her with the one she'd said yes to when he got down on one knee.

It seemed impossible.

'So what you're saying is that you wanted me to marry you, even if it would make me unhappy, just so you could do a business deal, show me off and brag about bagging the runaway bride?'

'What else do you think marriage *is,* Zoey?' David asked, sounding astonished at her naivety. 'It's deals and trophies. Marriage is the ultimate status symbol. You have to marry someone who enhances your own position.' He waved a hand in her direction. 'You might not have much social standing or money yourself, and your job barely qualifies as a career, but your parents' company makes up for that. Add in the fact that you're beautiful and charming, and suddenly you're of interest to people. But most of all you were a challenge. If I married you, people would know that I must have something other men didn't.'

Zoey sank back against the door as if she'd been punched in the stomach. '*That* was why you wanted to marry me?'

'Of course it was.' David's mouth twisted into a cruel, mocking smile. 'Oh, Zoey. You didn't *really* think it was *love*, did you? Nobody believes in that these days.'

I do, Zoey thought.

She knew that love was real—she'd seen it. And maybe she hadn't been lucky enough to find it for herself yet, but that didn't mean she had to settle for anything less.

And *definitely* not being a sign of manliness or a business deal for a guy like David.

Twisting her engagement ring off her right ring finger, Zoey held it out to David, who snatched it from her.

'I'm sorry this didn't work out,' she said softly. 'I'll pack up my stuff and get out of your way.'

'You do that. I'll stay on here for the next couple of weeks, like we planned. Give you time to get out of the London flat too.'

Pushing past her, David left the room and Zoey was alone for the first time since the desert island.

She took advantage of the solitude to crumple to the floor and sob.

CHAPTER EIGHT

ZOEY LET HERSELF cry until the tears stung her sore eyes and her chest hurt from wrenching sobs. If Grace had been there, she knew her best friend would have rubbed her back, handed her tissues, whispered encouragement and told her to *let it all out*.

So she did.

And then, when it was all out there, a mess of a life in tears and snot and misery, she picked herself up, washed her face and forced herself to face reality.

Grace wasn't there any longer to help her when she screwed up. To ask the important, searching questions that always led Zoey to her best path forward. Of course, if Grace had been there, Zoey wouldn't be in half the mess she was. Grace would have spotted what David was truly after long before Zoey had.

And if Grace was alive there was no way she'd have slept with Ash in the first place.

Still. Without her best friend on hand, Zoey would just have to do the asking *and* the answering.

'What do I want to happen next?' she asked herself aloud. 'I want… I want to go home. That's easy.' Except she didn't *have* a home any more. She'd been living in David's flat for months. So, back to her parents' house it was.

If they'd still have her.

'Worst case scenario, I find a hotel or something for a few nights until I can find somewhere—anywhere—to rent.' She'd picked herself up from nothing before, she could do it again. As soon as she was back in the right country, anyway.

'Okay, next question. What do I need to do to make that happen?' She could ask Ash to help her change her plane ticket home for a flight today. He could probably help her with a transfer off the island and to the airport on the mainland too, given his connections at the hotel and in the travel industry generally.

She already had her passport and ticket in her hand when reality hit, and she sank down to sit on the bed.

Yes, Ash would help her. He'd do whatever it took to get her home safely, she knew that. And he'd do it as a friend.

Except...that wasn't really all he was any more, however much she was trying to pretend otherwise. Sex changed things, whether they wanted it to or not. It was going to take some time to get them back to where they'd been before—if they ever managed it.

But that wasn't the worst part. The worst part was that it would be so, so easy *not* to go back to being friends.

So easy to let Ash travel back to London with her, if he wanted. To suggest she stay the night in his spare room, in that awful sparse flat he barely even lived in, only for them to end up in his bed together, recreating their finest desert island moments.

And from there it would be a short step into friends with benefits territory. She'd be a mate and a warm body in bed whenever he was in town. And she'd never ask him for anything more, because she already knew he couldn't give it.

It was good that Ash was getting back out into the world again, moving forward after Grace's death. But it couldn't be with her. Because she wanted so much more than that out of life.

Zoey knew—after one night or ten years, depending on how she looked at it—that it would be too damn easy to fall in love with Ash Carmichael. And it would break her heart when he couldn't love her back.

Which meant, for now, she had to do it without Ash. She had to take charge of her own life and move forward without him, without Grace, without her parents, without David or any other members of the Zoey's Exes Support Group.

Just Zoey.

Suddenly, the weight on her shoulders started to lessen, just a little. And the tears in her eyes were all dried up.

Maybe that was the key.

Maybe it was time to stop running away from her life, from her mistakes, and start facing them head-on instead.

She still wasn't entirely sure what she was going to do when she got back to London. But she knew she would be doing it alone. For herself, by herself.

* * *

Ash was just finishing packing his case when Zoey knocked on the hotel room door.

'How's David?' he asked as he stood aside to let her in. He scanned her face, taking in the red-rimmed eyes and dark circles, the pinched expression that made her look less like his Zoey, somehow. Less vibrant. Less alive.

He wanted to wrap her up in his arms and ask how *she* was, how he could make it better. And another, less civilised part of him really wanted to find David and hit him for making her look like that.

Except he knew that David wasn't the wrongdoer in this situation. He and Zoey were.

At least, that was what he thought until Zoey sat on the edge of his bed and filled him in on their conversation.

'Wait. He wanted to marry you for a *business deal?*'

'Oh, not just that,' Zoey replied airily. 'He had worse reasons, don't forget.'

'To prove he could get what other guys couldn't? To show you off as some sort of trophy?'

Zoey shrugged, her slim shoulders rising then slumping back down. 'Apparently my talent for screwing up weddings and relationships is legendary.'

'At least it is now David's been telling everyone your personal history so he can brag about overcoming it,' Ash muttered, the urge to punch rising in him again.

'Yeah. I dread to think what stories he's going to tell about me now.' She sighed. 'I can't see me getting asked out on a date again for a while.'

'Good,' Ash said without thinking. Zoey shot him a look and he groped for an explanation. 'I mean, maybe it's for the best. You can spend some time alone, figure out what you want, before you get back out there.' That sounded better than, *Now I've seen you naked I'm going to be insanely and irrationally jealous of anyone else who ever gets the opportunity, up to and including your doctor*, right?

'Right.' Zoey looked away as she answered and Ash forced himself to remember that she *knew* what she wanted. She just couldn't ever seem to find it.

And David was, most definitely, not the man for her.

Could *he* be?

The thought brushed through his mind like the sea breeze, stopping Ash halfway through the motion of folding a T-shirt.

It was tempting, he had to admit. The idea of letting Zoey into his life as more than a friend. Of being what she needed.

Except he couldn't.

She wanted true love, and he'd already given his heart away. Apparently death had a no returns policy.

He was too sad, too broken for Zoey's exuberant search for love.

As long as there were no consequences to their night together…

He needed to talk to her about it. But how was he supposed to bring it up?

Hey, Zo, you know I'm an idiot who hasn't had sex in two years and really only with my dead wife before that? Totally forgot about the existence of contraceptives as a thing. Appreciate that's totally on me but still… Kind of hoping it's one of those things you have covered…?

Given that he was dealing with a woman whose back-up plan to escape a wedding was climbing out of a window that was far too small for her, he wasn't sure what the odds were on that one.

Still. They definitely had to talk.

'What are your plans now?' he asked awkwardly.

'For dating?' Zoey asked, looking confused.

Right. He'd moved on mentally from their previous conversation, but not verbally. 'No. Well, yes, if you want to talk about that. But I meant more…now you're not getting married today. You're supposed to be having your honeymoon here, right? So, are you going to stay?'

Zoey shook her head so hard that her hair whipped round and caught him in the face as he sat down beside her on the bed. 'Definitely not. David will, apparently—he's paid for it, after all. So it's probably best if I was somewhere else. You know, like the other side of the world. At least until he's calmed down a bit. Besides, it'll give me a chance to clear out my stuff from his flat.'

'Where are you going to stay?' Ash wanted to offer her his spare room, but he wasn't sure she'd accept. And maybe she was right. Maybe they did need some distance between them for a little while.

'With my parents.' She said it like someone else might say, *In hell*, and Ash decided distance was over-rated anyway.

'You could have my spare room.'

She gave him a small sad smile. 'Thanks. But I'll try Mum and Dad's first, at least. If they're still talking to me by the time they get home. It shouldn't take me long to find a new flat anyway.'

It all felt wrong to Ash. 'Want me to sort a flight home to London for you at least?' What was the point of being heir to a luxury travel business if you couldn't fix something like this for a friend?

But Zoey shook her head again, less violently this time. 'I appreciate the offer, but I'll sort it. This is my screw-up. I need to fix it myself.'

Ash frowned. 'Hey, you didn't screw up.'

She flashed him a disbelieving look. 'I really did, Ash.'

'You made the right decision for you and your future happiness,' Ash corrected her. 'Your timing might suck, but you still did the right thing in the end.'

'I know,' Zoey replied. 'I mean, I knew it for sure when David told me all the reasons I should have gone through with the wedding anyway. He was the wrong man for me.'

'I'd argue he's the wrong man for anybody,' Ash said. 'But yeah, you're definitely better off without him.'

'Which is why I'm going to go and find someone to take me to the airport and get on the next plane back to London that my credit card can stand.'

'You're sure you won't let me sort it for you?' He couldn't fix anything else in her world, but this one he could. If she'd let him.

'Thank you, but no.' She sighed as she got to her feet. 'You know, I realised something. My whole life I've been looking for someone else to fix my life for me. Grace would take me in so I could escape my parents rowing. Then the two of you would support me every time I screwed up another relationship—relationships

I was only in because I was looking for some man to give me my happily-ever-after. Hell, I even needed you to help me escape my own wedding. Not just to get me off the island, but to prove to myself I was right to leave by—' She broke off, her cheeks pink, and Ash knew *exactly* what she wasn't saying.

By screwing you instead. Was that all he'd been? A way to be sure that she didn't want to be with David?

It hadn't felt like that to him.

'Anyway, the point is, maybe you're right. Maybe it is good I won't be able to find anyone willing to date me within a hundred-mile radius of David. Because...' She took a deep breath before continuing. 'Because it's time to stop looking for that happily-ever-after as if it'll fix my problems. It's time to make my life what I want it to be on my own, for a change.'

Ash swallowed. It wasn't that he didn't want Zoey to take hold of the reins of her own life. He did. So why did he feel as if he was being cast aside too?

'That's good. Really, Zo. Just…everyone needs a friend sometimes too, right?' he said. 'So don't forget. You don't have to do it all on your own. I'm here for you, if you need me.'

The smile she gave him was so soft and loving it made his chest ache. 'I know. You're my best friend, Ash. You're all I have left now. Which is why…'

'That's all we can ever be,' Ash finished, so she didn't have to. 'I get that. And I get you wanting to make it by yourself. But—'

She groaned. 'Does there have to be a but?'

'Hopefully not.' Ash tried to find a delicate way to

put what he had to say, and failed. 'Look, I'm totally on board with the pretending last night never happened and going back to being friends.' Well, not *totally,* since that meant never seeing her naked again. But he could work with it, for her sake. 'But I have to say something.'

'What, Ash?' She tilted her head to the side as she looked at him, as if she were waiting for some poetic or romantic pronouncement.

Boy, was she going to be disappointed.

'We didn't… We were reckless. I didn't use protection. Did you…?'

He knew her answer before she spoke. The colour drained from her cheeks, leaving her eyes huge in her face.

'David and I were doing this stupid abstinence thing for six weeks before the wedding. Plus he said he wanted to try for a honeymoon baby. So I went off the Pill two months ago.' Her words were a whisper.

Something seemed to freeze inside him at her answer. *There could be a baby.*

And of course Zoey wouldn't want that, just when she was taking control of her life again. But part of him couldn't help but imagine a whole new future for them, in that brief second before Zoey started talking again.

'I'm sure… I mean, the chances have to be low. What with all the stress and so on. I think that makes this sort of thing more difficult, right?' She looked up at him, chewing on her lower lip, and he realised that *he* was the voice of experience in this matter.

'Uh, yeah. I think so.' In truth, he could barely remember. After all, he and Grace had been focusing on trying to *get* pregnant, not hoping it wouldn't happen.

God, this was such a mess.

'Right. So, probably nothing to worry about.' The frown line between her eyes said she was worrying anyway, though.

'Probably not,' Ash said, in what he hoped was a reassuring manner. She was right. Grace had spent months planning to get pregnant—working out optimal times and strategies, adjusting their diets and habits, reading everything she could get her hands on about maximising fertility. There had been thermometers every morning to check when she was ovulating, calls for lunchtime quickies on optimal days—and still it had taken them nine months to get pregnant.

The chances that he and Zoey had conceived in one accidental hook-up—okay, two—had to be low. Surely.

'But…you'll let me know?' he asked, looking into her worried eyes. 'If there's, well, anything to know.'

'Of course,' she replied quickly. 'Of course I will. But right now I'd better get to the airport.'

'Can I take you?' Suddenly, he didn't want to let her out of his sight.

She shook her head. 'I'll get the hotel reception to help me. I'm hoping I can trade in my transfer and flight home from two weeks from now to today.'

'If you need any help, or anything…'

'I'll phone,' Zoey said. But he knew from the too-quick smile she threw him that she wouldn't. 'Give me a call next time you're in London for more than a night, yeah?'

'I will. We can…get dinner or something.'

'Sounds good.' Her smile grew strained. 'Bye, Ash.'
'Bye.'

And then she was gone. And Ash felt suddenly very, very alone again.

Pregnant.

The word echoed around Zoey's head the whole way to the airport.

She heard it in the waves around the speedboat that took her from the hotel island to the mainland, and in the rumble of tyres on the road of the minibus that took her to the terminal. It was in the roar of the planes taking off and landing.

'Pregnant?' the girl behind the counter at the drinks stall in the airport said. Zoey blinked until the girl repeated what she'd *actually* said. 'Coffee?'

Wasn't caffeine bad for the baby?

No. Because there was no baby. Even she wasn't that unlucky, right?

'Black,' she said. 'And strong, please.'

Sitting cradling her cup of coffee, she tried to think through all the events of the last thirty-six hours without her head exploding.

It wasn't easy.

But what it came down to was just what she'd told Ash. It was time to stop waiting around for someone to save her, love her, marry her, give her the family life she craved. Instead, she needed to fight for and carve out a life she could love for herself.

However hard that was.

That was why she hadn't let Ash help her get home—

or even see her off the island. She knew that if he'd come with her to the airport it would have been far too easy to start relying on him again. Even if she managed to avoid slipping into the casual relationship with him that she'd foreseen when she'd started planning her return trip, just needing someone else to save her rankled now.

She needed to go it alone. It was past time.

Which didn't mean she wasn't already missing him like crazy.

Zoey took another sip of coffee to stifle a groan. What had she been thinking? She'd screwed up in the past before, but never quite like this. Never 'run out on a wedding thousands of miles from home, got shipwrecked and had unprotected sex with my best friend' screwed up. This was a whole new level of Zoey catastrophe.

No wonder her parents drank so much.

She'd seen them again, on her way out of the hotel, and told them she was leaving. They seemed to agree that it was for the best. She expected they'd stay out there for the full week they'd planned—at David's expense, actually.

Zoey winced. She was quite glad she was missing that too. And if she was lucky, she'd have found a room in a shared flat or something and moved in before they even realised she'd been staying at home.

She wasn't particularly keen on the idea of going back to flat shares and tiny cramped accommodation after David's luxury apartment, but she didn't have much in the way of choices. She loved her job, but her salary didn't stretch far in London. And part of going it alone meant she really couldn't ask her parents for help, beyond a bed for a few nights while they were away.

She'd make it work. She always had before.

Stretching out her legs, Zoey stared across the airport terminal at all the holiday-makers coming and going. Happy families, loved-up couples, honeymooners, retirees, excited kids…all living the lives she wanted for herself. All with someone or a whole family of some-ones to love and support them.

And here she was, alone with her coffee and a sense of impending doom.

'This has to be rock-bottom,' she whispered to herself.

Then she straightened her back. Because if this was as low as she could get, that meant the only way forward was up.

Yanking her phone from her pocket, she opened up the notes app and started to type.

New Plan for Fewer Disasters

No disasters seemed a little ambitious, but fewer was surely doable.

1) Take responsibility for my own life and future.
2) Decide what I want from life that I can give myself, without needing someone else.
3) Quit dating for a while. Say, six months, mini-mum.
4) Say no next time someone proposes to me. Just for a change.

Hopefully number three would make number four a moot point for a while, but it still felt good to have it down there. Because it might have taken her a while, but she was finally ready to admit that marriage wasn't the be-all and end-all she'd always treated it as.

Yes, she still hoped to have that happy marriage and family life one day. But she was done putting off all the other life she could be living while she searched for it.

From now on, she was living *her* best life, on her own, on her terms.

And she didn't need anyone else to make that happen for her.

Zoey smiled. It felt good to be in control for once.

As the first boarding call for her plane went out, she stood in the queue, her bag at her feet, and started another list on her phone.

Zoey's Best Life List

Now she had hours in the air to think of fantastically fun things to add to it.

Things that definitely weren't *Sleep with Ash Carmichael again.*

CHAPTER NINE

HIS TRIP TO paradise was most definitely over, Ash decided, as he stared at the pile of paperwork sitting on his desk a week later. He'd headed back to the London office via a few other properties he needed to check, fully expecting to be sent straight back out on location to check on one of Carmichael's other existing or potential properties somewhere around the globe. But instead he'd returned to find expenses needing to be filed, reports to be typed up and his assistant absent without leave.

Plus, he was still thinking about Zoey.

She'd texted to tell him she'd arrived home safely, but that was all he'd heard from her since he'd put her on the boat to the mainland. No video call to check in, no funny emails about what she was up to, no new address details, not even a group chat inviting him out for drinks if he was in town this weekend.

Nothing.

It was making him anxious.

Maybe he'd call her tonight, if he wasn't preparing to fly straight back out again, as normal. They could have dinner, like they'd talked about. That would be good. And hopefully not too awkward.

Sinking into his swivel chair, he thumbed idly

through the stack in his in-tray and considered how the paperless office had never truly evolved. He'd dealt with all his emails while he was away, like always, but somehow that never quite covered everything that came up in a business day.

And there were no trips scheduled in his calendar. No flights booked or e-tickets waiting for him.

For the first time in two years, since he'd returned to work after Grace's death, he had nowhere to go.

He couldn't help but think this was some sort of a hint. And probably a sign he should go and talk to his father.

Or Zoey.

But no, his father first.

Wandering past his assistant's empty desk, he moved down the corridor, past wide windows showcasing the London skyline, towards the biggest office in the building. The office belonging to Arthur Carmichael, CEO of Carmichael Luxury Travel and very much still in situ as head of the company even at nearly seventy.

'Is he in?' Ash asked Moira, his dad's long-suffering assistant.

She nodded sagely, as if she knew something Ash didn't. Which she probably did.

Many things, actually. It was a standing joke that Moira knew the jobs of everyone else in the company better than they did.

'He's waiting for you,' she said with a sympathetic smile.

Oh. That didn't sound good.

Ash gave a perfunctory knock on the office door, then stuck his head around it. 'Dad?'

'Ash! Come in, son.' His father seemed in a reasonably jolly mood at least, Ash observed as he carefully shut the door behind him. He was still apprehensive as he took a seat, however.

It definitely felt as if he was missing something here.

'What can I do for you?' Arthur settled back into his seat, folding his arms against his chest as he leaned back, studying his son across the large mahogany desk.

'I was just checking in, really,' Ash said. 'Um, like I said in my email, the refurbishments on that one villa weren't complete, but I can go back in a few more weeks when they are. And, uh, I don't suppose you've seen my assistant, have you?'

It would help, Ash thought, if he could remember his assistant's name. But, in his defence, he'd only met her a couple of times. He'd not exactly spent a lot of time in the office lately. And her email address only had her initials... *R*, he thought. Rachel? Rebecca?

'Ruth has been reassigned,' Arthur said casually. 'Really, she was far too highly qualified to be just booking your flights and submitting your expenses.'

'But wasn't that sort of her job?' Ash asked, confused.

'Assistant to the company's second-in-command?' Arthur asked, his eyebrows raised. 'I rather think she was hoping to be a *little* more involved, don't you?'

This wasn't about Ruth at all, Ash realised suddenly. It was about *him*.

He was the one who hadn't been involved. Who hadn't spent more than a night or two in London in two years.

Because London was where he'd lost Grace.

He'd been coasting along on his grief ever since, taking every opportunity to fly away, stay away. And yes, he was working—but that wasn't why he'd been doing it. Not for the company. For the escape.

'Ash, your mother and I know the last two years have been unbearable for you.' Arthur bent forward, resting his forearms on the desk as he looked Ash in the eye. Ash made himself hold his father's gaze, however much he wanted to look away. 'And I appreciate that you needed time to grieve, to cope and move on. We've tried to accommodate that as best we can within the company. But your mother and I both think it's time, son. Time to come back to us. Not just to work, but to *yourself*. Stop running away and start moving towards something again.'

'So you reassigned my assistant?' Ash raised an eyebrow. 'Mum told you to talk to me about my personal life, so you gave Ruth a new job?' How like his father to make the personal professional.

'I figured taking away the person who booked the plane tickets might be the only way to keep you in the country long enough to talk to me,' Arthur said.

Ash looked away, conceding the point.

'It's just…been easier to be away, for a while,' Ash admitted. Then he thought about Zoey, picking herself up and starting over after the latest self-imposed implosion of her love life. She moved on, every time. Maybe his dad was right. Maybe it was time for him to do the same. He straightened up and caught his father's gaze. 'But I'm back now. And I'm ready to get back to doing the real work. Not just the busy work or travelling around checking on things that don't need checking on.'

A slow smile spread across Arthur's face. 'Well, that's good. Because I am rather hoping to retire one day, you know. And if you want to take this place over, we've got two years' worth of work to catch you up on.'

Looked like dinner with Zoey would have to wait. 'Let's get started, then.'

Zoey stared at the pregnancy test in her hand and forced herself to acknowledge the information it was giving her.

Outside the bathroom door, she could hear her two new roommates having a row about who had drunk the last of the vodka the night before. She tried to tune it out as she focused on the word in front of her.

Pregnant.

It said it right there in actual letters and everything. No *Is that one line or two?* or *Do you think that's really a cross?* questions about it.

And it wasn't the only one. She had three other tests that all said exactly the same thing.

She was pregnant.

She, Zoey Hepburn, disaster magnet extraordinaire, was going to be a mother.

Just when she was starting to get a handle on things.

She'd put off taking the test for as long as she could, but by the time she was three weeks late she hadn't even really needed the confirmation of the test. Her cycle might have been unpredictable since she came off the Pill, but not *that* unpredictable. And as much as she'd tried to ignore the exhaustion, the aching breasts and the nausea she felt in the early evening, she'd known what they meant—even if she hadn't been ready to confirm it until now.

Zoey tucked the test into the bottom of the bin, along with the other two. She didn't need anyone else finding out about this before she'd figured out what it meant for herself. Five weeks since she'd run out on her wedding. Five weeks since she'd decided to take control of her life and fight for the future she wanted and could make for herself.

And now this.

Zoey swallowed as tears burned behind her eyes. She'd only had four weeks of managing any semblance of a responsible grown-up life on her own. How could she possibly manage a newborn too?

She shook her head. There was no point whining about it. She'd made a vow to own her mistakes and take responsibility for her choices.

And she knew one thing for certain. No child was a mistake.

This was her baby. So she'd take responsibility for it. She'd love it and care for it and...and she should probably stop calling him or her *it* too, even in her head. She might give it—them?—a complex.

'We're going to be all right,' she whispered in the vague direction of her navel. 'I'm...well, I have no idea how yet, but we are. I've screwed up enough times that I have to start getting things right eventually, yeah?'

Okay. So she knew nothing about babies. Or pregnancy. But she could find out. The Internet held all the secrets and one of the things she *had* managed to do in the last four weeks was find a flat with actual functioning Wi-Fi. And nightmare roommates, admittedly, but she could stay in her bedroom and Internet search.

There would be websites and lists that she could read

and take notes from. She could figure out everything she needed to do, then break it down into manageable chunks and just do it. One small baby step at a time, so it didn't overwhelm her completely.

Easy.

Except…except the first thing on any list had to be telling the father, right?

Ash.

It could only be his. She and David hadn't had sex for over six weeks before the wedding—and even then she'd still been on the Pill. This baby could only be the result of her one unplanned, irresponsible night of passion with Ash.

She'd been avoiding him ever since they'd got back. No, not avoiding him. Just not going out of her way to see him. He was probably off jetting around the world as usual, anyway. He hadn't used to travel so much for work, that she remembered. But, ever since Grace died, he'd seemed to enjoy the excuse to get away. He'd even sold the house they'd bought when they'd married, buying a soulless flat somewhere fancy along the river, where he hardly ever spent any time. More often he'd been in her flat instead, especially when David was out.

But not since their return from paradise. She hadn't even told him her new address.

But she'd promised him she'd tell him if there were any…side-effects from their night together. And of course she would. Just not yet.

She wasn't ready. She needed more time to figure things out.

Like how she was going to cope with a baby on her own.

Zoey sank back down onto the toilet seat and tried to imagine telling him. Finding the actual words to let Ash know he was going to be a father, after all.

Oh, God, it would break him, she realised suddenly.

He'd had his true love, his chance at a family—and it had been cruelly taken from him. To offer him this now would be some poor substitute.

But this was his baby too. One thing she couldn't do alone, because she didn't have the right to. She couldn't cut him out of his own child's life that way.

She knew Ash, knew the way he thought, the codes he lived by. He'd do everything he could to support her and love their child, she had no doubt about that. And she wanted their baby to have him actively involved in his or her life. She'd never deny her child or her friend those things.

But she had to protect herself too.

If she was going to do this—have a baby with Ash Carmichael—she had to be very clear on what that meant and what it didn't mean.

But first she had to tell him.

Taking a deep breath, Zoey grabbed her phone and tapped out a text.

Are you in town? It would be good to catch up…

Ash smiled at the screen in front of him. Finally Zoey had got in touch. The message was just like the ones she normally sent when she fancied a night out, away from David usually. Obviously she'd meant what she'd said when she'd told him she wanted to pretend their time on the island had never happened.

She'd probably been waiting, he realised, until she was sure there were no consequences to their night together. If there had been, she'd have been in touch before now. He'd had an anxious couple of nights a few weeks ago, after some date-counting on the calendar. He couldn't know *exactly* when Zoey would be able to test if she was pregnant or not, but he'd done enough research on the subject to narrow it down. So he'd sat in his office, staring blankly at the computer screen, waiting to hear from her—but there had been nothing. Nothing except a strange sense of loss as the weeks passed—which Ash had tried to bury in work and ignore.

The bottom line was, Zoey would have got in touch sooner if there was anything he needed to know, he was sure. She wouldn't keep it from him. So she wasn't pregnant. That was good. Right?

Which meant they could just get back to being friends again. Perfect.

Picking up his phone, Ash tapped out a reply.

I am, as it happens. Want to get together tonight? I'll pick you up at seven. What's your new address?

No point giving her a chance to opt out, now they'd got this far.

He hadn't seen his best friend in weeks and he missed her.

Most of that was his fault, he knew. He could have

got in touch with her as easily as she had with him. But it turned out that not travelling didn't mean not being busy. His father had declared it time for a future planning meeting and dragged him, Moira and a variety of other essential staff off to the family manor house in Kent for several days of meetings and discussions about the direction the business should be taking next.

And then Arthur had casually dumped the whole thing in Ash's lap.

'You're the future of the company, not me. So this is your project. Stay here, or go and actually live in that fancy apartment on the Thames you bought. I don't care. Just get on with it.'

Then he'd left before Ash had even had a chance to object.

Not that he really wanted to. Suddenly, for the first time in two years, he was excited to be working again. Really working—not just escaping from his real life, or his memories. He had a purpose again, and it felt good to be getting stuck in. Even being back in London had been bearable—he felt as if he'd moved on to a different world, a different life. Starting over, just like Zoey was.

Suddenly, an unwelcome thought hit him. What if he was just replacing one sort of escape with another? He'd thrown himself into work and told himself that he was moving on, but he had to admit that the distraction it provided had been welcome too.

Because when he wasn't working, he was thinking about Zoey. Remembering that last moment they'd been alone on the beach together, before the boat had rescued them. Picturing her naked body beside him, sure, but more than that.

He kept remembering that unreadable look he'd seen on her face. The one that told him he was missing something. That there was something wrong, something she wasn't telling him.

Something, he reluctantly admitted to himself, that he was too scared to ask about again.

But maybe he didn't have to. Maybe they could just go back to being friends.

Starting tonight.

Pulling up his web browser, Ash started searching for somewhere fun to take her. Something *she* would enjoy. Something that would show her she was still important to him—just in a friendly way.

His phone pinged.

Pick me up at work?

The gallery. Ash frowned. Was that because she was still staying with her parents and didn't want a scene, or because she didn't think he'd approve of wherever she'd moved to next?

He'd figure it out later. Everything would be easier once they were spending time together again, talking again.

And her text had just helped him find the perfect place to take her too.

CHAPTER TEN

ZOEY STARED AT the three dresses she'd brought to work at the gallery with her and tried to decide which one put across her message best. Of course, it would be helpful if her message was less confusing.

Mother of your child, best friend and occasional lover, but that's all stopping now and we're just friends and co-parents from here on out was a lot of stress to put on any outfit.

At least she wasn't showing yet. Well, apart from being a bit more bloated than usual, but she doubted Ash would be looking closely enough to notice that. He might spot her swollen breasts though... Zoey took down the lowest cut of the three dresses from the rail in the back office, discounting it from her decision-making process.

If only all decisions were so easy. Like trying to figure out exactly how to tell Ash that she was pregnant.

Sighing, Zoey closed her eyes, turned around once, then grabbed the first dress her hand hit—a navy blue tunic-style thing she'd bought in a sale and never worn, for some reason. Perfect. It would cover any bloat bump *and* her enhanced cleavage. He'd never notice a thing.

Once the gallery was closed for the night, she

changed and did her make-up in the washroom mirror, glad to have peace and quiet to get ready alone. As soon as she'd read Ash's text about picking her up she'd known she couldn't invite him back to her current flat share. If her roommates weren't at each other's throats, then the state of the place would be enough to make him turn up his nose. Zoey had tried to keep things clean, at least, but it was an ongoing battle, given the slobs she was living with.

Another thing to fix before the baby came. She had to find somewhere better to live. Although how she was going to do that on her wages—especially once she was on maternity leave—she had no idea. The gallery's HR policies were a little lacking in that area, she'd discovered during her lunch break. Statutory Maternity Pay was the best she could hope for after the first few months. And if she had to pay nursery fees as well as rent…

One problem at a time, she reminded herself, as her breathing grew shallow and panicked. *First, tell Ash. Then panic about everything else.*

One thing was becoming abundantly clear the more she read up and looked into her options—her plans to go it alone, to be solely responsible for her own life, were suddenly a hell of a lot harder. Like it or not, she was going to have to swallow her pride and ask Ash for help if she wanted to keep her head above water.

And he'd give it, she had no doubt of that. She just worried what the cost would be to her heart.

At precisely seven o'clock Zoey heard a light tap on the gallery's glass door and, turning out the last of the lights and grabbing her bag and keys, she headed out to meet Ash, her chest tight and her shoulders tense.

This was it. And no dress in the world could make it any easier.

'Hey.' With a broad smile, Ash ducked his head to brush a kiss against her cheek. 'You look…lovely.'

Zoey's own smile stiffened. Had he noticed something? Or was he just awkward because the last time they'd been together she'd mostly been naked?

She wished she could just blurt it out now and get it over with, but Ash deserved to hear the news of his impending fatherhood somewhere a little more salubrious than a darkened London backstreet.

'Where's the restaurant?' she asked as he led her away from the gallery. She hoped it was close—if she'd known they'd be walking she'd have worn lower shoes.

He flashed her a secretive grin. 'No restaurant— well, not yet, anyway. We can grab dinner later. And there's bound to be canapés at this thing if you're really hungry.'

'What thing?' Zoey asked, her shoulders practically up around her ears with tension. They were supposed to be going to a restaurant. Preferably a quiet and discreet one where she could tell him her news in private. 'Where are we going?'

From his jacket pocket, Ash pulled out two tickets and waved them under her nose. 'You know that exhibition at the Hemmingslea Gallery everyone's been talking about? I got us tickets to the opening tonight.'

He looked so pleased with himself, so sure he'd done a good thing, that there was no way Zoey could tell him that, actually, the thought of standing up and making polite conversation with art-lovers for the next couple of hours made her miserable. Besides, that opening had been sold out for weeks, and it was definitely something Ash must have pulled some serious strings to get—because he knew *she'd* enjoy it. He'd never cared what everyone was talking about anyway, and the art world wasn't exactly his natural habitat.

He'd done this for her. So Zoey plastered on a smile and said, 'That's brilliant! Thank you,' as genuinely as she could manage.

She just hoped she didn't throw up over any priceless works of art.

Something was up with Zoey.

It had taken him a while to notice; she'd seemed fine at the gallery earlier, and gratifyingly excited by the tickets he'd managed to procure. But his first clue should have been the dress. It was dark and boring, and totally un-Zoey-like.

For a moment, he'd wondered if she'd gone out and bought something plain and loose cut to make sure he didn't get any ideas about how the night would end. Then he'd reminded himself that tonight was about rebuilding their friendship—not rekindling whatever they'd shared that night on the island. It probably hadn't even occurred to her. Maybe she was just going for a new look.

Anyway, the point was, he'd dismissed the dress from his mind. And then he'd been so enjoying spending time with her again, filling her in on his latest project at the company, how exciting it was to be moving on finally, finding his feet in the world again—that it had taken longer than it should to notice that Zoey wasn't her normal, sparkling self on their walk to the Hemmingslea Gallery.

As they wandered around the exhibition opening night party, however, there was no denying it.

Something's wrong.

As soon as he knew that, he could see the signs of it in every movement she made. The fixed smile on her pale face. The way she gripped onto a nearby chair too tightly, turning down a glass of champagne for the third time. The slightly green tinge she developed as another waiter brought round a tray of prawn canapés.

'Are you feeling okay?' he asked as she shook her head at the waiter.

'I'm fine,' she replied. But her smile didn't reach her eyes.

Maybe she was *physically* fine, Ash decided, but that didn't mean that there wasn't something else going on.

She was avoiding alcohol—because she was afraid that if they got drunk together again they'd make the same mistake they had on the island? Was she looking so stiff and was the conversation so stilted and one-sided because she still felt awkward around him?

Or was there something else?

Whatever it was, they definitely needed to talk about it. And not surrounded by priceless art and hundreds of other people, preferably.

'Where did you fancy for dinner?' he asked casually, hoping to build up to leaving early.

Zoey's eyes widened and the green tinge got stronger. 'Sorry. Be right back.'

And she was gone, through the crowds, towards the cloakroom.

Okay, she definitely wasn't fine, whatever she said. And there was something, a niggling feeling at the back of his head, that told him he knew what the problem was.

No. She'd have told me by now.

Following at a slower pace, Ash made his way over to the cloakrooms, where the girl who'd welcomed them waited, guarding jackets and bags.

'Did you see a beautiful woman in a navy dress come this way?'

She smiled and nodded towards the ladies' bathroom.

That made sense. At least she hadn't run out on him completely. That was always a risk with Zoey.

Leaning against the wall, Ash waited until she emerged again, still pale but less green.

'Want to try telling me you're fine again?' he asked, pushing away from the wall. 'Or do you fancy trying the truth this time?'

'Ash, really. I'm fine. Must have been something I ate disagreeing with me.' Another person might have found her words and her smile convincing—someone who didn't know Zoey as well as he did.

But he'd seen that look in her eyes before, and recently. That haunted, hunted look, as if she was desperately searching for an escape route, a way to run.

It was the same look she'd had when he'd found her

in a cupboard, trying to climb out of a window to avoid marrying David.

The fact she now displayed the same look and feel in relation to *him* was a stab to Ash's heart—and his pride.

'Don't lie to me, Zoey,' he said, his voice low. 'I'm not some fiancé you're running out on. I'm your friend. I want to help you. And I can't do that if you won't tell me the truth.'

'You want to help...' Zoey shook her head as she looked down at the floor, giving a low laugh. 'And I know I need your help. I just... I was so determined to do it on my own. And the moment I tell you, that's over. You'll want to fix everything for me.'

Fix everything. That meant there was something that needed fixing. *Of course* he was going to want to do that, then.

'Zo. Please. Just talk to me.'

Indecision flickered across her face. 'Not here,' she said finally. 'I want to tell you—I've been trying to figure out how all night. But not here.'

Grabbing his hand, she pulled him out of the main foyer and into a small side gallery he'd had no idea was even there.

The room was mostly in darkness—the rest of the gallery was closed for the evening, and Ash was pretty sure they weren't supposed to be there. But there was just enough light from the foyer for him to see her face as she looked up at him, chewing her lower lip.

'Just tell me,' he whispered. 'Whatever it is, Zo, we can fix it. Together.'

Zoey took a breath so deep he could see her chest rising. And he knew in that moment exactly what was coming next. But somehow he still wasn't prepared for it.

'Ash, I'm pregnant.'

And his whole world shifted again.

Relief settled over her the moment the words were out. She hadn't wanted to tell him here, or like this. But, however it had happened, she was glad that he knew. Glad that she wasn't keeping this secret alone any longer.

Glad that Ash knew he was going to be a father.

'That's why you messaged today? To tell me?' Ash asked, and she nodded. 'And how long have *you* known? Because I figured, when I didn't hear anything weeks ago…'

Zoey winced. 'I know. I'm sorry. But I couldn't work up the courage to take a test until this morning. I texted you as soon as I knew.'

Ash nodded, still looking poleaxed. She couldn't blame him. She still felt much the same way.

'So it's definitely… God, no. I'm not even asking that. Of course it is. You wouldn't be telling me otherwise.'

'Yes, it's yours,' Zoey confirmed for him anyway. 'No doubts there. Abstinence thing before the wedding, remember?'

'Right. Sure.' Ash ran a hand through his dark hair, his pale blue eyes still wide and wild beneath it. He shouldn't look so gorgeous right now, Zoey thought. Or at least she shouldn't be noticing it. There were kind of weightier matters to deal with. But it seemed her libido—or her heart—didn't care so much about those.

She stepped forward and placed a hand on his arm, looking up into his handsome, dear face. 'I'm sorry, Ash.'

Her words seemed to snap something in him as he shook his head firmly.

'You have *nothing* to be sorry for,' he said, his voice low and harsh. 'We were both there on that island together. I take my half of the responsibility too. And even then, it's a *baby,* Zoey. *Our* baby. We made a new life together. Neither one of us should ever have to apologise for that.'

Our baby. For the first time since she'd seen the word forming on the stick that morning, some of the tension drained out of Zoey's shoulders. She wasn't alone with this any longer.

Maybe we humans weren't made to do everything alone, anyway. Which didn't mean she was ready to give up her plan for taking care of herself. But it wasn't just her now, was it?

And it was kind of a relief to let Ash shoulder some of the responsibility from here on out.

'Are you okay?' He was close, Zoey realised suddenly. Very close. His hands held onto her upper arms as he studied her, but there was none of the lust and want she'd seen there last time they'd been together. Instead, he held her almost delicately, as if he were afraid he might break her. 'With the pregnancy, I mean. Have you seen a doctor yet? No, you only took the test this morning. Well, that's first up, I guess?'

Zoey nodded mutely, unsure how much he actually needed her to contribute to this conversation.

'And Zoey—' those pale blue eyes held hers in their

gaze, steady and sure and reassuring '—you're never on your own in this, okay? I'm here, for whatever you need.'

The nausea was starting to rise up again, as if now she was *officially* pregnant the morning sickness needed to up its game. 'Mostly I think I need to get out of here,' she admitted. 'Can you take me home?'

'No,' Ash said, smiling incongruously. 'Because if home was somewhere you were happy to be you'd have let me pick you up from there this evening.'

Zoey winced. 'I'll find somewhere new before the baby comes,' she promised.

'*We'll* find somewhere else,' he corrected. 'In fact, you already have somewhere else. Move in with me.'

'Ash...'

'I mean it. It's the obvious solution.'

She knew that he meant it; that wasn't the problem. But the idea of being there with him all day, every day, living in his space... How was she meant to keep resisting him if he was that close?

Another wave of nausea flowed over her and she realised the whole resisting thing might be easier than she'd thought if that carried on. Those damn prawns. She'd felt fine until a waiter had waved a tray of prawns under her nose. She was never eating seafood again.

'We need a plan, Zo,' he said, more softly. 'We've got, what, seven months or so to figure out how we're going to do this together. So we need to start now, right?'

'With me moving in?' Zoey shook her head. 'I think there have to be a few other steps we can cover first, don't you?' Stalling, that was the key. Until she felt less awful and could think rationally about all this.

Because right now the only part of her brain that was working was screaming for her to just let go and let Ash take care of her. And she was very afraid she might start listening to it soon.

'You're right,' Ash said, unexpectedly. But he was already signalling to the cloakroom attendant over her shoulder, asking for their coats. 'We've lots of things to talk about. So let's head back to my place and talk.'

'Ash…'

'There are no prawns, I promise,' he said, and she looked up at him suddenly. 'You turned green when the waiter brought those out. I think I started to guess then.'

'I hate seafood,' she muttered again.

'Just…come home with me tonight, Zoey. Please. Come home with me, I'll make you a peppermint tea to soothe your stomach and we'll talk as much or as little as you want. Okay?'

And really, how was a girl supposed to turn down an offer like that? The cloakroom girl's expression made it very clear that if Zoey didn't want to take him up on it, she would.

She was tired. She felt sick. And she really wanted someone to lean on for a while.

She wanted her best friend.

'Okay,' Zoey said, hoping she wouldn't regret it later.

CHAPTER ELEVEN

ASH HAD SPENT more time in his London flat over the last month than in the whole two years before, since he'd bought it. Still, opening the door and stepping inside now, with Zoey behind him, it was as if he were seeing it for the first time again.

The white, sleek flooring. The modern black kitchen, open-plan to the black-and-white themed lounge and dining area. There was no colour here, he realised suddenly. How had he never noticed that before?

He turned, expecting to see Zoey in her usual bright hues, but found that damn navy dress again, and an uncertain look on her face that made him nervous.

He needed to convince her to stay. And looking at the place he laughingly called his home, even he couldn't see any reasons why she would.

'I don't think I've ever actually been here, you know.' She stepped inside, looking around her curiously.

'Let's be honest, I've barely ever been here.' He felt as if he wanted to make excuses for the place. To promise that when the baby came there'd be softer edges and brighter colours.

Although just having Zoey there made everything feel softer and brighter, anyway.

As she settled herself on one of the high kitchen stools—and he resisted the urge to tell her to get down in case she fell and hurt the baby, because he knew it was irrational, but that didn't stop him thinking about it—he fixed her a peppermint tea and an ordinary cup for himself. Tea was soothing. Tea would help.

'So.' Zoey looked him directly in the eye over her mug. 'How do you want to do this?'

Ash knew *exactly* how they should do this. But before he got a chance to tell her, Zoey kept on talking.

'I mean, I assume you want to be involved in the baby's life, right? Not just one of those dads who sends money but never sees them. Not that I'm after your money or anything, but obviously it would help. But I can do it alone if I have to. And I know you travel a lot for work, so I'm not expecting that you'll suddenly become a stay-at-home dad or anything. But I would like to keep working, after my maternity leave, so there's that. And I know I need to move flats, and I guess there are probably a few things to change around here before the baby comes too. But basically, whatever involvement you want, I can work with, I think.'

'I want us to get married,' Ash said bluntly, the moment she stopped for breath.

Zoey's whole body jerked away from him so fast he reached out to grab her in case she really did fall off the stool.

'No.' The word came out on a sharp wave of disbelief and anger that Ash couldn't quite understand.

'Why not? It's perfect. You can move in here—or… or we can find somewhere new together. A proper family home.' Like the one he'd had with Grace. That would have been perfect. 'You'll have all the money you need if you're married to me, we can choose a nanny together so we can both carry on working as we normally do, and whenever I'm home we can be together as a family, without any awkward logistics. I don't see the problem.'

'Apart from the fact that that was the least romantic proposal ever?' Zoey asked, one eyebrow raised. 'Ash, I promised myself, after I left David, that I'd turn down the next proposal that came my way. Because weddings really haven't worked out that well for me in the past, remember?'

'But this one would be different.' Ash grabbed her hands and held them against his chest, staring down into her eyes as he tried to convince her.

This was his one shot, he realised. His one shot to live the life he'd thought had been ripped from him for ever. His chance at a future worth living—not through the company or money or a fancy flat. But with a woman he adored and a child they could raise together.

His one chance at a family again. And there was no one on earth he'd rather do it with.

'Zoey, this time we know what we're getting into. We *know* each other, better than you ever knew any of those guys you ran out on, I reckon. And we know what we're signing up for. This isn't some hopeful fairy-tale ending. This is something better. It's a family. You, me and our child.'

'Ash…'

'I can't promise you true love,' he said, his gaze darting away to the floor as he remembered why. 'You know that. But really, what good has that quest ever done you anyway? Yes, we both know it exists, but we also know it's rare as hens' teeth and that not everyone gets to experience it. But we could have *this*. Together.'

He slid off his stool to hold her closer, feeling her heartbeat racing against his chest. 'You're my best friend, Zoey. There's no one in the world I'd rather raise a child with. No other woman I'd want in my life the way I want you there. You're it for me now.'

There was a tiny sob. Was she crying? And was it too much to hope that it was tears of happiness?

He had to take the chance that it was. His heart thumping in his chest, Ash dropped to his knees, still holding her hands, and looked up.

'Zoey Hepburn, will you give my life meaning again and marry me?'

She swallowed, hard enough that he could see her throat bob, tears drying on her cheeks.

'Yes. I will.'

And Ash's world slid back into focus again.

There was a strong chance that Zoey might have made a terrible mistake.

As she surveyed Ash's apartment, her suitcase at her feet, she wondered if it was too late to back out now. Then she remembered the vintage ring on her finger, and the baby growing inside her, and realised that too late was about two months ago already.

The problem wasn't that she didn't want to marry Ash. It was that she was a bit afraid she wanted it too much.

'Is this really everything?' Ash asked as he lugged another suitcase through the door.

Zoey shrugged. 'I move often. I learned to travel light.'

Her whole life in two suitcases. She'd packed up and started again so many times now that she only kept the essentials. Every wedding she ran out on was a chance to slim down her possessions, if nothing else.

'I'll put these in your room, then.' He grabbed the other case—which she hadn't been allowed to carry up the stairs either—and headed in the direction of the bedrooms.

Your room. Not *our room.* Another reminder that this wasn't a real marriage.

Ash had been, as predicted, horrified by her flat share. And Zoey had to admit, as she sank down onto one of his black leather couches to look out over the London skyline, the view was much better from here. She was sure the place would start to feel homelier in time, anyway. Even if she still felt garishly out of place in her pink and white sundress.

The biggest problem was that *this*—the luxury flat, Ash carrying her suitcases—definitely wasn't doing things by herself.

She sighed, and made herself remember all the reasons she'd agreed to this.

It wasn't as if she hadn't followed through and said no the first time he'd proposed, anyway. But the second time…he'd painted such a perfect picture of their future together, she'd known that they could be happy together.

Although possibly happier if they were sharing the same bedroom…

The point was, she had a future now. A plan. And, more importantly, so did her child. And so did Ash.

This could be the last chance either of them had to find that kind of happiness—together. And while it might not be the happily-ever-after she'd been searching for, she had to admit it was pretty damn good.

Ash wanted this. Wanted her, and their child.

And when he'd looked at her, that longing in his eyes for something he'd never thought he could have again, that was when she'd realised.

She could never turn him down. Couldn't tear his life apart again and steal away that future once more.

Because she was in love with him.

Properly, truly, happily-ever-after love. And she knew he'd never be able to give her that back, but maybe that was okay. Maybe one of them feeling that way was enough.

He respected her, adored her, even wanted her still, she hoped. He was her best friend and he *did* love her, she knew. Just not *that* way.

But love was love. And when that love offered a future, a family, happiness, she was going to take it. For herself, as much as for Ash.

And for the baby. Because he or she was the most important thing in this whole situation now. And she knew that being with Ash would be the best outcome for their child, by far.

'Want to see your room?' Ash's head popped back into the room from the hallway, and Zoey pasted on a smile.

'Definitely.'

As she followed him down past the main bathroom,

she realised suddenly that there were *three* bedrooms down there.

'Mine's the one at the end,' Ash said, waving a hand. 'And I've put your stuff in here, if that's okay?'

Zoey nodded. But she was still looking at the third door, slightly ajar. 'What's in there?'

Was Ash *blushing?* 'Oh, well, I didn't want to do too much—I was pretty sure you'd have opinions on design and furniture and stuff. But…' He pushed the door fully open, and Zoey smiled.

The room was bright and sunny, obviously recently repainted in a warm and welcoming yellow. A silver-grey carpet had been put down over the hard white concrete floor. And hanging from the ceiling was a mobile, tiny planets and moons dangling from invisible strings.

'We can change any of it you want,' Ash said nervously. 'I just thought it would be good to have some things in place to start.'

He'd built the baby a nursery. Never mind her room, *this* was what she'd needed to see to be sure.

She flung her arms around him and hugged him tight. 'Thank you.'

'Anything for you,' he murmured into her hair. 'And the baby.'

And suddenly Zoey was sure that she wasn't making a mistake at all.

Everything was going to work out just right.

Ash stirred the pot on the hob and tried to remember if he'd ever actually cooked here before—something more than reheating last night's takeaway. Possibly not.

But now Zoey was here, everything was different. And she'd wanted Italian chicken, just like the one they'd eaten in a restaurant round the corner last week. Figuring that home-cooked food had to be good for the baby—even if it *was* cooked by him—Ash had finagled the recipe from the chef and was attempting to recreate it for her.

In the two weeks since she'd moved in, Ash's whole world seemed to have changed. It wasn't just the splashes of colour that filled his flat these days—a bright pink scarf left draped over the back of a chair, or a royal purple cardigan hung on the back of the door, or even the scent of Zoey's lavender perfume, lingering in a room after she'd gone to bed. It was the whole feel of the place. Hearing her humming to herself as she made them coffee in the morning—decaf for her, full strength for him—or watching her, feet kicked up under her on the sofa, as she leafed through an art catalogue she'd brought home from work. Suddenly, with the addition of an extra person in his life—two, if you counted the baby, and he did—his functional apartment felt like a home.

Yes, Ash was pretty sure that asking Zoey to marry him was the best thing he'd done in years.

Except they hadn't really moved on any further than agreeing to get married in the first place. Oh, he'd bought her a ring—a vintage sapphire and diamond ring, set in white gold, that he'd spotted in an antique shop on his way home one night and just known, without any hesitation at all, was meant to be on Zoey's finger. From the way her face had lit up as he'd presented it to her over Chinese takeaway that night, he'd been right.

But that was as far as they'd got. And time was moving on. If they wanted to get married before the baby came, they'd needed to get moving. Venues were probably already booked up, and dresses took forever to alter, he seemed to remember. Zoey would know what they needed to do. She was the wedding expert, after all—not that he planned to mention that to her.

Putting the lid on the pot to let the chicken simmer in the sauce, he crossed over to perch on the arm of the sofa Zoey was sitting on.

'Hey,' he said softly, drawing her attention away from the catalogue. 'I was thinking. We should start making plans—for the wedding, I mean.'

She gave a small shrug and smiled at him. 'I guess. I figured we'd just see what dates the registry office had free and go with that?'

Ash blinked. He'd been invited to five of Zoey's non-weddings so far—well, four if you discounted Harry, since the invitations were never actually posted for that one. Not one of them had taken place at a registry office. There'd been two in churches, one in a pagoda by a stream, one in some swanky hotel in central London, then the one out in the Indian Ocean that had brought them here.

The one thing they all had in common was, whoever she was intending to marry, Zoey planned to put on a show. A big display of love and happiness for everyone to share in. Not because she was trying to show off—he knew that wasn't her style. Just because she wanted her big day to be a big deal.

In her mind, it was always the start of the rest of her

life. 'And I want to start it off with a bang!' she'd told him once, when he'd asked about the fireworks on a village green somewhere, outside the perfect stone church.

But this time, marrying him, she was planning on the registry office? That didn't feel right.

'I thought you might want something a little…fancier?' he said tentatively. 'I mean, you know the money isn't a problem. And if this is the one wedding you actually go through with, I want it to be everything that *you* want.'

Her smile softened as she looked at him fondly. 'Ash, I don't need fancier. I don't need the show this time. A registry office wedding will be more than fine.'

He almost didn't want to ask, but he couldn't stop himself. 'Why? Why is this time so different?'

Zoey laughed at that, her face bright. 'Really? Ash, *everything* is different this time. I mean, I'm pregnant, you've been married before, and we're doing this because we're building a family together. It's practical, not romantic. We're not even sleeping in the same bedroom, for heaven's sake. So why make a big deal out of the wedding?'

Her words stung, even as he realised the truth of them. 'That doesn't mean it isn't important. Meaningful.'

She shrugged again. 'And it'll still be meaningful in a registry office, whether I'm wearing a white dress or not. Is that the chicken?'

The sound of the kitchen timer broke through his thoughts at last, and he dashed back to the kitchen to rescue dinner. But he couldn't shake her words.

It's practical, not romantic.

Yes, it was practical. But couldn't it be both? Why

did practical have to mean they stripped all the romance away?

He wanted this wedding day to be a fresh start for both of them. A new life together. Not just a piece of paperwork they needed to make the legalities and practicalities of being a family more straightforward.

We're not even sleeping in the same bedroom.

Ash dropped the wooden spoon onto the counter as those words drifted through his mind. Was *that* the problem?

He'd been holding back because he thought that was the right thing to do. She was pregnant, exhausted and nauseous a lot of the time. Plus they'd decided to be friends—but that was before they'd also decided to get married. He hadn't wanted to push the issue of what their physical romantic relationship might be when they were married, choosing to leave it up to her to define that when she felt ready.

But he knew what he wanted. He knew *exactly* what he wanted.

Did she, though?

Did she honestly not realise the battle he fought every day not to grab her and kiss her? The tight hold he'd had to keep on his self-control not to suggest she join him every night when they went to their separate rooms? How crazy it drove him catching her scent everywhere he turned and not being able to hold her close?

Perhaps she didn't.

And perhaps it was time he made that clear.

Ash turned off the heat under the pot. Dinner could wait.

CHAPTER TWELVE

'Is it ready?' Zoey asked as Ash approached again from the kitchen. She couldn't quite read the look on his face, but suddenly she got the feeling he wasn't coming to talk about the food.

He shook his head, confirming her suspicions. 'I need to talk to you about something first.'

Apprehension filled her, tightening her chest as she closed the catalogue in her hands. 'Okay.' Was he going to call the whole thing off? Tell her it would never work?

That he knew she loved him, and he couldn't ever love her back, so they should forget all this stupid marriage business?

This time, when he sat, Ash chose the seat right next to her and took her hand in his. She hoped he couldn't feel it trembling.

'You said that our wedding was practical. Functional, even.'

'Because it is,' she replied. 'Isn't it?' She couldn't quite keep the hope from her voice, but if Ash heard it he didn't show it.

'I suppose so,' he said. But then one of his hands drifted up her arm, along her neck, cupping her jawline and suddenly breathing became an awful lot harder. 'But that's not all I want it to be.'

Zoey forced herself to swallow down the hope that was building inside her. 'What…what were you hoping for, then?'

'This.' He gave her plenty of time to back away as he bent his head to kiss her. But all Zoey could think was, *At last.*

Oh, she had missed this so much. The feel of his lips against hers, his mouth, his tongue darting out across hers. Missed the heat that rose up to fill her at his touch. His arms, shoulders and back—so steady, hard and strong with muscle—under her fingers. His black hair, silky as she ran her hands through it. And the way he held her close—as if she was precious, but also greedily, as if he'd die if he couldn't have her right now…

Actually, *she* might die if she couldn't have him again. Now.

Ash pulled away and Zoey heard herself whimper at the loss of his lips. *So pathetic, Hepburn.*

'Uh, what I was trying to say…' He trailed off as if the intensity of the kiss had surprised him too.

'I think…' Zoey swallowed as her voice came out croaky, then tried again. 'I think I get what you were saying.'

He gave her a wicked smile, one that lit her up from within again, thinking of the last time she'd seen that smile, on a beach in paradise.

'I was holding back,' he said softly. 'I don't want to rush you into anything, but I'd hate for you to think for a moment that I don't still want you. That when I proposed to you I didn't hope that, one day, we'd have more than just a functional marriage.'

'I want that too,' she whispered. It wasn't love, of course. But to have Ash with her every day, and in her bed every night? That was close. It could be enough.

Couldn't it?

He kissed her again, lighter and happier, but no less arousing.

'So,' he asked. 'Dinner or bed?'

She didn't even have to think about the answer.

'Bed.'

Later—much later—as they lay in the darkness, Zoey tucked into the crook of his arm as he ran his other hand down her side, Ash wondered how he'd got so damn lucky.

'I never thought I could have all this again, you know,' he whispered to her, not sure if she was even still awake. 'I'm so happy I get to have it with you.'

'So am I,' she whispered back. But there was something in her voice—something that reminded him of her running away from him on that beach in paradise. Something that gave him pause, even while he couldn't put his finger on quite what it was.

'Are you okay?' he asked softly. 'Do you need anything?'

Whatever she needed, he'd give her, if it was within his power.

Zoey wriggled into an upright position, dragging the blanket with her so it covered those magnificent breasts he'd so enjoyed rediscovering. The fact that pregnancy had made them even more sensitive was only a bonus.

'Dinner?' she asked hopefully. 'We never got around to it, and I'm kind of hungry.'

Of course. Ash's worries floated away as he pressed a quick kiss to her lips and jumped out of bed, reaching for his trousers.

'Stay here. I'll bring it to you,' he said, whistling as he headed back to the kitchen.

Everything was going to be fine now. He was sure of it.

The next few weeks disappeared in a rush of wedding preparations and sex.

Zoey held firm on her registry office plan, and eventually even Ash seemed to agree it was the best idea.

'Apart from the fact it's the only way we're going to get this organised in time if you keep dragging me back to bed every time we have a moment free, I quite like it,' she said one Saturday morning as they lay together, naked under the sheets.

'I haven't heard you objecting to the bed part,' Ash commented.

'I'm not. But I am being practical. *And* romantic.'

Ash propped himself up on one elbow as he looked down at her. 'How so?'

Zoey grinned up at him, loving the feel of him so close. 'This wedding is about the future, right? Our lives together, with our child.' Her hand went automatically to her belly as she said it, and bumped into his as it rested there.

'Right,' Ash agreed. 'So?'

'So the actual wedding is the least important part. I'm less interested in the day itself, and more focused on everything that comes next.' His expression softened a little at that and Zoey felt it, tight in her chest. 'Plus, it means we can spend more time in bed and less time looking at venues.'

'I'm always in favour of that,' Ash agreed, swooping down to kiss her again. And then they had better things to do than talk.

Which was just as well, Zoey thought later. Because otherwise she might have ended up confessing her other reasons for wanting to keep things simple.

This wasn't like her other weddings. There was no hope for true love here—as much as she was still holding out for *content and sexually satisfied ever after*. She knew she needed to keep that at the front of her mind. Keeping the wedding to a simple registry office affair and lunch with Ash's parents afterwards was just one of the ways she was doing that.

Her heart ached with the knowledge that the man she loved more than anything in the world would never love her back the same way. He might be her prince, her forever love. But she'd only ever be his stand-in princess, the understudy in a role she was never meant to play for real.

And she could live with that, she'd decided, for the sake of their child. But she couldn't ever let herself forget her place. Because, if she did, she knew that the smallest reminder would break her, over and over again.

She and Ash loved each other as best friends, and co-parents to be. And as far as he and the rest of the world were to know, that was exactly how things would stay.

No one else needed to know her secret truth.

On the morning of the wedding, Ash kissed her

goodbye—a long, lingering promise of a kiss—as she lay in bed. 'I'll see you there, yes?'

She smiled lazily up at him. 'As long as I can bring myself to get out of this bed, yes.' When he still looked a trifle uncertain, she rolled her eyes. 'I'm marrying you today, Ash Carmichael, come hell or high water. So go pick up your parents and I'll see you at the registry office.'

He grinned. 'Okay. Your car will be here in two hours.' Another quick kiss and he was gone.

Zoey took her time getting ready—the plain ivory silk, empire-line dress she'd chosen was loose and flowing around her waist, but dipped deep at the neckline to make the most of her enhanced cleavage. It fell almost to the floor, but stopped just short to show off her bright pink heels. She curled her hair so it fell around her shoulders and applied her normal make-up rather than the extra brides were always recommended to wear, to last out the day.

Her day would end after the wedding lunch. Then, tomorrow, they'd fly out to the South of France for their honeymoon—something Ash had insisted they have, even if they were forgoing most of the other traditional wedding trappings.

'If this day is about starting our lives together, then I want to make sure we start it right,' he'd said.

'You mean by taking me away and keeping me in bed for a week?' Zoey had guessed.

'Exactly,' Ash had replied, with one of his most wicked grins.

Zoey hadn't felt it was worth arguing with, after that.

It felt surreal, preparing for her wedding alone—

for all that it was her choice. She hadn't even told her parents she was getting married, this time, let alone about the baby. She'd managed to move out again before they'd even returned from her last wedding, so she hadn't seen them since she'd left the island resort. They hadn't called, and neither had she.

I don't need them now. I've got Ash, and our baby. I've got a new future.

Maybe, if she kept repeating the words to herself, she'd feel less alone.

When the car arrived, the driver called the lift for her and she descended to the street in her wedding dress, waiting for him to open the car door before she got in. As he closed it behind her, she looked to the seat next to her, surprised to find it empty. She'd been expecting to see someone, she realised suddenly. Not her father, or even Ash...

Grace.

The name came to her lips before her brain, almost.

She'd expected to see her best friend since junior school, there on her wedding day to give her away—to give her blessing on her marriage to Ash.

But Grace was gone, and Zoey was alone.

But only until I marry Ash.

The car pulled away from the kerb and Zoey forced herself to focus on the future she'd made for herself—and leave the past behind for good.

CHAPTER THIRTEEN

'WELL, THIS IS a bit different from last time.' Ash's father, Arthur Carmichael, folded his hands behind his back and rose up on the balls of his feet as he surveyed the registry office, before dropping back down again.

'This is still the hallway, Dad,' Ash pointed out. 'I'm sure it's nicer inside.'

His mother had already disappeared to the florist she'd spotted a few doors down, when she'd learned that it was possible Zoey didn't even have a bouquet. He didn't think his parents quite embraced the idea of *simple but meaningful* the way Zoey seemed to have.

To be honest, it wasn't exactly his idea of a dream wedding either.

But he'd already had that once. This was something new. And that was fine.

'I wasn't talking about the venue, son,' Arthur said. 'I meant…this whole thing. Are you sure you really want to do this?'

That, Ash knew for certain. 'Absolutely.'

'For the baby.' Arthur sighed. 'I suppose that's the right thing to do, and your mother will be pleased. But these days, you don't have to, Ash, you know that, yes?

You can support her, of course, and be a part of the child's life, without marrying her.'

'I know that.' How could he make his father understand? 'She's…she's my best friend, Dad. I care for her. I want her to be happy. And honestly? She makes me happy too. I never thought I'd find that again.'

'After Grace,' his father said thoughtfully. 'Well, happiness is no bad thing to reach for, I suppose. Even in a place like this. Now, where is your mother? Aren't we supposed to be starting soon?'

'Zoey's not here yet either,' Ash pointed out. 'Don't worry.'

He wasn't worrying. She'd come, he was sure. Things were different this time, after all—wasn't that what she'd said? She could see their future together. He knew her, in a way all those other men she'd almost married didn't. He was her best friend.

She wouldn't let him down.

She'd be there. With or without a bouquet.

He didn't care. As long as she showed up.

'This is a bit different from last time.'

Zoey stopped outside the hallway as she heard Arthur Carmichael speak.

Last time. When Ash had been madly in love with his bride-to-be, and they'd had the perfect wedding and the perfect life.

She shouldn't listen in, she knew that. But she couldn't help herself. And as she heard Ash list the reasons he wanted to go through with the wedding…she couldn't stop herself hoping for words she knew she wouldn't hear.

Because I'm in love with her, Dad.

Of course, they never came.

Because he wasn't in love with her. And he never would be. And she *had* to come to terms with that.

'She makes me happy too. I never thought I'd find that again.'

She made him happy. That was something, wasn't it? *After Grace.*

Grace. Grace, who she loved and missed and wished she could see just once more every single day.

Grace, who held Zoey's fiancé's heart and would never give it back.

And so Ash was trying to recreate the future he'd lost, casting Zoey as Grace.

'I can't play that part,' she whispered to herself, realisation washing over her.

She'd known what he'd wanted—the life he'd had torn away from him. She just hadn't realised that she couldn't give it to him.

She couldn't be Grace for him—that wasn't who she was. And she definitely couldn't live knowing he was spending every day comparing her to the wife he'd lost.

She couldn't do this.

She couldn't marry Ash.

Oh, God, she was running out on another wedding.

She turned to leave, only to find Mrs Carmichael rushing up the steps behind her.

'Zoey! Perfect timing. I've brought you these.' She held out a large bunch of yellow roses and Zoey tried not to recoil from the offering.

Not yellow. Yellow is for friendship. She heard

Grace's voice in her head as she remembered helping her choose wedding flowers for Ash's *last* wedding.

'That's so kind. Um, could you just hold onto them for me? While I pop to the bathroom? Last-minute make-up check, you know…' She forced a smile, which Ash's mother returned.

'Of course. I'll wait here for you.'

'Lovely,' Zoey said weakly. No chance of escaping back out of the front door now, then.

Zoey hurried down the opposite corridor to where she knew Ash would be waiting, hoping there was a bathroom down there somewhere. Preferably one with a window that opened out onto the street.

'Ash?'

'Mum! There you are. We were supposed to start ten minutes ago,' Ash said as his mother bustled in carrying a bunch of yellow roses.

'Not that the bride's here yet,' his father put in.

'Yes, she is,' Julia Carmichael said. 'That's what I came to tell you. I saw her ten minutes ago as she came in, and she asked me to hold these for her while she popped to the bathroom. But she never came out!'

Ash's heart began a slow descent into his stomach. *She wouldn't. Would she?*

'I'd go and check on her but, really, I thought it might be better for you to do it, Ash?' his mum went on, looking concerned.

'Definitely better for me to do it,' he agreed. 'Wait here. Don't let them cancel or do *anything* until I get back. Okay?'

His parents nodded, and Ash stalked off towards the nearest ladies' bathroom.

He almost wasn't surprised to see a pair of hot pink high heels discarded by the door. Or the window above the sink pushed as far open as it would go.

Or even the bride, trying to climb out of it.

'Isn't this where we started?' he asked, keeping a tight hold of his temper. 'With you trying to escape through a window?'

Of course she was running. She was Zoey Hepburn. It was what she did.

Zoey jerked her head around, bashing it on the window frame as she did so. She winced, but didn't cry out. 'Ash…'

'No, don't even start,' he snapped as she climbed down from the counter. 'I know how this song goes—I've heard you sing it enough for others in the past, haven't I? It's not me; it's you. As if I didn't already know that.'

'Hey,' Zoey said sharply. 'Will you give me a chance to explain?'

'Like you intended to give me a chance to convince you before you climbed out of a window?' Ash shook his head. 'I can't honestly believe that I really thought I was different. That we were going to have some perfect life together. When the truth is I'm just like all the other men you ran out on, aren't I?'

'No! Ash—'

He laughed, the sound bitter in his throat. 'You're honestly going to deny it? Then tell me, Zoey. Please. How am I different? What makes this any different from any of your other non-weddings?'

'Because I'm in love with you!'

* * *

The moment the words were out, Zoey wished she could take them back again—could rewind her life, all the way back to that night in the hotel, with another window she couldn't fit through. She'd have walked out of that cupboard and married David, if it meant she didn't have to see the look of horror on Ash's face at her words.

But they were out there now. So he might as well know everything. Maybe it would help him understand—forgive her even, one day.

Maybe he'd realise what a lucky escape they'd had, right here, today.

'I'm in love with you, and I know you can never love me.' She sank back to lean against the bathroom counter, holding onto the Formica for added support. 'Grace was your true love; I get that. And I know you wanted the future you lost with her. But I can't do it, Ash.'

'Then why did you say yes when I proposed?' His voice was low with barely restrained anger. Zoey looked down at her bare toes to avoid seeing the hate in his eyes.

'Because…oh, because I wanted to be able to give you that. I wanted to be the one to give you your happily-ever-after. Your family, your future. Because I love you, and I wanted you to be happy.'

Was it her imagination, or did he actually flinch when she said the *L* word?

'So what changed?'

'I…' What was it? One big thing, or too many little things? Was it the way he kissed her goodnight and she always waited to hear him say *I love you*, and her heart broke a little more when it never came? Or was it her thinking of Grace in the car that morning? Or his father saying '*different from last time*'?

Or maybe it was all just the same, big thing.

Zoey swallowed, hard, and made herself say the words.

'I realised I can't spend the rest of my life trying to live up to a ghost, even one I loved as much as Grace. I love *you* too much, and knowing I'll never be enough for you would destroy me, in the end. So I'm sorry, but I can't marry you, Ash.'

And with that she picked up her shoes and, leaving them dangling from her fingers, walked out of the registry office, past Mr and Mrs Carmichael and a confused-looking registrar, and out into the street.

Time to start over. Again.

Ash stared after her as the bathroom door swung closed. Then, after a moment, he realised he was standing alone in the ladies' loos, and moved out into the corridor—only to find his parents and the registrar waiting for him.

'We heard shouting,' his mother said with an apologetic smile.

'The wedding's off,' Ash replied.

'Yes, we rather gathered that,' Arthur said, looking uncomfortable at the outpouring of emotion. Ash imagined he was wishing he was back behind his desk. 'And why, for that matter.'

His mother placed an arm around his shoulders, even though she had to reach up almost a foot to do it, even in heels. 'Come on, darling. Let's take you home—back to Kent with us. Everything will look a lot brighter in the morning, I'm sure.'

Ash let himself be ushered towards the door, his mind still reeling with Zoey's words.

She loved him. *Him*, Ash Carmichael.

She wasn't running because he wasn't enough for her—or, wait, maybe she was. Because he couldn't give her what she needed.

Because he wasn't in love with her.

Except…

'I have to say, son. A woman with a love and passion like that?' Arthur shook his head. 'I'm not sure I could let her just walk away.' Ash blinked. That might be the most personal thing his father had ever said to him.

And letting her walk away was what every other fiancé had done, wasn't it? They'd let Zoey walk out of their lives, and lived with the loss.

But he wasn't like all the others; she'd said so herself.

And now, faced with the prospect of a future without Zoey in it, he realised something else.

This wasn't about the baby. It wasn't about recreating the future he'd lost.

That wasn't why he'd asked Zoey to marry him. Or if it was at the start, it wasn't now.

Now, he wanted to marry her because of the way she brightened up his life—literally and figuratively. For the way his apartment was suddenly somewhere he wanted to be, now it was filled with her scent and her laugh and her everything in it. For the way she melted against him in bed at night, and he felt as if he'd come home at last. For the way her kiss made the world feel right. For how she made him laugh, or listened to him talk—and how he could listen to her for hours and never be bored.

Because she was his best friend.

And because he was in love with her too. Even if he'd been too much of an blind fool to realise it until now.

Grace would be rolling her eyes so hard right now, calling us both idiots.

And she'd be happy for them too, he was sure.

Because he knew now for certain what his happily-ever-after was—and what he hoped Zoey's was too.

He just had to find a way to make it happen.

Ash stopped suddenly in the doorway to the registry office. 'Dad? I'm going to need more than the week's leave I'd planned for the honeymoon. And there's something else I need that you can help me with too…'

CHAPTER FOURTEEN

SHE HAD NOWHERE to go. Again.

Zoey hailed a cab easily on the street, then sat in the back, uncertain of where to direct it.

'I do need an address, miss,' the cabbie said gently. Clearly he'd clocked the wedding dress and got an idea of how badly her day was going.

'Right. Yes. Um…' She gave Ash's address. All her stuff was still there, apart from anything else. Even if it did feel a bit like returning to the scene of the crime.

The door banged into the wall, the sound echoing around the flat as she walked in, alone. Her cheeks were wet, she realised as she brushed the tears away. She'd probably been crying ever since she'd left the registry office, and just not noticed.

She had a feeling there were a lot more tears to come.

Would Ash come back to the flat too? She thought not. He'd probably be whisked off by his parents for some TLC. And to give her a chance to get out of the flat. One of them would probably be here with an eviction notice before tomorrow.

Two suitcases leant against the wall by the door, packed and ready for the honeymoon they'd never take now. Ignoring them, Zoey moved through the flat like a

ghost, drifting aimlessly down the hallway to the bedroom she'd not used since the night Ash had cooked her
dinner and taken her to bed.

Her heart clenched as she passed the nursery, its
sunny yellow too happy for her mood.

Her child would never sleep there now, probably.
She had no idea where they *would* sleep, but she'd figure it out.

Because this wasn't like every other time she'd
walked out on a wedding. This time, there were more
consequences than moving out of a flat or giving back
a ring.

She was still pregnant with Ash's baby, even if she
hadn't married him. She couldn't just cut him out of her
life the way she had all the others.

They had to find a way to move forward together, but
apart. And that was a hell of a lot harder, she suspected.

But tomorrow. She'd figure it all out tomorrow.

Today, she just wanted to cry and sleep.

Reaching her bedroom, she flopped onto the bed
face first and let the tears fall in earnest.

Tomorrow she'd be an adult again.

Today, her heart was too broken.

The sound of the door buzzer woke her, hours later, and
she stumbled to it blearily.

'Hello?'

'Hello, Miss Hepburn. I'm here to take you to the
airport. If you could just buzz me in, I'll come collect
the bags.' It was the same driver from earlier, she realised, the one who'd taken her to the wedding. Ash

must not have cancelled the transfer for their honey-moon, afterwards.

'Oh, no, there's no need. We're not going away after all.'

'Miss Hepburn, Mr Carmichael called me twenty minutes ago and asked me to collect you and your bags and take you to the airport. So if you could just buzz me in?'

Twenty minutes ago? Zoey leant against the buzzer as she checked her phone. One message.

Zoey, get in the car. We need to talk. A

Well. She had no idea what was going on, but Ash was right about one thing. They definitely needed to talk.

'Guess I'd better get changed then,' she said.

Apparently adulting started today, after all.

Ash paced the main open-plan living space of the villa, from the wide glass bifold doors that led out to the sea and back to the floor-to-ceiling windows on the other side, looking out over the beach. And then he did it again. And again.

When would she get there?

At least he knew she was coming; he'd had confirmation of take-off and, having made it all the way out to the Indian Ocean, he couldn't imagine her turning back again.

But she wasn't there yet. Hence the pacing.

He'd known that if they'd flown out there together, they'd have argued. As much as he wanted to fix things,

Ash knew himself well enough to know he needed time to think his way through everything rationally—and Zoey probably did too. So he'd taken a commercial flight out, and asked his father to arrange the charter for Zoey and their bags.

Which meant now he had to wait.

The villa was almost unrecognisable from the place they'd stayed that fateful night. The renovations had been completed at last, and the whole place was the pinnacle of the luxury travel experience Carmichael's sought to provide. From the designer seating to the carefully selected palette of colours, everything screamed expensive—and, more importantly, the best.

Ash just hoped Zoey would understand what he was trying to do by bringing her here.

He wanted to start again. To give them a fresh chance to get this right. Whatever *this* turned out to be.

Ash knew what he wanted, what dreams kept him awake at night. But he also knew that the decision had to be Zoey's. If she wanted to run still, he wouldn't try to keep her.

But if there was a chance she really could want the same life together that he did…well, he had to take it.

As his pacing reached the glass doors again, he saw something in the distance, kicking up spray from the waves. A small motor boat, racing closer through the surf.

And there, right at the front, looking out towards him, was Zoey—her hair streaming back from her face, her sundress blown tight against her by the air current.

Ash opened the doors and headed out onto the jetty

to greet her, his eyes greedily drinking in every sight of her, even as the boat bobbed closer.

Was that a small bump, shown off by the thin fabric of her sundress? He thought it might be, and the realisation filled him with a warmth and excitement he barely recognised.

He was going to be a father. Whatever else happened between them, whatever the future held, that much was still true.

And yes, he was terrified of it being torn away from him again—and, given Zoey's history, he'd be an idiot not to acknowledge the flight risk.

But she'd said '*I love you*' and he believed her.

Which was why he had to give this his best shot.

The motor boat slowed and docked alongside the jetty, the driver hopping out to tie it up securely. Ash stepped forward and offered Zoey his hand to help her off the boat. She looked at him for a moment before taking it, and he wished more than anything that he could read her mind right then.

'You came,' he said.

She gave him a funny half smile. 'Seemed rude not to, really. Besides, I have a new rule. I came up with it on the plane. No more running away from things, however scary they are.'

Something tightened in Ash's chest. 'Good. Because I think we have a lot to talk about.'

It felt so strange, sitting inside such a high-end luxury villa—which was somehow also the shell of a building they'd spent the night in together.

'How was your journey?' Ash asked as he fussed around her—taking her bags, fetching her a drink of juice, finding more cushions for the sofa.

'Let's just say that it's a good job the morning sickness really did finally pass at twelve weeks.' She shuddered, trying to imagine that flight with the constant nausea that had accompanied her through the pregnancy so far.

Ash froze, halfway through plumping a pillow. 'I didn't even think about that. I should have done. I shouldn't have asked you to fly all this way when you're pregnant. I just—'

'Ash.' She placed a hand over his and pulled him to sit down next to her on the sofa. 'I know why you wanted me to come out here.'

'You do?' He sounded surprised.

Zoey smiled. 'Of course I do.' She'd had a lengthy flight alone to think about it, on one of the Carmichael's private planes. 'It's where it all started for us. And if we want to move forward as parents and friends, we have to go back and fix everything we got wrong between here and there.'

She should have known that Ash wouldn't give up their friendship, just because she was an idiot. And it wasn't as if he'd been in love with her anyway, so leaving him at the altar wouldn't have broken his heart or anything.

They could fix this. They might never be together again, and that hurt. But at least she knew they'd make things right for their child.

'Yeah, I guess that's pretty much it,' Ash admitted. 'So, where do we start?'

Zoey took a deep breath. She'd practised what she wanted to say on the plane, over and over. But saying it to his face, when he was watching her so carefully, felt like a whole different challenge.

'With an apology. And an explanation.'

'I think you said everything you needed to at the registry office,' Ash said. 'Well, apart from the apology.'

'I'm sorry,' Zoey said automatically. 'I should have talked to you, not run.'

'You should. But I'm sorry too.'

'What for? I was the one who tried to escape through a window. Again.'

'But I was the one who railroaded you into marriage. I should have known better.' Ash shook his head. 'I knew you were still looking for your true love, your happy ending. And as far as you were concerned I was asking you to give up all that to marry me.'

'I guess,' Zoey said, a large lump forming in her throat. She forced the words out around it. 'You're right—all I've ever wanted was a loving, happy marriage and maybe a family, one day. I wanted to do it all right—the way my parents didn't. I wanted what you and Grace had—and you already told me you couldn't give me that.'

'I did say that,' Ash admitted. 'Because I am an idiot.'

'I couldn't steal the future Grace was meant to have and lost,' Zoey went on, ignoring him. Then his words caught up with her. 'What?'

Ash moved across from her so his gaze could meet hers. He stared deep into her eyes, as if he was searching for the truth behind her words. Zoey made herself hold his gaze and let him look.

After all, her truths were already lying between them.

'Did you mean what you said? At the registry office?' he asked.

'Which part?'

'The part where you're in love with me?'

Zoey looked away. 'A bit. Sorry.'

Ash laughed, a low, husky chuckle. 'Love, don't be sorry. Hearing those words from you woke me up.'

Zoey blinked. 'What?'

'You made me realise how much I'd given up on. I'd tried to move forward, replacing what I'd lost—but I hadn't ever opened myself up fully to the future. I hadn't given myself the chance of finding something *new*. A different future for me—and for you.'

'I don't understand.'

'Then I realised that all your previous fiancés had something in common,' Ash went on, adding to her confusion.

'Yes. I ran out on them. Every time,' Zoey pointed out.

'With good reason.' Ash shuddered. 'I am *so* glad you didn't marry any of them. Not least because it would make it much harder for you to marry me.'

'I thought we agreed we weren't doing that?'

'I'm hoping what I'm about to say will change your mind,' Ash replied.

'You're talking about my ex-boyfriends,' Zoey said. 'I'm not really sure this is going to work.'

'Give me a chance.' Ash smiled—an honest, open, *happy* smile—and Zoey tried to remember the last time she'd seen that. When she was naked, probably.

'Okay.' Was that hope, tingling low in her belly?

'The point was, I realised that they all let you go. None of them followed you, tried to find out what you wanted and give it to you. So that's what I want to do now.'

The hope died. 'Ash, I told you what I need from a marriage and you can't give it to me.'

'You want love,' Ash replied. 'And the thing is... I always knew I loved you—you were Zoey, part of my family, of course I loved you.'

'Like a friend. Or a sister,' Zoey said glumly. 'That's not what I mean.'

'Yes. Except...not at all. Not even a little bit, it turns out.' Ash grabbed her hands and made her look at him again, and she saw something burning, deep in his eyes. Something she'd never even let herself look for before, or hope for.

'Ash?' she asked softly. She needed to hear the words.

'When you walked out on me, I realised I was so in love with you I couldn't think straight.'

It felt so good to have said it. To have the knowledge out there in the world, not stuck inside his head. And the warm glow of cautious happiness that Zoey was emitting at hearing it made every bit of the last couple of days worthwhile.

'I spent so long looking back at what I'd lost, I think I forgot how to look forward,' he whispered. 'But you showed me how again. And when you left I knew that I had to let go of the past and build a new future. I hope, with you.'

Reaching out, Ash pulled Zoey towards him, tracing a hand across her cheek to the back of her neck as he kissed her—gently but deeply, and hopefully full of all the words he still had to say to her.

She kissed him back, warm and loving, and Ash was filled with a sense of incredible good fortune. How could he be so lucky as to have found love like this not once, but twice?

A small part of him even wondered if this could be Grace's doing, matchmaking from the afterlife. He wouldn't put it past her. She always wanted her loved ones to be happy, more than anything.

Eventually, they broke the kiss. Ash rested his forehead against Zoey's and smiled down at her.

'So. Do you think I stand a better chance of convincing you to marry me now?' he asked.

Suddenly, Zoey's happy glow faded and she pulled away. 'Ash...'

'No.' He grabbed her hand and held it tight. 'No running, remember?'

She gave him a weak smile. 'I'm not sure I could if I wanted to. Give me another couple of months and I'll be hard pressed to even *waddle* away from you.'

And he couldn't wait to see it. To see her, heavy and blooming with his child. To know that they would be a *family,* just like they'd both always wanted.

But first he needed to figure out what the rest of her reservations were, and fix them. Quickly.

'You're beautiful,' he told her. 'Even green and vomiting, and definitely when you're nine months pregnant with my child. I promise you, I won't be able to get enough of you, even then.'

She gave him a disbelieving look. Maybe the bit about the vomit had been a little over the top.

'Zoey, tell me. What's the matter?'

Her teeth sank into her bottom lip as she chewed it, obviously weighing up her words. Her gaze didn't leave his, though, which he loved. He might not be able to read her thoughts, but he could see her emotions, passing behind her eyes.

She was still scared. He hated that she was scared of a future with him.

Ash knew better than anyone that the future could be a terrifying and unpredictable place. But he couldn't let that stop him hoping for better. He knew that now.

He hoped she did.

'I can't shake the feeling that I'm stealing Grace's place,' she admitted. 'Or that you're going to wake up one day next to me, and realise you're still wishing I was someone else. That I'll never be enough to replace her.'

'You're not replacing her. You couldn't.' He said it softly, but he saw the way his words made her flinch, all the same. 'Zo, do you think I haven't been thinking about Grace too? I do, every day. And I'm not going to stop—the same way you won't. But she's gone. She's been gone a long time now, and I know that we can't live our lives in a limbo, waiting in case of a miracle that won't come.'

'I know that too,' Zoey muttered, but she wasn't looking at him again now.

Ash tucked a finger under her chin and nudged her head up so she had to meet his eyes.

'Here's what I've realised,' he said. 'Grace will always be my first love. But that doesn't make my love for you any less. I love you, Zoey.'

Were those tears in her eyes? He hated to make her cry, but he needed to say this. And he had a feeling she needed to hear it.

'I'm not the same man I was when I married Grace. I'm not even the same man I was when she died. Two years of grief change a man. But, more than that, *you* changed me. Not just in one night here on this island, or even the months since. Before all of that, your love and care and kindness changed me. Every time you picked me up off the floor from a drunken, grief-filled stupor. Every time you sat all night with me and shared memories of Grace. Every time you called to check in, or texted a joke to make me laugh. *You* changed me, Zoey. Until I knew that if something happened in my life, you were the person I wanted to tell. Until you were the person I wanted to see last thing at night and first thing in the morning. Until you were the person whose opinion mattered, whose feelings counted most, who I'd drop everything and sail into a storm for.

'I might not have known that I loved you before this week. But, looking back, I can see my love for you— and yours for me—stretching back. The type of love it is changed that night on this island, when we realised how much we *wanted* each other too. But that wasn't where it started. That's only the latest part of it.'

'And now we have a whole new love story to tell.' Zoey placed his hand against her belly, where his child grew, and Ash thought his heart might explode from the rightness of it all.

'Yours might not have been the love I chose first, Zoey, but I promise you it'll be the last love I ever need. And I'll keep choosing you, and our family, day after day, for the rest of my life. If you'll let me.'

He could see her blinking away tears as she replied, 'Of course I will. You're my happily-ever-after.'

Ash smiled. 'I hope so. But, right now, our story is only just beginning.'

EPILOGUE

THE BEACH WAS packed with friends and family. At least she wasn't naked on it this time. Zoey winced, sparing a thought for the poor guys who'd rescued them off this very same island eighteen months ago, after the storm, when she'd waved her dress over her head as she ran towards them naked. Ash didn't seem to think they'd minded all that much, though.

When she'd asked Ash why he'd insisted on buying the villa—and the island—back from the company for his own personal use, he'd told her it was *their* place. Where it had all started, for real. And he couldn't imagine sharing it with anyone else.

But they were, this weekend at least. Of course, after the ceremony and the reception, Ash had laid on boats to take everyone away again to neighbouring island hotels, so they could spend their wedding night in peace, in their place.

Ash had flown all their guests out on the company plane, and somehow nobody had objected to attending yet another of her weddings, this time. Zoey imagined it was because of what they could see when they looked at Ash and her together, especially with little baby Charlie there with them too.

It was the same thing Zoey felt every time the three of them were together—which was as much of the time as possible.

Happiness.

True, happily-ever-after happiness.

It felt funny to think that after all those years chasing the perfect future, the ideal husband, she'd almost run away from the real thing when she'd found him.

Zoey smiled to herself. Maybe the reason it had all worked out was that Ash was the first one to actually chase *her*.

'So. Still want to do this?' Ash came up behind her, wrapping his arms around the waist of her bright pink wedding dress and holding her close.

'Where's Charlie?' she asked.

'Playing with his grandpa. He's having a great time,' Ash assured her. 'And I told Dad not to let him eat any more sand, so we're probably fine.'

Zoey wasn't entirely sure how thrilled Arthur would be about playing babysitter instead of enjoying the free bar, but it was true that Charlie adored his grandpa—and his grandpa loved him too. Maybe even more than Carmichael Luxury Travel, much to everyone's amazement.

'I ask you again. Are you sure you want to go through with it this time? Marrying me, I mean.'

Zoey twisted around in his arms and smiled up at him. 'Is that why you wanted us to stay here together last night? In case I decided to run again?'

Ash shook his head. 'No. I wanted to stay here with you because I can't bear to be apart from you. And if you want to run, I'd run with you, if you'd let me.'

'And if I wouldn't?'

'Then I'd let you go. Reluctantly, because it would break my heart. But seriously, Zo.' He looked down at her, all laughter gone from his eyes. 'If you need to run, just tell me.'

Oh, but she loved him. So much.

'Ash, you and Charlie, you're my home. My future.' She placed a hand against his cheek. 'Where on earth could I run to without leaving my heart behind? There is nowhere in the world I would rather be right now than here with you. Besides, I told you. No more running. Ever.'

'So we're getting married?' Ash asked.

She pressed a kiss to his lips. 'We're getting married.'

'Thank heavens for that.' Ash's gaze shifted away from hers and over her shoulder. 'Um, that no running thing, though. Does it still count if Charlie's eating sand again?'

Zoey glanced back at where her son was sitting at Arthur's feet, feeding himself sand as Arthur chatted to one of his many business contacts.

'Come on.' She grabbed Ash's hand and together they ran across the sand towards their son, the altar, and their happily-ever-after.

* * * * *

SWITCHED
AT BIRTH

CHRISTINE RIMMER

For MSR, always.

Prologue

"Happy birthday to me," Madison Delaney muttered glumly to her enormous and beautiful bedroom in which she slept alone. It was the second of March and she was officially twenty-seven years old. "Big whoop."

Still lazing in bed at ten in the morning, Madison finished the delicious almond essence latte whipped up for her by her excellent housekeeper, Ada. She set the coffee tray on the bed table and considered getting dressed.

But seriously, why rush? She had nothing to get dressed for. This year, she was spending her birthday at home—if you could call her huge, gorgeously decorated but essentially empty hilltop mansion in Bel Air a home. Really, she was almost never here. But due to a perfect storm of scheduling conflicts, ongoing script

changes and a bunch of big-time special effects set
pieces that required "further development," Madison
found herself with time off.

She didn't like it. Working, after all, was what she
did. Time off made her feel all prickly inside her own
skin, like there was something she should be doing but
she couldn't quite remember what.

Maybe she ought to call a couple of friends and go
out this evening. But then again, there was no one she
wanted to hang with all that much. She got along with
everyone, but that didn't mean she felt close to them.
And too often when she went out for a good time, it
ended up with her surrounded by photographers bark-
ing rude questions at her and her security team keeping them at bay. What fun was that?

"Goals," she grumbled, and climbed out of bed to
rummage through the drawers of the central-island
dresser in her embarrassingly large walk-in closet full
of fabulous clothes and designer shoes.

She didn't have to rummage long. Her notebook was
right where she'd put it a year ago today, in the back
of a lingerie drawer beneath a blue silk La Perla corset
she'd yet to wear. The pink spiral-bound notebook had
glittery butterflies on the front. Stuck in the binding
coil was a purple pen. The pen, which produced glittery metallic ink, was relatively new.

The notebook? A little tattered around the edges,
with a lot of the glitter worn off the butterflies. Her
mom had presented it to her the day she turned six.

Today, as she had every birthday since then, she
took the notebook and the pen and returned to the bed.
Sitting cross-legged on top of the covers, she pulled
the pen from the coil and opened the notebook to the

next empty page. Her objective: formulate three main goals to accomplish during her twenty-seventh year.

Frankly, she had zip on the goals front this year and she fully expected to squander a large amount of time staring at a blank page and trying not to think how uninspired she felt about life and work and just about everything else lately.

But then the weirdest thing happened.

Her pen seemed drawn to the page of its own accord and her three goals materialized as if by magic:

Lose virginity.

Retire from acting.

Get a life.

Whoa. Who knew? Apparently, this was a banner year. Up until this moment, she'd had no clue.

As she sat frowning at her totally unexpected annual objectives, she heard a faint sound downstairs.

Was the doorbell ringing?

Not that it mattered. Now and then an especially enthusiastic fan got past the front gate and made it to the door. Someone would answer, give the fan something with Madison's autograph on it and call security to escort the trespasser back outside the gate.

Madison recommenced staring at her new, glittery goals and wondering why she wasn't more upset at the very thought of turning her back on her megasuccessful career. After all, it was a career she'd pursued with single-minded purpose since her first set of goals written down slowly and laboriously with her mom's help in this very notebook on the day she turned six.

As for getting a life and dispensing with her V-card? Both of those made perfect sense. She would be thirty in no time at all. She needed a life *and* a sex life. She needed them yesterday, maybe sooner.

At the sound of a gentle tap on the outer door to the upstairs hallway, Madison glanced up. "Come on in!"

Ada, in a calf-length linen dress, her graying brown hair piled in a messy bun, bustled in through the sitting area. She marched to the bedside table and picked up the coffee tray. "You need to eat."

"I will." Madison chewed thoughtfully on her purple pen. "Soon. Did the doorbell ring?"

"Yes. Jonas Bravo is here." Ada wore a bemused sort of frown.

Madison frowned, too. "Did you say Jonas Bravo?"

"That's right."

Madison had never met the man. But she did know *of* him. Everyone knew about Jonas Bravo. His family was Los Angeles royalty. He had billions—the paps even called him the Bravo Billionaire. And he was her neighbor, more or less. He lived with his beautiful wife and their children in an even bigger house than Madison's, also in Bel Air, a world-famous house called Angel's Crest. Jonas Bravo was not in the movie business, but he and his billions were involved in just about every other industry in LA. And he sometimes invested in films.

"Sorry." Ada shrugged. "I don't know what got into me. I've been reading the stories about him since I was old enough to get a copy of the *National Enquirer* and I was so surprised to see him on the security monitor when he buzzed the front gate that I told Sergei to let him in." Sergei was on Madison's security team. "Then, when he rang the doorbell, I just stepped back and ushered him inside. He asked to speak to with you, so I put him in the sitting room. I really do apologize, Mad. It was not my call. But I mean, he is *the* Jonas Bravo."

"No. It's okay, really."

"He looks just like his pictures."

"It's fine," said Madison. "I hear you. You did the right thing." Madison glanced down at her rumpled pink sleep shirt and gray sleep shorts. "I need to change." She dropped her butterfly notebook and jumped from the bed. "Just let me put on a decent pair of jeans and a top that doesn't look like I slept in it. Go ahead and tell him I'll be right down."

Ten minutes later, Madison was shaking hands with the legendary Bravo Billionaire. He looked good, she thought, tall and broad-shouldered, with striking dark blue eyes and thick graying hair.

Once they'd said hello, he wished her a happy birthday. She thanked him, not finding it especially strange that he knew. The date of her birth was public knowledge, after all.

After the birthday wishes, the first words out of his mouth were, "Let me congratulate you on the protectiveness of your staff."

She backed off a step. "You've been trying to reach me?"

"This is my first attempt. But rumor has it you're a very hard woman to get in touch with. I confess, I hoped the element of surprise would work in my favor, that someone might just let me in."

"And someone did—coffee or something? Ada makes an amazing latte." When he shook his head, she cut to the chase. "What can I do for you, Jonas?"

"I was recently contacted by an elderly gentleman named Percy Valentine." Jonas said the name slowly and then fell silent, apparently waiting for her reaction. When she gave him none, he asked, "You've never heard of Percy Valentine?"

"No, I haven't."

Jonas launched into a story about how this Valentine guy was related to a branch of the Bravo family in a small coastal town in Oregon called Valentine Bay. "Percy's been trying to get in touch with you since last summer. He tells me he's spoken to your personal assistant, your manager, your housekeeper and also someone at your agency, but he's yet to get any of them to put him through to you."

"I'm sorry," said Madison, and she *was*—a little. Really, though, a lot of people tried to get through to her: journalists, fans, screenwriters, would-be producers with projects to pitch her, stalkers and other crazies, too. Her people protected her. If this Valentine person hadn't been able to get in contact, there was probably a very good reason her team had kept him away. "I work a lot and I've given orders that only high-priority calls get through."

"Which is why I'm here," said Jonas. "Percy hoped that I might be able to accomplish the impossible and actually get a word with you…"

Madison was starting to feel distinctly uncomfortable and she wasn't sure why. "Did this Percy Valentine happen to tell any of my people what he wanted to talk to me about?"

Jonas answered carefully. "It's sensitive information."

"So then, he never said why he needed to reach me?"

"He did, yes. He explained everything to your personal assistant."

"Rudy or Valerie?"

"Valerie Daws. Percy even sent proof of his claim. He never heard back. When he tried to call your PA again, he couldn't get through."

Valerie had been very ill for a few months the previous year. She'd ended up having to quit and Madison had hired Rudy Jeffries, her current PA. It was possible that the information Percy Valentine had sent had slipped through the cracks, somehow. "What kind of claim are we talking about here?"

Jonas slanted her the strangest look. "I think we should sit down."

Alarm flashed through her. People always suggested sitting down when they were about to come out with some horrible bit of news.

Madison squared her shoulders. "Of course." She gestured toward the nearest sitting area and followed him over there. He took an easy chair. Her knees wobbly now, she sank to the sofa. "All right. What?"

The Bravo Billionaire just looked at her. For a really long time.

"What?" she demanded again.

He glanced away and then back. "I'm just going to say it."

"Please do."

"There is good reason to believe that you were switched at birth and that your biological parents were George and Marie Bravo of Valentine Bay, Oregon."

A gasp escaped her as her stomach performed a forward roll.

It really was a good thing he'd made her sit down.

If she'd still been on her feet, she probably would have crumpled to the floor—and it wasn't true.

It *couldn't* be true!

But before she could cry out that he had to be wrong, Jonas added, "Percy said to tell you that the switch took place on a ranch called Wild River not far from Astoria, Oregon."

Wild River Ranch.

Okay, yeah. Twenty-seven years ago today, Madison had been born at Wild River Ranch. A few months after her birth, her dad had found another job in a different state and they'd moved on, like they always did.

But after her father died, when she and her mom moved to LA, they'd made a detour to northwestern Oregon—not to the actual ranch, but to the area. So that Madison would know where she came from, her mom had said with the saddest, strangest look in her eye.

In one of the few pictures Madison had of her father, Lloyd Delaney stood in front of the foreman's cottage at Wild River, smiling proudly, cradling a pink-blanketed bundle: Madison herself, just a few days after her birth.

No. It couldn't be true. Lloyd and Paula Delaney might have had their problems. But they had loved their only daughter unconditionally. Her dad was always saying how she had that "Delaney" look about her. Madison had no doubt that she was everything to him and to her mom, truly *theirs*, in every way.

"Yes," she gave out grudgingly. "I was born at Wild River Ranch in northern Oregon. But that doesn't mean—"

"Just let me say what I came to say." Jonas spoke very gently, silencing her arguments simply by being so patient, so kind.

"All right." She listened, her breath tangled, hot in her chest, her pulse racing, as the Bravo Billionaire shared what he knew.

At first, his words were a blur to her. She tried to focus, to understand.

Jonas said that a man named Martin Durand had made the switch. He did it because the other baby, the one raised by the Bravos, had been the result of Durand's secret affair with Paula Delaney. Durand, now deceased, was a married man. He'd been afraid that Paula would come after him and demand a paternity test.

"It was a totally out-there move on Durand's part," said Jonas. "The truth might very well have come out earlier if Paula had gone ahead and tried to prove Durand's paternity. The test would have shown that you were not related by blood to Durand or her husband, Lloyd—or even to Paula herself. She would have remembered that Marie Bravo gave birth to a child at the ranch on the same day that she did, would have put it together that somehow there must have been a switch."

"But I don't understand. If it all would have led back to Durand, anyway, why did he do it?"

"Apparently, he was freaked. He didn't stop to think it through. And then, after he'd switched you with Paula's baby, he had no opportunity to switch you back. You grew up with the Delaneys, believing that they were your biological parents, and if Paula ever told Lloyd that she doubted you were his—"

"Stop." Madison put up a hand. "I get it. That's enough, really."

"I understand. It's a lot to take in." Jonas stood from the chair. Moving on autopilot, Madison got up, too.

He held out a thumb drive.

She stared at it, shaking her head.

"It's all on there," he said, "everything I just explained to you and more, including pictures of your large family in Oregon and Martin Durand's final letter confessing what he did. I think you'll agree that the resemblance between you and three of the Bravo sisters is especially striking—and of course, when you're ready, there will be DNA tests providing conclusive proof. Also, you'll find contact information for Percy Valentine and your Bravo brothers and sisters. My numbers are there, too. And my door is always open to you, Madison." He took her hand.

She let him do that, let him set the memory stick in her palm and fold her fingers around it.

Was she dreaming? Her moorings to her life, her identity, her *self*—everything. It all felt torn loose and dangling.

The oddest thought occurred to her. "So then, are you saying that *we're* related, too, you and me?"

"Yes. You and I are second cousins. Your grandfather and mine were brothers. The extended family is a large one."

When her mom died four years ago, she'd lost the last of her family—or so she'd believed at the time. "And you said that the family in Oregon is large, too?"

"George and Marie Bravo had nine children." He turned for the door.

"Had?" she asked his retreating back.

He paused in midstep and faced her again. "George and Marie were very fond of traveling. One of the children, Finn, was lost on a trip to Russia years ago. The family continues to search for him."

"And George and Marie Bravo, what are they like?"

"I'm sorry, Madison, but two years after Finn disappeared, George and Marie died on another trip, that one to Thailand."

"Oh." The word came out wobbly, more breath than sound, as a wave of sadness washed through her for the lost boy—and for George and Marie Bravo. If they actually were her birth parents, she would never know them now.

"Listen." A look of concern had creased Jonas's brow. "How about if I stay until you've had a chance to check everything over?" He tipped his head at her white-knuckled fist and the memory stick she clutched in it.

"No!" she replied much too sharply. She needed to be alone for this. She needed time to absorb it all and reject it—or to claim it in her heart, take it under her skin. "I, well, would you please thank Percy Valentine for me?"

"Absolutely."

"Would you explain that you've spoken with me and given me all the information he sent you?" Her mouth felt so dry. She swallowed and forged on. "I'm going to need some time…"

Jonas Bravo understood. "You mean you want me to say that *you'll* call *him*?"

The weird, constricted feeling in her chest seemed to loosen a fraction. "Yes, please. Would you tell him that I'll be in touch as soon as I'm ready?"

"I'll do that. Thanks for hearing me out. Percy will be looking forward to your call."

Chapter One

A week after her life-changing visit from the Bravo Billionaire, Madison stood on the back deck of a cute shingled cottage on a pristine stretch of sand called Sweetheart Cove in Valentine Bay.

The sky was endless and overcast. Gulls wheeled and soared above the blue Pacific, filling the air with their drawn-out, plaintive cries. She could smell salt spray and a hint of evergreen from the tall trees on the cliffs that loomed behind the cottage and sheltered the private stretch of beach that formed the cove.

So far, she really liked it here, next to the ocean, on the Oregon coast. It was much cooler and wilder than in LA.

No, she hadn't reached out to Percy Valentine. But she would. Eventually. When she was ready.

Which wasn't quite yet.

To lie low, that was her plan. If she stayed incognito, the tabloid reporters wouldn't find her. She could have a little quiet time for herself while she worked up the nerve to reach out to the family she'd just learned she had.

And yeah. She might not have outed herself to Percy Valentine yet, but she'd studied everything on that flash drive Jonas had given her. She'd seen all the pictures, read all the explanations.

And now she *believed.*

Her parents—whom she still loved with all her heart—were not her biological parents. She had five brothers, if you counted the one who'd vanished in Siberia years and years ago. Five brothers and four sisters, three by birth and also Aislinn Bravo Winter, the real Madison Delaney—or at least, she would have been if not for what Martin Durand had done.

Everything seemed strange and new and scary. And it would probably only get more so. But she was coping. She was doing all right.

Right now, in the interest of not being recognized, she wore a floppy, wide-brimmed straw hat and a terrific pair of Bvlgari Serpenti Gradient Square sunglasses—the black ones with the snake's-head detail at the temples. It was just the kind of silly disguise she would never try in LA, the kind that wouldn't fool anyone there for a second. But here in the Pacific Northwest, where no one expected to run into a movie star, dark glasses and a big hat did the job just fine.

Yeah, okay. There was no one around who might recognize her, anyway. The beach was deserted and there were only the two houses in the cove—her cottage and the larger house next door.

But so what if the hat and glasses were overkill? She wore them anyway, to be on the safe side and also because wearing disguises was fun. She felt like she could be anybody, some Valentine Bay local who'd rented a beach cottage just to stand out on her deck and stare at the waves lapping the sand, stare and smile and feel no pressure to do anything but simply *be*.

Too bad about the Bluetooth device stuck in her ear and the grating voice of Myra Castle, her agent, talking too fast and too loud, as usual.

"Dare to Dream," shouted Myra. "Tell me you've had a chance to look over the script."

"Well, Myra, I just got here two days ago and—"

"You need to decide on it and we need to lock it in. They want you, but they won't wait forever."

"Myra, I finally have some time off and I'd really like to enjoy—"

"Exactly. Wasted time. You can't afford that. You're not getting any younger. I know that's a ridiculous thing to say to a twenty-seven-year-old woman, but that's Hollywood. And you pay me to give it to you straight. If you don't keep making the right choices, you'll end up last year's hot commodity. What about *Devious Intentions*?"

"No. Really. I'm not ready to—"

"Well, then *get* ready. I've discussed this with Rafe." Rafe Zuma was Madison's manager. "We agree, Rafe and I. It's perfect for you, the exact right next step after *Heartbeats* and *To the Top*..." There was more. Lots more. Myra was a world-champion talker.

Suppressing a sigh, Madison tuned her out.

The cottage came with a nice pair of field glasses. Snatching them from a pretty cast-iron table as she went by, she strolled toward the back of the wraparound deck, interjecting the occasional "Um," or "I understand," whenever Myra paused for a breath or suddenly put a question mark at the end of a sentence. At the back corner, Madison leaned on the railing and traded her sunglasses for the binoculars.

In the past two glorious, peaceful days, she'd had plenty of time to study the occupants of the other house. In residence were her hunky landlord, his wife, a pair of cute kids and an older guy who was most likely the landlord's dad.

She adjusted the binoculars, bringing the house next door into focus—the rear of the house, to be specific. In the last two days, Madison had been giving the field glasses quite a workout, mostly from her current vantage point.

And no, she wasn't bird-watching. She was observing the landlord, who had a workshop area back there under his house, a workshop with a wide, roll-up door. Right now, that door was up. On the concrete slab just beyond the open door, the landlord was busy measuring and sawing and hammering.

Did she feel guilty for using his own binoculars to peep at him? Not really. Yeah, okay, it was invasive of his privacy, not to mention pretty juvenile, but what red-blooded, straight woman wouldn't stare long and often at a guy who looked like that?

He was tall and sinewy and beautiful, with thick brown hair that tended to curl in the moist Oregon air and just the right amount of beard scruff. He was also very handy with a large number of manly tools. He even wore an actual tool belt, wore it low on his hard hips.

Right now, he had his shirt off, displaying a cornucopia of gorgeous, lean muscle, the kind a guy didn't get at a gym. Lucky for him, he was married, or she just might consider asking hunky Mr. Fixit if he would do her a big favor and help her check off number one on her list of birthday goals.

Madison snorted out a silly laugh just at the thought. As if she'd ever make a move on a stranger, even a single one. She could work a room like nobody's business and she had no false modesty about her talent as an actress or her pretty face and nice body. In public and on set, she was supremely self-confident.

But when it came to love and romance in Hollywood, who could blame a girl for being wary? Relationships imploded as fast as they began and it really was hard to know if a guy liked you for yourself or for what you could do for him. She didn't need the potential heartache, so she'd more or less relinquished the field on the sex and romance front—relinquished it right out of the gate. She worked hard and constantly. She became casual friends with her costars. But as for love, well, she didn't really have time for love, anyway.

Or she *hadn't* had time. Until this year.

This year, no matter what, she was *making* time. Making time to make time.

That brought another snort-laugh from her, which had Myra demanding in her ear, "What is so funny?"

"Nothing, Myra. Absolutely noth…" The word died unfinished as a random gust of wind lifted her wide-brimmed hat right off her head. "Crap."

She made a grab for it. Too late. The hat sailed over the railing. She set down the binoculars—and knocked her dark glasses off the railing in the process. The sunglasses plopped to the sand below and the hat wheeled off toward the ocean, vanishing from sight.

"Madison," Myra badgered in her ear. "What is going on there?"

Madison looked down to see how her favorite sunglasses were faring and found herself staring directly into the wide, wondering eyes of Mr. Fixit's little girl, who had been playing with her brother between the two houses while Madison peeped at their dad.

The little girl gasped. "Princess Eliza!" she cried and clapped her small hands with glee. "Princess Eliza, it's you!" Princess Eliza was the central character in a Hans Christian Andersen fairy tale, "The Wild Swans." Eight years ago, Madison, had played Eliza for Disney.

And that little girl? She was the cutest thing ever, with a riot of curly dark brown hair only partly contained in two braids. She wore denim overalls and a pink T-shirt. A jumbo-sized neon-green Band-Aid took up serious real estate on her left forearm. She beamed up at Madison, who beamed right back, not even caring that she'd just been recognized.

"Madison, you with me?" shouted Myra.

"Myra, sorry. Gotta go. I'll be in touch." The agent was still talking as Madison ended the call.

"I'm coming to see you!" The little girl waved madly. Madison waved back at her. "I'm coming right now!" And the child took off at a run.

Laughing, Madison pulled the device from her ear and her phone from her pocket. She whirled and headed for the main deck again. Resetting the phone to silent page, she dropped both it and the Bluetooth receiver on the cast-iron table as she passed it.

At the same time, the kid ran around to the steps

on the other side of the deck and started up them. "I'm here, Eliza," she called. "I'm here to see you!"

"Coco, stop!" Her brother followed after her. "That's not Eliza!" he shouted. "Eliza isn't real."

"Oh, you just shut up, Benjamin Killigan." The little girl paused in midstep and turned on her brother. "You don't know nothing."

"Anything," the boy corrected her. "And you know you're not supposed to bother the tenant."

Coco whirled away from him and ran up the remaining steps. "Eliza!" She reached the deck and raced for Madison, arms outstretched, pigtails flying.

Madison held out her arms. The little girl flew at her and landed, *smack*, against her middle.

"I'm Colleen." The child gazed up at her through shining blue eyes. "But everybody calls me Coco."

"Hello, Coco. My name is Madison."

"See?" crowed the boy as he skidded to a stop a few feet away from them. "She's not Eliza." He was a year or two older than Coco, with straight brown hair, serious brown eyes and a T-shirt with *Stand back! I'm going to try science!* printed on the front.

Coco let go of Madison to turn and deal with her brother. "Is so."

"No, she's not."

"Hold it," said Madison. The children fell silent. Two sets of eyes turned on her expectantly. "You're both right. I'm an actress who played the part of Eliza. So no, I'm not really Eliza, but yes, I am the one Coco remembers from *The Wild Swans*."

"Told you so," Coco gloated.

"All right, you two," Hunky Mr. Fixit said from the top of the steps. He'd taken off his tool belt and put on a T-shirt. Darn it. "What did I tell you about bothering the tenant?"

Benjamin seemed hurt. "Uncle Sten, I tried to stop her!"

Uncle Sten. Interesting. So the hot guy next door might not be married, after all?

Or maybe the kids were cousins and only the little girl was his.

"She waved at me!" cried Coco.

The hunk came toward them, his lace-up work boots eliminating the distance in four long strides. Up close, he had the same amazing blue eyes as Coco. "I'm Sten Larson." He offered Madison his big, manly hand.

"Madison." His hand was warm, dusted very lightly with dark hair—and rough in all the right places.

"I know who you are." He was so good-looking, with all that messy hair and those lips that made a woman think of kisses—kisses that start out slow, but then grow hot and wonderfully deep. "But you don't have to worry."

Her brain seemed to have gone off-line at his touch. "Um, worry? Why would I worry?"

He smiled then, a wry and beautiful smile. "I just mean that I'm sworn to secrecy concerning everything about you. I've even signed an NDA."

"Ah," she replied, the sound absurdly husky. "I can trust you then?" Was she flirting? She needed to cut that out. He could definitely be married.

"I'm not going to say a word to anyone," he vowed. "And neither are the kids. I'll make sure of that."

She still held his hand. They just looked at each other. The look went on for several seconds. Eventually, it became downright awkward. They let go simultaneously. "Really, it's no big deal," she said, trying really hard to control her totally out-there reactions to everything about this guy. "I waved at Coco. She recognized me from a Disney movie I did a few years back and she came running up to meet me."

"Yes!" crowed Coco with glee. "Princess Eliza is my most favoritest princess. She saved her brothers so they didn't have to be swans anymore. There were eleven of them, those brothers, and the wicked stepmother turned them all into swans and made them fly far, far away and Eliza had to—"

"Coco, settle down." A frown lowered the corners of Sten's distractingly kissable mouth. He seemed super cautious, the way people always did after they had it drilled it into them that Madison wanted privacy and she was not to be disturbed or to have attention drawn to her in any way.

"The beach is deserted," Madison said, feeling embarrassed at the rules she herself always insisted on. "I don't see a problem."

For several more endless seconds, he just looked at her. Really, he could do that forever, just stand there with those gorgeous eyes focused on her. She felt something lovely and magic with him, no doubt about it. It was absolutely delicious, that hot little spark of mutual attraction.

And for once, she was actually imagining acting on it.

At last.

But he just kept frowning. He turned to the kids. "All right you two, go on back to the house and check in with Grandpa."

Ben took Coco's hand. The little girl allowed him

to lead her to the stairs, but dug in her heels before following him down. Turning, she offered, "Eliza, you can come play with me at my house anytime!"

I'll be right there, Madison thought but didn't say. It probably wouldn't go over so well with Sten, who was watching her like he didn't quite know what to make of her, the supposedly reclusive movie star who suddenly found his grade school-age niece—or daughter—fascinating. "Thanks." She gave Coco a big smile.

"Come *on*." Ben pulled Coco on down the stairs.

Sten took another step backward. "I'm really sorry about this. I'll talk to the kids and their mom." *Their* mom. So then neither of the children was his? "I'll make sure they leave you alone and also that they understand not to tell people you're in town."

"Coco and Ben can come visit me anytime." The words were out of her mouth before she even realized she would say them—and now she *had* said them, she didn't want to take them back. The two children were charming and sweet and why shouldn't she get to know them a little?

As for hunky Mr. Fixit, well, Madison had shared on-screen kisses with some of the best-looking men in the world. But there was something about this one, with his slightly scruffy haircut and those lean muscles he had from doing actual work. He was so…natural, so *real*.

And definitely wary of her.

And just possibly, married.

She really needed to find out for sure if he was or he wasn't. "Your kids are just too cute," she said with a wide smile.

He almost smiled back, one side of his mouth curling up reluctantly. "They're my sister, Karin's, kids."

She kept a straight face, though inside she was happy-dancing. "You all live together, right?"

He nodded. "Bud, Karin's husband, died in a fishing accident more than three years ago now."

Her silly glee that this hot guy was almost certainly single vanished. "I'm so sorry."

He raked his hand back through all that unruly hair. "Yeah. It was rough. Coco was just three at the time. They're doing all right now, though. She and the kids moved in with Dad and me last summer. They're all downstairs together—Karin, the kids and my father. I've got the second floor to myself. There's plenty of room and my sister's a great cook. Dad and I pitch in watching the kids. I'm one of those single guys who likes having family around, so overall, it works out pretty well."

One of those single guys…

Yes! Inside, she fist-pumped like a crazy woman— seriously, what was she, twelve?

In some ways, yes.

She'd done a nude scene last year. Millions of people had seen her bare butt. But when it came to relationships in real life, Madison Delaney, America's Darling, suffered from a serious case of arrested development.

It was kind of sad. And not only that she knew nothing about men, IRL. But also, well, just imagining the house next door, with Sten and the kids, Sten's sister and his dad, too…

She envied them.

To have family. To have a brother or a sister, nieces and nephews, and to have them close. She'd always wanted that—and maybe, when she finally got up the nerve to get in contact with the Bravos, she would have what she'd always wanted.

After she got to know them all. Eventually. Over time...

Sten took a step closer. "What's wrong? You look so sad, all of a sudden." He lifted one of those fine, big hands. Her skin burned with the knowledge that he was going to touch her—brush a finger over her cheek, maybe smooth a loose ribbon of hair behind her ear.

Every nerve in her body had snapped to quivering alert.

But before his fingertips made contact, the glass door leading into the cottage slid open. Sten glanced over his shoulder as Dirk, her bodyguard, stuck his head out. "Everything okay?"

Sten lowered his hand.

Madison gave Dirk a tight nod with *get lost* written all over it. "All good."

Dirk pulled his big head back inside and shut the door, but he didn't go anywhere. He remained right there on the far side of the glass, legs braced wide, meaty shoulders back, watching. Madison was very fond of Dirk and Sergei and all of her bodyguards, but sometimes having round-the-clock security sucked—times like now, when she was not going to feel Sten Larson's hand brush her cheek, after all.

"I should get going," he said. "If you need anything, just let me know."

She tried to think of something clever and sophisticated to say to make him stay. But she was working without a script and her mind was a witless blank.

Over on the table, her phone started spinning in a

circle, the screen lighting up with a picture of Rafe in one of his bespoke suits, his dark face impossibly handsome, supremely confident. Resigned, she went to answer it as Sten headed for the stairs.

What the hell just happened?

Sten scowled as he ran down the steps. Did he get struck by lightning?

The movie star was freaking gorgeous, with those acres of streaky blond hair, that thousand-watt, dimpled smile. She was also friendly and outgoing and easy to talk to. No wonder they called her America's Darling.

He might have just come down with a serious crush on the woman. What the hell? Like he was fourteen again, all knees and elbows, overwhelmed and tongue-tied in the presence of Sharlee Stubbleman, a senior and the prettiest girl at Valentine Bay High.

Madison Delaney.

What was the matter with him? Talk about out of his league.

She'd looked so sad, though, there for a minute, hadn't she? Sad and a little bit lost.

And he'd wanted to pull her close, comfort her, maybe even taste those pillowy lips of hers. He might have done it, too, if not for the bodyguard shoving open the slider just as he was making his move.

She doesn't want to be disturbed.

He needed to remember that. The woman wanted to be alone and his job was to make sure nobody bothered her or found out that she'd rented his cottage at Sweetheart Cove. Madison Delaney had paid a lot of money for her six-week stay and for the total privacy he'd promised her assistant she would have.

Sten returned to his workshop, put his tools away and shut the roll-up door, smiling to himself as he thought of Coco and her little-girl crush on the star of her favorite Disney movie.

Too bad his niece wouldn't get to spend any more time with Madison. He would have to have a talk with Karin about how to make Coco understand that she was not allowed to pester the tenant or tell anyone else that a movie star was staying next door.

That night after she put the kids to bed, Karin joined him out on the deck. They sat in the comfy red cedar chairs he'd made a few years ago and watched the trail of the moon reflected, shimmering, on the ocean. The gulls were feeding, circling and calling and then diving for fish and just about anything else that happened to catch their eye.

There was a chilly wind blowing. Karin smoothed dark hair away from her face and wrapped her bulky sweater more tightly around her. "I'm guessing you'll want to discuss the movie star next door."

He grunted. "You noticed that Coco jabbered about her nonstop through dinner, then?"

"I did, yeah. What's up?" She turned her eyes to him. They were blue, like his eyes and their dad's and Coco's, too. In the moonlight, they looked almost black. Black and too somber. Three years since Bud died fishing the Gulf of Alaska. Sometimes Karin still looked way too sad.

"You signed the NDA, too," he said. "The tenant is not supposed to be disturbed and no one else can know that she's here."

"What? The big star got all offended because my little girl's a fan?"

"Whoa, Mama Grizzly. Take it down a notch. Madison really liked Coco. She said Coco and Ben could come over anytime they wanted to."

Karin leaned between their chairs and peered at him a little too closely. "*Madison?* So we're on a first-name basis with America's Darling, are we?"

"Stop."

"You like her." She slapped the side of his knee with the back of her hand. "Admit it."

"She seems like a good person."

"Right. You're attracted to her *goodness.*"

In some ways Karin was still the bratty little sister he'd grown up with. Mostly, he hoped she would never change. Times like now, though? Not so much. "There really is a point to this conversation and the point is that we need to keep the kids out of her hair and make sure they don't tell anyone she's staying here."

"All right. I'll handle it."

"How?"

"Well, Ben's no problem. He was born responsible and reasonable. He already knows the cottage is off-limits when a tenant is living there and that the tenants have a right to their privacy. Coco is a bit of a challenge. She's such a free spirit. But we've been talking about privacy and respect lately. I'll start with that. Ben will back me. Coco will fall in line, for her beloved 'Eliza's' sake, if nothing else."

He stared at his sister, thinking that beyond loving her, he really *liked* her. A lot. He was just about to tell her that when she sent him a slow, knowing smile. He knew that smile. It was her give-Sten-some-grief smile.

"You like the movie star," she said. "And not just because she's so *good*."

"Oh, come on." He tried to look really bored. "What guy with a pulse wouldn't like her?"

"Stennie. There's nothing wrong with liking the girl next door." *Stennie*. He used to chase her around the house with a squirt gun when she called him that. But now he was a grown-ass man and knew better than to let his sister's teasing get to him. Much. She leaned close again and pitched her voice low. "It's been more than a year since Ella went back to that loser in Seattle. Good riddance. Time to move on."

"Ella? Who's Ella?"

"Har-har. I know you don't like to talk about her. I don't want to talk about her, either. I never liked her."

"You didn't say so at the time."

"Because I'm a good sister who minds her own business and has sense enough not to give her big brother advice on his love life."

"Right. Like you're *not* doing now?"

"This isn't advice. It's a nudge. Sometimes you need a nudge."

"She wants to be alone. I signed the NDA."

"You're repeating yourself. And you *like* her. And you really ought to just go ahead and follow up on that."

That night and the next day, Madison started to wonder what she was even doing in Valentine Bay. She'd yet to work up the courage to reach out to Percy Valentine and the family she'd been born into.

And what was the point of getting away from LA when all she did was field calls from her agent and her manager? Myra and Rafe just never quit. They tagged-teamed her, pressuring her to sign on for this and think about that, to come back to LA for some high-priority meetings, to read a pile of scripts yesterday because time was flying by and she couldn't afford to lose momentum.

Madison could not have cared less about momentum. She needed a life—a real life, a life like most people took for granted. A life containing a family, a special guy and some friends she got together with outside of the movie business. Too bad she seemed stuck on hold lately, unable to take the necessary steps to make her goals happen.

Coco and Benjamin waved at her when they played outside, but when she tried to signal them up, they just waved again and ran off. She was pretty sure they'd been told to keep away.

And as for Sten? More than once, she faintly heard machines whirring down in his workshop. But his roll-up door stayed shut.

On the night of her fourth day in Valentine Bay, she'd had enough. She lay in bed in the dark and stared blankly at the shadows near the ceiling thinking that something had to give. She couldn't go on like this.

Bright and early the next morning, she called her manager and her agent and informed them in no uncertain terms that she was taking time off, having an actual vacation. And when a person took a vacation, she didn't want to constantly be forced to think about work.

They were not to contact her. If some emergency came up and they just *had* to reach out to her, they were to get in touch with Rudy, who would pass the word to her.

Next, she called Rudy and told him that while she

was in Valentine Bay, he would be dealing with Rafe and Myra. She also instructed him to call her security firm and inform them that she was sending Dirk back to LA.

"That's not going to go well," said her PA in his usual dry, unflappable tone.

"Do it. I'm serious. Dirk's the best. Make it very clear it's nothing against him. I just need to be on my own right now."

Ten minutes later, Rudy called her back to pass on the dire warnings from her security people. The team had not approved when she took only one bodyguard to Oregon, and they were even more concerned when they learned that she'd been using Dirk as a driver, too; security should stay focused on the main job.

And now she was suddenly ditching Dirk, as well? Her security team predicted that big trouble would follow.

"Let me send a driver, at least," Rudy pleaded.

"No. It's a dinky town. I'll find a way to get around."

"But you don't have a valid—"

"Rudy. I'll figure something out."

"I don't know why you won't let me send Ada. You're going to need someone to keep the fridge stocked and make the bed."

"I'm managing all that on my own."

"I really think you need to—"

"Rudy. Seriously, if I need help, you're a phone call away."

He argued some more. He was a sweetheart and very protective of her. She loved him for that.

But she also stuck by her decision to go it alone for a while.

At two that afternoon, Dirk got in the rented Hummer they'd been using since their arrival and drove away. Once he was gone, Madison tried again to work up the nerve to call someone in the Bravo family. She'd put all their numbers in her phone, but she'd yet to make use of them.

She dialed Percy's number twice. Both times, she hung up before it could ring. Then she tried texting her switched sister, Aislinn.

Same result. She began and then erased four texts without sending them.

For a couple of hours after that, she alternately tried to concentrate on reading a book, searched the Netflix menu for something to watch and paced the floor in exasperation at her own inability to complete a damn phone call or hit Send on a text.

At five, frustrated and fed up with herself, she did a very bad thing. It wasn't premeditated—at least, not exactly.

She entered the powder room off the kitchen innocently enough, used the toilet, flushed it and washed her hands. And it wasn't until then, as she rinsed and dried and glared at herself in the mirror over the pedestal sink, that it occurred to her that Sten Larson's phone number was right there on a little card by the landline in the living area.

In case she had a problem and needed him to fix it.

Carefully, she folded the towel and hung it back on the rack.

Then she took the lid off the toilet and set it on the seat. The mechanism within was simple enough. A chain pulled a rubber flapper up when you flushed.

The flapper lowered to seal the water inside once the tank was full again.

That chain? It could easily be unhooked from the bar that connected it to the handle. But wouldn't it be more realistic if the chain broke?

She stuck her fingers in there, got the chain in both hands and gave a good, strong yank.

Whoopsie.

She dried her hands again, after which she replaced the tank lid and then tried to flush. Nothing.

Madison grinned, feeling downright devilish. She was a movie star, after all, someone who pretended to be other people for a living, someone who had writers to give her words to say and staff to see to her every need, a person who couldn't be expected to understand how a toilet worked—let alone to have any clue what to do if something in there broke.

Before she had a chance to chicken out and hook the chain back together herself, she marched into the living area, picked up the house phone and punched in the number on the card.

Chapter Two

Sten was on his way home from Larson Boatworks when the call came in from the cottage phone. His pulse did a ridiculous, jittery little dance as he answered on his quad cab's speakerphone. "This is Sten."

There was dead air on the other end and for a moment, he relaxed, feeling certain it was the gruff bodyguard calling to ask for thicker towels or more coffee mugs or whatever.

But then she said, "Hi. It's Madison."

"Hey." He said it much too softly. Almost tenderly. *Somebody just shoot me.* "Everything okay?" That came out better. More brusque and businesslike.

"Well, there's something wrong with the toilet in the half bath. It won't flush. The handle thingy just flops around when I push it."

As he slowed the truck and turned onto the winding side road that meandered down the cliffs and into the cove, he was thinking that he really liked her voice.

Her voice was sweet and just a little bit husky—and come on. Everyone in America liked her voice. And her gorgeous, friendly, girl-next-door face. And what about that body? She had an amazing body—a *real*-looking body, soft and curvy, like a woman's body should be, with breasts that were average-size and completely natural-looking.

Stop thinking about her breasts, jackass.

But get real.

Who could blame him? Like most of the rest of the free world, he'd seen that recent romantic comedy, including the scene where she'd been stark naked in bed with her leading man, Brock Markovic.

Then again, how did he even know that was really her body? Maybe she'd had a body double.

Not that it was any of his damn business, either way.

"Sten?"

"Right here." *And definitely not thinking about you naked.*

"So, about the toilet?"

He was hugely tempted to launch into an explanation of what, exactly, might be wrong with the flushing mechanism and what he would do about it, just to show off what an expert he was on the issue of toilets—and yeah. He should face it. This girl had his brains leaking out his ears.

"Sten? Have I lost you?"

"I'll be there in five."

He drove the rest of the way to the main house, parked in the garage and grabbed a toolbox and the pair of sunglasses he'd found in the sand between the houses the day before. As he climbed the steps to the front door of the cottage, which faced the cliffs behind the beach, he reminded himself for the hundredth time that his job was to be happy about the enormous rent she paid and leave the beautiful creature next door alone. He would be fixing the damn toilet and getting the hell out.

She answered his knock wearing jeans and a snug shirt and looking like a couple of billion bucks. "I appreciate this." Her smile bloomed, dimples twinkling, and he almost forgot how to talk.

He held out the sunglasses. "I'm guessing these might be yours?"

She took them. "Wow, thank you. I love this pair and I thought I would never seem them again."

"No problem." He cleared his throat. "Let's have a look at that toilet." He sounded impossibly serious to his own ears. Like a bad actor playing a doctor on some cheesy soap.

She stepped back and ushered him in. He got a whiff of her scent as he moved past her. Sweet and peppery at once. Delicious. The scent conjured memories of his childhood, of all things, sent him back to the house on Dorcas Lane where he grew up.

Petunias. That was it. She smelled like his mom's petunias. In the summertime, they always overflowed the hanging baskets on the back deck. He used to love getting his nose right up in them, breathing in that scent that was so sweet it smelled sticky-good—sweet and yet sharp, too.

And why were they were just standing there in the entry area, staring at each other?

He broke the hold of her gaze and led the way down

the short hall to the half bath. She leaned in the doorway, slim arms folded across her middle, the sunglasses dangling from her fingers, watching as he set his toolbox on the floor. He almost told her she didn't have to hang around. He'd take care of the problem and let her know when he was leaving.

But if he told her that, she might turn and walk away. He didn't want that—even if he had been avoiding her since the other day. She was too tempting, too rich for his blood. And when she was standing close to him like this, well, the temptation was stronger. It overrode his caution.

He jiggled the handle and it flopped up and down uselessly.

"Not a big deal," he said.

"Great." Her dimples winked at him.

He took the lid off the tank and saw that the chain had been broken in two. That chain had zero rust on it or signs of wear. Doubtful it would have broken without help.

When he slanted Madison a glance, her blue-green eyes were wide and innocent as a cloudless sky. But her dimples told another story. She was trying really hard to hide a grin. She lowered her head and looked at her shoes, her shining hair flowing forward, covering her cheeks.

Was she blushing? "Where's your bodyguard?" he asked.

She straightened, guiding her hair behind her ear on one side. He saw the pink flush on her cheek. Definitely blushing. "I sent him back to LA."

"Why?"

"I've had security with me round-the-clock for

years. I wanted a little privacy for a change. It's kind of isolated here. And so far, nobody's bothered me, so…" She let a shrug finish for her.

He grabbed a pair of needle-nose pliers from the toolkit. "How is it, then, being on your own here?"

"Dirk's only been gone a few hours. Check in with me later. I'll let you know."

Sten saluted her with the pliers and then used them to reconnect the chain. "There you go." He worked the handle. The flapper lifted and the water flowed away, then was quickly replaced by more. They waited in silence until the water shut off. "It's working fine now." He dropped the pliers back into the toolbox and bent to latch it shut. Grabbing the handle, he straightened.

"How about a beer?" she asked, the words rushing to get out, her tone suddenly forceful.

He faced her. She gazed up at him, dimples nowhere in sight, looking defiant and determined now. Adorably so. He sucked in one more breath of her enticing scent and opened his mouth to say that he really had to go. What came out was, "A beer would be great."

In the kitchen, which looked out over the deck and the ocean beyond, she put the sunglasses down on the end of the counter, gestured for him to sit and then bounded to the fridge to pull out a couple of Breakside IPAs. The woman knew her beer—or at least somebody who worked for her did. She had chilled beer mugs, too.

"Help yourself." She set the full beer bottles and the frosty mugs on the table. "And I have nachos!" She looked so pleased with herself, like Coco with her kiddie oven that she baked imaginary cupcakes in and then made everyone sit at her kid-size table and pretend to eat them off miniature pink plastic plates. "What's so funny?" Madison was still standing by his chair, watching him.

"You're just so enthusiastic, that's all. It's cute."

She frowned, a line drawing down between her perfectly shaped eyebrows. "Thank you. I think. So... nachos?"

"I love nachos."

"Well, all right then."

She bustled around, heating the chips, adding stuff to the cheese sauce, popping it in the microwave. There were jalapeños and olives and onions and black beans that she sprinkled on after she'd poured on the sauce.

"Ta-da!" She set the platter on the table and gave them each a small plate.

"It looks great." And it did.

"Enjoy." She sat down in the chair across from him and held up her beer mug. He tapped it with his and they drank. "So, tell me," she said, tipping her head to the side, her hair falling like a wheat-colored waterfall along one shoulder. "Your name. Sten. Is that a nickname?"

"Nope. It's Swedish. Means stone."

"Ah." She seemed to ponder that. God, she was gorgeous. And sweet. And not innocent, exactly, but... open. She seemed fascinated by the most ordinary things. "I like it," she said. "Because you're not."

He waited for her to explain what she meant by that. When she didn't, he prompted her. "Not what?"

"Stone-like. Tell me more. What you *do*, what you love?"

He couldn't figure her out. The magic of her. And

that made him edgy. "Is it part of being an actress, to be so interested in every little thing?"

Those full lips thinned. "Everything I do is not about acting."

"Only *most* things?" It came out kind of snarky and he wished he'd kept his mouth shut.

Apparently, she did, too. She aimed a full-out scowl at him. "Don't make me get pissed at you. Maybe I just like you. Maybe I'm *interested* in you. Did you ever think of that?"

He wanted to laugh, of all things. Instead he teased in a flat tone, "Fine. You can like me."

She stared at him, her shining eyes narrowed. "I take it back about the stone thing. Now you're definitely coming off as stone-like. Stop it. Chill. Talk about you. About your family. About the things you build down there in your workshop."

He'd spotted her up there on the side deck more than once, wearing a big, floppy hat, using his own binoculars to spy on him. And he'd kind of liked it, her watching him. It had felt like a harmless, never-to-be-acted-on flirtation, somehow—until the other day, when he met her face-to-face and found her way too damn fascinating for his peace of mind.

"Sten," she tried again. "What do you make in your workshop?"

"Cabinets. Molding. Things you put in houses you flip."

"You flip houses?" She crunched another nacho. "Tell me about that."

"You're just going to make me ramble on about myself, aren't you?"

Her smile was slow and full of sweet devilment.

"Oh, yes, I am. You should tell me your life story. Just go ahead and get it over with."

He had the feeling she wouldn't give up on this, so he started talking. He explained that he'd flipped the cottage. "And then I decided to keep it and rent it out." He told her about his mom, who'd managed a local bakery and always kept a beautiful garden until she died five years ago. He shared way more than necessary about Larson Boatworks, the company his dad had started thirty-five years before. "We do fabrication and remodeling of sport and commercial fishing boats, mostly. I've been working with my dad for about six years now. He moved in with me after my mom died."

"And before you went to work with your dad?"

"In college, during school breaks, and for a while after, I worked on small fishing boats up and down the West Coast, from California to the Bering Sea. It's rough work, commercial fishing. But I loved it."

"Why did you quit?"

"It's good money, but not good enough. And my dad wanted me to come in on the family business. Eventually, the company will be mine—mine and Karin's. She runs the office now." She'd taken over when Ella quit. "I'm there when I'm needed and I can also fool around with real estate and construction."

"You're a busy guy," she said, and leaned in. "Got a girl, Sten?" She literally twinkled at him. A princess from a Disney movie, for sure.

"Damn." He took a long pull off his beer and set the mug down firmly. "You are nosy."

She laughed. "Well, I want to know, so I asked."

"There's no one. Your turn," he said, before she could ask another question about his currently nonexistent love life. "Make it good," he instructed. "Tell me something no one else knows."

"Wait a minute." She huffed a breath in pretend outrage. "All I asked for was a bio, but you want my deepest secrets?"

"That sounds about right to me." He gazed at her steadily and she stared right back. That special something swirled between them. It felt like a promise of what was to come. Right at the moment, he didn't care that it was a false promise and nothing was going to happen between them. He was having a good time and she seemed to be enjoying herself, too.

She leaned in again and stage-whispered dramatically, "You would have to swear never to tell a soul."

"I won't tell anyone." He put up a hand, to make it look official. "Not a soul."

And she launched into this crazy story about how she'd been switched at birth by some local rancher who didn't want his wife to find out he'd been fooling around. She said she was born into the Bravo family and the switch had happened soon after her birth. "My name should have been Aislinn," she said.

Sten knew the Bravos. They were a prominent family in town. He and the second-born brother, Matt, had been in the same grade in school.

The thing was, now she'd mentioned the Bravos, he really could see a family resemblance. Especially between her and the Bravo sisters, Harper, Hailey and Grace. She looked nothing like Aislinn, the oldest sister. Aislinn had dark hair and eyes—and come to think of it, none of the other Bravos looked much like Aislinn.

"I came here to get to know them, this family I

just found out I have. I've been here for days now." Her husky voice had turned plaintive. "Days. And I can't quite drum up the nerve to get in touch with them. I mean, they already know about the switch. *They* reached out to *me*. They *want* to meet me. I said I would call or whatever when I was ready. And here I am, in the town where they live. And somehow, I can't make myself contact them."

She looked so lost now, her glittery brightness dimmed. The most beautiful girl in the world, the girl who had everything. Except the family that should have been hers from the first.

"What can I do?" he asked, and realized he meant it. "How can I help?"

She sat a little straighter. "You mean that, Sten? Because I really, really want to take advantage of you."

"Whatever you want. Name it." So much for steering clear of her, for playing it cautious and smart. He'd just asked her to use him. And he couldn't wait for her to tell him what she wanted him to do.

She sucked in a long breath. "Okay, it's like this. I'm still not there yet. I'm not ready to go and see my lost family. I need more time. Time here, in this house. Without my PA or my driver or my housekeeper or my security team. They're all terrific, the best at what they do, but I just don't want them here, hovering. I want to change up some stuff in my life and I need the time and space to do that."

"Madison."

She gulped. At that moment she looked so young, young and confused and in need of a friend. "Yeah?"

"Just tell me what you want from me."

"There's a Subaru Forester downstairs in the garage." Before he could ask what a Subaru had to do with anything, she chattered on, "My security team had the car rental agency deliver it here before we arrived. It's actually a getaway car. See, if the media gets on to the fact that I'm here and I need to get away, I need one guy to drive, say, a Hummer or a limo—some big, fancy vehicle—as a decoy. The decoy rides off and the paparazzi chase after him. He leads them all the way to Portland International, where he drops off the Hummer and catches a commercial flight back to LA. And then, once all the reporters have followed the Hummer, another guy will drive me in the Subaru to the local airfield and the private jet that's waiting there to whisk me away."

"So you're warning me that you're planning an escape?"

She laughed. "No, I'm really just saying there's a Subaru down in the garage and I have the keys to it, but I can't drive it." Her cheeks flamed pinker than they had in the half bath, when she'd realized that he knew she'd broken that chain on purpose. "Okay, it's like this. I let my driver's license lapse a few years ago. It just never occurred to me that I might want to drive myself somewhere. But now, well, I don't want any of my people here. And that means, even though I have a Subaru, I have no way to get around. I'm afraid to call an Uber. What if the driver recognizes me? Things will get really hairy if word gets out I'm here."

"You want me to drive you somewhere, is that it?"

"Yeah." Those eyes of her could make a man do foolish things. "If you would, that would be terrific— well, I mean, when I do get up the nerve to reach out to this family I've never met. I'll pay you, of course, and I—"

"Stop. You're already paying me a bundle for this house. I'm not charging you any more than that. I'll drive you wherever you want to go." Had he lost it completely? Yeah, probably. But somehow, he couldn't stop offering to help. "And what about food? You'll have to get groceries while you're here."

"I've got that handled." She wore a proud little grin. "I can have everything delivered. My credit cards have only my first initial and my last name. Who's gonna care, as long as they don't see my face and put it together? I'll just wear a wig and dark glasses when I answer the door. I figure I can sign fast, grab the groceries and get rid of the delivery guy before he has a chance to see through my disguise."

He stared at her, kind of dumbfounded by everything—her, the situation, the way she planned to deal with it. She stared right back at him.

And then they both burst out laughing.

That felt good. So good. To be laughing with her at the sheer bizarreness of her world, at the idea that anyone would have to don a disguise just to answer the door.

When the laughter faded down and the room was too quiet, she waved a hand. "Talk about first world problems, huh? I've got a million of those."

He shouldn't ask. But he did. "What's really going on with you, Madison?"

She glanced away. But only for a moment. Then she seemed to steel herself. She looked him square in the eye. "Well, beyond finding out I apparently have a big family I never even knew existed, I guess you could say I'm having kind of a life crisis."

"How so?"

"From the age of six, all I ever wanted to do in my life was act."

"And you got what you wanted, right?"

"Yes, I did. I'm one of the lucky ones. I made my dream come true. In the process, though, I seem to have missed out on everything else, you know? So, I'm thinking of quitting acting—or at least of changing things up in a big way. And I, um…" She shifted in the chair, drank the last of her beer and set the mug down hard. "It's like this, Sten. I really need to get laid."

You got it, baby, he somehow managed not to say. But come on. When America's Darling says she needs to get laid, who wouldn't volunteer to help her out with that?

Her blush had deepened to cherry red. "God. I hardly know you and I'm not even drunk." She covered her face with her hands and squeaked, "I can't believe I just said that."

Her embarrassment only made her all the cuter—and he needed to reassure her, let her know that it was all right, that he liked a woman who said what was on her mind. "Hey."

With a hard sigh, she sat up straight and dropped her hands into her lap. "Now you know. I'm a lost cause."

"No, you're not. You're beautiful and smart and funny and…true."

She looked at him so intently then, as though she needed to see inside his head and be absolutely certain he wasn't mocking her. "Yeah?"

"Yeah. And believe me, I get it. I mean, I personally get it. I haven't been with anyone in over a year." He tried to be gentle and tactful with his next question. "So, you're saying it's been a long time for you, too?"

She took forever to respond. And when she finally did, he wondered for a second if he'd heard her correctly.

"Actually," she said, "I'm a virgin."

Chapter Three

Sten tried really hard to reconcile what she'd just said with the stunning creature sitting in the chair across from him.

She was beyond pretty. And she was a star. And what about that nude scene? Her sexy naked body on display at larger-than-life-size all over America. Yeah, she had a shy, little-girl side. But a virgin? No way would he have guessed that.

"Is it a religious thing?" he asked cautiously.

She shook her head. "I work a lot. Mostly, I've always felt I just didn't have time for a man. I try to be free and open when I'm acting. Ready for anything, you know? But I'm a lot more cautious in real life. I don't give my trust easily." She seemed completely sincere.

But maybe she was just messing with him.

It was as if she'd read his mind. "Nope." She flipped

a shining hank of hair back over her shoulder. "Not a joke. And I'm not screwing with your head. I just, well, I like you. You're easy to talk to. And here I am telling you way more than you ever could have possibly needed to know." She blew out her cheeks with a huff of breath and then pretended to study her fingernails. "You should run. Run away, fast."

"Madison." She looked up into his eyes—and he gave it up and said exactly what he was thinking. "I'm not going anywhere. You're too honest, too surprising and much too beautiful."

As her smile lit up the room again, someone knocked on the slider. It was Coco, her little face squished against the glass. "It's open!" Madison waved her in.

Coco shoved the door wide and announced, "Mommy says dinner's ready. It's lasagna and Eliz—I mean *Madison*, you're invited."

Madison jumped up. "I would love to have lasagna at your house." And then she sent him a look that dared him to come up with some reason she shouldn't go.

Not a chance. Karin was matchmaking and Coco was starstruck. And Madison seemed more than willing to go with the flow. Who was he to say no? "Well, all right, then." He stood, too.

"Hurry up," said Coco, getting bossy now things were going her way. "Mommy says right now."

Madison loved the house next door. It was as open and welcoming as the cottage, but a lot bigger, with comfortable furniture that invited a person to relax and stay awhile.

Both floors had full kitchens and large living areas, with tall windows framing the beach and the ocean.

There were three bedrooms upstairs and four bedrooms down.

She met Otto Larson. Sten's father was tall and lean, with a slight potbelly, thinning sandy hair and a lived-in face. "Pleased to meet you," he said in a shy, courtly way, taking her hand and pressing it between his two leathery paws.

Karin Killigan had wild dark hair like Coco's, a warm smile and just enough of a snarky attitude to make Madison feel at home.

They ate in the downstairs kitchen. As they shoveled in the pasta, yummy garlic bread and green salad, Coco told a rambling story about falling down at recess. "I had to go the nurse's office and get *two* Band-Aids to make it all better," she finished breathlessly, rising from the table and rolling up her jeans to show them off. The Band-Aids in question were bright yellow and neon pink, respectively, one on each scratched-up little knee.

Benjamin discussed his latest school science project and the book he'd decided to write about the life cycle of the razor clam. "Razor clams are highly sensitive to vibrations," he explained. "They can tell when a predator is coming just from that—the vibrations in the sand. Razor clams have very muscular feet and can propel themselves up or down in the sand to escape an attack. My book will have illustrations. I will draw them myself. I think it's going to be quite good, I really do."

Madison asked, "Have you ever eaten a razor clam?"

"Of course. They grow big here, not like the skinny ones on the East Coast. We get them with clam guns."

Karin laughed. "Not what you're thinking. A clam gun is actually a big piece of PVC pipe with a handle.

You wiggle the pipe into the sand and bring up the clam inside the pipe."

"You should go razor clamming, Madison," said Ben. "You can come with us Saturday."

"Yes!" Coco clapped her little hands. "Madison, you *have* to come."

"It's not far," coaxed Karin.

Madison slid a glance at Sten, who was seated to her left, to see if he was going to try to convince her that going clamming with his family was a bad idea.

He surprised her. "You'll love it," he said. And then he just kept looking at her. She gazed right back at him and never wanted to look away.

"We go at low tide," Ben announced. "Saturday, that will be at 5:57 p.m. But we want to get there two hours before the tide is lowest, so we leave in the afternoon."

"And it's really fun," Coco put in. "Except sometimes it's cold and it takes too long and I always have to promise I won't be a baby."

From down at one end of the table, Otto added quietly, with considerable dry humor, "We all go, together. Sten, too. I do hope you'll join us, Madison."

Reluctantly, Madison broke the hold of the mutual eye-seduction she and Sten had going on. "I would love to go clamming on Saturday."

"You'll need a license," said Ben. "You can get one online and print the receipt to use for Saturday. The real license will come in the mail."

That sounded complicated. "How about if I just observe?"

"Yes, you can," declared Ben.

After dinner, Ben wandered off to his room and Karin reminded Coco it was time for her bath.

"I know. I'm going—Madison, thank you for having dinner at my house."

"Thank you for inviting me. I had a wonderful time."

"Saturday, I will bring Spot it! and my rubber band ring kit. We can stay in the truck and play if we get all cold and tired."

"I would love that."

Coco gazed up at her, hesitating, before throwing shyness to the wind and grabbing her around the waist in a hug. For a sweet span of seconds, the little girl held on tight. And then she broke away and ran off toward the bedrooms.

Karin leaned close and whispered in Madison's ear, "My daughter's got a big crush on you."

"It's mutual, I promise you."

It was still early when Sten walked her back to her house.

"Saturday, then." he said, when they reached the glass door that led into the kitchen. "We'll leave at three. Wear something you don't mind getting wet and covered with sand. Got rain boots?" When she shook her head, he said that Karin probably had a pair she could use.

"Great." She'd spent a few hours with him, max. But she already knew that look on his face. He was preparing to make his escape. She caught his hand.

"Madison, I…"

She silenced him with a finger to her lips and then pulled him inside.

"What?" he asked, as she slid the door shut.

She simply stared up at him. His eyelashes were

so thick and dark and his eyes said he really did like her—but he wasn't sure that was wise.

He asked, "So, do you know how to get in touch with the Bravos?"

Still holding his hand, she stepped right in close, took his other hand, too, and twined their fingers together. He smelled so good, like wood shavings and cloves—and what had he just asked her?

Right. The Bravos and how to contact them. "I have phone numbers and addresses for all of them—and for the two elderly Valentines, Percy and Daffodil, as well."

"They're good people. You should just give one of them a call."

"I told you. I'm not there yet." And she wasn't letting him go yet, either. Slowly, each move careful and deliberate, she guided his hands to her waist. When he didn't pull back, she eased her fingers free of his hold, lifted her hands and pressed her palms to his chest. He was so warm. Even through his shirt, she felt the lean strength of him. "I like you, Sten. I like you a lot."

He frowned, and she just knew he was going to retreat. She steeled herself to accept that. But then he said, "You smell like the best things. Like petunias." He bent close. She tipped her head to the side, encouraging him, and shivered in anticipation as his nose grazed the side of her throat. "And roses and lemongrass, starch and sunshine…"

"It's my perfume," she said on a silly little hitch of breath.

He chuckled. And he brushed those sexy lips, up and down, right where his nose had been. "All that goodness is just perfume?"

Greatest. Moment. Ever. If only it would never have to end. "Well, maybe not the starch and sunshine part. I'm not sure where that comes from."

"I give." He pressed the words into her skin using those wonderful lips of his.

He gave what?

She didn't really understand what he meant—and truthfully, she didn't care. Not as long as he kept holding her, kept touching her in this tempting, perfect way. She pressed herself closer with a happy sigh.

And he lifted one hand from her waist. Before she could demand that he put it back where she'd so deliberately placed it, he cupped her chin and tipped up her face to him. His eyes were low now, lazy. Slumberous. "Can't resist."

That sounded really good. "Can't resist...what?"

"You." He dipped his head closer.

She surged up to meet him. "Sten." She kissed him.

And he kissed her back, all slow and gentle and just what she needed. She slid her arms up the solid shape of him and twined them around his neck.

Oh, it was everything. Kissing him was the best.

And it only got better, got deeper and wetter. Not quite so gentle, but all the more exciting. She eased her fingers up into his hair and closed the tiny distance between their bodies, pressing herself all along the length of him, loving the feel of him, lean and hard where she was soft.

But too soon, he was lifting that beautiful mouth away. "Pick one."

What was he talking about now? "One what?"

"A Bravo. Any Bravo."

"How many ways can I say it? I'm not ready yet."

She trailed a finger along the sculpted line of his jaw, enjoying the silky prickle of his beard scruff. "Want to spend the night?"

He seemed bemused. "You are too tempting."

She looked at him sideways then. "That's no answer."

"It's a fact. I *am* tempted."

"So then, what you mean is no."

"I didn't say that."

"But you're thinking it. Because I'm a virgin and that makes it awkward and probably messy and who needs that?"

"Madison." He said her name so sternly. A muscle in his jaw twitched with tension. "We hardly know each other."

"So?" She stepped back. Now they were facing off. The air seemed to crackle in the empty space between them. "People have sex all the time without knowing each other."

"*You* don't."

For a moment, she could almost regret telling him that she'd never had sex with anyone—but no. If she ever did have sex with a man, at the very least it would be a man she could say anything to. "What about you?" she challenged. "Ever had sex with a stranger?"

He actually smiled at that. "Okay. Yeah. I've had my share of casual hookups."

She took a guess. "But not anymore?"

He kind of nodded and shrugged simultaneously. "I got to that point most people reach, I think. That point where I wanted more. I wanted *the one*. I really thought I'd found her. We were together for two years, but it didn't work out."

"You still miss her." Oh, why did that make her stomach clench and her heart feel suddenly shrunken and sad?

"No." He said it too strongly. "I don't miss her. Not anymore."

"You're bitter, then?"

"Not bitter, just…" He seemed at a loss for the right word. She waited him out. And finally, he finished with, "I'm cautious. Once burned and all that."

"And you haven't been with anyone, not since who-ever-she-was?"

"No. I haven't."

"And you don't *want* to be with anyone?" she dared to ask.

The silence was deafening.

Okay, he didn't want to spend the night. He didn't want to answer questions. And he didn't want to talk about whoever-she-was. Fair enough.

Madison took the two steps to the door. "In case you've been wondering, yes, I did break the chain in the toilet to get you to come over here."

"Madison." He shook his head, but he was grinning again. Like she was just so cute and amusing.

Frankly, he was pissing her off. "People pretty much assume that when I'm not pretending to be someone else for way more money than such foolishness could possibly be worth, I lie around on a velvet couch waiting for someone to peel me a grape. And those people are not entirely wrong. I do have a great job, overall. I also make a lot of money and my people take care of me. But when I was a little girl, I lived on ranches all over the West. My dad—and I don't care that it's turned out he was no blood relation to me. He was my dad." Out of nowhere, her throat clutched and her eyes blurred with unwelcome tears.

She blinked those damn tears away. "He was the kind of dad who thought I was the most amazing little girl in the whole, wide world. My dad was a ranch foreman and all-around handyman. I was his 'assistant.'" She air-quoted that for him. "I had my own little pink toolbox and he taught me how to fix just about anything that might break around the house."

"Madison, I—"

"Don't." She gazed at him steadily, annoyed with him, but at the same time, finding real pleasure in the lovely pull of heat and energy between them. "Let it alone for tonight." She pulled open the slider. The breeze from the ocean blew in, fresh and moist with a hint of salt spray. "I'll be over Saturday. At three."

A half an hour later, Karin joined Sten out on the upper-level deck. "You're back early."

"What? You timed me?"

"Sheesh. Only thirty-one, and already a crabby old man. What's up? Did you blow it with Madison?"

He leaned his head back and stared at the clouds as they skidded across the moon. "Yeah. A little."

"Stennie. There is no 'a little.' You either blew it or you didn't."

"Okay, fine. I blew it."

"Why?"

"Oh, come on. Where's it gonna go?"

"You'll certainly never find out with an attitude like that."

"Karin. I don't want to talk about it. I mean that. Leave it alone."

"Fine. We won't talk about it." With a long sigh, she settled back. "But take a tip from Scarlett O'Hara."

He was not going to ask what the hell she meant by that. "What the hell do you mean by that?"

She reached across and patted his arm. "Tomorrow really is another day."

The next morning early, Sten drove to the two-bed-room starter home he'd closed on a few weeks ago. The drywall guys were hard at work. Things were moving along well. From there, he stopped in at the Boatworks, where his dad and Karin had everything under control.

Back at home, he went down to his workshop and finished up a few small projects he'd put aside earlier for larger ones. He worked outside, with the door open, shirtless.

Because it was a nice day.

And okay, yeah, maybe he was hoping to glance up at the cottage next door and see a pretty woman in a big hat with his own binoculars trained on him.

Didn't happen.

At noon, he put his tools away and went inside. He had a shower, pulled on clean jeans and a T-shirt and wandered out to the kitchen, where he opened the fridge and then stood there staring into it.

Nothing inside held any appeal.

And the house was too damn quiet, with Karin and his dad at the Boatworks, and both of the kids at school.

Was she even at the cottage right now?

Had to be. She'd said she was reluctant to go out for fear someone might recognize her.

Wasn't she getting tired of that, of being stranded in the house?

At least tomorrow, she'd get out for a while—she *had* said she was coming clamming with them.

Hadn't she?

Yeah. She'd promised she would be over Saturday as she showed him the door.

Really, he should check on her, see if there was anything she needed, anything he could get for her...

The house phone rang as Madison was standing at the sink spooning blueberry yogurt into her mouth.

Sten?

Who else would be calling on the house phone?

It rang a second time as she exulted in the high probability that it was him.

On the third ring, she set the yogurt on the counter and went to answer. "Yes?"

"Just checking on you."

She dropped to the sofa. "Why? You afraid I'm misbehaving?"

"If you are, can I come over?"

She stretched out, stuck a pillow under her head and gloated at the ceiling. "Actually, I just might be getting a little bit stir-crazy..."

"Not surprising. You've been in that house for, what, a week now?"

"Just about. And I need groceries. Maybe you could help me with that?"

"By...?"

"You could drive me to the store."

"But what if someone recognizes you?"

"They won't. I'll go in disguise."

"Who *are* you and what have you done with my tenant?" Sten teased when Madison answered the door in a short red-brown wig and the dark glasses he'd found in the sand and returned to her.

She made a pouty face. "I miss my big hat. Where are we going?"

"Safeway?" he suggested, and then realized she probably expected to go somewhere that only sold free-range chicken, organic produce and homeopathic headache remedies. "Sorry, you'll have to go almost to Portland to find a Whole Foods. But there's a great co-op in Astoria. We could try that."

"Are you kidding? Safeway is perfect. It's been over a decade since I went to a Safeway."

She cracked him up. "I'm so glad Safeway excites you."

She whacked him on the arm with the back of her hand, just like Karin would have done. "Knock it off with the hipster irony. It will be an adventure. Get with the program."

On the way to the store, she decided they needed a contingency plan. "Just in case someone recognizes me."

"Why am I certain you've already got that worked out?"

She turned his way slowly, dipped her head and gave him a look over the top of her enormous shades. "Because I do."

The plan was simple. If things got dicey, she would turn to him and announce that she'd forgotten something in another aisle and then run off in search of it. Meanwhile, he would keep whoever had recognized her busy while she hustled out of the store. As soon as the coast was clear, he would meet her at the truck.

"So then, you're counting on me to somehow keep

whoever knows it's you from running after you when you suddenly take off."

She sent him one of those irresistible smiles. "Yep. I'm trusting you to think on your feet. I know you won't let me down."

"Famous last words," he muttered under his breath and turned into the Safeway parking lot.

"One more thing," she said as he pulled into a space and switched off the engine. "How likely are we to run into someone you know?"

He shrugged. "It's a small town. It could happen."

"If it does, introduce me as Mallory Malloy."

"Sounds fake."

"It *is* fake. That's the point. But if you don't like it, make up something else. Just give the fake name and say I'm your tenant. I'll make friendly noises and then suddenly remember there's something I forgot. I'll rush off for another aisle and not come back."

"And then we meet here, at the truck?"

"That's it. We're set."

Inside the store, she had him push the cart. He happily followed along behind her, admiring the sweet sway of her hips as she tossed in produce and groceries, humming to herself as she went.

"What's that song you're humming?" he asked, when she stopped to grab pimiento-stuffed olives and a big jar of dill pickles.

"'I Love to Love.' Tina Charles sang it. Big disco hit in England way back in the day. It's essentially the theme song of the BBC series *River*." She leaned close and whispered with great enthusiasm, "Did you see *River*?"

He got a whiff of petunias and lemongrass and realized that right at this moment, he felt ridiculously happy about every little thing. "Sorry, didn't see that one."

"You should." She tapped his shoulder with the jar of pickles. "Murder. Love. Loss. And Stellan Skarsgård. Does it get any better?" She held up the pickles in one hand and the olives in the other and busted a few disco moves, singing that same song under her breath. An old guy down at the other end of the aisle stopped to watch, but quickly moved on when Sten gave him the evil eye.

And the old guy wasn't the only one who noticed her. A wig and sunglasses couldn't hide the sheer energy that radiated from her, or the infectiousness of her laugh. He didn't think anyone realized she was Madison Delaney, though. They just appreciated a pretty girl in tight jeans with a great laugh.

At the rear of the store, she found a straw-hat display stuck back with the metal racks of deep-discount merchandise. She went nuts over those and chose four of them to take home.

"Because who knows how long I'll be here?" she whispered to him. "What if I never work up the nerve to call the Bravos? I'm going to want to go shopping again just for the sake of getting out of the house and I'll need more than one good disguise."

"Just do it," he said.

"Do what, buy some hats?"

"Make that call. If you don't want to try one of your brothers or sisters, call Percy Valentine. He's a sweet old guy."

"What? Now? Right here in Safeway?"

"Yeah. I'll drive you to Valentine House, where

Percy lives with his sister. The house is older than they are and they're both in their eighties. You'll love it."

"Don't get pushy," she commanded, and tried on a wide-brimmed red sunhat. "What do you think? I love this one."

He wanted to grab her and kiss her, but settled for giving her a hard time, instead. "You are having far too much fun. You know that, right?"

"You can never have too much fun in Safeway." She tossed the red hat in the cart and plunked a pork-pie-style creation on her head. It looked good with her short, reddish wig. "Let's move on."

She wore the porkpie hat through the bakery area and on to the wine section and the deli.

By the time they made it to checkout, the cart was full to overflowing. She had to take off her hat for the checker, a twentysomething with word tattoos scrolling up and down her arms and *Fearless Dreamer* written in Gothic script on the side of her neck.

"Thanks." Madison took the hat back once the checker had scanned it and plopped it on top of her wig again.

"You know," said the checker, frowning thoughtfully, "you look a lot like Madison Delaney, the actress?" She leaned in to get a closer look and then, with a gasp, she covered her mouth with her hand, her dark eyes going wide. The people in line behind them were watching now. "Omigod," said the checker in sheer wonderment. "You *are* her, aren't you?"

Chapter Four

Did Sten expect his favorite movie star to freak?

Yeah, maybe. A little. He got ready to distract the checker so that Madison could sprint off down the paper goods aisle never to return.

But then Madison just laughed and clapped her hands. "Really?" she squealed in what sounded exactly like sheer delight. "*I* look like Madison Delaney?"

The checker squinted hard at her—and then relaxed. She grinned. "Yeah. You really do. Had me going there for a minute."

"Wow." Madison shook her head, as though stunned at the very idea that she might bear some resemblance to America's Darling. "Thank you."

"No, really," said the Fearless Dreamer. "You do look quite a bit like her."

"I wish," sighed Madison. "And I have to tell you, I love your ink."

The checker blushed. "It's just, you know, stuff that means something important to me."

"It's beautiful," said Madison, with feeling.

The checker beamed—and then seemed to realize that other people were waiting. She checked and bagged the rest of their purchases quickly.

Sten whipped out his credit card and paid before Madison could offer hers. Even if the card only showed her first initial, the sight of her last name would probably give the game away to the checker, who had recognized her once already.

"Good move with the credit card," Madison said, once they'd loaded the bags in the back and climbed into the quad cab. "I'll write you a check when we get home."

"You were brilliant." He backed from the space and drove them out of the parking lot. Once they were on the road again, he said, "I knew we were in big trouble, but you turned it right around."

"People see what they expect to see." She flipped down the visor and fiddled with her hat in the mirror, tipping it this way and that. "If they do happen to spot something they never imagined they would find in a particular place and time, it's not that hard to lead them back around to seeing what they think they *should* be seeing."

She continued to surprise him. "Did you learn that in acting school?"

"Sort of." She snapped the visor back up. "But there's a lot more to learn about acting than what you get in acting classes. You need voice—both spoken and singing lessons. You need dance—a little bit of everything, tap, modern, ballet."

"Disco?" He sent her a smirk.

"Absolutely. And mime. Improv. Stand-up. And I worked with a magician for a part I did a few years back. He taught me about misdirection—getting people to look where you want them to look, to see what you need them to see. That's essentially what I did back there at the checkout stand."

They rode without speaking for a while. She rolled down her window and braced her arm on the sill.

He broke the silence. "Did you really like that checker's tattoos?"

"I loved them." She took off her sunglasses and turned to him.

They shared one of those looks that stole his breath and had him thinking of kissing every inch of her, of waking up in the morning with her beside him, the sheets smelling of petunias and sex.

Reluctantly, he broke the hold of her gaze to focus on the road ahead.

She stared out the windshield, too. "But even if I hadn't loved that checker's ink, I would've said I did. And she would have believed me. I can be very convincing. Plus, *she* loves her tattoos, so why wouldn't some woman at the checkout stand who looks kind of like some famous actress love them, too?"

"You sound sad," he said, and resisted the need to take her hand and weave their fingers together.

"I am, a little. But only because I feel like I'm running in place."

He *had* to reach out then. She met him halfway and put her hand in his. It felt good there. Just right. "Call a Bravo," he suggested softly.

She squeezed his fingers and then let go. "Don't nag. It's not attractive."

* * *

For razor clamming the next day, Madison wore rain pants, a zip-up hoodie and Karin's spare rain boots. The weather was cool and misty, with a brisk wind that blew the wet sand into weird, otherworldly ripples. She kept her hood up to stay warm and reasonably dry and to help hide her identity.

Clamming was a hoot. Sten taught her how to look for the "show," the doughnut-shaped dimples in the sand that appeared as the tide retreated and indicated a razor clam in residence. He even let her try his PVC-pipe clamming gun, but only one time—because, he said, the rules were that you had to be licensed, you brought your own bucket and your own shovel or gun and you dug your own limit in clams, with nobody helping you.

"You're such a straight arrow," she teased him when he made her give him back his gun.

"You better watch out," he warned in a dire tone, grinning at her from under the headlamp he'd yet to switch on.

"Because…?"

He leaned closer, as though he had some big secret to share. "Your brother Matt is a game warden. He might come and arrest you."

The wind tried to blow her hoodie back. She pulled the drawstring tighter and retied it. "Matthias." She'd memorized all the names on the stick Jonas had given her. "Second-born after Daniel, recently married to Sabra Bond of Astoria."

"That's him. But most of us call him Matt. And you'll make a bad impression if you have to introduce yourself while he's booking you for poaching."

"Oh, come on. The most I would get is a citation, I'll bet."

He chuckled. "Just trying to keep you on the straight and narrow."

"And even if he did arrest me, at least I would be meeting him."

He leaned closer. His breath warmed her cheek. "A phone call. How hard can it be?"

"You're nagging again."

"Think of it as *encouraging*."

Coco, in a purple slicker and red rain boots printed with dinosaurs, came running up. She skidded to a stop in the wet sand. "Madison," she stage-whispered and then darted a glance around her at the scattering of strangers digging nearby. No one seemed the least interested in the little girl or the unknown woman in the turquoise hoodie gazing down at her. "Want to go to the truck and play? Mommy says if you pour it for me, I can have hot chocolate from the thermos she brought."

It wasn't full dark yet, but all down the beach as the tide continued to retreat, the clam diggers were switching on their headlamps.

Sten looked up from working his gun into the sand. "Go. Have fun."

The next half hour was perfect. Madison sipped hot chocolate and made rubber band bracelets with Coco in Sten's truck, watching the waning moon hanging over the water and the bright headlamps bobbing as the clammers hustled to take their limits.

Later, at Sten's house, Madison got a lesson in cleaning the catch. Then she helped Karin and Sten with the cooking. They dredged the tender parts in flour, egg and panko, fried them up fast and ate them with lemon wedges and tartar sauce.

Sten walked her back to the cottage at ten. She pulled him inside with her and kissed him. He tasted of the single malt Scotch and dark roast coffee he'd had after dinner. She longed to ask him to stay.

But she sensed that he wouldn't and why go hunting rejection?

When he said good-night, she let him go.

Even after a long, hot bath it was hard to sleep. She really was here for a purpose and getting absolutely nowhere with it. Sten annoyed her when he kept bugging her to reach out to old Mr. Valentine or one of her long-lost siblings—mostly because he was right. Damn it. She needed to make her move.

The next morning, Sten tapped on the sliding glass door at seven dressed in ripped-out jeans, flip-flops, a long-sleeved T-shirt that had seen better days and a serious case of bedhead. He had a half-empty mug of coffee in his hand.

She opened the slider. "What's up?"

"Got any eggs?"

"Of course, I have eggs. You saw me buy them the other day."

"Scramble me some?" Why did it feel like he was up to something? "Please?" he asked hopefully.

"Uh, sure. Come on in."

After refilling his mug, she fixed eggs for both of them. Sitting across from him as they ate, she couldn't help thinking that no man on earth had a right to look that effortlessly hot. The old T-shirt clung lovingly to his wide shoulders and lean arms.

It just wasn't fair.

He set down his empty mug. "What?"

"Why do I feel like you're up to something?"

"Because you're naturally suspicious?"

She glared at him. Suspiciously. "I know you have eggs at your house."

A slow, killer grin. "Yeah, but *you're* not at my house."

She grunt-laughed. "Can't stay away, huh?"

"You think you're joking, but yeah. That's about the size of it."

So he was here to seduce her? Somehow, she didn't quite buy that. She challenged, "Is this it, then? Is it happening at last? Are you finally going to give in and deflower me?"

"Damn. *Deflower.* Where did you come up with a word like that?"

"Hmm. Not sure. Shakespeare, maybe. Any number of really juicy historical romances, definitely—and you notice how you failed to answer my question?"

He studied her. She felt his gaze as an actual caress, tender. Purposeful. Arousing. "I just need to be sure that *you're* sure."

She got up, grabbed her plate, carried it to the sink and dropped it in there. It didn't break, but it landed with a clatter. She whirled on him. "Do we have to analyze it to death? Can't we just do what feels right?"

He picked up his own plate and came to her. "Madison." Without so much as a hint of a clatter, he set his plate down on top of hers. "Listen to yourself." He took her shoulders, turned her and made her face him. His eyes searched hers and his hands were so warm and strong as he held her in place. "I don't think you're sure."

She braced her hands on his lean hips, easing his T-shirt out of the way so she could hook her fingers in his belt loops. "You're making me crazy."

He bent close. She felt his breath, warm and sweet on her lips. "Is that such a bad thing?" And he kissed her.

With a hungry little cry, she flung herself hard against him. He wrapped those lean, strong arms around her as his lips played over hers and his hot tongue delved in. She felt him growing hard against her belly and her heartbeat throbbed, insistent and deep.

It was glorious. His big hands glided down her back to cup her bottom and pull her into him, closer. Harder. He smelled so good and he tasted like everything she'd been missing out on for way too many years—someone who really did like her just for herself. A guy with no agenda beyond what any guy has with a girl he's attracted to.

When he lifted his head, he said, "Go for a ride with me?"

She stared up at him, dazed in the loveliest way, her body humming, the world soft and blurry around the edges. "Sure."

"I'll put on some boots."

"And I shall formulate an effective disguise."

Ten minutes later, she had on a chin-length black wig à la Uma Thurman in *Pulp Fiction*, a straw boater and a great pair of retro tortoiseshell sunglasses. She ran around the back of Sten's house and found him right where he said he'd be, waiting by the open garage door.

They jumped in his truck and headed up the road that led out of the cove. He took Third Street south into the heart of Valentine Bay, where a pretty park appeared on the left.

A minute later, he was steering to the side of the street and pulling in at the curb. The engine went quiet as he switched it off.

She turned to him. "We're going for a walk in the park?"

"Look over there." He pointed at a rambling, three-story Queen Anne monstrosity across the street, on the edge of the park. It was a gorgeous old house in its way, with an excess of dentil moldings and several balconies rimmed in fussy iron lace.

"The big pale green one, you mean?"

"Yep."

It came to her then. She *knew* who that house belonged to. Whipping off her hat and the sunglasses, too, she whirled to confront him. "No."

"Maddy." He said the nickname so sweetly, for the very first time. It sounded so good. Only her mom and dad had ever called her Maddy. Unfortunately, he'd called her Maddy while trying to push her to do what she wasn't ready for. "I'm almost certain Percy Valentine will be at home," he coaxed. "Just go up and knock on the door—I'll go with you, if you want. You said he's been waiting for you to contact him. The old guy is going to be so happy to see you."

"Take me back to the cottage."

"Come on, take it easy." He lifted his hand to touch her, to soothe her and coax her some more.

She knocked his arm away. "Take me back or I'm out of this truck."

"Mad—"

"Stop." She unhooked her seat belt and grabbed the door handle. He caught her other arm. "Let go," she demanded.

He released her. "Nobody's forcing you. Just take a deep breath."

"You don't get to do this, okay?" She spoke to the dashboard. "I'll make a move when *I'm* ready."

"I just thought—"

"I do not want to hear it, what you thought, why you brought me here when I never asked you to. It's my life and my call and you just…no. Uh-uh. No. So just answer me. Are you taking me back or not?"

He let several awful seconds elapse before huffing out a breath. "Right. I'll take you back now."

Sten could feel her fury, like a separate presence in the truck with them, breathing fire. She didn't say a word during the ten-minute drive back to the cove.

When he pulled into his garage, she waited for the truck to come to a stop and then she grabbed her hat and glasses and took off.

Okay, maybe he was a little out of line, to go pushing her to do something she just wasn't ready for. But didn't somebody have to care enough to give her a nudge in the right direction?

She'd come here to meet her family. She needed to face whatever was holding her back and get on with it.

But she hadn't. And she wasn't.

And he wanted her to have what she wouldn't reach out and take. Because she was funny and sweet and kind. Because what he felt for her somehow already went way too deep.

"Where's Madison?" Karin asked him Tuesday night. The kids were in bed. It was raining, so they were having a beer in the upstairs great room—well, he was drinking real beer. Karin had a ginger beer. "Something happened with the two of you, right?"

He stared at the raindrops. They glittered like jewels as they skittered down the big windows that looked out on the deck. "Are all little sisters as nosy as you?"

"Probably. And I hear big sisters are worse. What's going on?"

"We had a disagreement, that's all—and don't ask me over what. It's something she told me in confidence, so leave it alone."

"That's good, that she would confide in you."

"Don't start."

Karen pointed at him with the bottle in her hand. "Madison's nothing like Ella."

"I never said she was."

His sister sent him a glance of infinite patience. "With Ella, it was simple timing for you. You were finally ready to get serious with a woman. You ran into Ella and she had that adorable little boy. You've always loved kids. You fell for the kid more than the woman."

"Why are you talking about this?"

"It's stuff I keep meaning to share with you."

"Share?" Truly one of the scarier words in the English language.

"Yes. Share. And tonight seems like a good time for sharing, given the situation."

"There is no 'situation' and tonight is not a good time."

"Ella used you. Get over it. Don't miss out on something great because of one crappy experience."

"Are you done?"

"For now?" Karin frowned like she had to think it over. Finally, she gave a slow nod. "Absolutely." And for a moment she was blessedly silent. It didn't last, though. "Coco keeps asking if she can go over there."

"Tell Coco to chill."

"All right—and come on. I'm only trying to help."

He chuckled in spite of himself. "Just tell me what Scarlett O'Hara would say."

"Fiddle-dee-dee." And she stuck out her tongue at him.

By Thursday, Madison still hadn't given him any kind of signal that she was ready to make up. He almost marched up the stairs to her back deck and pounded on the slider until she got sick of the racket and let him in.

But that would definitely be pushing and pushing was what had gotten him in the dog house with her in the first place.

He went to Larson Boatworks and helped out emergency rehabbing a shrimp trawler that the owner/operator wanted back in the water yesterday or sooner.

Then, home again, missing the girl next door way too much and at a loss as to how to proceed with her, he decided to get back to work on the shutters that would increase the curb appeal of his two-bedroom flip.

It was a perfect day for working outside, overcast and cool, but no rain. He got lost in the soothing, uncomplicated process of measuring and cutting and didn't even look up for over an hour.

He'd finished with the saw and turned it off to start laying out the pieces and assembling what he'd cut when a husky voice said, "Hey."

He glanced up and she was standing right there at the edge of the concrete pad that extended past the roll-up door of his shop. She wore loose khakis and a gray

T-shirt. No big sunglasses, no wig, no floppy hat. He took off his safety goggles and dropped them next to the saw. God, she looked good. Just Maddy, her streaky hair loose on her shoulders, a sheepish expression on her amazing face.

"I'm sorry," she said. "You were only trying to give me a little nudge in the right direction and I was a complete bitch about it."

Something happened in his chest. A tightness. And yet, a lightness, too.

She caught her upper lip between her teeth, nervous. Adorably so. "So, maybe, when you're through here, you could come over? We could talk?"

He really couldn't get enough of just looking at her. She was such a welcome sight.

"Sten. Would you please say something?"

"I need maybe five minutes to put this stuff away."

Those dimples winked at him. "Okay."

He started hauling everything back into the shop. She pitched in, carrying the shutter pieces and stacking them inside.

In no time, they were walking side by side between the houses. Her hand bumped his. He caught it and she let him.

Fingers entwined, they went around the back of the cottage and up the steps to the deck.

Once they were in her kitchen, he tugged on her hand. She came up against him with a willing little sigh, bringing the scent of summer flowers on this cool, cloudy day.

"I missed you so much," she said, her mouth tipped up like an offering.

He swooped down and claimed it in a long, much-needed kiss. "I wanted to come over here and pound on the door," he confessed when he finally lifted his head.

"I wish you had—but it's good that you didn't. I had some thinking to do."

"I get that, yeah."

She took his hand again, led him to the living area and pulled him down to the sofa with her. He wanted her closer, so he hooked an arm across her shoulders and gathered her in nice and snug against his side.

She snuggled in even closer. "So I really *have* been thinking about what's bothering me, what's keeping me from getting in touch with the family I didn't know I had."

"Did you figure it out?"

She put her palm against his chest, like she was feeling for his heartbeat. He laid his hand over hers, keeping it there.

And she said, "My dad taught me to ride a horse when I was younger than Coco. He had a deep sadness in him. But he was never sad when it came to me. I was his girl and his love for me was like armor, keeping me safe, making me feel like I was amazing, the best, the brightest, the prettiest little girl in the universe. I had confidence to spare, even though there was never enough money and he was always losing his job and we would have to move on."

She rested her head on his shoulder and he pressed a kiss into her silky hair. "My mom had a bad habit of falling suddenly in love with strange men," she said. "But my dad, well, he just loved her so much. He always took her back. And she was a good mom to me, the best. I decided I was going to be an actress when I was in kindergarten. That year, we were living near this dinky Wyoming town. My mom went straight into town and signed me up at Miss Sharonda's School of Drama and Dance. After that, wherever we moved to, no matter how short the money was, Mom and Dad made sure I got special classes to help me toward my goal of being a big star. When my dad died, I cried for a week. And then Mom said it was time."

"Time?"

"To move to Hollywood. She packed everything we had into a U-Haul and we drove to LA so I could get my start."

She tipped her head up to him. Her eyes were true turquoise right then, like the ocean on a clear and windless day. They glittered with tears. "I think I've been feeling guilty, feeling that getting to know the Bravos would be a betrayal of the parents who raised me, who did everything to make me feel important and special, like I could do anything."

"It wouldn't be betraying them, no way. They're still your parents—and you get to have brothers and sisters, too. The bigger the better, I think, when you're talking family." He watched a tear overflow. It trailed down her cheek. He bent close and kissed that tear away. "You know what? Never mind what I think. This is stuff you need to work out for yourself."

"Yes, I do." She sniffled as she swiped at another tear. "And I think I have worked it out. I think—I *know*—that I can still love and cherish the memory of my mom and dad. And I can get to know the Bravos, too. I read in the stuff Percy Valentine sent me that my oldest brother, Daniel, still lives in the house where my brothers and sisters grew up."

"Yeah. It's a beautiful old house, with a wide porch

and a big yard in back. It's up in the hills on the eastern edge of town."

"I was wondering if maybe you would drive me there?"

"Happy to. When?"

"How about right now?"

Chapter Five

It was almost five thirty when Sten eased his pickup in at the curb in front of the Bravo family house, which had a wide, well-cared-for front yard and stone pillars supporting the broad, deep front porch. Madison stared out her side window at the home where she should have grown up. She felt like a stranger inside her own skin.

"What do you think?" he asked and brushed the back of her hand with his.

She grabbed his fingers and held on, grateful for the warmth of his broad palm pressed to hers. "I'm terrified—but I'm going up and knocking on that door."

He gazed at her through those gorgeous blue eyes she'd started seeing her dreams. "You sure you don't want me to go in with you?"

She shook her head. "Thank you. But I need to do this on my own."

He let go of her hand, but only so he could ease his fingers around the back of her neck and pull her toward him across the console. They met in the middle. He brushed the sweetest kiss across her lips. "Text me when you're ready to go. I'll come and get you."

"I really could just call an Uber…"

"I don't think we have Uber here yet."

"So, a cab, then."

"Without a hat or a wig?" he teased. "We've got a quiet little town here. We don't need some rogue cabbie recognizing you and calling in the fleabag journos."

She laughed in spite of her nervousness. "Fleabag journos. Good one."

"I'm coming to get you as soon as you're ready to go." He kissed her again. And then, with obvious reluctance, he released her.

She grabbed the door latch and gave it a tug. A moment later, she was forcing her feet to carry her up the front walk and onto the big porch with a swing at one end. On the other, a grouping of comfy cushioned chairs and wicker tables invited a person to sit down and relax.

Marching straight to the wide front door, she punched the bell, giving herself no chance to chicken out. She should have called first, but she hadn't been able to make herself do it. This way, at least she was here.

Her heart did a somersault inside her chest as the door swung open. A cute woman with strawberry blond hair and a baby attached to the front of her in a sling, gave her an automatic sort of smile. "Hello?"

Madison stuck her hands in the pockets of her comfy old cargoes and managed a wobbly, "Hi." She meant to add, *I'm Madison Delaney. I wonder, is Daniel Bravo home*? But somehow the simple words refused to take shape.

That left her and the strawberry blonde just standing there staring at each other as the baby made goo-goo sounds, tiny fists stuck out from either side of the sling, waving randomly.

Madison tried again. "I'm, um, here to see—"

The woman silenced her with a gasp. Apparently, recognition had dawned. "Madison?" she asked. "Madison Delaney?"

"Um, yeah. I know I should have called but—"

"Omigod!" the woman shrieked, causing the baby to let out a bleat of distress and wave its little fists all the harder.

"Sorry, really. I *meant* to call, but somehow, I—"

"Oh, don't you even worry about that. I'm Keely, Daniel's wife. And this is Marie." She smiled down at the baby and stepped back. "Come in, come in."

Madison ordered her feet to carry her over the threshold. "I hope it's okay, I mean, that you're not busy or anything?"

"Of course, it's okay." Keely beamed. "It's more than okay. Everyone will be so excited that you're finally here." She moved in and offered a sort of half hug. Madison half hugged her in return, glancing down at one point to see the nearly bald head of the baby attached to the front of her. "Daniel will be thrilled," Keely went on. "He just got home a few minutes ago. He's upstairs in the shower but he'll be down any—"

"What's all the excitement?" A plump, gray-haired woman with excellent posture and a small child on either side of her stood at the top of the stairs.

"Auntie G!" exclaimed Keely. "It's Madison! She's finally here."

"At last." The woman started down the stairs slowly, the two children on either side of her, each holding one of her hands. They were maybe two or three years old, a boy and a girl. "Careful now," the woman warned.

"We are caweful!" exclaimed the boy.

"Mad-sen, hi!" said the girl, holding the railing with her other hand, getting both little feet on each step before taking the next one.

The boy echoed the girl. "Hi!"

They had to be Daniel's twins by his first wife, Lillie, who had been Keely's cousin. Lillie had died shortly after the children were born. Their names came to her. "Hi, Jake. Hi, Frannie."

Both kids shouted, "Hi!" all over again.

Keely chuckled. "What can I tell you? Never a dull moment around here. You'll stay for dinner?"

It wasn't that she didn't want to. But it all felt so surreal—and Keely was waiting expectantly for her answer. A no just wouldn't fly. "I would love to stay for dinner."

The older woman and the children made it down the final step and joined them. "This is my aunt, Gretchen Snow," said Keely. "She's also Frannie and Jake's grandmother."

Gretchen let go of Jake to offer a hand. When Madison took it, the older woman pulled her in for a quick hug. "I'm so glad you're here at last," Gretchen said. She smelled utterly amazing, like vanilla and almonds.

Jake chose that moment to dart off, giggling.

"That boy," said Gretchen on a huff of breath. Releasing Madison, she called, "Jakey, come back here, young man!"

"Jay, stop!" shouted Frannie. She braced her small hands on her hips, tipped her head up to Gretchen and announced sternly, "Gwamma, he's getting away."

Madison watched the action and tried to keep the relationships straight. The twins were first cousins once removed to their stepmother, Keely—who was their grandmother's niece. And this was just the beginning. There would be all those siblings to meet and remember. Madison wondered a little frantically how she would keep them all straight.

"Come get me!" crowed Jake from the room beyond the wide arch straight ahead of them.

"Gwamma, come on!" Frannie yanked on Gretchen's hand. "Wet's go get'im."

With a last wry smile at Madison, Gretchen allowed the little girl to pull her off in pursuit of the laughing boy.

"Come on in the kitchen," said Keely. Her baby had hold of both of her thumbs and Keely waved her hands gently in the infant's tiny grip. "Auntie G arrived today with four dozen sugar cookies she baked just this morning. I dare you to eat just one."

"Madison Delaney," said a deep voice from the top of the stairs. "It's about time." A tall, broad-shouldered lumberjack of a man stood at the top of the stairs, thick hair slicked back from his shower. He wore jeans and a flannel shirt and moccasins that made no sound as he started down the steps.

The baby cooed contentedly and Keely said, "Here's Daniel."

Madison stared as the big man came toward her. She

saw her own resemblance to him, around the eyes, in the shape of his mouth. *My brother*, she thought, the two simple words so alien to her. Alien and also wonderful. And heartbreaking, too.

He reached the bottom of the stairs and kept coming, stopping a few feet away, his golden brows drawing together in concern. "Madison. You okay?"

She nodded, struck wordless by this moment, by this serious-eyed man and his sweet wife, the baby and the two kids and their grandmother Gretchen, who smelled like a bakery.

"Good," Daniel said. "I'm so glad to see you." He lifted his arms, not really reaching for her, but kind of *offering* to reach. If that worked for her, if she was willing.

She felt awkward and out of it. But somehow, she managed a wobbly smile. "Good to see you, too." And then she took one weird, jerky step forward.

He did the rest, pulling her into his arms and hugging her tight.

In the big kitchen at the back of the house, Madison said yes to coffee and a couple of Gretchen's truly outstanding cookies.

Daniel visited for a few minutes, and then said he would be right back. "I'm going to make a few calls, see if I can get more of the family over here tonight."

Madison swallowed down her apprehensions at meeting more long-lost relatives and reminded herself that she *wanted* this, to finally get to know the people she should have grown up with. He left the kitchen and returned about fifteen minutes later.

Within an hour, the house was full of Bravos. Percy

and Daffodil Valentine arrived, too, both of them trim and spry, with white hair and the wrinkles a person gets from eighty-plus years of life. Madison was hugged and exclaimed over. Everyone seemed so happy to see her.

She met Harper and Hailey, who were seventh- and eighth-born of the siblings. They almost could have been twins, the physical resemblance between the two of them was so strong. And they both looked like Madison—or maybe she looked like them.

Hailey laughed about it. "Wait till Grace gets home for spring break next week. We'll take pictures of all four of us. No one will be able to tell us apart." It was an exaggeration, but not *that* much of one.

The last arrivals came at a little before seven, Matthias and his wife, Sabra, who lived on Sabra's farm near Astoria. And Aislinn and her husband, Jaxon Winter, the adopted son of Martin Durand. They'd driven over from Wild River Ranch, which Jaxon had eventually inherited after Martin Durand died.

Included on that memory stick Madison had studied so thoroughly was a copy of the final letter written by Durand to accompany his will. In the letter, he not only laid out how he'd switched two innocent babies at birth, but also that Aislinn and Jaxon had to marry for three months in order for Jaxon to get the ranch. Apparently, the forced marriage had turned into the real thing.

Which was great.

Martin Durand, though? Talk about a piece of work.

Aislinn was slender and small-boned, with an angular face, huge dark eyes and dark hair. She bore no physical resemblance to the rest of the Bravos. She didn't look all that much like the mother who'd raised

Madison, either. But there was something about her that felt so familiar. Something in her voice, in the way that she moved—it all whispered to Madison of Paula Delaney, somehow. Just being near her had Madison feeling at home and also missing her lost mom all over again.

Once everyone but Grace had arrived, they shared a potluck dinner of dishes brought by the various members of the family. There was roast chicken and mac and cheese with ham, ribs from a local restaurant and a variety of sides.

Sweet old Percy took Madison aside just before the food was served and explained that Martin Durand had left a DNA sample with a reputable lab. Aislinn had already been tested. The test proved she was Durand's biological daughter.

"I don't think any of us have much doubt who your blood parents were," said Percy. "Still, it never hurts to take advantage of the proof that's so readily available these days. Would you be open to sibling testing?" When she said that yes, she wanted to be tested, Percy asked if she would be available on Sunday. She said that she would, after which Percy called for everyone's attention and got their unanimous agreement that they could make it on Sunday for dinner. Grace would be home for spring break by then, so all the siblings could be there. Percy would bring the test kits and all of them would provide DNA samples. Results would be available online sometime in the following week.

After three hours of intense togetherness with people she'd only just met, Madison needed a breather. She slipped out to the front porch and dropped gratefully into one of the comfy, cushioned chairs. It was dark by then, but not too cold. The porch lights cast everything in a golden kind of glow.

She texted Sten that she was ready to go whenever he could come pick her up. He answered immediately.

—Ten minutes?

—Perfect. I'll be waiting on the front porch.

She stuck her phone back in her pocket and was about to go back in and tell everyone goodbye when the door opened and Aislinn came out. "Everything okay out here?"

Oddly, although Aislinn was the only Bravo in town to which she had no blood relationship, Madison felt a certain bond with the woman who should have grown up calling Lloyd and Paula Delaney her dad and mom.

"Join me." Madison patted the chair beside her.

Aislinn came and sat down. "You look a little shell-shocked."

Madison gave a sheepish laugh. "I think my head is literally spinning." She admitted, "It's a lot to take in, that's all."

"Tell me about it. After I got the news, I spent months wandering around in a daze, trying to figure out who the hell I really am. I read up on you—but not in a stalkerish way, I promise." And they laughed together at the sheer unreality of the situation. Then Aislinn grew serious again. "I just, well, I felt as though I'd stolen your life from you."

"What? Aislinn, you were a newborn baby, completely innocent. No way you're to blame for what Martin Durand did."

Aislinn tapped her temple. "I know that in here." She put her palm against her chest. "In my heart, though, I just had to work through it, you know?"

"Yeah. I do. I truly do."

"But, Madison, I read that your parents adored you and I hope that it's true."

"They did, yes. They loved me. I never doubted their love. And I loved *them*. I still miss them every day." She had to ask, "How about George and Marie Bravo?"

"I was their little princess," said Aislinn with a faraway smile. "And a very happy little girl. I felt safe and cared for and…precious, you know?"

"I do. And I'm glad."

"And I wonder, would you want to come out to Wild River for dinner?" Aislinn fiddled with the filigree heart she wore on a silver chain around her neck. "Say, Saturday? You can see the ranch where you were born."

It surprised Madison how much she wanted that. "Yes, definitely. What time?"

"Five? I'll show you around the place before we eat. Bring a friend if you'd like."

"I'll be there," Madison promised just as Sten's pickup pulled in at the curb. He gave her a wave from inside the cab, leaning forward enough that the streetlamp above cast his face into sharp relief for a moment. She waved back, her heart suddenly lighter, somehow. "And here's my ride…"

"Isn't that Sten Larson?"

"The one and only. I guess I'm not surprised you know him. Sten mentioned that he was in the same grade in school as Matt."

"Yeah. And Liam and Karin are the same age." Liam was fourth-born, after Daniel, Matt and Connor.

"I'm staying at a cottage Sten owns out at Sweetheart Cove. He's been terrific, playing chauffeur when I need a ride, taking me razor clamming. Karin even had me over to dinner. I really like the family."

"I know the cove. It's a beautiful spot."

"I love it. It's pretty isolated, which works for me because I've been trying to keep a low profile so that word won't get out I'm in town. If the tabloids get hold of the news that I'm here, well, some of those reporters can get pretty rabid."

"I won't tell a soul. And I'll warn the rest of the family to keep quiet about your being here."

"Thanks." Madison rose. "I'm just going to run down and tell Sten I need to go in and say good-night to everyone."

Aislinn got up before suggesting, "Or I could say goodbye to them for you?"

Madison hesitated. She really was anxious to get away, get a chance to decompress. But not to at least thank Keely and Daniel for the evening seemed rude.

"They'll understand." Aislinn took her by the shoulders and pulled her in for a goodbye hug. When they stepped apart, Aislinn said, "It's a lot to deal with, being switched. I promise you, they get it. They've already been through it once with me."

"Honestly, tonight has been great."

"But maybe just a *little* overwhelming?"

Madison sighed. "I'm that obvious?"

"Hey. It's totally okay for you to need the space to process, or whatever. Just remember we're here for you. Call any one of us, anytime."

"Thank you." Madison got out her phone. She brought up Aislinn's cell number and sent her a text confirming dinner at the ranch on Saturday. "Now you can reach me whenever you feel like it. I'll group text everyone so they can get hold of me, too."

"About Saturday…" Aislinn wore a knowing little grin.

Madison didn't get it. "What?"

"Bring Sten."

She stifled a groan. "So I'm not only obvious, but transparent, as well."

"He's a good guy. And hot, which never hurts."

"We're just, um, friends."

"Like I said. Bring a friend."

Sten leaned across the passenger seat to push open the door when Madison came down the walk. She climbed in and buckled up.

"You got here fast." Her gorgeous smile seemed forced.

He started up the engine again and headed for home. "I had some errands to run in town, then I grabbed a burger at a little place I know that's not too far from here."

She stared at the darkened street ahead. "You really should let me pay you to ferry me around."

He responded in a flat tone. "Maddy."

She sent him a snooty little glance. "What?"

"Knock it off."

They rode in silence for a few minutes. She said, "That was Aislinn, on the porch with me."

"Yes, I know. She's a sweetheart."

"You should've come up, said hi."

"I thought about it. But tonight, well, it was for you, to meet your family. I didn't want to butt in to that."

"I should've come and gotten you."

"I think that's three times you've said 'should' since you climbed in this truck. What's going on?"

She folded her hands in lap and gazed down at them, pensive. "They were wonderful, all of them. I like them a lot and I'm really glad you pushed me to finally go and meet them."

"But...?"

"It's just weird, that's all. To be in that house I would have grown up in, with all the people I would have known all my life, to have all these might-have-beens whirling around in my brain."

"Is there something I can do—you know, to make it better, make it a little less weird?"

Her head came up. He turned to meet those turquoise eyes briefly before focusing on the road again.

"I'm going out to Wild River Ranch on Saturday, for dinner." She kept her gaze on the street ahead. "Aislinn invited me. When she saw it was you coming to pick me up, she said you're a good guy and you're hot."

"That Aislinn. She knows what she's talking about."

"She also said I should bring *you* with me on Saturday."

"Oh, did she?"

"Sten, will you come out to Wild River with me Saturday?"

Her invitation pleased him. It also made him a little nervous about where things were going between them. But not nervous enough to get him to beg off. "Yeah. I will." He stole another glance at her.

Her dimples were now on full display. "You just said yes to me."

"Yes, I did." He could look at her forever. But he made himself face front again before he got them in a wreck.

"Come inside with me," she said.

They stood at the front door to the cottage, the cliffs behind them, the porch light bringing out bronze streaks in her pale hair. He wanted to kiss her—oh, who was he kidding? He wanted to do a lot more than kiss her.

And what was so wrong with that? She wanted it, too. She'd said as much more than once.

"'Thank you, Maddy. I would love to come in,'" she answered for him, faking a man's deep voice. And then she turned, stuck the key in the lock and pushed open the door. "Please. After you."

He went in and led the way through the small entry to the great room in back.

"Beer in the fridge," she said, pausing to flip on a light. "One for me, too?"

He got out two bottles, uncapped them and carried them over to where she stood by the slider. "Here you go."

"Thanks." She took the beer and pushed the slider open, letting in the chilly night air and the long sigh of the waves gliding into shore out there beyond the stretch of beach. "To families." She raised her beer. "They can make us crazy, but where would we be without them?"

He tapped his bottle to hers and teased, "You look like someone just stole your dog."

She tried a grin, but her eyes were full of shadows. "I'm a downer tonight. It's the simple truth."

"Talk to me. Tell me everything."

"It's too depressing."

Easing a hand under her hair, he pulled her close. "Talk." He breathed the word against the velvet skin of her forehead and then, reluctantly, let her go.

She leaned back against the doorframe, her mouth so soft, her gaze cast down. "Just thinking about my dad—the one I grew up with, not the one named Bravo."

He wanted to touch her again, so he did, brushing a finger down the perfect line of her nose, guiding a lock of hair back behind her ear. "Thinking about your dad makes you sad?"

"Tonight, it does. He was tall, with blond hair and blue eyes—which is why, I'm guessing, he believed I was his child, even though my mom messed around behind his back more than once. She was small-boned, with dark hair and eyes. They both always claimed I got my looks from the Delaney side of the family. He loved me so much. I really don't think he ever had a clue that I might not be his."

"You *were* his. He loved you. And it's obvious that you loved him. That's what matters."

"Yeah. Or at least, that's what I keep telling my-self." She laughed, but it wasn't a happy sound. "It's just, well, I have this feeling and I've had it for a while now, this feeling that I'm a fake, that I have no real life at all."

He kind of wanted to grab her and shake her. But he made himself say mildly, "You're being way too hard on yourself."

She shook her head. "I don't think so. Ever since I was Coco's age I've been so focused, so set on a certain course. But lately—and I mean, in the past couple of years, long before all this switched-at-birth business—

it's like the ground has been slowly giving way beneath my feet. I honestly do want a different sort of life now."

Did he believe her? Not really. No way was she giving up the dazzling career she'd worked so hard to create. She was just going through a tough time. It would pass and she would go back to Hollywood to make another megahit movie and accept a second Oscar to keep the first one company.

He would miss her when she left. Miss her a whole hell of a lot. In the week and a half since he'd first come face-to-face with her, she'd wormed her way under his skin. How had he let that happen?

Not that it mattered at this point.

What mattered now was that it was too late to get away from her painlessly.

He might as well enjoy himself for as long as it lasted.

"Here," he said. "Give me that beer."

She wrinkled her nose at him, bratty and contrary, the way Coco got sometimes. "I'm not finished with it."

"I'll return it to you later." He snatched it from her hand.

"Hey!" She tried to grab it back.

He held on. They scuffled over it, laughing like a couple of witless idiots. She got hold of his arm and shook it hard enough that she ended up with beer all down the front of her shirt.

"Now look what you did." She stepped back and braced her hands on her hips, going full-out Coco in a snit. "Sten Larson, I smell like a brewery."

He took the bottles by their necks, one-handed, and used the other hand to shove open the screen. "We'll fix that. Come on." He set off across the deck.

"Sten!"

He kept walking, aware of her footfalls behind him as he ran down the stairs and across the beach, not pausing until he was a few feet from where the waves slid in and retreated, leaving lacy trails of foam behind. Bending, he twisted the bottles into dry sand so they stood upright, side by side.

Maddy came even with him just as he was pulling off one of his boots. "What are you up to now?" She had her head tipped to the side, her hair blowing every which way, watching him.

"I'm going wading in the ocean." He slipped off his sock and stuck it in the top of the boot.

"Are you crazy? The water's got to be freezing."

"It's fine. Around fifty degrees this time of year. You'd have to be submerged to get hypothermia and it would take an hour or so for that to happen."

"Well, aren't you the expert? And fifty is cold!"

"Don't be a big sissy," he said under his breath as he pulled off the other shoe and the sock, too.

She stuck out that obstinate chin at him. "What did you call me?"

He dropped both boots next to the propped-up bottles and crouched to roll up his pant legs. "Your beer's right there when you want it." He grabbed his from the sand and waded out into the leading edge of the next wave, not looking back or stopping until the water lapped at his shins.

She was right. It was colder than usual. He wouldn't last that long barefoot. But he was counting on her to get her shoes off and join him.

His toes were only half-frozen when he heard her

splashing behind him, giggling as she approached, shrieking, "Oh! Cold! Yikes! Chilly."

He turned, whipped out a hand and grabbed her—catching the wrist that didn't have a beer attached to it. She shrieked again as he pulled her close and kissed her. She tasted so sweet, of laughter and beer.

"Cold," she giggled against his lips, her hair blowing in both their faces, getting caught between their mouths as she launched herself upward. He read her intention, catching her with his free hand, giving her a boost as she hitched up her legs and hooked her ankles around his waist.

Carrying her now, he forged off along the water's edge, the waves lapping at him. He had one hand under her fine little butt, the other still clutching his beer at her back, still kissing her as she clung like a barnacle to the front of him.

"Yum," she said when he lifted his mouth. She opened her eyes and grinned at him as she shoved her flying hair back behind an ear. It quickly blew free and plastered itself across her mouth again. "Suddenly, I feel much better about everything."

He kissed her again, a quick one that time. "A walk along the water's edge will do that for you."

"Oh, really? I thought it was kissing *you* that made all the difference."

He faked a thoughtful frown. "We probably should test your theory."

"Well, yeah. Just for, you know, science and all that."

"All right then. Here's the plan. This time I won't walk. I'll just stand right here, holding you—which feels amazing, FYI." His feet were numb, but who cared at this point? "Afterward, we'll decide if the walking made a difference."

"Go for it." She puckered up those beautiful lips at him and squinted her eyes closed.

He took that gorgeous mouth.

There was no laughing this time.

Just the sweet taste of the right woman, all eagerness, so soft and welcoming. He speared his tongue in and she met it. The constant roar of the ocean, the frozen state of his feet, the smell of seaweed and wet sand, it all flew away.

They might have remained there, kissing into the next morning—if not for the sudden, big wave that came out of nowhere, flinging cold seawater on them, soaking them from the shoulders down.

She screamed and he let out a bellow. Then they both started laughing again.

"Look at it this way." He nudged a string of seaweed off her shoulder and nuzzled her wet, salty neck. "I think that wave washed the beer off your shirt."

She dug the fingers of her free hand into his hair and pulled, so he lifted his head to her. "Smart-ass." And she kissed him, quick and hard. "Okay. Let's get moving before a bigger wave comes and drags us out to sea."

He lowered her feet to the sand and they ran up the beach, away from the untrustworthy waves.

"Well?" he asked when they reached the little pile of his boots and her shoes. "Walking or kissing? Which is responsible for your attitude adjustment?"

"Let me see." She made a show of considering the weighty question, bracing a thumb under her chin and tapping a finger against her cheek. All the while, she was shivering, wet to the ends of her hair. "Scientifically speaking...."

"Scientifically. Of course."

"Kissing. No doubt about it. In fact, I'm thinking that we should do it again in order to keep my spirits up."

Now that was an excellent idea. He pulled her close and she lifted her angel's face to him.

That kiss was slow and deep and endlessly sweet. He didn't want it to end. He forgot his frozen feet and their waterlogged clothes.

But eventually, they came up for air and she started shivering again.

He bent, grabbed her shoes and handed them to her. "Let's get you inside before frostbite sets in."

Chapter Six

They dropped their shoes outside the door.

Sten gestured Madison in ahead of him, pulling the door shut once he was inside. She continued to shiver, feeling glad he was with her, hoping he would stay.

"Give me your beer," he said. "And your phone, too."

She pulled her phone from her dripping pocket. The screen lit right up when she swiped it, none the worse for getting wet. She handed the phone and the beer over.

He set them on the table along with his beer, checking his phone as she had hers and then leaving it, too. "Come here." Those blue eyes of his promised all manner of scary, wonderful things.

She stepped up close. He took her soggy T-shirt by the hem.

"Lift your arms."

She did and he eased it up and away. And there she

was, in her wet bra and her baggy canvas pants, no doubt looking like a drowned rat.

But he just tipped up her chin and kissed her, short and sweet. "You're still shivering." He picked up a remote from a side table and turned on the gas fireplace. "That'll warm it up in here. How 'bout a shower?"

"Yes, please." She had her arms wrapped around herself, but it wasn't helping much. Her teeth had started chattering.

"Come on."

She followed him into her bedroom and on to the en suite bath.

It was easy between them, natural and uncomplicated, somehow. Not overtly sexy, just effortless and right. Not like when she used to try to date in LA, and it always felt so fake. Like it was all about being seen and admired, a photo op more than a way to get to know someone.

With Sten, it just felt real.

They stripped off everything, leaving it all in a soggy pile near the open door to the bedroom.

Yeah, she felt a little awkward. She was at home in her body, but she'd never been naked like this before, with just a man that she wanted, the two of them. Alone.

He turned on the shower and glanced over his shoulder to find her watching him. How could she help it? He was all hard planes and strong angles, his back layered in lean muscles leading down to an amazing rock-hard butt and powerful legs dusted with dark hair.

She was blushing. She could feel it, her neck and face going hot.

And then he turned to her fully. He was beautiful

all over. She tried not to stare at the proof of his desire for her.

"Maddy." Her name on his lips was like a gentle touch, soothing her nervousness, easing her fears. "Words can't do you justice." He held out his hand.

She took it and let him pull her into the shower stall, under the wide rain showerhead so that the wonderful, hot water poured down over them, taking all the chills away. A sense of ease stole through her. She lifted her hands and placed them against his chest, which was as sharply cut as the back of him, with a perfect T of hair across his pectorals, and in a soft trail down the center of him.

He felt so solid, so strong and male. And she was glad, so glad right then.

That she had waited.

That he would be the one.

She tipped up her chin to him and he took her mouth in a light, easy kiss. She felt the tip of him, hard and hot against her belly.

But then he stepped back and reached for the soap.

He bathed her and washed her hair, touching her everywhere, but not lingering, not trying to arouse her, more like soothing her. Pampering her. And getting to know her with his hands.

She returned the favor, chickening out a little over the naughty bits. He smiled when she skated the soap around his erection and then took over for her whenever she seemed shy.

A quick mutual rinse-off and they got out together and dried off. He tucked a towel around his hips. "I'll put our wet clothes in the washer."

"Thanks."

He gathered them up and left her to blow-dry her hair.

Once that was done, she put on her favorite cozy terry cloth robe and went looking for him.

He hadn't gone far. She found him in the great room sitting by the fire wearing busted-out jeans and a worn T-shirt. He held out his hand and she went to him, pulling his arm across her shoulders, snuggling in good and close.

"Did you go back to your house to get dressed?" Grinning a little, she pictured him running across the deck in the moonlight wearing only a towel.

He pressed his lips into her hair. "Uh-uh. There are some boxes of old clothes stored in the attic here."

She tipped her head back so she could see his eyes. They were dark blue and endless, sucking her in, making her feel like she wasn't alone, like her life *could* be different. Simpler and richer, both at once—and she just had to ask, "Stay with me tonight?"

He smoothed her hair, guiding it off her shoulders and down her back. "I don't have condoms with me. But I could go next door and get some."

Condoms. Such an unromantic, practical consideration. Still, his mention of them made a glow of happiness all through her.

Not because of any possible hot, sexy times. But because he really was giving himself up to her the way she'd fantasized he might since the day she'd lured him to the cottage to repair the toilet she'd broken on purpose.

She liked everything about him. He was not only a pure pleasure to look at, he was a good guy, thoughtful. Kind. With a great sense of humor. Someone who took care of his family and tried to do the right thing.

Even when he pissed her off, she was pretty much all in on Sten.

How could she not be? He treated her like royalty, ferrying her around wherever she wanted to go, putting up with her silly disguises and her paranoia about the possibility that she might be recognized.

Too bad he'd also maintained a certain emotional distance between them.

Until now.

Until tonight.

But…*condoms*?

Was she ready for that?

She shook her head. "Just to sleep—or is that too weird?"

"Not weird in the least." He was stifling a chuckle, she just knew it. He kissed the end of her nose. "And yeah, I would love to stay."

A phone was ringing—the landline phone.

Madison opened her eyes. The light through the curtains told her it was morning. She picked up the handset. "Hullo?"

"Hey, Madison. It's Karin. Just wondering if maybe my brother is there?"

Turning her head slowly on the pillow, Madison met a pair of sleepy blue eyes. They grinned at each other. "Who is it?" he asked.

"Karin," she mouthed at him, and then, into the phone, "Yes, he's right here." She handed it to him.

"What?" he grumbled into the mouthpiece. Karin said something that brought a snort from him. "Right… Sure, I'll ask her." He covered the speaker with his palm. "My sister says she just *happened* to notice that my truck was in the garage, but I wasn't at the house. She's all smug."

"Smug?"

"She's been after me to make a move on you since the night you broke the toilet to get my attention."

"Really?" Karin was on her side. That pleased her no end.

"Really. And we're invited to breakfast in the downstairs kitchen next door. You like blueberry pancakes?"

"I love them."

"We'll be there," he said to Karin and then went up on an elbow to reach over Madison and drop the phone back on the base. Once that was done, he showed no inclination to return to his side of the bed. "Good morning."

"Morning."

He kissed her chin, a quick, sweet little peck, and then they did the eye thing, smiling and staring at each other. "You are gorgeous."

She smiled wider, knowing she had bedhead and probably morning breath. "Flattery. I'm all for it."

He dipped closer to nuzzle her neck and nip at the collar of the T-shirt she'd worn to sleep in. "But you have too many clothes on."

She wrapped her arms around his neck and kissed his cheek, indulging her imagination, picturing what her life might be, if she could wake up in the same bed with this man every morning for the rest of their lives. "I have two words for you," she whispered in his ear. "Blueberry. Pancakes."

He levered up on an elbow. "Seriously? You'd rather have breakfast than me?"

"It's a really difficult choice. However…"

* * *

"Uncle Sten, did you have a sleepover at Madison's?" demanded Coco, who was already at the table with a half-eaten pancake on her plate and syrup on her chin when Madison and Sten entered the downstairs kitchen.

Karin, at the cooktop flipping pancakes, tried to nip that line of questioning in the bud. "Eat your breakfast, sweetheart."

Coco was not deterred. "But *I* want to have a sleepover with Madison."

Chuckling, Otto patted the little girl's shoulder and dabbed at her chin with his napkin as Madison took the chair Sten pulled out for her.

Ben, buttering his pancakes with careful, even strokes, remarked, "Grown-ups don't have sleepovers with kids."

"Unless the grown-up is your *friend*," argued Coco. "And Madison is my friend, aren't you, Madison?"

"Yes, I am," Madison replied automatically.

Her blue eyes going big as Cinnabon rolls, Coco amped up the charm factor. "So then, Madison, can we have a sleepover, you and me, at your house, please?"

Madison knew the proper answer to that one. "We'll have to talk to your mom about that."

Coco turned those big eyes on her mother. "Mommy, Madison says yes. So can we have a sleepover? Please."

Karin turned from the cooktop and asked sweetly, "Do you need the answer to that question right now?"

Coco stuck out her bottom lip.

Ben turned to Madison and stage-whispered, "That's Mom's big move. When she says that, you can't say yes, or Mom just says, 'All right then. The answer is no,' and you don't get whatever you're asking for."

Coco knew the drill, too. "No, Mommy," she said with exaggerated politeness. "I don't need an answer now, but I would 'preciate it if you would think about it."

"Fair enough." Karin flipped a couple of golden-brown pancakes onto a plate. "Madison and I will discuss it and we will let you know."

That evening, Karin got a rare night to party with friends and Madison, Coco, Sten and Benjamin rolled out sleeping bags on the cottage's great room floor. They had popcorn and hot chocolate with marshmallows and watched a couple of movies—science fiction for Ben and *Mulan* for Coco. Later, Sten told them a long ghost story about a demented clown who lived in a cornfield.

It was well after midnight when the kids finally fell asleep.

Sten joined Madison in her sleeping bag. They whispered together like a couple of naughty kids and shared more than one smoking hot kiss. Finally, at a little before one, he returned to his own bag and they settled in for the night. Madison drifted off to sleep with a smile on her face.

She wasn't sure what woke her. Voices? A car door slamming?

She sat up in her sleeping bag. It was still dark, past three in the morning according to the digital clock on the stove in the kitchen area.

Sten sat up and whispered, "What's wrong?"

"Don't know," she whispered back. "I think I heard something outside."

"I'll check." He got up. She rose, too. "You stay here," he instructed.

"No way. I'm going." And there it was again—people talking. Arguing, maybe, coming from the cliff side of the house. She put up a hand for silence. But now all was quiet. "Voices, I think."

He pointed toward the slider. She followed him on tiptoe, trying not to wake Coco or Ben.

When they reached the glass door, he pushed it open with agonizing slowness and closed it behind them the same way.

It was chilly out—and very dark, too, with the moon no longer visible in the overcast sky. They were both barefoot, in sleep pants and long-sleeved T-shirts. Hopefully, they would solve this little mystery quickly, and not be out in the cold for long.

He whispered, "If there's anything suspicious going on, I'm sending you back inside and you will go. Understood?"

She was tempted to argue that he wasn't the boss of her—but she wanted to find out what was going on at the front of the house more. "Agreed."

He led her around to the side deck. They'd just turned the corner when they heard the murmur of voices again. Sten pulled her back against the outer wall of the house, into the shadow of the eaves, where they wouldn't be spotted. They crept along the wall, stopping before they reached the corner that would lead them around to the front of the cottage where the light by the front door could give them away.

From the darkness under the eaves, they could see

two figures down in the parking turnaround on the cliff side of the house next door. The two stood facing each other by a large, dark-colored SUV. They were somewhat illuminated in the muted glow of the lights on either side of the workshop's roll-up door.

A man and a woman.

"I just can't," said the woman in a pleading tone. Her voice was familiar. She turned her head a little and Madison knew for sure. It was Karin.

The man argued, "It's been three years. Come on, Karin. You've got a right to a life."

"Don't—" she began.

"Damn it, it's not—"

"Liam, keep your voice down."

Liam? The man moved just a fraction and the light found his face.

It was him, all right. Liam Bravo, the third-born brother Madison had met for the first time Thursday night.

And whatever was going on between him and Karin was obviously none of her business or Sten's.

Sten must have come to the same conclusion. He signaled that they should go back. She nodded and led the way, keeping quiet and close to the house, out of sight from down below.

When they reached the slider, she turned back to him and whispered, "Karin and Liam?"

He shrugged. "It's news to me. I mean, they dated for a while in high school."

"They did?"

"Hey. It was high school. It was a long time ago."

"Wow."

"Karin loved Bud." He sounded defensive. "Bud

was a good guy and he was crazy about her. She was a wreck when he died."

"Hey." She touched his arm. "You don't have to explain anything to me. I get that it's none of my business. But I do think Karin's the best. And what Liam said to her does make sense. She's single now and she's got a right to find a little happiness for herself."

"True." He lifted a hand and ghosted a slow touch down the side of her throat, leaving happy, warm shivers in his wake.

She stepped in closer, wanting somehow to ease him, though he didn't seem troubled, exactly. "You okay?"

He shrugged again. "It's just weird, after all these years, thinking of Karin with anyone but Bud. Plus, I kind of feel like a creeper, spying on my sister."

She had to stifle a laugh. "Well, we had no idea we were butting in on anything. It might have turned out to be something we really needed to deal with."

"Right."

She reached up and put her hand against his warm, scruffy cheek. "So no harm done?"

"Maddy," he whispered, fond and gentle and full of desire. Happiness filled her.

She pulled him down to her. They shared a slow, sweet kiss.

"Let's go on in," he said when he lifted his head.

Inside, they crept to their separate sleeping bags and settled in for what was left of the night. It took Madison a long time to fall back to sleep. She kept thinking of Karin, wondering what, actually, had been going on between Karin and Liam out there in the dark. And then she started considering how short life really was, how a person could have the love of her life and lose him in a heartbeat.

How when love found you, you needed to reach for it—reach for it and hold on tight and make the most of every moment fate granted you.

The next afternoon, in the main house at Wild River Ranch, Aislinn led Madison up the stairs to the second floor.

"It's this one." Aislinn stopped in the doorway to a small bedroom. Madison stopped beside her.

Late afternoon sunlight poured in through the one window on the opposite wall. The room was painted a soothing dove gray. It had a double bed with a bright quilt, a rag rug and a dresser topped with a gorgeous Craftsman-style lamp. Colorful pictures decorated the walls.

Aislinn explained, "Like a few of the other rooms in the house, it needed a generous dose of TLC. It was a dark room, depressing, you know? I brightened it up a little."

"It's nice," said Madison. "Cheerful."

"Thanks—so anyway, the story goes that Claudia, Martin Durand's wife, acted as midwife that night. Your mom and mine each had one of the rooms to either side of this one. They gave birth within a few minutes of each other. Once we were born, Claudia put us in makeshift cribs made of dresser drawers on a bed in this room while she looked after the new mothers."

"I remember all this from Martin's letter." Madison stared at a beautiful wall hanging sewn with twining flowers that Aislinn had hung above the bed. "He wrote that it was storming that night, really bad, with power outages, flooded roads and no way for Marie and George Bravo to get home when she went into labor, let alone make it to the hospital in Astoria or Valentine Bay. Martin Durand snuck in and switched us."

Aislinn nodded. "Our blankets were identical and we were both about the same size. I had wisps of dark hair and you didn't, but he switched us anyway, got away with it, and when he started to feel guilty, it was too late."

"He had no way to switch us back without someone finding out what he'd done."

Aislinn turned to her. "So. Here we are." Her dark eyes gleamed with unshed tears.

Madison felt an answering rush of emotion, filling her heart, blurring her vision. She reached out an arm and drew Aislinn to her side. They stared at the room together, arms around each other's shoulders, for a long string of quiet seconds.

Aislinn broke the silence. "Does it help any? Seeing the room where it happened?"

Madison didn't really know how to answer her. "I did want to see it…"

"But?"

"Well, I wouldn't say it helps, exactly. What does help is to know you a little. To see that you're happy, that your life works for you."

Aislinn drew in a slow breath, as though gathering courage. "I admit, I've been wondering—how *you* are? If you like the way things have turned out for you?"

"I've got no complaints. I got everything I ever wanted."

"But are you happy?" Aislinn anxiously scanned her face.

"I'm not *un*happy—and don't look at me like that. I'm fine, honestly. I'm just ready for a change, that's all."

Aislinn turned fully toward her and took both of her hands. "Anything I can do to help you make that change, just say the word."

"You *are* helping," Madison said. "A lot. By reaching out, by inviting me here, to the place where we were born. By being the one who really understands what I'm going through." She tugged on Aislinn's hands. "Now come on, let's go back downstairs before the guys start wondering why we've deserted them."

They found Sten and Jaxon in Jax's study and they all four trekked out to the stables, where Madison and Sten met Burt, the ranch foreman, and his dog, Ace. Dinner was an excellent prime rib prepared by the housekeeper, Erma.

After the meal they met Aislinn's pet rabbits, who lived on the enclosed side porch of the ranch house. They went back inside for dessert and hung around until after ten.

"You're quiet," Sten said as they were driving back to Valentine Bay.

"Just thinking." She leaned her head against the window with a sigh. "About Aislinn and Jax, how happy they seem together. I want that, you know? Love. Real love, with the right person…" She dared to sit up and look at him then. The dashboard lights cast his features into sharp relief. He was staring straight ahead, like the road might jump up and bite him if he dared to glance away. "Oops." She tried to make a joke of it. "I have mentioned the dreaded L-word and I've only known you for a couple of weeks. Talk about awkward. So sorry. My bad."

It took him far too long to figure out how to reply. And when he did, he spoke grimly. "Madison, I'm crazy about you."

"Try to say it without clenching your teeth—and you know what? Let's not do this, okay?"

"Fine with me." He never once took his gaze off the road.

She leaned back and shut her eyes.

He cued up some music and they listened to soft rock and power pop the rest of the way. At the cove, he parked his pickup in the side garage of the main house.

"Thank you for taking me to the ranch," she said. "I had a great time." And she got out and left through the wide-open garage door, her heart aching with each beat. Really, it was kind of amazing how fast everything had gone to crap.

But then she heard the garage door go down and his footsteps behind her. Her pulse pounded faster. Maybe he was planning for them to actually talk about what had just happened—about their feelings for each other and how they were getting closer and she wanted them to get closer still. It would be good to talk honestly about all this, right?

Oh, but it didn't feel good. She almost whirled on him and said something provoking.

But she remembered last night, the sounds of Karin and Liam arguing outside, having no idea how far their voices carried.

Better not to go there until they were indoors, at least.

She led the way up the steps to the front door of the cottage, unlocked it and went in. He was right behind her. Dropping her purse on the narrow entry table, she kept going to the great room, where she flipped on a couple of lamps and then went and stood at the slider, staring out at the sliver of moon hanging high above the ocean.

"Madison, come on."

She turned and faced him, though it hurt to look at him right now. Why did he have to be so gorgeous? Why did it seem like he just kept getting better-looking every time she saw him? She knew it was her heart doing that, seeing the beauty of him ever more clearly as she grew to love him.

And no, she'd never been in love before. And she really hadn't known him very long. She was pushing too fast, she got that. But she recognized it already, this love she had for him. She accepted it as real and right and true. In the space of two weeks, she'd come to love Sten Larson.

Too bad he didn't love her.

He put up both hands and then dropped them. "We just need to be realistic, okay? As I said in the truck, I'm gone on you. You're like no other woman I've ever met before. And this feeling I have for you, it's strong. But you really need to look inside yourself, deep down, to who you really are, to all you've accomplished so far in your life. You've got to know that you're not going to give up being America's Darling to settle down on the Oregon coast with a house-flipping shipbuilder any more than I'm going move to LA to live with a movie star."

She wanted to haul off and smack him a good one. "That's just your fears talking, Sten."

"No, it's…"

She whipped up a hand. "I'm not finished."

He glared, but he gave it up. "Go ahead."

"Thank you, I will," she said with quiet fury. "You're wrong. All wrong. And just to be clear, I would never ask you to leave your family and the home that you love, so don't get yourself all worked up on that score. On the other hand, if I were to move here, that would be *my* choice, not yours. If I were to move here permanently, it would be because that was what *I* wanted, what worked for me. And it wouldn't just be as a home base, a place to come back to between movies. I'm talking about quitting acting, Sten, I really am."

He stared at her so bleakly. "You say all that now."

"Because it's true."

"And just what would you *do*, if you quit acting?"

"I have no idea. Yet. But I would find something that suits me. And I have great money managers. Frankly, if I don't want to work, I never have to work again— and you and me? We could totally happen. But not if you won't *let* us happen. Not if you close your mind and your heart to all that could be."

For a moment, he just stared at her. She almost started to hope he would say something positive. But no. "I just don't get it."

She knew she shouldn't ask. "What don't you get?"

"How can you possibly be so naive?"

That capped it. "Okay, look. I should never have mentioned the word *love*. We're not there yet." *Well, you're not there, anyway.* "And we may never be there.

Right now, I don't know what to say to you except that whatever that woman who hurt you did to you, I am not her. No way, no how— Oh. And one more thing. Good night, Sten."

Chapter Seven

Karin dropped into the deck chair beside Sten.

She tapped his shoulder with a tall cold one. Sten took it, had a long sip and stared at the new moon, thinking how lucky he was to have such a great sister.

But then she had to go and ruin it by talking. "Don't tell me you're in the dog house with America's Darling *again*."

"Fine. I won't tell you."

Karin gave him a look, like he was just such a chucklehead. "Put yourself out of your misery. Go say you're sorry."

"Drop it."

"Stennie, it's time you learned to love again." She said it so sweetly.

And that made it hurt even more—enough that he opened his big mouth and said, "Yeah, well, it's time you started taking your own advice." The words got out before he made himself stop them.

And Karin knew exactly what he meant by them—or at least, she suspected. She took a long pull off her ginger beer and then asked, "What are you getting at?"

He tried to backpedal. "It's not my business. Sorry."

"Just say it. Please."

And then he turned and looked at her and, well, he never had liked lying much. "Last night, when you got home…" He explained about hearing voices, and that he and Madison had gone outside to see what was up. "We saw you with Liam Bravo."

"Ugh." She drank more fake beer. "It's complicated."

Now that he'd gone and put his foot in it, he at least had to offer, "You want to talk about it?"

"Um, no."

He felt relief that she wasn't going to unburden herself to him, which probably made him a terrible brother. "Well, I'm ready to listen if you ever do."

"Thanks—but like I said, no. Liam did tell me, though, the real reason Madison's here in town." She leaned her head back and watched the wisps of clouds high above, like smoke trails in the dark sky. "She looks like the Bravos. I probably should have guessed—and don't worry. I won't say anything to anyone. I haven't forgotten that she's trying not to let the world know she's here—and anyway, who would I tell?"

They gazed out at the ocean together until he asked, "So where's my quote from Scarlett O'Hara?"

"Sorry." She set her half-empty bottle on the little table between them and gathered her legs up onto the chair. "Scarlett's got nothing worthwhile to say tonight."

* * *

The next day, Madison stewed a little over whether or not to call Sten and ask him for a ride to Daniel's house.

Somehow, she kept herself from doing that. Really, she'd been using him as a car service and that just wasn't right. Plus, they were now on the outs and she had no desire whatsoever to ask him for anything at the moment, anyway.

She put on her dark wig, sunglasses and a big hat and called a cab to take her to the DNA party, making a stop at a drugstore downtown along the way. An unnecessary stop, probably.

But so what? It was her life and her body and if she ever spoke to Sten again, she intended to be ready for anything that might happen.

Was that wonky reasoning? Absolutely.

She stopped at the drugstore anyway.

No one in the store recognized her. She could have been invisible for all the attention the clerk and the few other customers gave her. And the cabbie? He never looked twice at her.

All of which had her thinking she needed to get over herself.

If somebody found her out, so what? She would just ask the person to please respect her privacy—and if they didn't and a few paparazzi showed up in town, well, so be it. She'd been hounded by relentless photojournalists before and lived to tell about it.

At Daniel's, she stuffed her silly disguise in her giant tote and visited with her newfound family. She played Old MacDonald Lotto with the twins and kissed a really unsanitary-looking stuffed animal when Jake stuck the thing in her face. Keely let her hold the baby. Little Marie cooed and waved her tiny hands. She smelled like milk and clean cotton sheets dried in the sun—well, until she dumped a big load in her diaper, anyway.

Keely laughed. "She's so cute until she poops."

Madison handed the little girl to her mother and spent a few minutes getting to know the youngest of her new siblings, Grace. Everyone's phones got a workout as they took a bunch of group shots.

Harper asked about Brock Markovic, who'd been Madison's leading man in more than one film. "Okay, Madison. It's tacky, and you probably don't want to hear it, but I just have to know. Are you and Brock a thing?"

She thought of Sten, felt a painful twinge of longing in the vicinity of her heart. If only he were here with her, nobody would be asking about her and Brock. "Sorry to break it to you, Harper, but Brock and I are not a thing and never have been."

Hailey let out a moan. "We were so sure you two were crazy in love."

"Nope. He's a great guy, and everyone says we have killer chemistry on-screen."

"Oh, yes, you do." Harper made a show of fanning herself.

"Yeah, well. In reality? Never gonna happen."

The DNA was collected without much fanfare by Percy and Great-Aunt Daffy. A simple swipe of the inside of the cheek and it was done.

Percy had a kit for Madison and each of the Bravo siblings, including Aislinn, who already knew she was Martin Durand's daughter. By testing against the other siblings, Aislinn could eliminate herself once and for all as a Bravo by blood, thus getting as close as possible to proving that Paula Delaney had been her biological mother.

After the meal, Madison tried to get a little face time with her newly found brothers—starting with Liam. She found him charming and full of questions about her life in LA and the movie business. He didn't talk much about himself, though, and he said zero about whatever was going on with him and Karin. Not that she really expected to learn anything about his private life. After all, they hardly knew each other and she was reasonably certain he had no clue what she and Sten had overheard the other night.

Third-born Connor, who worked with Daniel at Valentine Logging, revealed a little more about himself than Liam had. Connor had been married, he said, to his best friend's only sister. His ex-wife had left him to make it big in advertising in New York City.

Madison was outraged on his behalf. "So you're saying she just divorced you and left?"

Connor's expression turned sheepish. "Well, not exactly…"

Madison figured it out about then, and accused, "You wouldn't go."

"Why am I talking about this?" Connor was suddenly all about his empty glass. "I think I need another drink."

Madison moved on to Daniel and then chatted with Matt and his wife, Sabra. Later, she ended up sitting in the kitchen with Aislinn and Keely, drinking really tasty cinnamon tea and hearing great stories about what it was like growing up in Valentine Bay.

By nine, the kids were in bed. Percy and Daffy and

a few of the others had already left. Madison got out her phone to summon another cab.

"Put that phone down," ordered Aislinn. "Jax and I go right by Sweetheart Cove on the way back to the ranch. The truck is a crew cab, so there's plenty of room."

Aislinn waited until they were on the road before she remarked way too casually, "I was surprised that Sten wasn't with you today."

Madison almost lied and said he couldn't make it. But already, she felt close to Aislinn. She trusted her—and Jaxon, too. And that lifted her spirits a little. She'd begun to create real relationships in Valentine Bay. "Not much fun to bring him with me when I'm not speaking to him."

Jax and Aislinn shared a glance. Madison watched them from the back seat, feeling suddenly envious—of their closeness, their intimate connection.

She wanted that, an intimate connection with a man, she really did. And not just any man. With Sten.

Maybe. If he ever started taking her seriously.

"I keep meaning to ask," said Aislinn. "How long will you be in town?"

"Three more weeks and five days." She wasn't even at the halfway point in her stay.

Still, it felt like her hiatus was flying by much too fast. Even if she did hold firm on her birthday goal to leave acting behind, she still had contracts to honor. Unless her current project suffered more delays, she would be back on a soundstage by the first of May.

"Plenty of time for you and Sten to work things out." Aislinn said it as though she honestly believed it.

And Madison couldn't help but hope she was right.

* * *

For Sten, the day had crawled by. He spent hours in his workshop, getting a lot done and feeling zero satisfaction about it. Mostly, he was just trying to keep his mind from straying to thoughts of the movie star next door.

After dinner, he went to check on the flip house, where the list of what still needed doing went on and on. At least they were on schedule, a rarity in his experience.

Twenty minutes was all it took and he'd seen everything he needed to see. So, what now? Nothing at home to look forward to. If he had a beer with Karin, she'd be on his ass to work things out with Maddy. The alternative—sitting around by himself trying not to think about Maddy—didn't thrill him either.

He knew a quiet bar in the center of town, but halfway there, he remembered the place was closed on Sundays. Instead, he went to the Sea Breeze on Beach Street and took a seat at the bar.

Ingrid Ostergard, the owner and Keely Bravo's mom, served him a beer. Ingrid used to be a bona fide rock star. She was fun, with lots of attitude, her hair a different color every time he came in. Tonight, it was a deep magenta. They made small talk for a few minutes and then she moved down the bar to pour refills for a couple of guys in Rip City T-shirts.

Sten nursed his beer and did exactly what he would have been doing if he'd gone home—missed Madison. He wished he hadn't been such a douche to her last night and he wondered if she'd had any trouble getting a ride to the Bravo house for the DNA dinner. Taking her where she needed to go and protecting her from any possible hassling was supposed to be his job. But instead, he'd pissed her off and left her to scare up a ride for herself.

He was currently trying to tell himself that staying away from her was for the best. The woman presented a lot more temptation than he was ready to deal with.

When Ingrid asked if he wanted another beer, he said no, thanked her and put his money on the bar. He didn't realize he'd left his phone in the truck until it buzzed at him from the console as he got in behind the wheel.

Maddy?

He grabbed for it, almost dropping the damn thing in his eagerness to see what she had to say.

But it wasn't Madison.

It was Ella Robson. His ex-girlfriend had sent him four texts while he was in the bar.

—Guess who? How have you been?

—Been thinking of you lately, missing those big hands of yours and all the amazing things they can do.

—Joey still asks about you. I swear he's grown a foot since you last saw him.

—Sten? Come on. Only joking around. Can't we just talk?

He felt nothing—well, nothing beyond annoyance, that she'd contacted him again, that she'd stooped so low as to drag poor Joey into it. The kid didn't need his mother pulling that kind of stuff.

Did she think she could start something up with him

again? Had she split with Darrin for the second time? Or was she texting him behind her husband's back?

Whatever she was up to, he wanted it stopped.

He'd thought the world of her once, a single mom, newly divorced, trying to take care of her young son after her husband had left her. Joey was a great kid. Sten had wanted to help her, wanted to make things better for her and her boy.

He'd been the one to hire her as the office manager at the Boatworks. Joey was four then.

It was pretty much what Karin had said the other night. Sten had fallen for both the mom and the kid—and that had surprised the hell out of everyone who knew him.

After all, he was the guy who loved his freedom. When he wanted family around him, he had a sister, the kids and his dad—and Bud, too, before they lost him. He'd liked things with women to be simple and uncomplicated. But when it came to Ella and Joey, right away he was thinking forever with a ready-made family.

Ella had refused to go out with him at first. She'd said it was a bad idea to date the boss. He'd thought that showed so much integrity.

Soon enough, though, she was saying yes. The morning after their first night together, Sten asked her to move in with him.

But she wouldn't come live with him—not out in the open for the world to see, anyway. When Darrin, who lived in Seattle, had custody of Joey, though? That was a different story. She would play house with Sten while her son was away.

He'd asked her to marry him over and over, been such a sucker for her brave single-mom act. She'd always said no, always claimed that she was wild for him, but she wasn't "ready" for marriage again yet. That she just didn't think getting married again would be good for Joey.

Then, out of nowhere—at least, from Sten's point of view—Ella and Darrin had reconciled. Ella broke the news to Sten right there in his private office at Larson Boatworks.

She marched in, shut the door and came to stand at his desk. Head high and a noble expression on her pretty face, she'd quietly informed him that she appreciated what a good guy he was, not to mention how great they were together in bed.

But sex wasn't everything. She was quitting the Boatworks and she and Sten were through. Darrin wanted to get back together and they were going to remarry. Ella and Joey would join Darrin in Seattle. It was the best thing for Joey, after all. She collected her last paycheck, put her stuff in a box and walked out. Sten hadn't seen her since.

It had taken him a while to accept the depressing fact that he'd been little more than Ella Robson's dependable booty call for three years. Her goal had always been to get back with her husband.

Now she had what she'd been after—and she was screwing it up?

I'm done, he thought.

And the best part? It was absolutely true. He'd been telling himself for months that he was over Ella.

Now he knew it for a certainty.

He considered just blowing off her texts.

But ghosting was for wimps.

He texted back: Leave it alone, Ella. You and I are

done. Don't contact me again. And then he blocked her number—after which he still felt like he had ants crawling under his skin.

His irritation really had nothing to do with Ella Robson.

He was pissed off because it wasn't Maddy who'd sent him four texts in a row.

What was this thing he had for unavailable women, anyway? First a single mom determined to get back with the husband who'd walked out on her.

Now a movie star—and yeah, okay, Maddy claimed she was leaving her big-time career behind. Sten actually believed that *she* believed she would do it.

He just didn't think it would happen. She'd dedicated her life to becoming the best of the best at what she did. It made no sense for her to walk away from all that at the top of her game.

In the end, she would return to LA and get on with her real life. He could just picture her, looking back with wistful fondness on her time with him at Sweetheart Cove.

So yeah, Sten had no illusions about how things would shake out with Maddy in the end. After she'd sent him away last night, he'd been telling himself that avoiding her from here on out was the best course.

And it might have been.

Except he was already in too deep.

The cottage seemed so quiet and empty when Madison got home.

She dropped her bag on the narrow table by the front door and went on through to the great room. She was just about to turn on a light when she saw the tall, broad-shouldered figure standing out on the deck.

Sten. He was leaning on the railing, staring off toward the beach and the restless ocean beyond.

Her heart lifted and her skin felt all prickly, her blood suddenly hot as it raced through her veins. She left the light off and went straight to the slider, where she hesitated, her hand on the latch, in delicious indecision.

Because she was still mad at him and she wasn't sure she even wanted to talk to him—except, well, she did. So much. She wanted to feel his hard arms around her, his soft lips on hers. She wanted him to admit that he'd been so wrong, that they had something special and he was actually willing to give them a chance.

Either he'd heard Jax's truck out in front or he'd somehow sensed her presence in the dark house behind him. Straightening and turning, he locked eyes with her through the glass.

A long, lovely shiver went through her, a shiver that felt like surrender. She pushed the slider wide.

It was all the encouragement he needed. He came for her, blue eyes burning, long legs eating up the distance in quick, determined strides.

"Maddy." He stopped a foot away from her. "I'm sorry. I was jerk."

She willed him closer.

And he took that last step. He cradled her face in those big, rough hands and lowered his beautiful mouth to hers.

She sighed at the wonder of it—at all of it. At his coming to find her, at the way he'd admitted right off that he'd behaved badly.

And even more than his apology, she melted at the way he made her feel, at the warmth of his breath across her skin, the hungry look in his eyes as his palms coasted out over her shoulders and down her arms. He cupped his hands around the back of hers and eased his fingers in, lacing them together with hers.

And he kissed her for a long time, right there in the open doorway, kissed her gently—and yet not. Kissed her with a kind of leashed forcefulness that had her wishing he might never stop.

As his mouth seduced her, his hands were on the move again, touching her, stroking her, causing a riot of lovely sensations as his fingers skimmed her shoulders, glided along her neck and eased up into her hair.

He gathered the mass of it into a fist, pulling her head back to kiss her more deeply.

She moaned. With a low growl in response, he loosened his grip and combed through the strands in long, soothing strokes.

"All day, all I've wanted is to be with you," he whispered. "I was pretty sure I'd blown it for good this time."

"Uh-uh. No way. I'm so glad you're here."

"I kept telling myself it was the best thing, anyway, to leave you alone."

"No. Wrong. That would be the *worst* thing."

He kissed the tip of her nose and the space between her eyebrows. "How did it go at Daniel's?"

"It was great. Aislinn and Jax asked where you were. I said we weren't speaking. They seemed to think we would work it out."

"Were they right?"

"I'm still back there with how you thought leaving me alone was the best way to go."

"Yeah, well. I'm here, aren't I?"

She faked a sulky face. "And I probably shouldn't be so glad about that."

"Maddy." He bent closer. His warm breath ghosted across her skin. "Won't you please forgive me for being a doucheberry?"

She chuckled against his beautiful mouth. "Douche-berry. That's pretty bad—and of course I forgive you. The truth is, when you're kissing me, I could forgive you just about anything."

"I just want you closer." He hauled her even tighter against him. The kiss got deeper and wetter.

What he was doing to her? She'd never known anything like what she felt with him. His kiss stole the breath right out of her lungs.

"I just want this time with you," he whispered, the words rough and ragged against her parted lips. "Every minute we can steal."

Steal? They weren't stealing anything. She wanted him and he wanted her and it was all wide-open, above-board, wasn't it?

Then again, who cared what word he used?

What mattered was that he was here and she was here and this perfect moment would never come again.

"It's all right." She meant it, she did. He'd been a jerk, yeah. But she'd pushed things too fast. And she wanted what he wanted, anyway—to be with him, right now, however it worked out when her time in Oregon was through.

At some point in life, a woman had to let go, take

what was offered, give up the goals and the planning and just let the good things happen for once.

He framed her face again. "Can I come in, then?"

She grinned. "But you're already in."

He glanced left and right. "Currently, we are standing on the threshold."

"Hmm."

He frowned down at her. "I'm not sure I like the way you're looking at me. Like you can't decide whether to let me stay or make me go."

"Hmm," she said again, but then she took both his hands and stepped back, pulling him with her as she cleared the doorway.

"Come here." He kissed her some more, a hungry, exciting kiss. He smelled like cedar and the cool night wind off the ocean. She couldn't get enough of just breathing him in.

"Do not leave this spot." He stopped kissing her, but only to shut and lock the slider. The moment he faced her again, she made her move, whipping off her light sweater, dropping it to the floor, kicking off her shoes and unzipping her jeans.

"I really like where this is going." His eyes looked so dark right then, full of dangerous promises. Sparking heat as he went, he traced a slow, sweet caress down the middle of her body, into the valley between her breasts, over the little bow at the center of her bra—and lower, to the top of her red panties revealed between the open zipper teeth. "But, Maddy. Are you sure?"

She nodded, her breath coming a little frantic, her skin on fire. "I even went to the drugstore and bought condoms, which is pretty crazy given that I was still angry with you when I did it. I took a cab." She said it with pride.

His fingers skated upward again. He cradled her left breast, easing his thumb under the lace at the top of the cup, guiding it down so her breast, with its puckered, dusky nipple, was bare. A rush of arousal flooded through her and her knees went all wobbly. He did the same thing to the other breast.

She felt pliant, easy—weak, in the most wonderful, dizzy sort of way. "Nobody noticed me, not the cabdriver, not anyone in the drugstore."

"Taking the big chances now, are you?" He bent close and took her nipple in his mouth.

"Ungh." She let her head fall back. He drew on the tight bead of flesh and then licked her in a circle, bringing another needful sound rising from her throat.

"Wrap your legs around me." Eagerly, she obeyed, jumping up into his arms. He helped, boosting her so she could hook her ankles at the small of his back. He kissed her some more. "The condoms?" he asked against her mouth.

"My bag. Front hall," she managed, as she clutched his wide shoulders and kissed him as fervently as he was kissing her.

He took her to the front door. She reached out a hand and grabbed the big tote, sliding the handles into the crook of her elbow.

And then they were moving again, the bag bouncing against his thigh as he carried her, still kissing her, down the short hall to the main bedroom and straight to the bed. Gently, he lowered her so she was sitting on the mattress. Only then did he break the kiss.

Rising to his full height, he turned on the lamp as she pushed down her jeans and dropped them on the far side of the bed. He didn't move, just stood there by the lamp, watching her, in only her bra and panties now.

She felt more naked than naked. The panties were no more than a strip of lace. And the bra? It wasn't doing much, with the cups pulled down so he could see both her breasts—more than just *see* them, really. The bra seemed to hold them up for display.

Don't squirm, she commanded herself. *You're doing this. Own it.*

She sat as still as she could, breathing only a little bit frantically, her tote still hooked in the crook of her elbow.

Oh, the look on his face…

It was everything. Tender and hopeful and scared. Needful. Cautious, too. His way too kissable mouth curved in a hint of a smile.

The condoms, she reminded herself and got busy hauling her wig and her hat out of the bag, tossing them toward the bedside chair, finally coming up with the box of Trojan Magnums she'd bought. "I really hope I got the right ones. They have about a thousand different kinds. It's very confusing for a first-time condom buyer."

"Those will do fine," he said. She handed him the box. He removed a couple of condoms, set them on the night table and put the box beside them.

"Hold on," she said, abruptly enough that he glanced up at her in surprise.

"What?"

"I bought lube, too. It's in here somewhere." She had to stick her head in the tote to find it, but she wrapped her fingers around it at last. "Ta-da." She whipped out the tube.

He played along. "Yay." They stared at each other and then both of them smiled.

"Okay, then." She put the tube near the two pouches and dropped the tote over the edge of the bed. It landed with a plop on top of her jeans.

There was a moment, kind of awkward but also knowing and true. They stared at each other. This really was happening. They really were doing this.

Her first time.

It would be with Sten and that made her glad.

"Yeah?" he asked.

"Yeah," she whispered, her throat tight with emotion. "No doubt."

Chapter Eight

Sten dropped to a crouch and unlaced his boots.

Kicking them off as he rose again, he got rid of his socks, unzipped his pants and shoved them down along with his boxer briefs. The whole time, he held her gaze. The cream-colored cable-knit sweater he wore came off last.

And that was it. He was naked.

Madison scraped her teeth across her lower lip and sighed. He was so easy to look at, that handsome face, all those lean, hard muscles. His penis was half erect, the sight of it causing a stab of uneasiness as to what would actually happen here tonight.

"I'm nervous." There. She'd confessed it.

"Change your mind?" He asked it quietly, and the way his gaze held hers was reassuring, even soothing. "You only need to say so."

She drew in a shuddery breath as she shook her head. "No way. I'm, um, in."

He came down to her and gathered her close, pulling her onto his lap as his lips covered hers.

She could feel him growing harder and bigger against her hip. Her anxiousness ratcheted up again. But he just kept on kissing and caressing her in a way that was somehow an end in itself. His body said he wanted her. But still, he wasn't pushing her. He kissed her like it was enough for him—more than enough. Like it was everything.

Her nerves slowly settled. It was better, easier, with him wrapped all around her, holding her, skin to skin.

He pulled away enough to kiss the tip of her nose and each of her cheeks. And then his mouth touched hers again, lightly and then going deeper. He lay back on the pillows, pulling her with him. She ended up on top of him, kind of draped all over him. The long, drugging kiss continued. At the same time, he lavished her with long, slow caresses, down her back, over her shoulders, along her arms.

He took her bra away and then pushed down her panties—which got hung up around her knees. She wiggled to kick them off, but they hardly budged and that made her feel awkward and bumbling.

Because really, how it could possibly work, the mechanics of this thing called sex, if her panties were keeping her knees from opening?

But then he swept a confident hand down the outside of her thigh, turning her on top of him as he guided both of her legs to one side of him. In a slow caress, he brought that same hand beneath her other thigh and then lower, until his fingers touched the soft under-curves of her knees—and the unbudgeable panties. Just like that, the swatch of lace and elastic glided down over her shins. With a silly little giggle, she kicked them off at last.

Things got kind of hazy after that. She felt loose and easy, at home in her skin, with him all around her, stroking her, those wonderful fingers sliding down to cup her mound. She moaned when he did that. It felt so natural, so right.

He rolled them, so she was lying on her back. And he touched her some more. Her legs just fell open, kind of by themselves. He eased a finger in and then another. She was very wet and it felt really good and she kind of wished he would just keep doing what he was doing and never stop.

She moaned, rolling her head away from his drugging kiss, murmuring, "Sten. That. Right there. Never stop…"

He caught her lips again, kissed the words right off her mouth, his tongue sweeping behind her parted lips, arousing her almost as powerfully as the things his fingers were doing down below.

She came without a hint of warning, rising and hitting the crest on a cry of surprised delight. It wasn't her first orgasm. She might be a virgin, but she was intimately acquainted with her own body. It wasn't her first, but oh, it was glorious. It felt good to be with him, to let go in his arms—so very good.

Sten kissed her some more. Really, he was a master at this. He kissed her as though kissing her could never get old for him, and as for those hands of his…

The guy had mad skills, no question about it.

She lay there in afterglow, thinking that it couldn't get any better than what had just happened.

But then he kissed the curve of her jaw. He dropped a string of hot, lovely kisses along the column of her throat.

And lower.

Down and down and down he went, now and then pausing to nip at her with his teeth, bringing a gasp of excited surprise followed by a low hum of pure pleasure when those velvety lips of his were on her again.

She closed her eyes in lazy delight—only to lift her head and stare down the length of her naked body. "Oh!" she cried at the sight of her thighs draped over his broad shoulders, his mouth right there where his fingers had been before.

He glanced up. Their eyes met, but he just went on kissing her most private place.

With a sigh of surrender, she let her head drop back to the pillow. It was all too hot and urgent and wonderful. She felt the edges of her control fraying.

Control of what? she asked herself with another breathless little moan.

She had no control. She was flesh and bone and pure sensation and Sten played her like he knew every inch of her, like all of her—body, mind and heart—was his and his alone.

She let it happen, let another climax shudder through her, leaving her limp, utterly satisfied.

He eased out from between her thighs and wrapped her close in his arms again. She settled into his embrace with a sigh.

Paradise. Really. She'd gone to bed with this man who somehow spoke to her heart—and ended up in paradise. She rested her head against his hard chest, listened to his heartbeat and thought how she really ought to show some initiative. She might be inexperienced, but she could take the lead at least a little.

Then he tipped up her chin and kissed her again. She tasted herself on his tongue and all her good intentions to give him at least a fraction of the delight he'd given her faded like morning mist in the light of the sun. For this time, her first time, she would be totally selfish, let him show her the way.

He reached for the tube on the nightstand and squeezed some on his fingers. She watched him, thinking that she trusted him, and how easy that was for her—to trust this particular man. She'd been wondering, in recent years, if there was something wrong with her that she couldn't take a chance on a guy. She'd been lonely, in LA, where it just seemed safer not to give her trust at all.

Like breathing, to trust him. As natural as taking in air.

The lube was cool. At first.

But it quickly turned warm. The wonder started all over again, her pleasure rising as he worked his special magic on her willing flesh. She felt that lovely, building urgency and shut her eyes in surrender, knowing he would take her over the edge yet again.

When he pulled away before that happened, she moaned in protest and let her eyes drift open.

He had a condom in his hand. She watched as he rolled it down over his thick length and then spread some of the lube on it. His big hand looked so naughty to her, stroking himself.

She probably should have been worried. It was most likely going to hurt.

But her body was so loose, so easy and willing. Her heart beat with a deep, slow, hungry rhythm. She was much too turned on to be worried. This was exactly what she wanted—her first birthday goal, realized.

And best of all, with him.

She reached for him. He came to her and she opened to him. He guided himself to her core and began to ease himself into her ready heat.

It did hurt. But he went so slowly, lifting up on his forearms, his eyes commanding her, holding her, calming her. A muscle in his jaw flexed and he groaned her name as he held himself in check.

"So tight," he whispered, dipping his forehead down to hers, letting out a heavy sigh. A bead of sweat trickled from his temple onto hers, cooling as it slid back into her hair. "Maddy, you have to tell me. You have to say if you want me to stop."

She framed his face between her hands and locked her gaze with his. "No. Don't stop. Don't you dare."

He pushed in a tiny bit more. She must have winced because he went still again. He waited for her body to relax around him—and then he pushed in some more.

It took forever. But finally, it did happen. At last they were fully joined. Pressed deep within her, he held himself still and claimed her mouth with slow, drugging intent, kissing her endlessly as he gave her body time to fully accept him.

Only then did he begin to rock, but cautiously, withdrawing barely a fraction each time, coming back to her with measured care. The pain slowly turned to mere discomfort and from there to warmth and a good kind of fullness.

She wrapped her legs around him and pulled him down hard and tight to her.

That did it. "Maddy, I…" Whatever he'd meant to say turned into a groan.

He began to rock into her in steady, forceful strokes. It felt…not painful. But he was stretching her to the limit each time he filled her. She made herself breathe deep, go with it.

And it worked. Her body adjusted, opening around him. It still felt like a lot, like the very edge of too much.

But now it had also begun to feel good.

A moan escaped her.

That seemed to drive him onward. He came into her harder, increasing the pace.

After that, it was all she could do just to go with what was happening, to hold him and breathe into each stroke and keep herself willing, *there* in the moment, free in her body, fearless.

Open to him.

"I can't hold out," he growled down at her as his body rolled into her. "Maddy. I wanted this to be for you."

"It's okay."

"I'm letting you down…"

"No. You aren't."

"I have to…"

"It's okay, I promise you," she whispered, stroking his shoulders. "It's good." She gathered him closer.

"Maddy," he said. And nothing more.

He surged into her hard, bringing a guttural sound

from her, a sound of shock at how deep he was—and of submission, too.

Submission to him, to her feelings for him that were so strong, so real to her. She was lost to him, all his.

How had he done it? He'd busted through everything, torn down the walls she'd so carefully constructed so that no one could hurt her the way her mom had hurt her dad.

He had claimed not only her willing body.

He owned her heart.

Going utterly still in her arms, pressing himself so very deep, he came. She felt him pulsing within her.

She felt him everywhere.

"Maddy," he whispered on a final, deep sigh.

Chapter Nine

There was a knock on the slider as Madison, in sleep pants, a tank top and a stretched-out cardigan sweater, was choosing a pod for her morning coffee. Her phone, on the end of the counter, gave a buzz with an incoming text.

Paying no attention to the phone, she glanced over her shoulder toward the door to the deck. It was Coco, looking totally pulled-together in pink jeans, pink tennies and a pink-and-white-striped sweater. Really, the cuteness factor was off the charts with that kid.

Madison left the pod on the counter and went to open the door. Outside, it was foggy. She breathed in the moist coolness of it. Somewhere in the mist that obscured the water, a gull gave a long, fading cry.

"You and Uncle Sten had another sleepover without me, dincha?" the little girl accused. At Madison's easy shrug, Coco gave up on the attitude. "It's okay. Did you have fun?"

Oh, sweetheart. You have no idea… "Yes, we did, thank you."

Sten appeared from the short hall to the bedroom, his hair sleep-scrambled, barefoot and without his sweater. At least he'd pulled on his pants. Madison's belly got all fluttery just at the sight of him. They shared a long look, a lover's look full of intimate secrets. It was all new to her, to have a morning-after with a man, with *this* man. She could definitely get used to waking up in bed with him.

"Uncle Sten," said Coco sternly.

His bare feet whispered across the hardwood floor as he came and stood next to Madison. He draped one of those lean-muscled arms across her shoulders, so casually, as though putting his arm around her was something he did every day. She loved that he did that—loved it almost as much as the morning-after look they'd just shared.

"What's up, Coco-Puff?" he asked.

Frowning a little, her big blue eyes straying kind of nervously toward the other house and then back, Coco said, "Come over for breakfast—and hurry. We have to get ready for school, you know."

"Colleen!" It was Karin's voice from down between the houses.

"Uh-oh." Coco scrunched up her face.

"Up here!" Sten called to his sister as he gazed down at Coco, shaking his head.

"Well," Coco said, as if in answer to words he hadn't spoken. "You have to eat breakfast. Breakfast is good for you."

About then, Karin materialized out of the fog as she sprinted up the stairs on the far side of the cottage. "Okay, young lady. What did I say?"

Coco let out a long, exhausted-sounding sigh. "That Madison and Uncle Sten prob'ly wanted to fix their own breakfast." She parroted her answer as if by rote and then added hopefully, "But you didn't 'zackly say no."

"You didn't give me a chance." Karin glanced up from her daughter. "Sorry, you guys. She snuck over here while I was busy frying eggs."

"No problem." Madison tried to keep her expression serious, though everything Coco did just seemed completely adorable to her.

"So can they just come over, then?" Coco asked, raising her arms out to the side and then dropping them so hard her palms made twin slapping sounds against her pink jeans.

"Not this time. Your food's on the table. Go on back to the house and eat. I'll be there in a minute."

"But, Mom…" Coco whined.

"Now."

Dragging her feet, Coco trudged to the stairs and started down.

Karin said to her brother, "When you didn't come down for breakfast, she just knew you were over here. She started in on me to let her invite you both to join us. I put her off, but you know Coco."

Sten did know. "She took matters into her own hands."

Karin turned to Madison. "Holding the line on my little girl? Talk about a full-time job."

By then, the little girl in question was out of sight.

Still, Madison pitched her voice low against the chance that the child might overhear. "I don't know how you do it. I couldn't refuse her anything."

Karin made a humphing sound. "With kids, it's learn fast, or die—and now I can't invite you two over for bacon and eggs this morning without encouraging her to get sneaky when things don't go her way."

Sten's arm still rested across Madison's shoulder. She reached up and wrapped her hand around his, leaning into him, because it felt natural to do that. It felt utterly right.

"We get it," he said. And he nuzzled her hair, which she'd piled on the top of her head in a haphazard bun.

Did life get any better?

Doubtful.

"How 'bout this?" suggested Karin. "Just come over at breakfast-time any morning the mood strikes. That way, when Coco starts in on me, I can tell her you have an open invitation, that when you can make it for breakfast, you will."

Madison thanked her and Sten said, "Works for me."

Karin started for the stairs—but then stopped and turned back. "I have to say it." She pointed a finger at Sten then at Madison and back to Sten again. "I like where this is going. I truly do." With a low laugh, she left.

Sten shut the slider. "Ignore my pushy niece *and* my matchmaking sister."

She stepped right up to him and kissed him with a quick press of her lips to his. "Maybe I like where this is going, too."

He was silent. But his expression told her way more

than she wanted to know. As far as he was concerned, this special magic between them was just for now.

And no way was she ruining an absolutely perfect morning by getting into it with him about what might happen next. There didn't need to be a next—scratch that. There definitely did need to be a next. There *would* be a next.

But they didn't have to talk about that now.

She gave him a slow smile.

He put a finger under her chin. "Those dimples. You could finish a man off with those dimples, you know that?"

She kissed him again, taking her time about it, resting her palms on his warm, hard, bare chest.

He said, "Oh, and by the way. Just so you're aware. Liam told Karin why you're here, that you're a long-lost Bravo sister. Karin has promised to keep it to herself."

"All good," she said. "Want some breakfast?"

"You cook?" he teased.

She didn't roll her eyes, but she considered it. "I've cooked you breakfast once before as I recall, so you are well aware that I have a few life skills beyond memorizing other people's words and hitting my mark, thank you—scrambled and sausage?"

He gave her one of those looks containing equal parts fondness and desire. "Yes, please."

Sten brewed himself a pod of coffee and set the table as Maddy bustled around the kitchen getting the food on. It was fun, just being with her, doing simple, everyday things—waking up together, sharing breakfast.

They sat down to eat. "This is really good," he said, after his first bite.

"So, then. It's confirmed. I can fry sausage and scramble eggs. Yet more proof that I'm a woman you shouldn't underestimate." She sipped her coffee and looked downright smug.

He wanted to jump up, grab her, slam his mouth on hers and carry her back to the bedroom again. But he had to remember that last night was her first time. She was probably sore.

Over on the counter, her phone buzzed with a text. She ignored it.

"You need a ride anywhere today?" he asked.

"Nope. And really, you don't have to drive me everywhere. I'll just call a cab."

"Cab service around here isn't the best," he warned. "Sometimes it takes them forever to show up."

"I can wait. It's not like I'm on a tight schedule or anything."

"Maddy. You need a ride, you call me."

She spread marionberry jam on her toast, taking great care to spread it out to the crusts. "Are you saying you *want* to drive me?"

"I'm saying I'm my own boss and my schedule is flexible. I'm saying just call me and I'll take you where you want to go."

She set down her knife. "So many things I love about Oregon, including the amazing marionberry jam." She took a bite, chewed it slowly and swallowed. How could the sight of her eating toast be so sexy?

Was he over-the-moon for her? Definitely.

But it was okay. It was fine. As long as he kept things in perspective, why shouldn't they both have a really good time together?

She studied her toast as though considering where to bite it next. "But do you *want* to drive me?"

He wanted to do a lot more than drive her. Why not just admit it? "Hell, yes."

She slanted him a glance. "Because you want to be with me every minute you can, right?"

"That's right." It came out sounding like a growl.

"And I want to be with you." She showed him those dimples. He was a goner, no doubt about it. "Fair enough, then. I'll call you when I need a ride."

Her phone buzzed. She just sipped her coffee and enjoyed a bite of scrambled eggs. Then the phone rang.

"Fine," she muttered to no one in particular. She got up and answered it. "What is it, Rudy?" Her lush mouth a flat line and her turquoise eyes stormy, she listened to whatever her assistant had to say. "Just tell Myra that no, I haven't had a chance to read it. I am on vacation, and she knows it. I've told her like five hundred times— and you know what? I give up. Just have her call me. I'll tell her myself. Again... Yeah. Thanks... It's not you. You're the best. Mmm-hmm, bye." She ended the call. "Sorry," she said. "My agent is about to call and when she does I'm not going to say what she wants to hear. Myra's a powerhouse. She's not nice when you tell her things she doesn't want to hear."

"You want me to leave?"

"No. Although, I confess, you will probably wish you had."

Maybe he would. But he stayed where he was. This was her life and it wouldn't hurt for him to witness a reminder of that.

The phone hadn't finished the first ring when she

answered it. "Myra. Rudy said it was urgent. What can I do for you?"

The woman on the other end was a fast-talker. And a loud one. He could almost make out what she said even though Maddy hadn't put her on speaker. He got, "...to dream." And "...read it?"

"Myra, I told you. I'm not reading anything right now. I'm taking some much-needed family time."

Myra took issue—vehemently. He understood enough of the words to get that the agent didn't know Maddy had a family.

Maddy sucked in a tight breath through her nose. "Sorry. Figure of speech. Vacation, then. You *have* heard of those?"

Myra snapped back with something sassy.

Maddy said, "I realize I don't take vacations—not until now, anyway. And that is why I'm due one, wouldn't you say?"

Myra didn't sound like she would say that at all. She fired off a string of sentences, like the rat-tat-tat of a Gatling gun.

And Maddy replied, "Well, then tell them I understand. Thank them for thinking of me for the part. I'm not going to read it until I'm back in LA and I guess that means—no, wait." Maddy drew herself up tall. "Myra, just turn it down for me. It's as simple as that. Tell them it's not for me."

Myra squawked like an outraged duck.

"It's a movie," said Maddy. "Not world peace."

Myra disagreed. At length.

"Well, that is my answer, so there's nothing else to say right now. Anything else you need, reach out to Rudy. I'll call you as soon as I get back. We'll do lunch, talk about, um, the future…"

Myra started squawking again.

Maddy didn't let her get rolling. "I have to go. Take care, Myra."

The room seemed deathly quiet when she ended the call. She let out a long sigh.

Not really sure what to say, he asked, "You okay?"

Her slim shoulders were slumped. She rubbed the space between her eyebrows like she was getting a headache. "Just thinking about the people who depend on me for their livelihood. If I do walk away from acting, I'll need to start considering how and when to tell them that I'm not taking on any more projects."

"So, you're Myra's only client?"

That made her smile. "Hardly. She represents several big names. It's not really Myra I'm worried about. It's more, well, Rudy's a treasure and so is my house-keeper. And they're not the only great people who work for me. I'll need to start talking to them about where they might go next."

He shouldn't even ask. But he did. "Would you leave LA, then?"

"I'm thinking about it. I'm mostly there because that's where the film industry is. If I'm not in the in-dustry, well, why not try somewhere else?"

Somewhere else like, say, a small town in Oregon where her newly discovered family lived?

Why was he even letting himself think it?

She went on, "Then again, it will be a while before I have to let anyone go. I've got those two projects I'm already signed on for. And the house in Bel Air isn't my only property. I'll still be needing staff for at least the next few years—maybe longer, depending on what I decide I want to do next."

Staff? Last night, he'd had the best sex of his life with a gorgeous virgin—who had staff.

Talk about putting the situation in perspective.

And come on. He'd known her for two weeks. It was way too soon to be worrying about the future, anyway. They were having a great time and he needed to focus on that.

She seemed to have come to a similar conclusion. She asked brightly, "So what's up for you today?"

"The usual. I'll stop in to check on the progress at a house I'm flipping and then spend the afternoon at the Boatworks."

She gave him that look, the one that made him forget his own damn name. "I would love to see your flip house and I've been dying to look around the family business. Take me with you."

He tried to talk her out of it, tried to get her to see that drywall and tile wasn't all that interesting and a tour of the Boatworks would take ten minutes tops. Plus, he had a few hours of work he needed to do there.

Maddy was undeterred. "I'll read a book or take a walk or check in with my investment banker. Sheesh, Sten. Believe it or not, I know how to amuse myself." Her dimples were flashing and those eyes could coax a guy to jump off a cliff and smile all the way down to the canyon floor below.

Sten knew he was in big trouble. It was official: he could refuse Maddy nothing. "You sure?"

"What part of 'Take me with you' didn't get through to you?"

He surrendered. "Wear something you don't mind getting paint on."

"I need a shower. Care to join me?"

He folded his arms across his chest. "That's just mean and you know it. If I join you in the shower we'll spend the whole day in your bed." Which sounded pretty much perfect to him.

Her grin said it sounded good to her, too. "So that's a no?"

His pants were getting tighter. "Stop it."

She waved a hand. "Fine. Go...put on your tool belt. I'll meet you down at your garage in twenty minutes."

He didn't expect her to make it in twenty, no way. But seventeen minutes later, she was waiting in the driveway when he opened the garage door. He pulled out and she jumped in on the passenger side, looking ready to lay tile in a plain white T-shirt, old jeans and a pair of high-tops. She'd tucked her hair up in a short wig and finished the look with a Mariners cap and a pair of aviator sunglasses.

At the flip house, the painters were hard at work, inside and out. Sten gave her a quick tour, explained that the floors were covered in the main room because he was keeping the original hardwood. In the kitchen, he planned on refinishing the cabinets, installing quartz countertops and putting in new appliances.

"The yard's pretty bare," she said, dipping her head and peering at him over the tops of those flyboy shades. "What about curb appeal?"

"You've been watching those home improvement shows."

"I love them. Especially *Property Brothers*." She

pointed her thumb at herself. "Team Jonathan, all the way, baby."

He happily launched into way more detail than she could possibly need about driveway resurfacing, water-conserving irrigation systems and what would be planted, and where.

Marcus Dunbar, who ran the painting crew, stuck his head in the front door. "Sten. Got a minute?"

"Go ahead," Maddy said. "I'll be fine."

He wasn't outside for long. But when he came back in, she was nowhere in sight.

"I *love* you..." The voice—a guy's voice—came from down the hallway that led to the bedrooms.

What the hell? Sten turned the corner to the hall and spotted them down at the other end—a muscled-up guy with long hair knotted up in a manbun, and Madison. The guy had her cornered against the far wall. "I've seen all of your movies. *Heartbeats* about finished me. And *The Deepest Lie*? You were amazing."

"Hey." Sten practically shouted it as he strode toward them. The guy didn't turn. "Back off. Now." Sten grabbed the guy by his brawny shoulder and yanked him around.

"Dude." The guy had a beard—or the skimpy beginnings of one. Just a kid, one who apparently did a lot of lifting. He looked to be maybe twenty, tops. He put up both hands. "No offense. Seriously. Chill."

Maddy lifted her chin in Sten's direction. With the dark glasses, he couldn't tell if she was scared or not. "It's okay, Sten."

"No, it's not." He released his grip on the kid and demanded, "Name?"

"Uh. Darby Williams."

"I'm Sten. I own this house. You're on Marcus's crew?"

The kid finally had the sense to get nervous. "Uh. Yeah. New today—and man, I'm sorry. It's just, you know, *Madison Delaney.*" He said her name like that explained everything: all manner of unacceptable behaviors, up to and including boxing her in at the end of a hallway to gush all over her.

Sten shot another glance at Maddy, seeking a signal as to how he was supposed to deal with this fool.

She took off the dark glasses. Her eyes were calm—resigned, even. "Darby just wanted me to know he's enjoyed my movies."

"Enjoyed?" Darby was outraged. "Doesn't even come close."

"Listen, Darby." She turned those amazing eyes on the guy. "I'm kind of on the down-low here, so if you could maybe—"

"Madison." He plunked his fist on his paint-spattered Imagine Dragons T-shirt, right over his heart. "No one is gonna hear anything about you from me."

"Thank you." She blasted him that megawatt smile.

"God. It's an honor. Words are not enough."

Sten was thinking that maybe he ought to just fire the guy on the spot. That, or punch his lights out.

"Darby!" It was Marcus—at the front door, it sounded like. "Where'd you get off to?"

"On my way!" Darby turned to Sten. "Sorry, man. Really." And then to Maddy, "What you do? Never stop." And then he spun on his heel and sprinted off, leaving Sten and Maddy staring at each other.

"You told him who you were." He didn't mean to

sound accusing, but the sight of her boxed in by a strange guy had his adrenaline pumping.

"Remember what I said about misdirection? Didn't work on Darby. He spotted me and he *knew* it was me, so I had to go with it."

She could have been hurt. "Was that smart?"

Her eyes got frosty. "I did the best I could, Sten."

"The guy had you backed up against the damn wall."

"He was a fan. It's not a big deal."

"I shouldn't have left you alone in here."

"Please. You had no way of knowing someone would recognize me. He wasn't even in the house when you went out. I heard him come in the back door right after you left looking for that Marcus guy."

"How did he get you boxed into the hallway?"

"I was already in the hallway. He spotted me as he went by and stopped to ask if I knew where that Marcus guy was. You should have seen him when he realized it was me. He did this double take and his mouth fell open." She chuckled. "Really, it was kind of cute."

"Cute? He boxed you in."

"You keep saying that."

"I'll say it again. He boxed you in because I left you alone."

She let out a groan. "Now you're beating yourself up. Don't. It's not your fault. It can happen. And if I want to change things up in my life, I'm going to have to start developing coping strategies that don't involve a round-the-clock security team."

"Coping strategies? Some people are crazy. There's no coping strategy for dealing with a guy who's come unhinged."

"Darby is not unhinged."

"Close. Did you see that look in his eye?"

"It just surprised him to see some film star, here, in a half-finished flip house in Valentine Bay, that's all."

"Did he put his hands on you?"

"No, he did not—and as for coping with crazy people, yes, there are strategies for that. There are coping strategies for just about any situation."

"Yeah, and you can cope your ass off and things can still get out of hand."

"But they didn't. It all worked out."

His heart still pounded way too fast. He wanted to put a fist through the freshly hung drywall.

And yeah. He did know he was overreacting.

It was just, well, he couldn't stand it if anything happened to her. The need to take care of her, to protect her, keep her safe had become an imperative.

When had that happened? He wasn't sure.

But somehow, at some point, he'd become completely invested in her well-being.

He kept telling himself that he saw the situation realistically. He liked her a whole hell of a lot. And he wanted her safe. Add to that, he just plain wanted *her*. Bad. And constantly.

And as of last night, they were lovers. A man needed to protect his woman.

Even if it wasn't meant to last.

And it *wouldn't* last, he reminded himself for the umpteenth time. In a few weeks, she would return to LA, make her next movie, work things out with that pushy agent of hers and realize that being a big star wasn't such a bad gig, after all.

All her talk about making a different kind of life was just that—talk.

If he had any sense of self-preservation at all, he ought to get some distance from her.

Yeah. Distance. Good luck with that. All she had to do was smile at him and he forgot all the reasons he shouldn't have let her get under his skin.

"Sten." She hooked the sunglasses in the neck opening of her T-shirt and took a step closer.

Even with the smell of fresh paint heavy in the air, he got a whiff of petunias, sweet and yet sharp. Her mouth was tipped up to him. He was aching to take it.

"Sorry," he said. "Darby freaked me out."

She lifted her arms and propped them on his shoulders. "You okay now?"

"Yeah." He dared to rest his palms on the swell of her hips. Back in the day, before he'd had the bad judgment to try to find love and happiness with Ella Robson, he'd had his hands on a good number of pretty women. Not one of them—Ella included—had felt the way Maddy did, like the curve of her waist was just made for his hands.

She was smart and funny and kind and beautiful. And he wanted her. Who wouldn't?

It's not deathless love. Get over yourself.

He kissed her, slow and sweet and just deep enough to ease the coiling tension inside him, to reassure himself that she really had taken the encounter with that Darby kid in stride.

"So no harm done," she said when he lifted his head. "What's next?"

Madison was having a fabulous time.

The flip house really interested her. She'd always thought it might be kind of fun, to fix a house up to sell, to figure out cost-conscious ways to make it better, make potential buyers want to live there.

Plus, Sten had just kissed her. Kissing Sten was one of the premier experiences of her life, an experience she planned to repeat. Frequently.

They went to Larson Boatworks next.

The family business consisted of a series of hangars and a row of boat slips on the Columbia River not far from Astoria. Most of the boatbuilding was done in the larger two hangars. The smaller hangar was the office.

They stopped in at the office first. Karin was busy behind the counter. She gave them a wave and a smile.

Sten led the way to the full-size hangars and showed her the projects they were working on now, including a sixty-six-foot commercial fishing vessel called the *Lady Defiant*. The *Lady* was getting a major refit. When the work was complete, the boat would be seventy-eight feet long and six feet wider than originally, with what Sten called a bulbous bow.

Otto Larson was at work on the *Lady Defiant*. Madison greeted him, but she also took care to keep a low profile with the guys who worked for the Larsons. She wore her hat and glasses the whole time.

Once Sten had given her the tour, he had work to do.

Madison left him to it and strolled around the property, keeping to herself. She found a nice spot on a little dock in sight of the hangar where she'd left Sten.

For a while, she played games on her phone. Then she switched to the reading app and dug into a bestselling mystery she'd been meaning to read for months now and never had time for. It was peaceful on the dock, with the sound of the river lapping around her. When she got tired of reading, she just sat there in the mild sunlight, watching the giant boats out on the wide river.

After a half hour of boat-watching, she almost nodded off. Time to get up and move around a bit. She texted Sten to let him know she was dropping in on Karin and headed for the office at the other end of the yard.

A woman she didn't remember seeing earlier stood behind the front counter. Madison introduced herself as the Larsons' tenant and asked if Karin was anywhere around.

The woman stapled a stack of papers and handed them to a guy in overalls and a tan cap. "There you go, Denny. You're all set." She pointed back over her shoulder. "Karin's taking a break. Through that door there."

The door in question led to an empty employees' lounge with a basic kitchen setup in an L-shape along two of the walls and a table in the center of the room, five molded plastic chairs around it. One of the chairs was pulled out. On the table in front of it sat a half-finished sandwich and a can of ginger ale. No sign of Karin.

Directly across from the door to the office area, there was another door with a restroom sign on it. Karin was probably in there.

Madison pulled out one of the chairs. But before she could sit down, she heard the sounds from the other side of the restroom door. Someone was being sick.

Karin?

Who else could it be? Madison almost rushed to her aid.

But then, what if it wasn't Karin? That could definitely be awkward. It could be awkward even if it was

Karin. Sten's sister might not appreciate a woman she really hardly knew knocking on the bathroom door when she thought she was alone.

So Madison just stood there by the table, wanting to help and not knowing if she should.

Finally, the heaving noises stopped. The toilet flushed. She heard water running.

Karin emerged. Her cheeks were red and her eyes watery. She held a damp paper towel to her mouth. "Madison." She lowered the towel and smiled in a wan sort of way.

Madison met her midway between the table and the restroom door. "Are you sick?"

"It's a long story."

Madison wrapped an arm around her. Karin didn't resist the attention. They went back to the table, where Karin dropped into the chair with the food in front of it.

"Ugh," said Sten's sister as she glared at the leftover sandwich. "That's enough of that." She shoved it away and then drank from the can of ginger ale, setting it down with great care and bringing the wet towel back to her mouth.

Madison hovered at her elbow. "Are you going to be sick again?"

Karin shook her wild, dark hair and laughed—or at least, Madison thought it was a laugh. Sten's sister still had the towel pressed to her face. Maybe she was gagging.

"How can I help?" Madison cast a frantic glance around the room, seeking a wastebasket or some other appropriate receptacle in case Sten's sister really was about to hurl.

But then, Karin lowered the towel and took a few

slow breaths through her nose. "I'm okay," she said. "Really. I think it's stopped for now."

Cautiously, ready to leap to Karin's rescue at the first sign of heaving, Madison lowered herself into the next chair. She took off her hat and her sunglasses and set them on the table.

Karin tossed the towel down and put her hands to her flushed cheeks as if to cool them. Slowly, her eyes lifted to lock with Madison's. They stared at each other.

And it was right then, as their gazes collided, that Madison *knew*.

Chapter Ten

"Liam's?" Madison asked in a whisper, wondering what was the matter with her to ask such a thing. Not only was it no concern of hers, the question made no sense.

Except it did make sense. To Karin. "Yep. You're going to be an auntie." Karin caught her trembling lower lip between her teeth. Her eyes gleamed with tears.

But Karin didn't cry. She grabbed Madison's hand between both of hers. "Listen. You can't tell anyone. Please. Not Sten. Definitely not Liam. I'll do it. I will. Eventually."

"I promise you I won't say a word."

"Thank you. I'm just not ready to get into it with anyone yet. I'm still dealing with the fact that it's even happening, you know?"

Madison nodded. "I totally get it. I mean it. No one is going to hear anything from me."

"Good." Karin released her grip on Madison's hand and grabbed the ginger ale. "It was just supposed to be a one-night thing, you know?" She drank. "But there was more than one night. There were several nights. I kept saying never again. I'm so full of crap. Because anytime I could get away, I would call him. And each time I would remind him—and myself—that it was the last time." She glanced up at Madison again. "I've known him forever, since kindergarten, can you believe it? We're the same age."

"I know. Aislinn told me you two were in the same grade in school and Sten mentioned that you and Liam dated in high school."

"High school." Karin stared into the middle distance. "It seems like a million years ago. Sometimes I…" Right then, Madison's phone buzzed with a text. Karin blinked. "You should check that. It could be Sten."

Madison pulled the phone from her pocket.

Karin was right.

Ready to go. I'm on my way to the office.

"I hate to leave you." Madison scooted closer to Karin and gave her arm a reassuring squeeze. "I can put him off."

But Karin just shook her head. "No. You go on. Thanks for holding my hand. It helped. You're a keeper."

Madison sighed. "Maybe tell your brother that."

"Believe me. I have."

A few minute later, Sten came through the door from the front office. "What have you two been up to?"

"None of your business," his sister said.

* * *

That night, Sten took Madison out to a nice restaurant on the river in Astoria. She wore a red wig and red-framed glasses—glasses she'd once used in a movie role. They had regular glass for the lenses. He said she looked hot and someone was bound to recognize her.

She shrugged. "Whatever happens, I'll live."

What happened was nothing. Nobody recognized her. Or if they did, they either respected her privacy or plain didn't care.

It was a great little restaurant, with windows framing a view of the river. Old pilings stuck up out of the water, seagulls perched on them contentedly. From their table, they could also see the Astoria-Megler Bridge arching over the wide Columbia all the way to the Washington side.

They shared a nice bottle of wine and she snapped a lot of pictures of the river and the seagulls.

"Just like a tourist," he teased.

She took pictures of him, too, so sexy and handsome in his gray fisherman's sweater, his hair kind of windblown, looking back at her through her phone's camera lens as though he wanted to eat her right up.

And he did, too—but that was much later, in her bed at the cottage. They made love for hours. Past midnight, as she drifted off to sleep, she realized she had never felt this close to anyone.

Or this happy.

Thursday first thing, she got a call from Percy. The DNA results were up online.

"Oh, Percy." She giggled like a nervous kid. "Just tell me."

"Well, all right then. It's official. You are my great-niece and you have a great-aunt, our dear Daffodil. You have five brothers and four sisters. Because of course, we count Aislinn, though the results show she is no blood relation to you or the others. And we include Finn, as well. He may have disappeared years ago, but we all have faith he will return to us in time."

She thanked Percy, hung up and grabbed Sten in a celebratory kiss.

And then she called Aislinn.

"Madison, hey!" said the sister of her heart.

"I just… I needed to hear your voice. Percy called. The DNA results are in."

"Yeah. He called me, too. He's such a sweetheart. I think he wanted to make certain I was okay with the news."

Madison wanted the same thing. "And, um, are you okay with it?"

"It's taken me a while to get there," Aislinn admitted. "But yes. I am—and you?"

"The same. Kind of jazzed, in fact. To have a whole family when I thought I had no one. It's pretty spectacular."

"Excellent. And you know I have to ask. Things with Sten?"

He'd disappeared into the master bath. She could hear the shower running in there. "Good," she said. "Really good."

"So then, you two made up—as I predicted."

Madison groaned. "You think you know everything, don't you?"

"Just don't you dare break the poor guy's heart."

"You assume the heartbreaking will be done by me?"

"What?" Aislinn put on a tough voice. "Is he giving you grief? And I always thought he was such a great guy. Just say the word. I'll have a long talk with him."

"Um, we're having a good time, that's all." Hey. It was the safest thing to say. Because they definitely were having a beautiful time and who knew what would happen in the future, anyway?

"You are such a bad liar," Aislinn chided.

"And you, Aislinn Winter, are a hopeless romantic."

"Yes, I am and damn proud of it."

Madison no sooner hung up with Aislinn than Daniel called to welcome her to the family all over again and to remind her that she was invited to dinner on Sunday. She promised to be there.

"Bring Sten," he added.

She didn't even ask how he knew about her and Sten. The family seemed to have a very effective communication grapevine. "I'll invite him," she promised.

As they said goodbye, Sten emerged from the bathroom in clean jeans and a fresh T-shirt, his hair still wet from the shower.

"The DNA results are in," she said. "I am officially a Bravo."

"Great news." He grabbed her and spun her around.

"It's not really a surprise," she said when he set her down. "But still. It feels good to know for sure."

He kissed her and then asked, "Breakfast at the other house?"

"I'm in."

In Karin's kitchen, Coco had set places at the table for them. "Madison, you sit by me." She patted the chair beside her.

Madison took the chair she offered as Sten grabbed

the coffeepot and filled them each a cup. It was the usual, with the kids talking over each other and Otto smiling benevolently.

Sten filled the empty mug at Karin's place, too. But when his sister finished dishing out the eggs and sat down to eat, she left the full mug untouched and only had a few bites of the oatmeal she'd fixed for herself.

Sten frowned at her. "You okay?"

Karin waved a hand and said she was fine, after which Ben launched into a detailed description of his latest science project.

Coco waited impatiently for her brother to finish, and then told Madison all about the birthday party she was attending that Saturday. "There will be face-painting and maybe even pony rides..."

As Coco chattered away, Karin got up and carried her barely touched oatmeal and full mug of coffee to the sink. When she returned to the table, Madison managed to catch her eye. Karin smiled at her. *I'm fine*, that smile said. *Don't worry about me.*

Madison *would* worry. But she would keep the other woman's confidence as she'd promised to do.

Fifteen minutes later, Karin was herding the kids toward her SUV to drive them up to the bus stop for school. Otto left right after her. Sten had stuff to do at the flip house and then he would go on to the Boatworks, too.

Back at the cottage on her own, Madison actually tried to read a couple of the scripts she'd brought with her from LA. Maybe one of them would thrill her and she'd suddenly realize she couldn't give up acting, after all. And maybe she was feeling just a little guilty about Myra's last call. The agent was only doing her job. Until recently Madison had been grateful to have someone like Myra making sure the best roles always came her way.

Tried. That was the operative word when it came to reading those scripts. She just couldn't get herself to focus. Her mind refused to cooperate. She yawned a lot as she read, though objectively she knew that the material was excellent.

Around eleven she gave it up and went for a walk on the beach. After that, she called a cab, chose a wig and a hat and went to Safeway on her own. It was great. Nobody bothered her.

Back at the cottage, she put her groceries away and considered calling Myra—and then wondered if maybe she was losing her mind. What good would calling Myra do? The woman was a shark and calling her now would just be leaving a trail of bloody chum on the water. Myra would be after her all over again to fly back to LA ASAP and sign on for the project Madison didn't even want.

It was just…

Well, getting the DNA results somehow seemed to make everything so clear and final. She was a Bravo. Whatever lingering doubts she might have had were gone now. She really did have a whole family right here in Valentine Bay. She *liked* them. Over time, she wanted to get to know them better.

But the real goal in coming here had been accomplished. She'd found her family. Sunday, at Daniel's, they would celebrate that.

And then…

Well, then there was her life that she still wanted to change up completely.

Her life—and Sten. He mattered to her. A lot. She wanted to talk with him about what they might have together going forward.

Was it too soon to talk about that?

Not to her.

Sten, though? She had an uneasy feeling that he was a long way from ready to discuss the future with her.

Sten was in his office trying to come up with a workaround for an issue with the refit of the *Lady Defiant* when Karin stuck her head in the door.

"You've got company," his sister said. She seemed really pissed off. "It's Ella Robson," she added, and Sten understood the reason for that sneer on her face. "Happy to tell her to go pee up a rope."

Was he tempted to let Karin get rid of her? Absolutely. But it wasn't her problem. "Thanks. Send her in."

A minute later, Ella strutted in dressed to kill in itty-bitty short-shorts and a silky top, her long sable hair loose on her shoulders. The look was a far cry from the low-key button-downs and dressy jeans she used to wear.

She shut the door and kind of lounged back against it. "You blocked me."

"Because we're through."

"I had to see you. Oh, Sten. I was afraid you would refuse to talk to me."

"I asked you never to contact me again before I blocked you. So yeah, I don't want to talk to you."

She tipped her head to the side and gave him a flirty little smile. "But you *are* talking to me."

"It seemed unfair to leave my sister to deal with you. Please. Just stop with the head games and leave."

The flirty smile morphed into a sad frown and pleading eyes. "It's over with Darrin. Really, truly over. Forever."

"I'm sorry to hear that." And he was. He supposed. For poor Joey, at least.

"I'm trying to tell you I made a huge mistake breaking up with you. You're the best man I ever—"

"Ella. You need to put on your listening ears. I'm not interested."

"Oh, come on. If you would just—"

"No. It's time for you to go now. Please don't come back."

"But, Sten, if only we could—"

"There's nothing more to say. Please go."

It went on like that, with her trying to convince him that he should give her another chance and him trying to figure out new and more emphatic ways to say no. The problem was, she wouldn't go. Asking her to leave, *telling* her to leave—well, the words just weren't working.

And yet grabbing her and dragging her out of the building to get rid of her? That had to be an assault charge in the making.

Finally, there was a tap on the door.

"Don't answer that." Ella spread her arms wide, blocking the door. "Please."

"Open the door, Ella."

"Sten, I'm trying to *talk* to you."

Another knock. Karin called, "Sten? You okay in there?"

"Ella, move away from the damn door."

"This is your last chance," she said. "If you don't talk to me now, you'll never see me again."

"That's what I want, Ella. Never. To. See. You. Again." He made each word a sentence in hopes of finally getting through.

And maybe he did. At least she peeled herself away from the door and came toward him. "You really mean that?"

"I don't know how to make it any clearer to you." He dodged around her and opened the door.

Karin was standing on the other side. "Whoa." She blinked at him in surprise. "Need some help in here?"

At that moment, he forgave his baby sister for every one of the million and one ways she could drive him crazy. "Thanks. Ella's just leaving."

"Omigod," Ella whispered, bringing her hand to her mouth in what looked like pure shock. "You really mean it. You…you don't want another chance with me…"

How many times did he have to say it? He parroted flatly, "I really mean it. I don't want another chance with you. Goodbye, Ella."

"Oh, Sten!" Ella cried.

Karin chose that moment to burst out laughing.

Ella whirled on her. "Bitch," she proclaimed, after which she tossed her head. Her silky hair fanned out and settled, just so, on her shoulders. She aimed her scowl at Sten. "That does it. I am so done with you, Sten Larson. Forever." And she marched out the door.

Karin, still laughing, sagged against the doorframe. Sten scooted past her and followed Ella out into the front office, just to make she was actually leaving. She kept walking. Rounding the counter, she flung the outside door wide, stormed through and slammed it behind her.

"You're enjoying this way too much," Sten said to his sister, who kept right on laughing.

Outside, he heard a car start up. Through the window next to the outer door, he saw Ella's Jetta speed away.

Karin peeled herself off the doorframe and went to her desk. "I'm sorry for laughing." She dropped into her chair.

"No, you're not."

"Okay, okay. I couldn't help myself. But you are so right. I'm not sorry in the least. That was just too perfect." She waved her hand in front of her face as a few more random giggles escaped her. "Really brightened my day, you know?"

Sten shook his head. "You said you never liked her, but I guess I didn't realize how *much* you didn't like her."

"Actually, I did like her at first. She was nice to me then, because she was sucking up to you. Once she had you, she didn't need to make an effort with the rest of us."

"So what you're saying is that I was a complete idiot for ever getting involved with her."

"You're no idiot. You're just a man who was finally ready for the right woman when the wrong one came along."

"Okay, on second thought maybe I'd rather just be a damn idiot." That brought another giggle from his sister—and he was still kind of worried that he hadn't seen the last of Ella. "Tell me honestly. Do you think she's really gone for good?"

"Yeah. I do. How can she manipulate you if you

don't buy her act? That drama queen has gotten your message and she is never coming back."

Madison heard Sten's truck drive in at a little after six that night. A few seconds later, her phone beeped with a text: Want some company?

With that lovely rising feeling in her chest just at the prospect of seeing his face, she texted back: I do. Especially if the company is you.

When he showed up a couple of minutes later, he took her in his arms and kissed her until her head was spinning. She pulled him inside and they tore at each other's clothes.

After a breathtaking interlude in the bedroom, they got dressed again and went out to the kitchen.

She fried the pork chops she'd bought that day and served them with baked potatoes and a green salad. They ate. After the meal, when she asked him if he wanted coffee, he got up, grabbed her hand and led her back to the bedroom again.

What was it with her clothes around him? They seemed to fall off of their own accord. Once he had her naked, he knelt before her on the bedside rug.

Oh, the things that man could do with his lips and his hands. The aftershocks of the pleasure he brought were still rocking through her when she pulled him onto the bed with her, rolled on top of him and kissed her way down to where he jutted up hard and ready from the nest of dark hair between his powerful thighs.

It wasn't the first time she'd used her hands and her eager mouth on him. But it was the first time she felt strong and confident making love to him that way. It not only turned her on, it also felt natural and right.

Afterward, she cuddled up next to him, pulled the sheet over them and invited him to dinner at Daniel's on Sunday. "It's kind of a DNA-results party. Daniel specifically said I should invite you to come—and don't ask me how he knew about us. I never said anything. Believe me, I would have. But I haven't had a chance. Maybe Aislinn told him."

He braced an elbow on his pillow and rested his head on his hand. "Isn't that more of a family thing?"

She got the strangest feeling then. A sense of his retreat from her.

It hurt. Like he was taking away something she needed to live: water, food. The very air she breathed.

And she might have been short on real experience with men when she arrived in Valentine Bay. But she was learning fast.

If he was pulling away, she was going to make him say so right to her face. Yeah, she was new at this romance thing. But she'd never been afraid to come out with whatever was on her mind.

She captured his blue gaze and wouldn't let go of it. "Right. It's a family thing. Like breakfast at your sister's is a family thing. And razor clamming. Those are *your* family things and you and your family were kind enough to include me. Me and my family want to include you in Sunday dinner. Are you saying you don't want to go?"

He stared at her for a long time. Finally, he said, "God. You are so beautiful."

"Thank you. But you didn't answer my question."

"I just think we should kind of watch it, that's all, be realistic about this. Not get in too deep."

Did that piss her off?

Oh, most definitely.

At first. She let the hurt and anger wash through her, waited for it to settle down to a dull throb in the vicinity of her heart before she asked, "You really meant what you said Sunday night, didn't you? That you just wanted this time with me, every minute we could *steal*?"

It took him way too long to answer. And then it got worse because he answered with one painful word. "Yeah."

"But you're *crazy* about me?" She tried not to pile on the irony and knew that she didn't fully succeed.

"I am, yeah. I think it will probably mess me over really bad when you go."

She sat up, pulling the sheet with her to cover her breasts. Because it was like that between them suddenly. All at once, he was someone she didn't want to be bare in front of. "It doesn't have to end when I go back to LA. You know it doesn't. We could—"

"Maddy. Leave it alone. Let's just enjoy what we have for right now. Please."

"I don't understand you."

"What's to understand?"

"It's like you're trying to prove that things can't work out with us. One way or another, you'll make sure it all goes to crap and then you can say you knew that it would all along."

"Look." He lied with his eyes. He watched her so tenderly, begging her to understand that he knew best and what he knew was that she would go and he would stay and that would be the end of them. "I'm the first guy you've been with. There are going to be other guys.

The day will come when you look back on this time
we had together and—"

"Ungh!" She cut him off with a hard groan aimed
at the ceiling. "Please. Believe it or not, there are still
people in this world who have one sexual partner their
whole lives and are totally happy about that. So can
we not talk about my next boyfriend while I'm still in
bed with you?"

He nodded. Slowly. "You're right. Sorry."

And really, why was she pushing this? Hadn't she
promised herself she would take this thing with him
one day at a time, enjoy every moment and not weigh
it all down with expectations?

She wanted him, *loved* him even. And that meant
she wanted *more* of him—of his kisses and his tender touch. Of that fine body of his that felt like home
when he held her tight. Of his time and attention, his
great laugh, his kindness and that way he had of seeing things that made the world all new to her, made the
path before her clear and bathed in light.

So, all right. She wanted him and imagining the two
of them together into the future seemed utterly easy
and right to her.

It just wasn't that way for him.

And the guy had a right to his doubts. He was only
trying to be honest about them, trying to put the brakes
on a little. Could she really blame him for believing that
in the end the big movie star from LA would eventually return to her Bel Air mansion and her amazing,
perfect, big-time career, leaving him far behind?

She made herself put away her frustration with him.
"All right then. That's a no-thank-you on the post-DNA
party."

"It's just better that way."

"Wrong. But you're certainly entitled to your opinion. I really don't want to fight."

"Neither do I." He pulled her close again. She settled her head on his shoulder.

And then he asked, "What time do you need to be there?"

She rubbed her palm against the light dusting of hair on his hard chest, enjoying the springy feel of it against her skin. "Around three."

"I'll drive you. You can call me when you're ready to come home."

"I'll get a cab." Before he could argue, she pressed her hand harder against his chest, communicating that she meant what she said. "If you're not going, you're not driving me."

"Maddy…"

"Forget it. Let it go."

Sten's goal was to keep his outlook realistic when it came to him and Maddy. The whole point was to not get in too deep.

He knew it would be bad when she left. But maybe, by drawing the line on her now and then, he could make his future misery a little less so.

That was his plan.

Didn't really shake out that way, though.

When he got home Friday afternoon, he went straight to her. A bee to honey? Moth to a flame? Yeah. That was him. A walking, talking, can't-get-enough-of-her cliché.

But he couldn't stop thinking what a dumb-ass he'd been over Ella once. Having to come face-to-face with her again had brought it all way too sharply home. Three years of his life he'd wasted thinking he was in love with that woman.

And now, well, he couldn't even remember what he'd seen in her. He'd made up a woman to love and put Ella's face on her.

Screw love.

Simple as that.

Yeah, he knew Maddy was nothing like Ella. Maddy was generous and kind and good. She was beautiful inside and out.

But she would leave. She would leave for completely different reasons than Ella had. The kind of career she'd built, well, she might be going through something of a life crisis, what with learning she had a family she'd never met and finding out that her parents had no blood relationship to her. She might tell herself she needed a big change in her life to cope with all the shocking revelations that had come her way lately.

But in the end? Nobody walked away from Maddy's kind of success. And he, well, he didn't fit with her, not really. She needed to be free to find the kind of man who liked the high-powered life she led.

He didn't resent that she would go. And no matter what she said about wanting to be with him when her time in Valentine Bay was through, she didn't need him trailing around after her as she got on with her real life. And he'd never planned to live anywhere but here.

And that was what it came down to. Valentine Bay was not her life. She was on vacation, pure and simple. In the end, she would leave.

And he would stay.

Sunday afternoon, she rode off in a cab and didn't come back until after two Monday morning. He knew what time she returned because he was wide awake—in his own bed, damn it—and heard a car pull in at the front of the house. A car door closed and the vehicle drove away.

He lay there staring up toward the dark ceiling, reminding himself that he was not getting up to go make sure she was all right.

If she needed him for some reason, she would let him know.

Three minutes later, his phone lit up.

Grinning like the fool he was for her, he grabbed it.

R U worried? Don't be. I'm home safe. She included a selfie taken in the cottage kitchen. Her eyes looked kind of bleary and she had a goofy grin on her face.

Are you drunk?

Not exactly. Nice time at Daniel's. Went out afterward with Hailey and Harper to Keely's mom's bar. I got kinda reconized. Had to autograph some napkins. But it's OK. Everone was relly nice. Wish U were there.

You're drunk.

If I send U a sexy pic will U come over?

Don't tempt me.

Silly. That's the point. 2 tempt U.

Even drunk, she made him laugh. I'm on my way.

Wait. I didn't send the pic yet.

And she sent one. It was a close-up. Her eyes were crossed and she was sticking out her tongue.

He responded, I'm coming.

Told ya. I'm super hot. You can't resist me.

She thought she was kidding. He chuckled to himself as he pulled on his pants and headed out shirtless in flip-flops.

She was waiting with the slider open, barefoot, her body braced against the doorframe. Those blue-green eyes were low and lazy. She looked a little wobbly, like she needed the doorframe to keep her from slithering to the floor. "Did I ever mention that you look really good without your shirt?"

"Thanks." He took her by the shoulders, kissed her forehead and turned her around. "Bedtime."

"I don't know. My feet are tired of walking."

He bent and scooped her up against his chest. With a soft little sigh, she wrapped her arms around his neck and rested her head under his chin. He carried her to the bedroom.

"It's fun to have sisters," she said when he laid her on the bed and set to work undressing her. "We talked about starting a business together, Harper, Hailey and me. Creating kids' parties. We would play clowns and magicians, provide the entertainment, you know? Oh, and we're keeping it quiet, that I'm a Bravo, for the time being. News like that would put the paps in a frenzy.

We don't need that. I told them I was quitting acting. They might even have believed me. Unlike some people I could mention." She fell silent. Unresisting, she let him turn her this way and that to get her out of her clothes. Eventually, she piped up with, "At the Sea Breeze, we did Jell-O shots. They were too sweet. But it's a funny thing about Jell-O shots. The more you have, the better they taste."

He had her down to her bra and panties by then. "Sleep shirt?"

"Yes, please. Top drawer, left. Gimme the black one. It's really soft." She was wiggling around trying to unhook her bra as he went to get it.

When he returned, she'd gotten rid of the bra. On her back, naked from the waist up, she stared dreamily into the middle distance.

"Can you sit up and raise your arms?"

"I'm not incapacitated," she replied with great dignity and popped to a sitting position. Fisting her hands, she shoved them high in the air. He eased the shirt on, smoothing it down over her gorgeous body. "Thanks." She scrunched up her face. "Tomorrow, I prob'ly won't feel so good."

He went to the bathroom and came back with a couple of aspirin and a full glass of water. "Take your medicine." She downed the pills and drained the glass.

He put the glass on the nightstand. "Come on. Under the covers."

"'Kay." She dropped back to the pillow. He settled the blankets over her. "You come to bed, too," she commanded.

As if he could tell her no.

He kicked off his flip-flops, got rid of his jeans and slid under the covers with her.

"There we go." She rolled to her side and assumed the small spoon position. He wrapped himself around her. Peace settled over him and he drifted toward the sleep that had eluded him all night.

"I love you, Sten," she said in a near-whisper and snuggled in closer.

The words sounded unbearably sweet. He almost returned them. But that wouldn't be wise.

Chapter Eleven

Three days later, in the afternoon while Sten was still at the Boatworks, Coco knocked on the glass door of the cottage. She had a temporary tattoo of a butterfly on her left cheek and a plastic pail in either hand, each containing shovels, scoops and rakes of various sizes.

"Ben's at soccer practice," she announced when Madison slid open the door. "Grandpa said I could come over and see you but not to be a pest."

"You are never a pest."

Coco beamed. "That's what I said." She held up the pails. "You want to go make a sandcastle, maybe?"

"What a stellar idea."

"Here." Coco handed her one of the pails. "Look." She peeled down her lower lip. "I lost a tooth."

"Wow." Madison admired the empty space where the baby incisor had been. "Your first?"

"Yep," replied Coco proudly. "C'mon. Let's go." She headed for the stairs. Madison followed her down to the sand.

Several feet from the shore, they dropped to their butts and removed their shoes and socks, leaving them there, away from the waves.

Barefoot, they got to work, hauling wet sand up to the spot they'd chosen near their shoes, packing it down, then going for more. Madison enjoyed Coco's chatter as well as the sound of the waves and the misty sweetness of the wind that kept blowing her hair into her face.

She wasn't sure what alerted her that they weren't alone, but all of a sudden, a shiver skated along her arms. She looked up and there were two guys not forty feet away, each with a camera plastered to his face.

The paps had found her.

"Coco," she said softly. "Let's get all our stuff and go back to the cottage."

Coco glanced up from the sand she was patting. "But we're making a sandcastle."

"I know, but we have to go now. I will explain everything as soon as we get back to the house."

Coco frowned. But then she shrugged. "Okay. I'm kinda thirsty anyway." They put the tools in the buckets, snatched up their shoes and headed for the stairs.

"Madison!" called one of the cameramen.

"Who's that?" demanded Coco.

"I don't know his name, sweetheart. But I want to talk to him for a minute. Meet you on the deck?"

"But I want to come with—"

"Please."

Something in her expression must have gotten through. Coco took off.

Photojournalists were not allowed to trespass on private property—not that they necessarily always obeyed the laws. However, nobody owned the ocean and the two men were staying very close to the waves.

Madison marched right up to them. They just kept snapping as she approached. "No photos of that child," she said. They weren't supposed to take pictures of children, anyway—except for child actors.

And actually, the rules she kept reassuring herself they had to follow were California rules. She hoped they applied in Oregon, too.

"Not interested in the kid," said one, camera still over his face.

"Why does it matter?" the other fired back, adjusting his giant lens. "Who is she?"

"A local," Madison said and added with emphasis, "Not an actor."

"Show us those dimples," the second guy demanded.

"What brings you to Valentine Bay?" asked the first.

It was only going to devolve from here. Madison turned on her heel and headed for the cottage again, not once looking back.

Coco, leaning on the railing above, was waiting for her. She ran up the steps. They left the pails of castle-making equipment at the door along with their shoes, brushed the sand from their feet and went inside, where Madison explained as simply as she could that the men on the beach were photographers taking pictures of her because she was an actress.

Coco listened attentively and then asked for a cold drink. "Or a Popsicle. Do you have Popsicles?"

Madison gave her a glass of orange juice and then walked her back to the other house, using the front door this time. The paps were nowhere in sight. That didn't mean they weren't lurking nearby.

When Sten got home, she told him what had happened. He went out and looked around, but found no sign of anyone else in the cove. They went over to the other house to report the incident to Karin and Otto, who seemed no more concerned than Sten had.

The Larsons didn't understand. Two guys with cameras was just the beginning.

The next day, shortly after the Larsons and Killigans left for the day, six photographers appeared. Madison watched them from behind the glass door of the cottage. They appeared out of the mist from way down the beach somewhere and they stayed close to the water. She had no way of knowing if there were more of them lurking on the cliffs above the front of the house.

Madison remained inside. She Googled herself. Yep. There she was playing in the sand with Coco, who was shot from the back and unrecognizable, thank God for small favors.

The caption read: America's Darling makes sandcastles in the Pacific Northwest.

The copy was minimal, just that she was enjoying some time off in the charming seaside town of Valentine Bay. But it wouldn't stay minimal. If she remained here, eventually someone would get a shot of her and Sten. Once they figured out that she was romantically involved with someone, well, talk about a feeding frenzy.

No. It was no good. The Larsons loved their quiet,

private life here in the cove. She didn't want to mess that up.

And what about her newfound family? She and Harper and Hailey had gotten pretty loose Sunday night. Loose enough that she'd been recognized. She wasn't sure how much they'd said about being sisters, now she thought about it. Anyone in the Sea Breeze might have overheard. Plus, well, you only had to look at all three of them together to notice the family resemblance.

That would be one hell of a scoop: America's Darling: Switched at Birth.

Yeah, okay, it would probably come out at some point, anyway.

But if she left now she would have at least a chance of saving her family from the chaos of a media circus.

It was time for her to go.

Time to go and she was in love with Sten and whenever she tried to talk to him about how much he meant to her, he came back with a gentle reminder that what they had was just for now.

Or worse, he would pretend she hadn't said anything. She might have been a little wasted from the Jell-O shots, back there in the early hours of Monday morning, but she clearly remembered saying she loved him.

As well as the resounding silence that followed.

Was she a fool?

She couldn't help but think that maybe she had it all wrong and he was right. That what they had was a fantasy, beautiful but temporary. An interlude and nothing more.

She called Rudy.

Four hours later, Dirk and Sergei arrived in a rented

Hummer. They chased the paparazzi away —at least temporarily—and checked the cottage and the perimeter for points of vulnerability.

She explained to them that the Larsons were to be given free access to her and the cottage, that she had grown close with them over the past few weeks. She did not need security from them. They were not to be intimidated or questioned. If they knocked on the door, she would let them in.

As for Sten, he wouldn't knock. And Sergei and Dirk were to do nothing about that except maybe say hello and shake his hand.

At a little before six, Sten passed the Hummer parked in front of the cottage as he came down the driveway headed for his garage. Was the bodyguard back?

Had something bad happened that would make Maddy call in security?

His pulse ratcheted up several notches.

Maybe he should have taken her more seriously when she seemed so worried about those photographers who'd shown up on the beach yesterday.

He parked the truck and headed for the cottage, letting himself in through the front entrance. A giant, muscled-up Slavic-looking guy was standing, feet wide, massive arms crossed over his enormous chest, a few feet from the door.

"Hi," the guy said, and actually cracked a reasonable semblance of a smile. "I'm Sergei."

"Sten."

"Yeah. I know." He offered a hand the size of a frying pan.

Sten shook it as Maddy appeared. She looked a little anxious, but otherwise okay.

"Hey," she said.

Sergei stepped aside and Sten went to her, taking her by the shoulders. "You all right?"

"Yeah. Long story. We'll talk." She kissed him, just a quick peck, but it helped to ease his general feeling of apprehension. A little.

He glanced toward the main room and saw the other bodyguard, the one he remembered from before, Dirk.

Dirk gave him a wave.

Maddy said, "Dirk. Sergei. Walk the perimeter, or whatever. Just find something to do outside for an hour."

The bodyguards didn't look happy, but a few seconds later, they were out the door.

Maddy turned a too-bright smile on him. "So. How 'bout a beer?"

He pulled her close again and gazed steadily into those aquamarine eyes. "What's going on?"

She scraped her pretty teeth along her lower lip. "Let's at least go in the great room and sit down."

His general uneasiness growing once more, he followed her in there and dropped down on the couch beside her. "Okay. What?"

"The paparazzi showed up again today—out on the beach. And I know how this goes. Today, there were six of them. Tomorrow there will be more." She looked so worried. He didn't really get why a few eager-beaver reporters alarmed her. At the same time, he needed to protect her, to know that she felt safe. Thus, he wanted to break a few expensive cameras just on principle.

"Hey." Sliding a hand under the silky fall of her

hair, he tugged her close and brushed a kiss between her brows. He kept his voice gentle when he asked, "Did they harass you?"

"Other than the general annoyance of knowing they were out there lurking, waiting for a chance to get the perfect shot of me doing something sexy, illegal or outrageous, no. I stayed in the house where they couldn't use their telephoto lenses on me. They aren't allowed on private property, so they never left the beach—until Sergei and Dirk arrived to scare them away."

"If you were that freaked about it, I wish you had called me."

"I wasn't freaked. I know how this works, that's all. I was lucky, really, to get a whole month here before they found me."

"So, we'll have Dirk and Sergei in the spare rooms from now on?" It didn't sound great, but if she needed them to feel safe, she should have them.

"Sten."

Leaning close again, he pressed his forehead to hers and breathed in the spicy-sweet scent of her skin. "You look so down. Why?"

She pulled back. Reluctantly, he released her. "It's time for me to go back to LA."

Every nerve in his body rebelled at that. And suddenly there was a weird ache in the center of his chest. She wasn't going anywhere. Not yet. They still had time. "What are you talking about? You have the cottage for two more weeks."

"I know. But I can't stay."

"Yes, you—"

She silenced him with two soft fingertips against his lips. "I know you don't understand. You live in this beautiful place and nobody bothers you. Well, as of now, you will be bothered if I stay here. They'll descend in force and they'll not only be looking for pictures, they will want the story, to know *why* I suddenly decided to go incognito for a month in some tiny town in Oregon. It'll just be a circus and I'm not up for that. I've called my family and let them know I'm leaving. They weren't any happier about it than I am, but at least we connected. I have some time yet, before my next movie. Harper and Hailey might be able to make it for a visit to LA."

He couldn't sit still. He jumped up, went to the window and stood staring blindly out. "I guess I'm just not ready for you to go." He faced her then.

She was on her feet, so beautiful, with those eyes he would never get enough of staring into, that mouth he couldn't wait to kiss. "I'm leaving tomorrow."

He went to her, took her by her slim shoulders. "This is just crazy. Come on, you don't have to go."

Her soft lips were trembling. "Oh, Sten. Are you...?"

"What?"

She scanned his face as though seeking the answer to some major question. "I mean, well, it would be different. We could take a different approach to this problem, if we were in it for, um, more." What she said wasn't clear.

But he understood her anyway. He let his hands drop to his sides. "More."

She tipped her chin higher. "I think I told you, I have two upcoming projects I can't get out of. That could add up to a year, possibly longer, of work I'm committed to. There will be media, PR stuff I have to do after that, promotion for both projects, awards seasons, all that. If we were together, we would essentially find a way to come out as a couple. Maybe a magazine interview, maybe a press conference, whatever. You would have to deal with the media, at least to a degree. For a while, I mean. But give me the next two or three years, and I'm done. I'm not doing another film. It won't be that long before I'm old news. We could make a plan to settle here, in Valentine Bay."

It sounded so *possible* when she put it like that. He really needed to watch it, keep both feet firmly on solid ground or she'd have him convinced that it was all going to magically work out and they could wander off into the sunset together. "Come on. You don't really mean that. You won't really like the quiet life. You're Madison Delaney, damn it."

She drew herself up. "I've been telling you since I got here what I'm going to do and I've meant it every time I've said it. I've loved my career and I know I've been spectacularly fortunate. I've had all the breaks. It's been great, but I'm so done. I want a *real* life now, to walk down the street and have nobody care. To be with my family, to have friends I can count on who can count on me back, to…learn to lay tile. To open a kids' party business with my sisters. I want to get married—to *you*, Sten. I want us to have kids. I want to yell too loud at our little girl's soccer games and cry with love and pride when our son has a solo in the school Christmas show. I want an ordinary, everyday life—with you, I hope. But one way or another, I am making big changes, making a new kind of life for myself, I truly am."

"Maddy…" He reached for her again.

She came into his arms with a soft cry. He lifted her stubborn chin and he kissed her.

So sweet, that kiss.

He wished it might never end.

But it did. She pulled away and looked up at him, her gaze unwavering. "I love you, Sten Larson. I love you and, no, I'm not sure how it would work, exactly, given the zoo that is my life, but I think if we both just started with agreeing that we want to stay together, that we both want to *make* it work, we could take it from there, we could start figuring out how to create something that feels like forever."

"Maddy," he said. He had no idea what to say next.

But she knew. She got it. She caught her lower lip between her teeth and whispered, "So, then. That's a no?"

He didn't want to say it. But he knew that he had to. "I'm just not a Hollywood type of guy."

"And I'm not asking you to be one."

He wished he could believe her. But she wasn't facing the way the world really worked. "Look, eventually, you're going to start thinking about how the life you say you're done with matters to you, after all. You're not going to want to give up what you've worked so hard for, the kind of life most people would kill for. You've earned what you have. Why should you leave it behind?"

"I just told you why. Because I want something different now."

"Uh-uh. Maddy, come on. It's not going to work out for us. You're America's Darling and I'm just a regular guy. We need to face that, not start making promises we know we won't keep."

"I *would*," she insisted. "I would keep my promises to you, Sten. I swear to you I would."

It was so hard, not to grab her close, not to start promising things back to her, not to join in her delusion that love could magically make everything right. "No, Maddy. I can't."

Madison longed to keep trying, to keep pushing, start begging.

But she not only loved him, she *knew* him. Already. In just a few short, beautiful weeks.

He was her guy, her forever.

But he couldn't—or simply wouldn't—open his heart and let her in.

And she was no miracle worker. She couldn't make a blind man see. She wouldn't convince him of anything if he was set against believing in all they could be.

Somehow, she spoke reasonably. "I don't know who broke your trust, Sten. But I really hope someday you realize that there are women in this world who actually mean what they say."

He only stood there, saying nothing, looking at her with bleak acceptance in his eyes.

She longed to ask him for this one more night.

But please. A girl needed to have at least a little pride.

"Thank you," she said, knowing she sounded stiff and fake and not really caring all that much. "Thank you for everything, for all the ways you've made my visit here amazing. I will always remember this time we've had together."

"Goodbye." He kind of growled the word at her. "That's what you mean, right?"

"Yes." Her heart was in a million pieces. But she wouldn't start crying over that. Not till he was gone. "Goodbye."

Chapter Twelve

A raw emptiness in his chest, as though he'd somehow scraped his own heart out with a rusty spoon, Sten went home.

He knew he'd done the smart thing, to refuse her. It really couldn't work with them. He was right to say no.

He also kind of wanted to strangle himself.

Because in the few weeks he'd known her, Maddy had managed to fill every corner of his life. He'd fallen so hard and so deep. How had he let that happen?

Why hadn't he stopped himself, somehow?

He entered through the front door of his half of the main house and went on through the empty great room all the way to the wall of windows that faced the sea. The clouds had cleared off and the sky was a pure, uninterrupted blue.

Four short weeks they'd had together. And now he could not imagine his life without her in it.

* * *

"Where's Madison?" Karin asked when Sten went downstairs for dinner.

He explained in a rational, calm voice that Madison was worried about all the photographers that had been showing up. She'd decided to go. "She's leaving for Los Angeles tomorrow."

Coco jumped up. "I need to go see her."

"Sit down, honey," said Karin. "Eat your dinner. I'll give her a call later. We'll all say goodbye before she goes."

"But, Mommy. I don't *want* her to go."

"She can't stay forever," said Ben in his best Little Professor voice. "She's a movie star. She has acting she has to do."

"But we didn't even get to finish our sandcastle." Coco's big eyes welled with tears. "It's not fair. It's just not fair!"

"Honey…"

"It's not fair!"

"Oh, sweetheart." Karin held out her arms.

Coco flung herself into them. "Mama. She's my friend. She's my friend and now she's going." The tears overflowed.

Karin got up. Coco clung to her, lifting her legs and wrapping them around her waist as she sobbed against her neck. "We'll be back," Karin said, and turned for the hallway that led to the bedrooms.

Sten's dad asked gruffly, "You tell Madison that you love her?"

Across the table, Ben's eyes were big as Frisbees.

"Dad, come on," Sten replied and had no idea what

to follow up with. He finished lamely, "Time and place, man."

"So that's a no?"

"It, um, didn't work out."

"That's a no." His father seemed to stare right through him. "Pass the broccoli," he said, adding, "fool," so low it was almost inaudible.

But Sten heard him. And judging by the way his nephew's eyes got even wider, Ben heard him, too.

Karin flopped down in the deck chair next to him. She handed him a beer and then tapped it with her can of Hansen's Natural Grape Soda. It was twilight, the last sliver of the day vanishing out there over the waves.

For several minutes, they just sat there, staring off at the ocean.

But his sister's silence couldn't last. "I talked to Madison. They're leaving for Executive Airport at eight in the morning." The small airstrip where the private planes took off was about five miles outside of town. "Dad and I and the kids will go over to the cottage at seven thirty to say goodbye." She stopped talking, probably waiting for him to admit what a blockhead he was to turn Maddy down.

He said nothing.

So of course, she said, "You need to go over there, Sten. Work it out with her. Don't let the best thing that ever happened to you just ride off in a Hummer."

"She'll be in the Subaru that's hidden in the garage, if you really want to know."

"What in the world are you babbling about?"

"Nothing. Just leave it, Karin. Just leave it alone."

She sipped her soda. "I get why you're mad. You're

mad at yourself. And you know what? You *should* be mad."

"Let me finish that thought for you." He stared furiously at the last light of day as it winked out to nothing. "I'm a dolt and a dunce, a real birdbrain and a total schmuck to let her get away."

"True," said his sister. "But the good news is, she's not gone yet. It's not too late. You know that, right?"

"Oh, yeah?"

Karin sank down in her chair. "You exhaust me. You really do. And if you don't work this out with her, if you don't go after her and beg her to give you another chance, well, I don't know what to tell you, except that you deserve all the misery you'll be suffering once she's gone. I mean, just look at yourself. You're miserable already. And you're *choosing* to be miserable."

He turned and gave her a glare. "Karin, that's enough."

She just kept talking. "I mean, think about what you're doing. The wrong woman, a woman who didn't deserve you, broke your heart. And your response to that, your way to make sure that doesn't happen again? Refuse to give the *right* woman a fighting chance."

"How do you even know she asked for a chance?"

"Oh, please. Like I haven't seen the two of you together. Like I don't know a true love match when I see one. She asked, because that's who she is. She's brave and true and honest about her feelings—and you go ahead, Sten Larson. You go ahead and try to tell me I'm wrong."

"Are you finished?" he muttered, his teeth clenched so hard his jaw ached.

"Sten." Now she gave him a pleading look. "Don't do it. Don't throw love away."

He faced the ocean again and stared into the darkness wondering what the hell had ever made him think that living with his family was a good idea.

Somehow, Sten got through the endless, sleepless night that followed.

At seven thirty the next morning, his family all trooped over to the cottage to say goodbye. He remained upstairs at his house. But he heard them all come back, heard them leave again, his dad and Karin for the Boatworks, the kids to catch the school bus.

A few minutes later, the Hummer drove off. He stood at his front door watching it go. Besides the driver, there was someone sitting in the back seat and also in the passenger seat, though it was hard to say who with the windows tinted. Dummies, maybe? He had to give her security team credit. They knew how to pull off a fake-out, all right.

Twenty minutes after the Hummer headed up the twisting driveway, the garage door of the cottage opened and the Subaru Forester backed out. A man was driving. There was no one else in the car—or at least, that was how it looked.

He went back inside and poured himself a third mug of coffee.

Standing at the windows in the great room, looking out at the gray day and the restless ocean, he sipped his coffee and tried not to feel so raw and hollow inside. When his cup was empty, he filled it again and went outside. He sat in his favorite deck chair staring out at the waves, wondering how long it was going to take him to get over the woman he'd just sent away.

A *long* time.

Like, say, maybe…forever.

This was so much worse than what had happened with Ella. This was *Maddy* he'd lost.

And it was his own damn fault she was gone.

A misty rain started to fall. Still, he sat there and considered how badly he'd screwed up.

He kept hearing his sister's voice in his head. *The wrong woman, a woman who didn't deserve you, broke your heart. And your response to that, your way to make sure that doesn't happen again? Refuse to give the right woman a fighting chance…*

It pissed him the hell off when Karin was right.

Because Maddy *was* good and honest and true—and he was letting her get away, why, exactly?

What excuse had he given her?

Because he wasn't a Hollywood type of guy?

Weak. Feeble. Downright pathetic.

What was his fear here, really? That she would long for her career if she gave it up?

The truth was, he didn't think she *should* give it up.

But really, that was up to her.

What about him, then? If he wanted to be with her, where would he fit?

Say it turned out the way he was so sure it would. Say that, given more time to consider her own future, she realized that she just wasn't ready to quit, that she wanted to make more movies?

The real question for him was could he live with that? Could he maybe go visit her on location now and then, do what he needed to do to help Karin and his dad with the Boatworks and also kind of keep the home fires burning in Bel Air?

Why not?

Seriously. Why the hell not?

For a woman like Maddy, the least he could do was learn to be a little damn flexible.

If she would even have him now.

If he wasn't already too late.

He got out his phone to text her. Fine drops of rain spattered the dark screen as he stared down at it, finger poised to swipe.

But he didn't swipe.

Because a text or a phone call?

Uh-uh. That wouldn't be near enough.

Leaving his empty mug on the arm of his chair, Sten jumped to his feet and ran back inside to grab the keys to his truck.

It was a ten-minute drive to Valentine Bay Executive Airport.

He made it in seven. Yeah, he was begging for a speeding ticket. But a miracle happened and he didn't get stopped.

Tires squealing, he spun into the small parking lot at the airfield and slammed to a stop beside the familiar Subaru. It was empty now, just waiting for some guy from the rental place to come pick it up. The rain fell, soft and steady.

He turned off the engine and jumped out just in time to see a Gulfstream lift off the end of the runway and sail upward into the gray sky. It had to be her.

And that meant he was too late.

With his heart like a lump of lead in his chest, he watched the plane vanish from his sight.

He'd blown it. She was gone. He hung his head and let the disappointment wash over him.

Now what?

He wasn't giving up, but it was going to take some work to get to her. Yeah, it was only what he deserved for being the world's biggest dumb-ass, but still.

If he hadn't sat there on the deck in the misty rain pondering his own idiocy for so long, he might have at least had a chance to get down on his knees to her before she left for LA.

He took his phone out of his pocket.

It lit up with a text in his hand.

A text from Maddy?

Not possible. No way could he get that lucky. His blood roared in his ears and his heart did something impossible inside his chest, as he read, Turn around.

What the…?

Slowly, hardly daring to hope, he faced the tiny terminal.

And there she was, inside the terminal, her unforgettable face pressed to the glass.

They took off at a run, simultaneously. She burst through the glass doors as he reached the walkway leading up to them.

"You came to get me!" She squealed like Coco did when he tickled her, and threw herself into his wide-open arms.

"Maddy." He gathered her in, hard and tight, buried his face in her hair and breathed in the scent that belonged only to her. The rain kept drizzling down. Neither of them cared. "Maddy…"

She lifted her head to breathlessly explain, "I sent Dirk in the plane, back to LA. I couldn't leave without trying one more time. I thought, well, if that makes me a crazy, love-addled nutjob, I don't care. I thought,

I've got two weeks in that cottage and I'm taking them. Your sister said she didn't give two shakes about the paparazzi. So did your dad. They said to stay, that one way or another, we would work it out, together. That all I had to do was just *not* to leave yet. And the more I thought about that, the more I thought they were right—oh, Sten. Were they? Were they right?" Those turquoise eyes searched his.

"Yeah." He cradled her precious, rain-wet face between his hands. "But it wouldn't have mattered in the end if you'd flown off before I got here. One way or another, I would have tracked you down to tell you that I love you, Maddy. That you're everything to me, that I was so wrong and I know that now, and would you please just give me a chance to make everything right?"

She let out a cry and surged up to press her sweet mouth to his.

That kiss? It was everything—a promise. A vow.

For now and tomorrow and all their tomorrows.

When she dropped back to her heels, she said, "There *was* someone else, wasn't there? Someone who hurt you?" At his slow nod, she commanded, "Tell me. All of it. I need to know."

And he did tell her. He explained everything about Ella—or at least, he made one hell of an attempt, right there in front of the terminal, as the misty rain dribbled down on them. "She, well, she texted me that Sunday night when you were at Daniel's for your DNA party. And she showed up at the Boatworks last week to try to get something going with me again."

She gulped. "Were you...tempted?"

"Hell, no."

"But you said that she was between us..."

"Uh-uh. It was my failure with her—that was what got between me and you. That she was the wrong choice for me all along and I refused to see it. It screwed with my head, to have to realize how completely I'd misjudged her. While I was with her, I wouldn't let myself admit the truth about her. I ignored all the signs that it was never going to work with her. Because I had chosen her and by God, I needed to be right in my choice. My pride wouldn't let me see that I was only a convenience for her, a placeholder until she could get the other guy to take her back. Then he *did* take her back and I had to face what a chump I'd been."

She put a hand to his cheek. "Too bad for her. She blew it. Her loss, my gain." Maddy's smile was slow and full of satisfaction—but then she frowned and chided gently, "You should have said something, explained all this earlier. It would have helped me to be more patient, to understand."

"Yeah." He turned his face into her hand and pressed a kiss against her soft palm. "I messed up. And I am so sorry. I hope you can forgive me."

"Of course I forgive you. I love you and I always will."

He took her hand and kissed the back of it. "I'm so glad. That you're here. That you didn't go."

"But see, that's because I'm not like that other woman. I don't have secret goals. I *own* my goals out loud and proud. I go after what I want and for me, *you* are the goal, Sten Larson. You're the one that I want."

"You mean that." It wasn't a question.

And she knew it wasn't. "I love you."

"Maddy, you were incredible yesterday, telling me you loved me, trying to reassure me that we could work it out. And me? I was nothing but a coward. But not anymore. I get it now. I do. *You* are the one for me. I just want to be beside you, whatever the future brings. I understand now, how it is, how it will be. You are always with me. In here." He pressed their joined hands to his heart. "I love you. And I want everything with you—to marry you, to have kids with you. All of it."

"Yes," she whispered prayerfully. "Yes, to all of it. I want that, too."

"But for right now, the simple fact that you're here. That you love me, too. Maddy, that's what counts, that's what really matters. That's the beginning."

"The beginning." Her eyes shone so bright. "Yes. Today, right now, here in the drizzling rain, you and me, telling the truth, making our promises to each other that we are bound to keep—this is the real beginning. The beginning of *us*."

Epilogue

Madison remained in Valentine Bay until the end of April.

Right away, it got inconvenient, with the paps popping up every time she turned around. She called her security team. They sent Dirk, Sergei and two other guys to patrol the cove and keep the press at bay.

After that, it wasn't too bad, really. Sten and his family took it all in stride. Mostly, they pretended the photographers weren't even there. It became kind of a game with them, to behave as if it was nothing out of the ordinary having people with cameras plastered to their faces everywhere they turned. Coco and Madison built the biggest sandcastle ever, with technical advice from Ben and plenty of help from Sten.

The Bravos handled all the excitement well, too. Madison had them over to the beach cottage for din-

ner. And another night, she and Sten met Harper and
Hailey, Aislinn and Jax for drinks at the Sea Breeze.
The bodyguards came with them for crowd control.
Only one pap got in. Ingrid Ostergard escorted him
right back out.

When Madison returned to LA, Sten went with her.
By then, the world had kind of figured out that America's
Darling had a special guy. Together, she and Sten gave
an interview to *People*, a full-color center spread, just to
make it official.

She had a five-day break from filming in mid-June
due to the necessity for emergency script changes.
They flew home to Valentine Bay and got married in
the little church where all the Larsons had been bap-
tized. It was beautiful and media-free, a small, private
ceremony, just the Bravos, Karin and the kids, Otto
Larson and Percy and Daffodil Valentine.

Her security team made that happen with the clever
use of a decoy limo. Once the limo had driven off,
Madison, in her wedding gown, stretched out on the
back seat of a Hyundai Sonata. Sergei gently settled
a tarp over her. She giggled all the way to the chapel
at the sheer absurdity of going to get married under a
tarp. Sten, in jeans and a T-shirt, drove his truck to the
church. He changed to his tux when he got there.

"Forever," he whispered, as he slid the sapphire ring
that had once been his mother's onto her finger.

"And always," she vowed.

Two years later, Madison had completed both of
her final films. She'd also received a nomination for
her second Oscar.

Sten, looking super hot as always in a gorgeous tux,

was her date for the Academy Awards. Six months pregnant with their first child, Madison wore a clinging gold gown that showed off her baby bump. When Robin Roberts asked her what she had coming up next, she reached for Sten's hand. He wove his fingers with hers and moved in close.

"Married life," she replied. "You know, the man I love and babies, lots of family nearby."

Robin smiled and congratulated her.

Madison won that night. She thanked everyone who had made her win possible, including the parents who'd raised her to be bold and fearless, to chase her wildest dreams. She and Sten skipped the after-parties. They went straight back to the house in Bel Air where she could put her feet up.

Three weeks later, they flew home to Valentine Bay and settled in to raise their family on Sweetheart Cove.

It never got out to the world at large that Madison Delaney Larson was a Bravo by birth. And that suited her just fine.

On Madison's fortieth birthday, Sten and Jax threw a party at the cove for her and for Aislinn. It was a gorgeous almost-spring day. They spent most of the afternoon out on the beach, with a big family dinner later up at the house.

Madison had a great time. Her life was as she'd dreamed it might someday be. She had it all—a big extended family, four beautiful children and the man she loved at her side.

* * * * *